Tony Shill[...] [...]th
Australia, [...]

He gr[...] [...]ith
a Bachelor of [...]ma
of Education. He subsequently [...]d a
Bachelor of Education degree through Hartley
College.

Tony has been a teacher of English since
1977, first at Stuart High, Whyalla, and then at
Aberfoyle Park High, Adelaide.

He lives in Adelaide with his wife, Anette,
and two daughters, Jaimee and Kim.

He is the author of the *Andrakis* trilogy:
Guardians, *Kingmaker* and *Dragon Lords*.

THE LAST WIZARD

TONY SHILLITOE

PAN
AUSTRALIA

First published 1995 in Pan
by Pan Macmillan Australia Pty Limited
St Martins Tower, 31 Market Street, Sydney

National Library of Australia
cataloguing-in-publication data:

Shillitoe, Tony, 1955– .
The last wizard.
ISBN 0 330 35600 3.
I. Title.
A823.3

Typeset in 12pt/14pt Perpetua by Post Typesetters, Brisbane
Printed in Australia by McPherson's Printing Group

For Jaimee and Kim

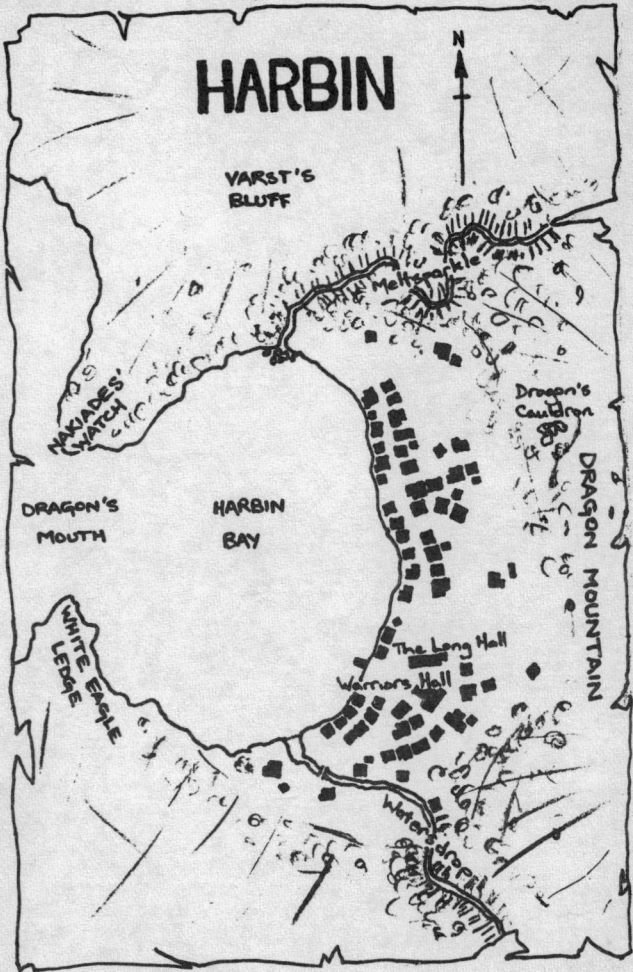

HARBIN

N ↑

VARST'S
BLUFF

Mellbranke

NAKIADES'
WATCH

Dragon's
Cauldron

DRAGON'S
MOUTH

HARBIN
BAY

DRAGON MOUNTAIN

WHITE EAGLE
LEDGE

The Long Hall

Warriors Hall

Waterdrop

GODS AND GODDESSES OF HARBIN

Varst
Lord of all things, creator of the universe, judge of mankind, god of wisdom and anger.

Procra
Varst's wife: goddess of procreation and fertility, mother of all existence.

Ecg
Varst's son: god of strength and courage and warriors.

Fler
Varst's daughter: goddess of renewal, of animals and plants, and of beauty.

Arkamroth
The Earthfire Dragon: bringer of fire and earthquake, his home is in the heart of a volcano.

Blitzart
The Great White Dragon: bringer of winter, storms and bitter cold; his home is in the frozen wastes.

Shaddho
The Dragon of Darkness: bringer of night and death, his home is in the darkness.

FESTIVALS AND CELEBRATIONS

Spring
Celebration of Fler—Festival to herald the rebirth of living things and new growth.

Ecg's Feast—Recognition of the youths who are embarking on manhood.

Summer
Sacrifice to Varst—(Varst's Feast) Feast held to farewell the

dragonwarriors on their annual pilgrimage to hunt dragons.

Dragon Feast—Celebration held to welcome the returning dragonwarriors who sailed on the dragonship.

Autumn

Procra's Dance—Fertility ritual at which the single dragonwarriors may choose wives from the single women in Harbin.

Procra's Feast—Ritual gathering of foodstuffs to be shared between villagers.

Winter

Blitzart's Feast—(The Mad Wizards' Dance) Mid-winter gathering of the village to share food and company and break the long monotony of winter.

VILLAGE LEADERS

The Dragon Head

Held by the most highly respected warrior of the village. He commands obedience from all members of the community, leads the Dragon Fang, and can only be deposed by his own choice or by a stronger challenger in one-to-one combat.

The Dragon Heart

The village priest. His duties are mainly to teach the people the functions of the gods, the legends and their meanings, and to sing the Words of Passage to speed the spirits of the dead to Varst's Eternal Paradise. The role is handed down from father to son.

The Dragon Fang

Every warrior in the village is a member of the Dragon Fang. Apart from defending the village, a role the Dragon

Fang has never had to play in Harbin, its other duty is to train throughout winter and spring in readiness to sail south during summer and hunt dragons. It is a matter of status for all men to belong to the Dragon Fang, because no-one can claim manhood until he has sailed on the dragonship journeys.

The Dragon's Wrath

The Law Council of Harbin. Seldom assembled except to resolve rare disputes or determine a new law, the Dragon's Wrath is formed by the Dragon Head, the Dragon Heart, and three elected senior members of the Dragon Fang. Any decision made by the Dragon's Wrath is considered absolute.

The Legend

Na-Kia-Des' tiny ship sped out of Blitzart's jaws, the great white dragon's frozen breath thundering in its sails. All round the storm churned the wild sea white with fury. And lurking, lurking at the edge of the maelstrom, great Shaddho, dragon of all darkness, waited to claim Na-Kia-Des and his people. Long raged Blitzart's storm. Dark was Shaddho's night. Na-Kia-Des' helpless craft rose and fell on the mountainous waves, and his people, terrified Na-Kia-Des had indeed called the dragons' merciless wrath down upon them, huddled like water-rats in the flooded hull.

Only Na-Kia-Des defied the storm. When the vicious winds tore away the sail, he lashed his body to the broken mast, turned his face into the full breath of Blitzart the storm dragon, and cried out, 'Hear me, Lord of all dragons! Hear me almighty Varst! Look down and see that I am not afraid of your servants! Know I am Na-Kia-Des, first-born son of Esa-Ra-Tha. Know I am a warrior, a mighty warrior. I alone will stand before you and not kneel or cower in fear. I am not afraid of you. I am not afraid!'

Hearing Na-Kia-Des bellow into the face of Blitzart's breath, seeing him roped to the shattered mast like a mad-man, the people in the boat were filled with even greater

1

fear. Here was their mightiest warrior, Na-Kia-Des, screaming at the dragons and calling on the highest god of all, Varst, Lord and Creator of everything, as if he was merely challenging an ordinary man to single combat. All night Na-Kia-Des yelled his anger and his challenges into the wind and the rain, until it seemed his breath had mingled with that of the great white dragon, and all was one.

When morning broke, the first of the people woke to find the storm gone and the ship rocking on a gentle swell. Grey though the skies remained, the worst had surely passed. When they turned to look upon Na-Kia-Des, they saw his wild eyes were gazing straight ahead, as if fixed on a wondrous sight. Filled with curiosity, the people scrambled onto the deck and stared. They saw mountain peaks, forests, cliffs; a new world.

'Behold!' said Na-Kia-Des as they stared in awe at the vision before them. 'Almighty Varst has heard. He has looked down upon our people and blessed us with a new home. He has seen our courage and welcomes us into his world again.'

Amazed and grateful, the people gathered and knelt before great Na-Kia-Des. They thanked him for his protection, and for their deliverance, but he waved them aside, saying, 'Offer your prayers to Varst. He, not I, brings you here.'

And so it was that Na-Kia-Des' people came to live at the foot of Dragon Mountain. Na-Kia-Des' battered ship drifted into the bay and there was much joy when the people at last set their feet on dry land. They found pasture, and building stone, and a fruitful forest, and crystal waters to drink. It was as if they had found again the fabled paradise of Te-Akra-Sen. Soon those with craft set to building, and the village of H-Ara-Bin—the place of peace—rose from the earth. Such was the happiness in those first days that Na-Kia-Des took a wife, the beautiful Se-Lese-Rin, daughter of Ku-Ra-Las, and in no time the laughter of children echoed around the mountainside.

But Blitzart and Shaddho watched with envious eyes. Na-Kia-Des had flouted their greatness. He had called upon their lord and master to rebuke them. Angered and frustrated, they took their grievance to their elder brother, great Arkamroth, the Earthfire dragon.

'Brother, come. Look at the men children at play in our world,' they beseeched. 'See how they strut and frolic as if the world was their own.'

Wise Arkamroth, hearing his spiteful brothers, came to look as they asked, and saw the people of Na-Kia-Des at play in their new life.

'Does this not anger you?' his brothers asked.

Arkamroth turned and smiled, and answered them by saying, 'No, brothers, it does not anger me.'

Dismayed by his response, they tried to persuade him to act on their behalf. 'Help us brother,' they pleaded. 'Use the earth and its fires to drive them back into the sea.'

'No,' replied Arkamroth. 'I see no reason. Men have only a brief moment before they are dust, and there are but few here. What are they to trouble such as us?' So saying, he left his brothers, and flew south and west to tend to his own matters.

Infuriated by their elder brother's indifference, they went to complain to the Master of all dragons, almighty Varst.

'O Great One,' said Blitzart, his massive white head bowed low with respect before his master, 'O Greatest of All, hear us.'

Varst turned from his tasks and saw his creatures before him. 'Speak,' he commanded.

'It is not our place to question your wisdom, mighty Lord,' said Blitzart cautiously, 'but we feel you have done us a terrible wrong in letting the pitiful seed of Na-Kia-Des ruin our beautiful garden. He taunted us, showed us no respect, and spited us when we were playing. Now he goes unpunished.'

Great Varst opened wide his golden eyes, and they shimmered in the light of the radiant sun. 'Are you saying I have done wrong?' he asked.

Shaddho knew well the mood of his master. He eased away from Blitzart's side, sensing how unwise it would be to proceed. But Blitzart, blinded by his own intense desire for revenge, did not heed the master's tone.

'I think it is wrong to let so arrogant a man live without fear,' he insisted. 'I would not have let that be so.'

There followed a long and fearful silence. Varst stared at Blitzart, his golden eyes shining. Only then did Blitzart realise the foolishness of his words and wish he had never spoken. His heart suddenly as cold as his breath, Blitzart slunk from his master's presence. Shaddho silently followed.

'Then we are cursed to endure this braggart Na-Kia-Des.' Shaddho hissed when they were safely out of Varst's hearing. 'Still, as brother Arkamroth has reminded us, a man's life is but a passing instant. Soon the name of Na-Kia-Des will fade, and his people will wither and die. What is humankind to dragons? Dust in the wind.'

'It is not enough!' Blitzart spat angrily. 'Na-Kia-Des must be punished.'

'Then let him face a dragon's wrath,' Shaddho declared. 'If you are so determined this Na-Kia-Des must die, brother, send one of our children to taste his flesh and burn his bones to ash.'

'Yes,' agreed Blitzart. 'I will send one of the children to teach these people of Na-Kia-Des that respect must always be shown to us.'

Of course Na-Kia-Des knew nothing of the dragons' plans for vengeance. He watched his new home grow, and his children bloom like forest roses, and felt indeed he could at last put away his warrior's sword and be at peace once and for all. Happy that all was well, Na-Kia-Des told beautiful Se-Lese-Rin that he would travel east into the mountains to see what lay beyond. He gathered a few young men who were willing to travel with him, and provisions, and the small band set out to discover what greater mysteries Varst had hidden beyond Dragon Mountain.

In the days while Na-Kia-Des explored, the people of H-Ara-Bin continued to thrive and prosper. Then one night Shaddho threw a great darkness across the face of the moon. The people cowered in fear as they watched the Dragon of Darkness sweep across the sky and steal away the light. And down from the mountain came a breath so cold it turned the earth white and the water froze in the wells. The people knew then that cruel Blitzart stalked the land.

'What will become of us?' they cried. 'The dragons have come, and we shall all perish. Where is Na-Kia-Des?'

Out of the darkness, across the waters, a shape loomed,

a scaly shape with eyes of fire and jaws of flame. It burned the buildings of the village and took whatever fresh meat it could find—animals or people. Again it came, and again, burning, killing, eating what it pleased. Each night it came, Shaddho hid the moon and Blitzart froze the air. The people cried and hid in terror, but still the monster came to feed and destroy.

In desperation, some of the braver men waited in hiding to ambush the ravaging creature. When it arrived, they leapt out, brandishing their stone-sharpened spears, only to see that they faced a shining dragon of silver—one of Blitzart's earthly spawn. Undaunted, they heaved their weapons, but sharp war spears bounced off its scaly hide as if they were nothing but children's wooden play spears. Enraged by the futile attack, the dragon tore the hapless warriors limb from limb and left their heads behind on the shore as a warning to the people of H-Ara-Bin not to dare oppose a child of Blitzart. Then it slid back into the sea.

Fearing rightly the child of Blitzart would soon return to plunder their homes, the people called a meeting. Several put forward bold schemes for driving the creature off, but they had all seen the terrible fate of the warriors who had faced the silver creature and knew they were in greater peril than ever before.

'There is no point fighting,' the men claimed. 'The dragon will come and take until there is nothing left to take.'

'Then we must stop it,' argued Se-Lese-Rin. 'Na-Kia-Des would.'

'But he is not here. And we are too weak ourselves to

stop it,' the people said. And they asked the fair Se-Lese-Rin, 'Where is your husband?'

'I do not know,' she whispered forlornly. 'I do not know.'

At that fateful moment, the roof of the meeting hall burst into flames and a silvered head appeared. Its eyes burned like the coals of a blacksmith's forge. Its sharp teeth glittered like diamond spear-points. The people screamed and scattered in fear, running to the safety of the forest and the mountain. Some even put out to sea in their tiny fishing boats to escape the wrath of the hideous child of Blitzart. For three days the people hid, too frightened to return to the village lest the dragon be waiting for them.

When at last they crept back into the ruins of H-Ara-Bin, it was discovered that Se-Lese-Rin was not among them. Na-Kia-Des' four sons had returned with the old woman Er-A-Bos, and they told the people they had not seen their mother since the night of the dragon's attack. Then, in the ashes of the meeting hall, the old woman found the ivory wedding bracelet Na-Kia-Des had given the beautiful Se-Lese-Rin, and all feared Se-Lese-Rin had perished in the flames. A great sorrow descended. Mourning songs rose to the heavens.

So long and so deep was the sound of sorrow that it brought Na-Kia-Des down from the mountains seeking the reason for his people's bitter sadness. When they told him of the coming of the silver dragon and the fate of his beloved Se-Lese-Rin, he snatched up a spear from the earth and vowed he would slay the child of Blitzart and save his beautiful wife and once again make H-Ara-Bin a place of peace. Those who had been his companions on the mountain journey asked to stand beside him, but Na-Kia-Des refused their offer, saying that it was his responsibility to face Blitzart's child since it was he who had foolishly neglected his duty to protect his people by going away into the east in the first place. Then, taking only the spear, his sword, and his armour, Na-Kia-Des left the village.

Na-Kia-Des strode to the peak of Dragon Mountain and there he screamed a challenge to Blitzart to meet him face to face and be done with it. For five long nights he waited for Blitzart's answer, but the Storm Dragon ignored his challenge. Then on the sixth night Na-Kia-Des came back down from the mountain and went to the head of the bluff which we now call Nakiades' Watch, and waited for Blitzart's child to slink out of the sea. When the dragon came, it was heralded by a day of freezing cold breath from Blitzart's jaws, and it rose from the waters with its silvered scales glittering and eyes of coal-bright fire shining full of death. Mighty Na-Kia-Des strode down from the bluff to meet the enemy in battle. He stepped into the path of the terrible dragon and brandished his spear.

'Hear me, death-spawn of Blitzart!' he called. 'Where is my Se-Lese-Rin? Where is the beautiful wife of Na-Kia-Des?'

The dragon's eyes burnt with hunger as it gazed down upon the solitary figure standing defiantly in its path. Its ugly maw opened, and a hissing, twisted sound issued from it, the sound of a thousand tortured souls caught in Arkamroth's fires.

'Man-thing!' it spat. 'You are nothing to me. When I have torn the flesh from your bones, ground your bones to dust beneath my feet, and eaten my fill of your people, then shall I answer you.' So saying, the dragon sucked in its breath and spat a stream of blue fire at Na-Kia-Des. But Na-Kia-Des leapt aside, feeling the fiery heat rush past his shoulder. Then he raised his spear and launched it at the child of Blitzart. True was the warrior's aim. Strong was Na-Kia-Des' arm. Where the spears of lesser men bounced harmlessly off the dragon's silver armour, Na-Kia-Des' spear struck home, piercing the smaller, softer underarm scales of the startled creature and lodging deep in its flesh. A strangled scream of pain rent the air and the dragon sent green spouts of fire flaming into the sky as it staggered backwards. Seeing his chance, Na-Kia-Des rushed forward and plunged his sword deep into one of the dragon's red eyes. Though mortally wounded, Blitzart's child wrenched itself free of the warrior's death embrace, tossing Na-Kia-Des aside like a discarded dinner bone, and stretched its blood-spattered silver wings to take flight. It retreated towards the top of the hill we call Varst's Bluff. Na-Kia-Des followed its ever-weakening flight until he too reached the summit of Varst's Bluff. There he stood over the dying dragon. He pulled his sword from its eye and let the dark green dragon blood ebb into the earth.

When Na-Kia-Des came down to the village, holding his sword aloft with dragon blood still steaming on its blade, the people rushed out to greet him joyfully. They praised his courage, and carried him to the centre of H-Ara-Bin, and showered him with gifts, and bowed before him as if he was mightier than even great Varst, father of all dragons. Na-Kia-Des, though, was deeply troubled. One among the people, the warrior Te-Era-Vis, kneeled before Na-Kia-Des and said, 'Why are you not happy? You have brought peace again to H-Ara-Bin. The people shout your name to the heavens. Mighty Varst himself could not deny your greatness. Why are you so full of sorrow?'

Na-Kia-Des lifted his weary eyes to Te-Era-Vis and replied, 'I have lost what I most loved.'

Then everyone remembered that Se-Lese-Rin had not yet returned. The most beautiful flower of all the village had not been found. The joy sank and the celebration ceased. The people of H-Ara-Bin left great Na-Kia-Des to his sorrow beside the dying embers of the fire, and went quietly home to their own hearths.

The next morning they found Na-Kia-Des at the water's edge. He was busy cutting, binding, and shaping wood. Ropes and raw sailcloth lay beside him.

'What is it you are doing?' they asked.

'I am building a boat,' he answered, but he did not look up, and he did not slacken in his work

'Why do you build a boat?' some asked.

'Because I am going to the land of dragons,' Na-Kia-Des told them.

His answer stunned those who heard it, and some even stole away shaking their heads, believing that Na-Kia-Des must have been maddened by his battle with the dragon, but good Te-Era-Vis bent beside the great warrior and asked, 'What will you do in the land of dragons, mighty Na-Kia-Des?'

'Se-Lese-Rin is there. I will go to her and bring her home again.'

'How is it you know this?' Te-Era-Vis asked.

For the first time, Na-Kia-Des looked up and caught Te-Era-Vis' eye. 'Blitzart's dying child told me it is so. So I will go to the south lands and take back what is mine. And I will punish Blitzart's children for what they have done.' Thus, having spoken, the mighty warrior returned to his task. Te-Era-Vis then took up a crafting tool and began to work beside Na-Kia-Des.

When word spread that the great warriors were building a boat, a dragonship, more people came down to the water's edge. First they came to watch, but then some bent to work with Na-Kia-Des and Te-Era-Vis, and soon the whole village was working as one. And Na-Kia-Des' dragonship grew from the lumber and the hemp and tar. The great sail was sewn by the wives and daughters of H-Ara-Bin while the craftsmen laboured over the boat. Na-Kia-Des released Te-Era-Vis from construction and directed his companion to teach all the young men the skills of a warrior, the skills of Na-Kia-Des the Dragonslayer, for they would be sailing with Na-Kia-Des into the land of dragons. There they would face the children of Blitzart, and Shaddho, and even great Arkamroth's offspring, and they would need to know how to fight and kill the fire-breathing creatures.

When the first dragonship was ready, Na-Kia-Des ordered that the great sail be coloured with the red dye of the bloodflower which grows on the high slopes of Dragon Mountain. This would be a sign to the children of the dragons that Na-Kia-Des was coming to avenge the murder of his people by Blitzart's child. Then he gathered about him the warriors whom Te-Era-Vis had taught, and in the first weeks of summer they set sail.

Though he searched and searched, Na-Kia-Des did not find his beloved Se-Lese-Rin. Each year thereafter, before Blitzart's breath swept down from the mountains, Na-Kia-Des returned to H-Ara-Bin with riches and spoils gathered from the hordes of dragons slain by his warriors, and each summer when Arkamroth's warm winds drove Blitzart's icy touch from the waters, the band of warriors took to the sea in search of Se-Lese-Rin. On his death-night, Na-Kia-Des made his warriors swear an oath before almighty Varst that they would never cease their search for Se-Lese-Rin nor end their war with the children of Blitzart and Shaddho until he and Se-Lese-Rin were reunited. And so it is still that each year the warriors of H-Ara-Bin, the Dragon Fang, take to the dragonship in summer and journey south to the land of dragons. So it is that the law of mighty Na-Kia-Des is with us and makes our days strong and prosperous. We are the dragonwarriors. We are the Dragon Fang. We are the children of Na-Kia-Des and the people of H-Ara-Bin.

Chapter One

Marc had stood sea-watch for ten full days on the promontory his people called White Eagle's Ledge. He rubbed the thick stubble on his chin, feeling the edge of a long white scar that ran from his left eye to his collarbone. The late summer weather was warm, and only a lazy westerly breeze drifting in from the empty reaches of the ocean broke the day's rising heat. The dragonship's return would be slow, he mused. In the absence of a strong southerly, no-one could truly estimate its exact time of return. He imagined the Dragon Head, Kevan, chafing at the lassitude of the elements and cursing the delay. The dragonwarriors would be tired and bored.

Marc stretched his left arm in the warm afternoon light and stared across the deep grey bay towards the village. The huts and cottages and halls of Harbin were a single dark smudge against the light green forest fringe. It seemed to him that the village clung like a bramble vine to the long strip of fertile land nestled beneath the steep shoulders of Dragon Mountain. The people had waited nearly ten weeks for the dragonship's return. Those who liked rumours of tragedy and misfortune were already spreading tales of disaster—warriors torn asunder by a mighty dragon, rocks ripping the heart out of the dragonship in a surging storm. Marc was too old to listen to morbid imaginings of woe. Before he received the near-mortal wound that left him scarred and unable to wield a battleaxe or pull an oar, he had spent fifteen summers on the dragonship. He knew the vagaries of the wind, and where the ship would be heading. More than most others who stayed in Harbin while the warriors searched for the fabled dragon treasures, he understood what was delaying the ship—the weather.

He sighed, shifted his stance against the granite rock, and squinted into the sun's glare on the grey ocean. Gulls dipped and rolled out near Varst's Bluff on the northern side of the bay. They were little more than tiny dots, flashing white when sunlight caught their feathers. They were free creatures, scavengers perhaps, but they were able to come and go as they pleased. He wondered if they ever considered the affairs of men, ever wondered why he and others stood sentinel on the spray-moistened rocks while they wheeled and dipped above the ocean. 'Foolish thoughts,' he chided himself. But then he had a lot of time for foolish thinking while he was on sea-watch. So many strange ideas invaded his mind while he was alone that he sometimes wondered if great Varst himself was playing tricks with him. He shook his head as if that would clear his mind, and turned his gaze back to the south.

That's when he saw the square rig of the dragonship's single red sail rise into view. He blinked and checked again. It was the dragonship. He knew it well. Hadn't he sailed in that craft's belly for fifteen summers? Even for a man of thirty plus winters he still felt a surge of elation at the ship's appearance. Given the fickle breeze, he estimated the dragonship would make Harbin by nightfall. In a few short hours the whole village would leap into celebration. How he loved to dance and sing the old dragon-hunting songs! There would be new stories tonight; new tales to add to the already rich history of Harbin.

He reached into a small cleft beneath the granite rock and withdrew the ivory horn that had been handed down through the generations from Nakiades' era. It was stored there for the seawatcher to alert the village to approaching ships. He ran his callused fingers across the fine carvings on the horn, the pictures of powerful warriors locked in mortal combat with fearsome dragons, and felt a pang of regret that the old days had gone long before he was even born into this world. He would have been keen to be a hero, to have his likeness carved into the artefacts of his descendants. Then he pushed the daydream from his mind. Too many foolish thoughts again, he reminded himself sourly. He sucked in a chestful of air, lifted the horn to his lips, and blew hard and long. The sound raced across the expanse of water and echoed against the small islets and the great mountains. Summer was closing. The dragonwarriors of Harbin, the Dragon Fang, were coming home.

The seawatcher's distant signal was taken up in Harbin. An exclamation of joy passed from mouth to mouth, shared by the women and children. Outside the Dragon Head's residence, Eesa slapped a paddle against the interior of her heavy wooden butter churn and muttered an oath to Procra, the Mother Goddess.

'Chasse!' she called to the closed door of her cottage. 'Chasse!'

A moment later the wooden door swung open, hinges whining at the movement. A willowy, broad-shouldered youth emerged, rubbing his eyes against the bright mid-afternoon sunlight. He flicked back a loose lock of blond hair and stared at his mother's hunched figure at the churn. Then he heard the familiar sound of the horn across the bay and the cries of excitement swelling throughout Harbin. The blood raced through his veins. This time next year, a full sixteen winters old, he would be coming home aboard the dragonship. He would be a dragonwarrior, a man who had faced the wrath of a dragon and taken a dragon's hoard to mark his victory over the beast.

'Are you listening to me?' Eesa waggled a butter-smeared finger in front of the boy's face to break his reverie.

'Yes, Mother,' he answered.

'Then do as I ask and find that girl. I need all the help I can get to prepare for the men's return. You make sure she's back here.'

Chasse suppressed a smile at the sight of his mother. She was first woman to the Dragon Head, his father, and his father was the most powerful warrior of Harbin. Yet here she was, standing with her sleeves rolled up and goat fat smeared up to her elbows and across her forehead and cheeks, looking like any other common village woman. Eesa was still considered a beauty by all the men, Chasse knew that, but it was hard to see the beauty when she dressed like a drab.

'Chasse!'

'I'm going, Mother,' he replied hurriedly and scampered away.

From the mountain ledge where she sat cross-legged, Tamesan watched the solitary red sail. It hung above the bay's dark grey waters like a statement of intent, moving painfully slowly, yet inexorably closer in the gentle breezes eddying above the vast western ocean. Beneath the red square, the ship's hull remained only a darker suggestion on the watery mass, a shadow. Already fractious gulls were stooping and circling the ship, acting as winged heralds to its approach.

The last sail she saw in Harbin Bay had been moving rapidly out of it ten weeks earlier, carrying the village's dragonwarriors and a handful of hopeful would-be-warrior youths. They had headed into the untamed world of heaving seas and dragon tales, to treasures and adventure and manhood. Tam had watched the ship leave with her usual mixture of exhilaration and concern—and envy. Her father had

17

stood perched on the curving prow, his mane of greying hair and full beard seeming to emphasise his status. As Dragon Head, Kevan led the men on their annual pilgrimage to slay one of the fearful dragons that lurked in the wilderness and terrorised less fortunate villages elsewhere along the coast.

Tam studied the sail's progress. She decided it would be late afternoon before the ship docked at the wooden jetty jutting from the stone embankment below the village. Then there would be rejoicing and reunions as families welcomed the return of fathers and sons, brothers and husbands. The night's celebrations would be neither lavish nor long. The dragonship's return was a mere forerunner to the Dragon Feast, the annual Harbin festival during which the treasure gathered from the slain dragon's den would be shared. Then there would be a good deal of food and wine consumed while the men related stories of their most recent adventure, and sang older ballads about the past deeds of great dragonwarriors like Tamesan's father. And there would be the traditional tales told of the ancestors who first sailed into the bay with Nakiades, the first warrior who fought the silver dragon so that his people could settle and have a new life. At the end of the festival, the men would present the initiated warriors who had sailed away for the first time to battle the legendary dragons. They would no longer be regarded as eager, immature boys like her brother Chasse. They would be true dragonwarriors, with all the rights and trappings of the men who belonged to

Harbin's Dragon Fang, because they had played their part in gathering the defeated dragon's treasure.

A pebble rattled above Tam, then clattered down the rocky escarpment to her left. A second pebble ricocheted off a flat rock to her right. She shook out her finely braided red-gold hair and glared at a clump of bushes directly below.

'I know where you are, Chasse,' she said with mock anger. A third pebble arched out of the thick clump and clunked harmlessly against the granite rock face behind her. 'Chasse!' she warned. Her voice was more insistent. A blond head popped into view from behind the largest bush, and a broad bright grin creased the youth's face. Her brother's comic appearance disarmed her. She broke into a smile and asked, 'What do you want?'

'The ship's coming,' he said.

'I know that,' she answered. 'I can see it from here.'

'Mother is calling for you.'

'Let her call,' she abruptly replied.

'I'm coming up, Tam,' Chasse informed her. He disengaged himself from his cover and scrambled up the rocks towards his sister. A moment later he was sitting beside her in the early afternoon sunlight, gazing towards the sun-speckled bay that glittered like mica flecks in blue-grey granite.

'It's a dark sea they return on,' he murmured absently.

Tam nodded and glanced up at the patchy ceiling of light grey clouds. The blinding sun hung in one brilliant patch of azure blue sky as if determined to light and warm the world, and she reflected on the village lore they had grown up with but not always understood. A dark sea heralded a storm or conflict. The old village women spoke in riddles of red sunsets, and grey seas, and ice on summer ponds, as if these things were sure portents of events, but Tam had seen little to prove the accuracy of their predictions. She recalled that many so-called confirmed predictions made by old crones like Sharmine, or the bent and wizened Marissa, who preached that the bad of the world to come could be read from fish entrails, were worked back to an earlier sign they claimed to have observed, rarely forward. The one time she mentioned her scepticism to her mother, Eesa sharply informed her she should respect her elders and be less critical of others until she was perfect herself. Then she had handed Tam the small mucking shovel to clean out the chicken roost to make her point clear. Tam never broached the subject again in her hearing.

'Do you believe all that stuff?' she asked Chasse.

Her brother turned his bright blue eyes towards her, and she found herself feeling sorry for all the girls who would fall victim to his handsome looks.

'Sometimes,' he answered cryptically.

'Meaning what?' she asked.

'Meaning I don't know,' he grinned. 'Sometimes things happen and it's easy to see there was a warning about it. Like when Defra fell into the stream at Watersdrop last year. The old women said Sharmine had seen a red flower in the stream only two days before. She called it an omen.'

'I don't believe it,' Tam snapped. 'The old women just make it up to feel important or something. It's like they want to keep everyone else aware of their presence and place.'

Chasse didn't pursue the argument. He had grown too used to Tam questioning every value their mother and father held sacred. Although he often enjoyed provoking her by taking their parents' side in discussions, recently he found her criticisms of village customs and beliefs too passionate to be fun any more. She seemed to be brooding on an anger deep within that was becoming more passionate, more determined. He had always been close to his sister, being barely a year older, even despite her being a girl, but lately that closeness had changed. There was someone else emerging from inside his normally effervescent sister: a stranger who swung into moods of deep contemplation on a whim or a thought.

Tam shifted her focus from the dragonship tacking in the mouth of the bay to the spread of slate-shingled roofs clustered along the strip of curved shore directly below her mountain perch. She could see the small finger of planking and poles that jutted into the dark water forming the jetty. The incoming boat would berth there. Fishermen's boats moored at the jetty bobbed like fishing floats on the ocean swell. She could just make out moving dots of colour which would be the first people preparing for the dragonship's arrival.

No doubt her mother would be among them. In her station as wife of the Dragon Head she would ensure the jetty was clear of fishing tackle and any unnecessary clutter that might hamper the disembarking dragonwarriors. Other wives would be there, too. They came to help and be bossed around by Eesa because in their husbands' absence they answered to her. Eesa would be cursing Tam's tardiness. She frequently despaired of a daughter who lacked the necessary sense of duty expected of a girl-child of the Dragon Head. Tam was hoping the importance of the occasion would subsume her mother's rage by the time she descended to lend a reluctant hand.

Further up the steeply sloping bank, other people moved between the wooden huts. Some were simply going about their menial daily duties, as if they were ignorant of the dragonship's return—especially the few remaining men—but Tam knew most would be readying for the dragonship's arrival. People were gathering nogs of wood for a fire in the Long Hall, carrying fresh sheeting and furs to the Warriors' Hall, and taking food and mead to the Long Hall for the night's celebrations. The goat herders were busily mustering their free-ranging stock from the lower hillside, and driving the multicoloured animals towards the rough-hewn pens used to hold them until those to be killed and prepared for the night's feasting were selected. The bustling activity would intensify as the ship neared mooring.

'Coming down?' Chasse inquired, tilting his head and cocking an eyebrow at his sister.

'Have I a choice?' she responded.

'You're a girl,' he mocked. 'You have no choice.'

She laughed politely at her brother's condescending observation. She knew it was meant to be nothing more than shared humour, but the truth of his statement rankled. She *was* a girl, and as far as the village was concerned she had no choice but to do as she was told. That was the law.

'I'll come down, brother Chasse,' she said with feigned diffidence, 'but only because *I* choose to.'

'I'll tell father that when he gets in,' Chasse threatened with a snigger. He began to slide down the rockface. 'You know what will happen then.'

'You won't live that long, my cheeky brother!' she retorted, and with an attacking cry she scrambled over the lip of the ledge in pursuit.

By the time the pair reached the base of the mountain their faces were flushed and they were breathless. Though Chasse was a summer older, he barely escaped her. Her agility amazed him. She knew the paths down the mountainside and through the forest better than anyone. He knew she spent a lot of time wandering there, a habit that made their mother more than angry with her. She was his sister, but he loved her because she was so unlike other village girls. Sometimes he wished she was a boy, a brother, because she was always willing to play the games he enjoyed. The difficult thing was, now he was out of childhood, almost a man, that it was unseemly for him to be seen too often in her company, especially sharing games. She would be a poor brother anyway, he decided. She was too different, not because she was a girl, but because she had different ideas, different habits. Tamesan was unique. That was the word that best described her.

One day last summer he had overheard the old woman Sharmine whisper it to another woman. She thought no-one would overhear, but she hadn't seen Chasse bent over a fish barrel retrieving a leather-wrapped ball he had been throwing with Aska and Marron, and he heard the old women talking about Tam.

'Eesa will rue the day she bore that child,' Sharmine had said with a solemn face. 'She doesn't want to be a woman. She sees too much of this world already and I fear she doesn't like what she sees.' The other woman—Chasse remembered she was called Laryssa; she had died just last winter—shook her head and made a harsh whispered reply. He didn't understand her comment, but it made Sharmine's crusty old face wrinkle with laughter, and she answered, 'I remember well enough what it was like. Oh, but I did infuriate my father then, and mother swore she would take me and throw me off Watersdrop to purge the village of my ways.' Her laughter subsided to a chuckle. Then she made a strange sign in the air with her open hand, the same sign she always made when she claimed to foresee an event. 'But this girl of Eesa and Kevan is not like we were, Laryssa, not like us at all. We had a place here and knew it. It just took us a little time to settle down, the way it does for some girls. This one is different. There is something in her presence, in her bearing, something that makes her unique. I fear she will bring great sorrow to her household. Some things I have seen are trifles, but this I know to be true as if Procra herself had whispered it to me.' Laryssa also made a similar clearing motion with her open palm, but Chasse had to move away because his friends were calling.

The word 'unique' was new to him then. He asked Eesa what it meant and she explained, and when she asked him why he wanted to know, he simply replied that he had heard someone use it. But the word merged with his vision of Tamesan from that point onward, and he couldn't look at his sister or think of her without remembering Sharmine's prediction. She was unique, but he was also afraid of the sorrow she might one day bring to herself and to her family.

'Come on, Chasse!' Tam cried. She sprinted across the open pasture where the village goats grazed, her red hair streaming behind her like a banner. He heard the challenge in her voice and took to his heels after her, drawing on his boyish pride not to be beaten to the village outskirts by a girl.

They reached the junction of paths just inside the village, side by side, but the sight of their mother, arms akimbo, in the middle of the road, stopped them short. The Dragon Head's wife fixed them both with an angry glare for a brief moment, then focussed her attention directly on Tam. The girl met her mother's steady gaze. Without shifting her eyes, Eesa addressed her first words to Chasse.

'Your father returns. Get down to the jetty with the other boys and do whatever tasks are required of you to ensure the dragonwarriors can leave their ship unhindered by the garbage of mundane village life.'

Chasse mumbled his reply, touched Tam's hand briefly as if to reassure her that he was only going because it was his duty, then ran past Eesa and disappeared into the depths of the village.

Eesa's green eyes narrowed. 'Are you too proud to answer the call of the sea-watcher's horn?' she asked.

'I came,' Tam replied carefully, trying to judge her mother's mood and intent. She was certain both were going to be unpleasant.

'I had to send your brother to get you. I had to send for you like a servant seeking her mistress. Your brother is nearly a man. Men do not chase after foolish girls who think life is for nothing better than sitting on mountain tops gazing at the sky. Your brother has more important things to do. And so do you. The men are coming home. Your father is coming home. And you will prepare for him and for all the other men of Harbin like every other girl in this village. Do you understand me, girl? No more foolishness. You are the Dragon Head's daughter. Behave accordingly!'

Tam nodded in silence. She knew better than to publicly protest when her mother was in such a mood. Her mother's will was also law. She had no choice but to be patient and obey her.

Chapter Two

Tam carefully squared the sharp knife above the salmon before pushing down and severing its head. Scales and bone crunched under the blade. She scraped the fish head into the wooden bin at her feet, then she slit the fish's belly and dragged out its slippery entrails.

Eesa's intention had been as unpleasant as her mood. She set Tam to the task of helping to clean fish for the night's feast. The task was menial, but Tam knew the daughter of the Dragon Head could not be seen to be above doing such work. Normally, however, Eesa would have arranged for her daughter to be involved in less odoriferous duties, like preparing vegetables, or cleaning out the Warriors' Hall—the duties expected of younger girls and the dragonwarriors' women. Cleaning and gutting fish, being both smelly and dangerous, was traditionally the lot of widowed harridans, or fishermen's wives whose husbands did not travel south in summer on the dragonship. Careless slips of razor-sharp fishing knives had cost the women more than the tips of their fingers over the years, so it was obvious to Tam that her mother was determined to punish her. But for what? Choosing to spend time alone? What was wrong with that?

'Watch yourself, girl,' a cracked voice warned. Tam lifted her head and looked into the glinting eyes of Amarti, wife of old Berikan the fisherman. The woman pointed with the stub of a lost finger at Tam's knife. Its sharp edge was dangerously close to her hand. With her dark shiny pupils above her sun-cracked cheeks and snub nose, Amarti looked just like a crab, an observation that secretly amused Tam. The Dragon Heart, Harbin's lore priest, ironically chose the old language words 'A-Mare-Ti' for her name. They translated approximately to mean 'tough little crab', and Amarti certainly *was* a tough little crab. Tam slid the gutted fish aside and pulled another from the pitted bucket on the bench. The fish scales glinted like armour in the brittle sunlight. She set to sliding her knife back and forth across the fish's loose and slippery body, and contemplated the names of her family to ease the boredom of her job.

Her father was Kevan. In the old tongue he would be called 'Ka-Evar-Une'—'the man of rock'. His was a name of strength and perseverance. She could not argue with the Dragon Heart's choice of name for her father. He was strong, a veritable pillar of Harbin; the rock of its foundation.

Her mother's name came from 'Ere-Eesa' and it meant 'daughter of fortune' in full translation. As much as she tried, she found no connection between the priest's choice of name for her mother and her life. She knew from family gossip over the years that her mother was the only daughter and only child of Maruki, a widow, meaning the family had no men to carry the family heritage or bring fortune to the family name. Perhaps fortune had favoured Eesa through marriage to Kevan.

Her brother Chasse was named by the priest from 'En-Chai-Se' which meant 'he who triumphs'. Tam grinned as she remembered the choice. Cynicism told her that her brother's name had been given by a priest who wanted to impress her father with a promise that his son would rise to greatness. Not that she doubted Chasse would be a great warrior. But he was not from the same mould as their father. Chasse was softer, but in a positive way. He was warm like a cosy autumn fire where his father was cold like a rock. If Chasse ever rose to be a leader, he would only ever lead by example, not by force or threat. He would listen to the needs of others. Not like his father at all.

Tam considered her own name. The Dragon Heart chose 'Te-Amen-San' from the old language for her. It literally meant 'the dawn's light'. As a little girl, when she learnt her name's true meaning, she loved to hear its sound on her mother's lips. It tied her to sunrises and their beauty. As much as anything, her name drew her to the natural world. As a child, she sometimes rose before the first rays of daylight began to colour the eastern skies over the backs of the mountains, slipped outside and sat on the shingled roof of her parents' cottage, watching the sunrise set the world ablaze with its golds and reds. 'Te-Amen-San—dawn's light.' Mystified by it, she used to whisper the words softly at the sky. She wondered why the Dragon Heart had chosen that special name for her. Even her red-gold hair matched her name. She began to believe she was destined for something more than the mundane fate shared by all the other women in Harbin—cleaning and cooking and mending and bearing children for men.

She checked her thoughts. Not quite all the women. Those who were truly ugly, like old Asmae, who lived in isolation at the northern reach of the village, could never attract a man, and were never blessed with children. But even Asmae carried a woman's burden in her working life. She turned her share of pots, mended her share of fishing nets, cooked her share of meals for the single men in the Warriors' Hall. With her sight dimmed, her back bowed, her hands gnarled and scarred from years of servile work, Asmae spent the long winters alone, and the short summers with few visitors except for the young girls Eesa sent to feed her. Tam felt a chord of pity whenever she thought of the old woman. She fully understood Eesa's reason for sending young girls to tend Asmae, though. It was a blunt social lesson. The choices young women had were limited to this: accept the care of a strong husband and his burden of marriage, or live forever alone and dependent on the goodwill of strangers.

'You'll daydream away your fingers, girl,' Amarti

rasped. Tam raised her left hand to brush aside a wisp of hair that dangled annoyingly across her cheek, and swept the fish head into her bucket. As she bent to extract another salmon from her basket, she heard a voice. Someone was sniggering. She glanced up to see three girls sidling past, carrying freshly cut reeds in their woven baskets.

'Oh, excuse us,' the tallest girl said with pouting dignity. 'We didn't mean to disturb the daughter of the Dragon Head from so important a task.' She smiled sweetly at Tam and her ice-blue eyes sparkled maliciously.

Tam forced a return smile and scooped another fish from the basket, letting it land on her benchtop with a smack.

'I do hope you're being very careful with that knife, Tamesan. It looks wickedly sharp,' the tall girl said with mock concern. She shook her long black plait and nudged one of her companions.

With a deft swing of the knife, Tam hacked off the fish head and smiled again at her antagonist. 'Pray to Procra I don't slip and cut the tip off your wagging tongue, Katris,' she warned.

Katris' two friends stifled their laughter. Katris nonchalantly shrugged her shoulders and replied haughtily, 'Oh well, can't stay to gossip idly with the fisherwomen. We have the Long Hall to prepare for the men. We have to leave you to it.' She turned and led her friends up the slope, away from the pebbled beach and the fishermen's quarters.

'Good riddance,' Tam muttered under her breath, glad to be free of Katris' taunting face.

After a few paces though, the dark-haired girl turned and shouted, 'Please do bathe in some scented oils before you come to the feasting tonight, Tamesan. I think our men will be sick of the stench of fish after so long at sea.' She wheeled, laughing, and the three girls continued up the foot-worn pathway towards the village centre.

'You be paying no heed to them, girl,' Amarti croaked, waggling a limp fish at Tam. 'They've no call to be teasing you like that. Your mother would tan their rumps if she heard them.'

Tam watched the receding figures, thinking of all the answers she should have called after Katris, before deciding she was better off not speaking. Katris had changed so much. Two summers ago they were close friends, laughing together, playing games, sharing secrets, looking for any excuse to spend time in each other's company. Only Chasse had been as close to her as Katris. She remembered taking Katris to the higher slopes of Dragon Mountain. There, she shared her private aerie, and from it, they could view the entire bay and see all the islets out to Dragon's Mouth, where the deep ocean filled the horizon. It was the one place where Tam could escape from her mother's constant demands for work and help. Village girls rarely ventured up the mountain beyond the trees bordering the cattle pasture, but Tam took Katris higher to show her the world from a different perspective. From the heights of Dragon Mountain, Tam shared with Katris her love of the world surrounding Harbin, revealing to her the serenity and beauty of the forest, the strength of the mountains, the moodiness of the ocean and the pastel-painted sunsets, the secret of the dawn's light. Katris had sat staring in silent wonder, and Tam made her promise not to share the secret with anyone else. As a pledge of trust, they shared the translations of their names in the old tongue. Katris came from 'Ke-Atry-Sis' meaning 'she of moon beauty'. With her pale skin, blue eyes and black hair, Katris was indeed growing into a beauty of a full fourteen summers. She was as tall as Tam, and as sharp of mind, so they were natural friends.

But the friendship waned when Katris' interests became less adventurous, and more like those of the other girls. She stopped asking to go up the mountain, and then began making excuses not to go whenever Tam invited her. While Tam sought opportunities to avoid women's work, Katris started going out of her way to learn the cooking craft, and how to weave, and care for little children. The adolescent girls, Katris foremost, chattered incessantly about boys and men. They compared the men's respective merits, their physical attractiveness, their reputations as warriors. Tam feigned interest in their conversations to stay in the crowd. Initially, she even took nervous delight in sneaking down to the hot springs at the Dragon's Cauldron with Katris and the others when the men bathed, to study them secretly, but she quickly tired of that fervent, furtive game. She tried to entice Katris away, but her friend laughed at her, calling her a little girl still. Hurt, Tam tried to cling to the outer edge of the girls' group. But something had changed; she could sense it. Katris snubbed her frequently, especially when Tam showed no interest in girls' talk. Then the snide and poorly disguised remarks began. The girls didn't approve of Tam spending time with Chasse, playing boyish games. They accused her of turning her brother—someone they all agreed was very handsome—into more of a girl than a boy. They chastised her for ducking her responsibilities and being slow in learning craft and cooking skills. Her first period came later than Katris', so they teased her for being slow to grow into a woman. Embarrassed, and sick of the harassment, she spent less time with the girls. Instead, she chose to share her loss of social identity with the solitary beauty of the mountainside.

Alone on the mountain, staring across the expanse of the bay into the sweeping ocean beyond, the taunts and ridicule of Katris and the other girls receded. Tam lost herself in watching the gulls wheel over the fishing shoals. Every now and then a gull would swoop and settle on the water, dip its head, then fly off with a tiny sparkling weight hanging from its beak. She observed how the sparrows, flitting from bough to bough, chased and caught butterflies and other insects. In their turn, insects swarmed above delicate mountain blooms, gathering pollen or nibbling at the fresh petals and green leaves. There was balance and purpose to everything, a harmony in the natural world that made the teasing games of the village girls seem trivial. Tam could lie against the warm flat granite of her favourite mountain perch and almost feel the pulse of the earth in the morning sunlight. High above Harbin, the whole world fell into perspective, and her tiny village diminished in significance.

When she tried to slip back into the group near the end of her twelfth summer two years ago, more bored with isolation than desiring their company, Katris deliberately told the others about Tam's mountain hideaway, and the secret hope she held that her name marked her for things greater than being the common wife of a Harbin dragonwarrior. The girls' ridicule trebled. They laughed in Tam's face and accused her of thinking she was above everyone because she was the Dragon Head's daughter. Hurt by Katris' broken trust, Tam stormed away and vowed to have nothing more to do with their idle activities and frivolous chatter about who was the best-looking man, and who would pair with whom when the time came for choosing. She again sought the mountain's solitude, and occasionally the company of her brother Chasse.

Tam sensed a presence, interrupting her thoughts, then saw a small shadow. Her little brother, Jaysin, stood beside her, staring at the knife she held above a silver-pink fish. She waited for him to speak, but he seemed reluctant to do so. For a six year old, Jaysin was intensely quiet and reserved. He often sat at the edge of the children's games. Tam felt immensely sorry for her auburn-haired little brother. He was so much like herself—a thinker, unable to mix easily with his peers—but unlike her, he always seemed desperately unhappy.

'Well?' she inquired when it was obvious Jaysin would not speak first.

'Mother wants you to feed Gramma,' he said in his reed-thin voice. He didn't lift his eyes from the knife.

'Do you want a turn?' she offered. She lifted the knife carefully towards Jaysin's hand.

'No,' the boy blurted and ran off towards the jetty.

'Now that there *is* a strange one,' laughed Amarti as she lifted a gnarled hand to her forehead, feigning confusion.

Tam ignored the old woman's comment and watched Jaysin's receding form. Sometimes she just wanted to hug and hold her little brother to keep him safe from the harms of the world. Sometimes too, like everyone else, she simply saw him as an odd little boy, and then she felt guilty for thinking like that.

'I have to go,' she announced. She picked up an old rag and wiped the scales and fish juice from her hands. Then she dipped her hands in a bucket of water used to rinse the scaling knives and shook them dry before heading up the path towards the village centre.

People were engrossed in organising for the return of the dragonship. Girls bustled in and out of the

Warriors' Hall. Some swept, others carried linen and straw. Women carted woven baskets of new-baked breads into the Long Hall, and armfuls of firewood, while an older man hobbled along the upper path bearing a pair of freshly killed chickens for the coming feast. Most did not even see Tam pass, but some, like Banni, waved or smiled. Banni was barely three summers older than Tam. She had come of age the previous summer and the dragonwarrior Jared had taken her for his wife, as everyone in the village expected. Though she was older, she was always friendly towards Tam, more so than Tam's own peers. In fact Banni never seemed unhappy or angry with anyone. She was a calm spirit, at peace with everyone and everything. Tam returned her wave, then continued towards the narrow wooden bridge that spanned Watersdrop and led to her home.

As she approached the bridge, she saw boys milling on the path. They were gathering into a circle. At its centre two boys faced each other. One was tall, strongly built, with a shock of dark hair. She recognised him immediately—Marron, Trask's son. Trask was a fierce member of the Dragon Fang, a dragonwarrior considered by many villagers as second in prowess only to Tam's father. Marron was the same age as her brother Chasse. Next summer both he and Chasse would be initiate warriors on the dragonship. The other boy had his back to her but she was certain it was Derin, the third son of old Galt, the herdsman. He had long, dirty blond hair that he always let hang free. Marron's head bobbed. Derin sidestepped. In his hand he held a solid stick, fashioned like a crude sword. The boys were fighting again. Hardly a week seemed to pass lately without a brawl erupting. They were obsessed with proving who was strongest, who was the better fighter. The circle rotated across the path and cut Tam's access to the bridge. She shifted her feet impatiently, forced to watch.

Marron and Derin had fought more times in the past four weeks than anyone could count. Marron won every encounter but Derin did not accept defeat. Even Eesa intervened at one stage, as each fight became more bloody and determined. Not that she entirely disapproved of the fighting. After all, she told Tam, they were boys, and boys had to sort out who was strongest and who would lead. No. Eesa's concern was more with the developing viciousness. The village could ill afford to lose a potential dragonwarrior to boyish games. Derin had emerged from the last fight with a long cut across the side of his neck, a broken nose, and a wound on his thigh. But as expected, with no dragonwarrior men to back her authority in the village, Eesa's complaints fell on deaf ears. Without the men, the older boys were a law unto themselves.

Marron suddenly lunged. Derin leapt backwards, escaping Marron's first attack, but he was caught in a tangle of spectators. Tam heard him grunt as Marron struck. A cheer rose from the circle. Several boys threw Derin out of their midst and he stumbled forward,

clutching his stomach and gasping for air. He dropped
the stick weapon. Marron looked up and saw Tam was
watching. He smiled. Then he spun with excessive
bravado and swung his right leg up in a kick. His shin
caught the doubled-over Derin smack under the chin
and almost cartwheeled the boy backwards. Derin collapsed amidst a roar of approval from the audience. He
did not move. Marron turned to face Tam with both
hands held high and then executed an exaggerated
bow. She was horrified. Derin was still lying motionless, and no-one stooped to help him. The circle of
boys were jostling around Marron, patting him on the
back, congratulating him. Derin could be badly
injured, or worse, and they didn't even care. She
ignored Marron's smile and pushed through the group
to kneel beside Derin. When she touched his bruised
arm he groaned, sucked in a lungful of air, and
coughed violently.

'Leave him alone. He'll be all right,' said a voice
above her. She looked up into Marron's dirty face and
dark glittering eyes. A dozen boys of all ages stared
down at her, curious. Derin groaned again and spat a
mouthful of blood into the earth. A broken tooth
gleamed in the mess.

'You've hurt him,' she accused, struggling to make
Marron sorry for Derin's plight.

Laughter burst from the boys. Marron grinned and
replied, 'Of course I've hurt him. It was a fight.
That's what you're supposed to do in a fight.' More
laughter greeted his sarcasm. Some boys complained

that they wanted something else to do. Then a voice alerted them that Derin's father was coming. They began to drift away.

'So you're all going to leave him here?' Tam asked in amazement.

'His father is coming,' Marron sneered. 'I'm sure a shepherd knows how to look after hurt animals.'

Derin winced. The muscles bunched in his legs as if he was going to stand, but the fight was long gone from his body and he groaned again and relaxed.

Tam glanced up angrily at Marron, who still stood over her. 'Can't you stop taunting him?' she implored.

'I'll stop when he's had enough and knows his place,' Marron asserted. He stared at Tam. His face, set in a strong, determined expression, defied anyone, even her, to doubt that he was the best fighter and natural leader of the boys. But his eyes, dark and defiant, seemed to have deeper purpose, as though he was studying her face for the answer to a very different question. Inexplicably, she suddenly felt uncomfortable and vulnerable. Before she could move though, she heard the rhythm of running feet, heavy feet. Derin's father, Galt the herdsman, came lumbering towards them.

'Get away from my boy!' he snarled as he pushed past Marron and knelt beside Tam. Marron sniggered. Galt's weather-worn face flared with anger at the youth's stifled laughter and he rose to face Marron, growling, 'If you don't get out of my sight before

I lift my arm, I'll break your smirking face with my fist, you cocky little rooster.'

Marron retreated instinctively but he didn't turn to leave. Instead, he fixed the old man with an acid glare, and sneered, 'I'll go, old man, but not because you frighten me. I just don't like the smell of goat dung.'

Galt lifted his fist, but Marron skipped away, laughing, and jogged towards the village centre.

'When your father returns you will hear more of this!' Galt shouted. 'Mark my words! You will hear more!' He watched until the youth joined the waiting pack of boys and they gravitated towards the jetty. Then he turned to his son. Tam had helped Derin sit up, but he wobbled groggily and constantly moaned.

'Here, girl,' Galt said gently, while firmly pushing her aside. 'Leave my son to me. He does not need a woman's touch. You run along and do whatever it is your mother has set you to do.'

Tam wanted to object, but the old man was already bending to cradle Derin in his arms, and she could see the mixture of anger, hurt, and sorrow competing for control of the old man's lined face. Instead, she rose and moved back, and she watched while Galt walked unsteadily away, bearing the weight of his beaten son towards their simple home on the outskirts of the village, beneath Dragon Mountain. Then she crossed the wooden bridge towards her own home, scattering a flock of chickens as she passed through them.

From her doorstep she could see across Harbin Bay. The water remained grey. The more adventurous fishermen were rowing towards the gap to meet the dragonship. The ship's red sail was a large square now, and the long low hull was visible above the waterline. Her father would be home soon. Kevan would reassert his authority and her mother would revert to being the Dragon Head's wife. Tam wondered how her mother really felt each time her husband left her in charge of village affairs, then returned to take back the responsibility and status. Every woman in the village must experience something like that. When their men were away, they made the decisions, they controlled their own lives; when their men returned they fell back into place, letting the men decide, letting the men rule. Last summer she dared to ask Eesa why it was like that. She received a scolding for her curiosity, and a lecture on how it was that men were born to lead and women to follow. Later she overheard her mother talking with the other women and they were laughing about what Tam had asked.

'That child asks too many questions,' Eesa said. 'If her father heard her, he would go mad.'

'We all would like to ask too many questions,' another woman replied. 'Thank Procra for summer and dragon journeys,' she added. Then they all laughed. Tam didn't understand what was so funny about the dragon journeys, but she learned that her questions weren't hers alone. She just happened to ask them aloud. She was surprised to learn that the women were almost glad to be free of the men during summer, though, because she had never heard that sentiment publicly admitted.

Tam hesitated at the door to her home. She wondered what mood her grandmother would be in. The old lady had long outlived the rest of her generation, almost as if she was defying death as fervently as Marron defied any boy to better him. But she was thin, and feeble-minded, and couldn't feed or dress herself unaided. As soon as Tam was old enough to cope, she was put in charge of Gramma Harmi. It was her chore, her duty. That, and looking after little brother Jaysin, although he was taking care of himself adequately this summer. Lately she seldom saw him, except in the morning and when she came home in the evening. She had to do the family chores. Jaysin always disappeared during the day. Chasse went out and explored, and played, and sometimes fought. Because they were boys, it was accepted they could do these things. And she worked. Because she was just a girl.

'Is that you, child?' Gramma Harmi's croaky voice rasped from within the cottage. The old lady persisted in calling her 'child'. Never once did she call her Tamesan or Tam. She wondered if her grandmother even remembered her name at all.

Tam toyed with the idea of sneaking away back up the mountain. She could just sit there alone, in peace, and watch the sun set over the bay as the dragonship drifted to the jetty, surrounded by torchlight flickering on the water. At least that was how she imagined it might look. Then she could turn into an eagle and climb high into the night. She would circle above the merry band of homecomers and welcomers and watch her people celebrate the close of summer. No-one would know it was her soaring above them against the tapestry of stars. She would feel free. She would be free.

'Girl?' the old lady's voice asked tremulously, 'Have you come to feed me?'

Tam pushed aside her daydream with a shrug and lifted the smooth doorhandle. She breezed into the darkened cottage, calling sweetly, 'Yes, Gramma, it's me, come to feed you.'

Chapter Three

The western sky was a patch of scarlet embers when the dragonship docked at Harbin's jetty. Flickering torches, teased by a fickle sea breeze that had eluded the ship throughout the day, bobbed along the jetty and threw glittering light across the dark water. People moved about with purpose. Some called for and caught the hawsers to lash the ship to its moorings. Others dragged a crude wooden gangplank into position to receive the disembarking Dragon Fang, the village's glorious warriors.

As Tam pushed through the throng, she felt the collective anticipation of the women waiting to welcome their menfolk who had been ten weeks away from their hearths. She had missed her father despite the fact that he was frequently surly and aloof when he was home. She wondered if the dragon they pursued this time had proven a tough adversary.

The scrape of wood against wood and a raucous cheer from the men on board drew her attention to the ship. She pressed towards Eesa, who was foremost on the jetty to receive her homecoming husband, and saw a dozen eager hands slide the gangplank over the dragonship's gunwales. Dark shapes swarmed at the edge of the torchlight, and for a moment Tam imagined them to be the frightening figures of her nightmares. Then one large warrior stepped onto the gangplank and into the light. Tam knew his full greying beard and hair, and heard the people let out a great spontaneous cheer to welcome her father, Kevan, Dragon Head of Harbin. He lurched heavily off the ship and gave Eesa a hearty hug. He ruffled Jaysin's hair, patted Chasse on the shoulder, and nodded to acknowledge Tam.

Before anyone could speak, more cheers broke from the crowd as other figures, lighter in stature than Kevan, clambered across the plank. Four young men, still wearing battle armour and carrying their spears, joined the welcoming party. They were the newly initiated dragonwarriors. Tam knew them. There was Harly, Karl's son; Kerik, son of Jon; the lanky and awkward Garret, whose father had been killed by a dragon four summers before; and Ion, who had the same name as his father. All four tried to look intensely serious for an embarrassing moment before they were greeted by the open arms and affection of their waiting families. The remaining men then emerged from the semi-darkness of the dragonship to be met by their people.

Tam was getting caught in the crush, so she eased away from her family momentarily and shifted to the jetty's furthest reach, amongst the fishing tackle and baskets that had been stacked up during the day. The noisy welcoming party began to gravitate towards the shore, heading up to the Long Hall where a small feast had been prepared for the village's mighty warriors. In the midst of the crowd she could just make out her father's head and shoulders. She was about to follow in their wake when she noticed a motionless figure at the head of the gangplank. One woman remained staring into the dragonship's dark depths as if held there by an invisible rope. Even in the dwindling light Tam recognised her. She stepped forward and gently said, 'Banni?' The older girl did not move. Tam moved to her side and glanced into the empty hold of the dragonship. Waves lapped against the jetty's wooden pylons, gradually subsuming the receding noise of the revellers.

'Banni? Are you all right?' Tam asked gingerly. Banni stifled a sob in the darkness. Tam reached out to touch her shoulder.

'Where is he?' Banni asked into the empty air. 'Where is my husband?'

Tam had no answer. Jared had not disembarked. Banni had not missed him in the crowd. She knew Jared would have found her. Jared had not come home. Banni sobbed again, and the shoulder on which Tam had placed a gentle hand began to shake violently. The young woman suddenly collapsed onto the planks of the jetty and wept for her lost husband. Tam knelt, wanting to comfort her, but she felt awkward and confused. She had seen other women cry when their men had not returned from the summer journey, but she had never experienced the loss of someone close, so she did not really know what to do or say. Worst of all, she felt a need to cry, too. Banni's sorrow was her sorrow. The tears welled in her eyes, and she shared Banni's grief as the distant, dancing torches of the joyful home-comers disappeared into the Long Hall.

'We crept up to the dragon's lair and fanned out in a big circle. Everyone had a spear ready. When Salmon whistled, Kevan strode from the bushes into the dragon's lair as bold as Varst himself and said, "Who dares to challenge the Dragon Head of Harbin?"'

The eyes of the listening audience in the Long Hall turned their admiration on Kevan. The Dragon Head smiled and nodded to Chasse as if affirming the truth of the tale. Jon, the storyteller, paused for effect and a mouthful of sweet mead, then continued.

'The foul dragon heard his challenge and stirred. Its eyes opened, one at a time. Its teeth bristled and its blue scales shone. With a deep-throated roar, and a flash of fire, it rose to the fight. But the Dragon Fang had planned well. As the beast showed itself, thinking it faced but a single warrior, a flight of Harbin spears darkened the morning sky. Some bounced harmlessly from its scales, and some missed their mark—'

Here Jon paused again to cast a shrewd wink at

another dragonwarrior. His attention fell on Theo, a warrior closer to Kevan's age. An outburst of friendly but derisive laughter greeted Jon's action and Theo lifted his fist in mock anger, replying, 'At least I hit something!'

'It has to be the deadest bush I've seen!' yelled Raven, and a roar of laughter echoed through the hall.

'It was a very dangerous bush, that one,' chimed in another warrior, and more laughter erupted.

'Tell the story!' Theo growled, keen to shift attention from his own shortcoming in the adventure. When he noticed his two sons grinning up at him he cuffed both behind the ear, and said, 'We'll see who laughs when you grinning idiots face your first dragon.' More laughter followed.

'Enough spears found their marks,' Jon announced. 'The dragon was sorely wounded. But still it made one last attempt to attack the source of its anger. Mighty Kevan had to fight bravely to save himself from its dying wrath. Then Trask stepped forward and cut off its head, and the fight went out of the beast. The dragon of Etkuan curled up and died. The Dragon Fang of Harbin has conquered another of the foul beasts that stole away great Nakiades' beautiful treasure.'

A discordant cheer of approval greeted Jon's conclusion of the tale. Congratulatory remarks followed, and individuals dropped into recounting fragments of the adventure to their family and companions that particularly pertained to themselves. Tam listened patiently while Theo told Chasse for the third time of how Kevan stood toe-to-toe with the dragon in its lair. She had seen the long scar on her father's left arm inflicted by one of the dragon's vicious claws. He dutifully rolled up his sleeve and allowed Eesa and his family and friends to trace its puckered white path from biceps to wrist, while Theo described in detail the crimson blood that flowed freely from it during the battle. Tam found herself staring absently at a small scar on her father's forehead, no doubt the legacy of a minor wound during the battle, but her mind strayed constantly from the tales of heroes to Banni and her lost husband, Jared.

Banni was not in the Long Hall. She had returned to her empty, cold, dark hut to deal with her grief. Tam had walked with her as far as the door, but once there Banni simply said she would be all right and went inside alone. Tam had no choice but to go to the Long Hall. She walked reluctantly, and stood outside the Long Hall for a long time, listening to the laughter and storytelling, until Chasse came looking for her.

'Tam, where have you been? Father has noticed,' he informed her.

'With Banni,' she quietly replied. 'Jared isn't home.'

Chasse shook his head. 'I didn't know. Those things aren't mentioned tonight. But come inside, Tam. Father wants us all to be with him. He has done brave deeds.'

So Tam followed her brother into the warmth and noise and celebration of the Long Hall, but she could not forget Banni's sorrow.

In all the storytelling, Jared's name was not mentioned. It was as if the warrior had never gone on the summer journey. But Tam knew that was the sacred rule of the first welcoming feast: it was meant to be a time of joy and happiness, a moment for reunion and hope; the names of those who had not returned, who fell before the dragon, or perished in the cruel seas, were taboo for that single night. There would be time for loss and grief later, when the dead were honoured. The ceremony, those summers it was needed, was always held five days after the dragonship's return. Then the family and friends of the dead congregated with the Dragon Heart priest at Watersdrop to sing the Words of Passage. The singing was a prayer asking Varst to keep the dead person's soul safe from the great dragon Shaddho's maw as it journeyed through the dark world of death to Varst's Eternal Paradise in the heart of the sun. She knew all this, but still Banni's grief hung over Tam as the people around her related their adventures.

Someone nudged her kneecap. She blinked and looked up at her father. His face was solemn as he directed where she should look with a subtle shift of his dark blue eyes, but his voice was not unkind as he spoke.

'It would seem my daughter has an admirer.'

She turned her attention in the direction her father

indicated, and saw Trask's family seated on the floor with several dragonwarriors. No-one in particular was looking at her. Then she noticed Marron. He turned and stared at her across the smoky space. When he saw Tam watching him, a faint smile played across his face. She looked away.

Her father nodded knowingly and patted her knee, saying wisely, 'All things in their time, Tamesan. Trask's son would be a fine match for you.'

She lowered her eyes to stare at a half-eaten portion of bread, and blushed against her will. She heard Theo laugh and say, 'Your young maiden glows with pleasure. You have an uncommon beauty ripening in your house, Kevan,' and her father replied with a complimentary comment she barely heard.

She wished she hadn't blushed. She couldn't decide whether she was embarrassed by her father pointing Marron out to her, or angry. Marron was not a boy she could be interested in. He was an arrogant bully. His beating of Derin earlier in the day was sickening proof of that. She had watched him swagger about the village for years. Even as a small child, Marron dominated games and pushed other boys around until they followed him like sheep. And he always teased the girls. He was cruel. Now that they were nearing adulthood, girls like Katris raved about his long dark hair and his muscles, although they were quick to remind themselves that the older dragonwarriors were even more desirable. But of the boys in the village nearing manhood, Marron was widely considered one of the best catches. In fact, although she spent much less time now with Katris and her friends, Tam knew Katris openly hoped Marron would choose her for his wife once he was a dragonwarrior. She thought they would be a perfect match. As far as Tam was concerned, Katris could have him.

'Are you all right, Tam?' Chasse was leaning forward, concern on his bright face.

'I'm fine,' she replied. 'Thanks.' She chanced a quick glance across the hall at Marron but he was thankfully engrossed in another tale being told by his father. Tam took a deep breath and spoke to her mother. 'Should I go back and see that Gramma is still all right?'

Eesa hesitated and frowned. Tam had interrupted her as she had been listening to yet another variation on her husband's part in the slaying of the Etkuan dragon. Then she nodded and said, 'Of course, Tamesan. I had forgotten Gramma in all the excitement. Run along.' Then she tilted her head towards the wall where a small body lay curled asleep. 'Take Jaysin with you. I think he's had too much food and too much news tonight.'

Grateful for the excuse to leave the smoke and noise of the Long Hall, Tam bade goodnight to her father and mother, then scooped up little Jaysin's sleeping form, and made her way towards the main door, accompanied by Chasse. Marron looked up as she passed but she made no attempt to acknowledge him.

When she reached the door, Chasse opened it and asked, 'Do you want me to come home with you?'

'No,' she answered. 'No. You would disappoint father if you left this early on the welcoming night. Stay. I know how to see to Gramma and Jaysin.'

Chasse smiled appreciatively as she stepped by him. Then he closed the door and returned to the circle between Kevan and Theo.

The air outside was cold. Her warm breath escaped in misty clouds as she cradled Jaysin's weight in her arms and climbed the gentle slope towards the bridge spanning Watersdrop. She stopped to adjust her heavy sleeping bundle at the bridge and stared across the village. A patch of silver moonlight scudded across the scattered collection of buildings, chasing shadows. The yellow light of the Long Hall sat at the centre. Down at the water's edge three tiny lights wavered. Some fishermen, already making their way home from the celebration, perhaps. She wondered what it must be like to be a fisherman in Harbin. Some had been dragonwarriors as young men, who serious injuries had forced to abandon the summer journeys and remain home. They were seldom happy while the dragonship was away, and talked constantly of the old adventures, as if they longed for those times to return and dissolve the drudgery of their fishermen's existence. They were sad, bitter men. She also knew others, like Amarti's husband, who chose to be fishermen. They had never hunted dragons, had never been accorded the status of manhood sought by all the young boys.

Yet they enjoyed their work and their place in the village, taking pride in what they did and ignoring the condescending comments made by certain dragonwarriors about those men who stayed with the women and children. She would like to know why they chose to be different. Perhaps one day she would ask.

A tiny point of light bobbed in the bay. One fisherman was already at work. The water was a patchwork of light and dark, shining like metal wherever the moon forced its beams through the clouded night sky. It had a troubled, uncertain look to it, Tam thought, and she was suddenly afraid for the lone fisherman out there on the mysterious ocean. She could imagine the broad black wings of Shaddho, the great Dragon of Darkness who had pursued Nakiades and Tam's ancestors into Harbin, spread across the face of the moon as the beast hunted for prey. And out there in the darkness a solitary man went about his simple work, heedless of the danger sweeping in around him. Tam shivered.

She drew her eyes away from the ocean and stared towards the dark smudge that was Banni's hut. Was that how poor Banni felt now, she wondered, alone in a sea of darkness? And was Jared's soul already somewhere out there in that greater ocean of darkness called death, equally alone, frightened that no-one would sing the Words of Passage to bring him to the light of Varst's Eternal Paradise? Tears crept inside her throat again, a rising veil of sadness she felt but couldn't really explain, or even understand. She hugged Jaysin's tiny body to her breast and hurried home across the bridge.

Chapter Four

'I have no idea where the old man is,' replied Eesa. Tam heard the rising irritation in her mother's tone.

'He is needed here,' Kevan insisted. He banged his fist against the door jamb to emphasise his point. 'The Dragon Head wants him here.'

'You know as well as I do that he is as easy to compel as the wind on a windless day,' Eesa responded.

'It is unlike him not to come down the first morning after the return of the dragonship. He knows his skills and herbs are needed,' said Theo. 'Perhaps I should send one of my boys to fetch him.'

'No,' grumbled Kevan angrily. 'I am Dragon Head. I will send for him, though it infuriates me to have to do so.' He turned to Eesa and glanced towards Tam, who was feeding Gramma Harmi. 'As soon as the girl finishes with the old woman, send her to fetch the Herbal Man. I want him in the village today. There are men who need his healing and advice. Am I understood?'

'Yes, husband,' Eesa answered dutifully. 'She will go.' She gave Tam a stern look that warned her to be obedient or face terrible consequences.

Kevan then beckoned Chasse, who was loitering by the window. 'You, lad, will come with us to the Warriors' Hall. There you can see the spoils of the dragon's treasure. If you intend to be a man next summer it is time you spent more time with men.' With that, he led Chasse and Theo out of the cottage.

Eesa waited until they left. Then she collected three pottery bowls and fixed Tam with a glare. 'You heard your father. When you have finished with Gramma, go up to the Herbal Man's hut and bring him to the village. Bring him straight down, understand? No dilly-dallying on the mountainside, or playing games, girl, or by Procra you will be sorry. Hear me?'

'Yes, mother,' Tam replied as she lifted another spoonful of gruel to the old woman's lips.

'Make sure you have. Your father is home and he won't abide nonsense from a girl, especially his own daughter.'

Tam bit her lip. She desperately wanted to shout, 'Yes, mother! I know, mother! Father's word is law, and I'm only a girl so it doesn't matter what I think, does it?' but instead she merely said, 'Yes, mother, I'll bring the Herbal Man,' and started wiping the dribble from Gramma Harmi's chin with an old piece of cloth. The old lady gave Tam a crooked toothless grin.

'When you get back, you can come down to the fish tables and help,' Eesa instructed as she stepped out of the doorway. 'If I am not there, I will be in the Long Hall cleaning and mending. You can come and help there.'

Tam watched her mother disappear before she put down the half-empty bowl of gruel and cloth. 'Can I get anything else for you Gramma?' she asked.

The old lady shook her head, and mumbled, 'Little boys.'

Tam smiled weakly at Gramma's comment. She assumed she was thinking of Chasse and Jaysin. The old lady seldom seemed to keep track of conversations any more. She drifted from sleep, to feeding, to sleep. Sometimes she had something to say, but no-one took much notice when she did, because what Gramma said was rarely connected to what was happening around her.

'That's all they really are,' the old lady added as Tam drew a light blanket over her legs.

'I'll be back a little later, Gramma,' Tam explained as she straightened and headed for the door. 'Mother wants me to run another errand.'

'You just be mindful of that dragon,' Gramma said firmly as Tam closed the door.

'There is no dragon on the mountain,' Tam thought to herself. She wondered why Gramma Harmi always had a fixation about a dragon.

Once over the bridge, she felt the weight of tiredness and boredom lift. Being sent to find the Herbal Man was at least an interesting task—though it wasn't fetching the old man that inspired her. In fact, she really didn't cherish the thought of knocking at his hut and then walking down the slopes of Dragon Mountain alone with him at all. He was creepy. He lived in isolation high on the mountain, even during the frozen months of winter when the mountain was locked under the weight of snow, and only rarely came down to the village during the year. His visits were customarily brief. He either came to barter for food and sometimes minor provisions, or to answer the urgent request of a villager who needed his healing. He wore a long dark cloak, as black as Shaddho's legendary hide, and he was old. Some people in the village believed he was older than Gramma Harmi. Tam doubted that.

Adults in the village viewed him with distrust. No-one knew anything of his family. He had no wife, no children, and had lived on the mountain for as long as anyone could remember. He had no true name. Rumour-mongers like Sharmine and Marissa claimed he was a servant of Shaddho, an evil man cursed to use his healing powers to atone for some wicked misdeed in the past. Tam could never see the logic in their tale, but there were many in the village willing to listen. A few, like Amarti, believed the Herbal Man was really being punished by Varst for some basic mistake, and that his penance was to live alone and friendless until he died or expunged his evil through good deeds.

For the children of Harbin, the Herbal Man was a vengeful fairy. Parents told naughty little children that if they didn't behave the Herbal Man would come down from the mountain in the middle of a storm like a demon and carry them away to his hut. There he would boil them in a vat and feed them to the beasts he kept locked in a cave beneath his bed. Tam remembered how, when she was very young, she lay awake, rigid with horror, during a raging winter storm after her father had threatened her with the Herbal Man's visitation. She did not dare fall asleep for fear of being stolen away. It was little wonder, then, that village children screamed in terror when the Herbal Man appeared to treat their ailments. Those he successfully treated were left confused about his true nature, and that confusion bred a strong distrust in some, who rationalised their confusion by clinging to the tales told by Sharmine or Marissa.

Tam never had the loathing for the Herbal Man of her peers. She had seen what the old man could do with his herbs and broths when her brother Chasse lay close to death six summers ago. Chasse had caught a strange malady that spread through the village one summer after the return of the dragonship. It started as a dry feeling in the throat and then became a raging fever. Untreated, the victims died within five days. Two dragonwarriors and six other village people were first to die. They refused the Herbal Man's treatment. Only after Kevan accepted what the old man wanted to do to his son Chasse, did others relent and allow the Herbal Man to treat them. Recovery was slow for those who hesitated, and some still died despite the old man's efforts. Anyone treated early in their sickness recovered very quickly. Yet grateful as people were to the Herbal Man for curing the ill and saving lives, many remained suspicious and distant because he had not saved everyone. So too did the old man. He chose to be aloof and secretive in his ways. The old fears and rumours were unchanged.

Tam was happy to fetch the Herbal Man because it meant she could spend time on the mountain. It meant she didn't have to feed Gramma Harmi, or baby-sit Jaysin, or clean fish, or mend clothes, or mould pots or weave baskets, or do any of the endless, mindless jobs her mother Eesa set aside for her. It was early morning, and it would take until almost midday to reach the Herbal Man's hut; it would be mid-afternoon before she returned with him. Most of the day was hers to enjoy without drudgery.

She spied Katris and a group of girls outside the Long Hall, but as she was headed away from the village and across the pastures, they did not see her pass. She crossed several foot-worn paths that led to outlying huts owned by goat herders, and climbed a wooden railing fence used to keep the goats near the buildings at night. As she crossed the wide pasture, she saw three youths driving goats out of a pen onto the hillside. Each goat was a splash of black, white and tan against the light green summer grass. She followed the tree line at the far side of the pasture for a short distance until she joined the path that led up the mountain towards the Herbal Man's hut. Her goatskin boots and the lower half of her skirt were damp from dew. She could have taken the main path from the village, but it was much quicker to cut across the pasture, and she simply enjoyed walking through the patches of long grass.

The mountain path cut back across the lower slope in a lazy pattern, making it a leisurely walk between the tall fir trees. She was in no hurry. Her mother had warned her not to waste time, but she couldn't complain if Tam chose to walk slowly to avoid slipping over. As she walked, she watched for glimpses of the wildlife she loved to study on the mountain. Not much appeared. She spied a rabbit, and the usual birds flitted between branches higher in the tree canopies. She thought she heard a larger creature crunch through a clump of bushes, and she tensed in preparation for an encounter, but whatever it was avoided her. She found plenty of scratchings and spoor and droppings to show the woods were thickly populated, but the animals themselves were busy deeper in the trees or asleep in their lairs.

At one point she stumbled upon three straying goats. The goat herders would no doubt be worrying where they were, although goats frequently wandered. If they were still here when she descended later, she would at least try to drive them back down to the pasture. It would be dangerous to leave the animals wandering because there were bears on the mountain, and occasionally wolves. In the late days of autumn and early days of spring, driven by starvation, the predators sometimes came to the edge of the village and stole goats or chickens. Wolves were rare visitors. Tam had seen wolves from the safety of her village one warm evening two summers ago. A pack appeared as if by magic on the edge of the goat pasture as the sun dipped into the western ocean. Lit by the last rays of golden light, the wolves skirted the tree line, then melted into the woods. Bears were more common. She watched two cubs playing near her mountain hideaway for most of a morning once, until their mother lumbered out of the underbrush and led them away. Bears seemed harmless enough, their great grey shaggy coats looked soft and warm, but she remembered the firm warnings all village children received to keep out of the woods and off the mountain, especially at night when the bears roamed.

After a while the path made a definite upward turn, becoming quite steep as it climbed the mountain proper. The ground was rockier, trees appeared to cling to the ground rather than grow from it, and cliffs rose into view. Tam had only been on this section of the path once, last summer, when she had accompanied Chasse to take a message to the Herbal Man on Kevan's behalf. Beyond this point the path snaked between rocky outcrops, crossing a shallow section of the mountain where the Herbal Man's hut lay on a narrow, densely wooded plateau.

She stopped halfway up the steep section and clambered onto a gigantic outcrop of boulders that erupted from the mountainside and tumbled over each other like excited puppies. Her own hideaway wasn't this high. From her perch she could see across the entire bay. The sun forced its way between the thin layer of clouds and lit the whole view for her. The deep blue ocean sparkled. She could see the forested peaks of Varst's Bluff and Nakiades' Watch on either side of the entrance to Harbin Bay, called the Dragon's Mouth, and visible directly below her was Harbin itself, nestled between the curves of shore and forest. White gulls circled above the fishing huts and tables. Lines of hearth-fire smoke curled lazily upward. Tiny figures moved on errands through the village. The people looked so small and insignificant in contrast to the wider world surrounding them. She sat and soaked up the warmth of the mid-morning sun for a short time, enjoying being able to look over everything without reproach from an intrusive adult concerned with more mundane matters. Finally, though, her conscience pricked her—she had a duty to complete. She climbed down to the pathway and continued up the mountain.

The sun was nearly overhead when she reached the plateau. As the path levelled, the foliage thickened, and the trees pushed closer together as if thankful for a flat space in which they could safely plant their roots. The ground was damp underfoot, and the soil rich. Tam could almost taste the increased moisture in the air. Last summer, when she had reached this point with Chasse, she felt as if she had entered another world. The trees glistened with moss and lichen, and broad-leaved ferns, some as tall as Tam's father, grew abundantly between the trees. There was a profusion of colourful birds here as well. They filled the air with their chirruping and chatter, and the beating of their wings as they flew swiftly between the tree trunks just above Tam's head. Some birds were flashes of brilliant blue and red and yellow as they hurtled past and disappeared into the mass of thick green. The plateau was a beautiful lush garden, and it fascinated Tam. The place was eerie, but she couldn't reason precisely why it made her feel like that. Perhaps it was because the whole plateau was so different to everything else on the mountain and in her village, as if it really didn't belong to the world of Harbin. She had dreamed of this forest several times since her last visit. Always, in her dream, the forest was silent, full of expectation, as if awaiting some great event—caught in the moment between seeing and comprehending. It was a question waiting for an answer, an answer she did not have. Perhaps that was why the place felt eerie to her.

The path wound gently through the luxuriant forest, rising and falling where rivulets cut their own paths across the plateau. Just above the tree canopy she could see the face of the upper mountain and its craggy peak looming like a god. Even at the end of summer, snow clung doggedly to the peak, reminding everyone that winter would soon return to bury the world under its icy blanket. Tam tried to imagine the plateau forest deep in snow, the trees and ferns coated white, but somehow the image eluded her, as if the concept could not belong there. It was impossible to imagine this place as being anything other than what it was now. The thought added depth to her peculiar sense of the eeriness pervading the forest.

Tam paused at a rill and cupped her hands to scoop up a mouthful of sparkling fresh water. It tasted cool, and reminded her just how thirsty she was, so she drank three more scoopfuls before continuing. Within a few metres, she reached a small clearing on the crest of a rise. At the far edge of the clearing stood a hovel. It was the Herbal Man's home. The building was so overgrown with creepers and moss that it almost blended into the surrounding forest. It looked older than any hut in the village, and its ramshackle appearance suggested it had been badly thrown together out of discarded pieces of wood and broken stone by a drunk or a lunatic. In fact, Tam believed if it wasn't for the creepers and vines festooning the building, the dilapidated structure would collapse altogether.

Tam's uneasiness increased as she approached the hut. A soft tinkling of bells and wind chimes drifted on the faint breeze. It was like a haunting melody, full of strange harmonies and erratic rhythms and discordant notes that both pleased and jarred her senses. The fear she couldn't quite control spread through her and made her throat sticky and her legs weak. She reminded herself that the nightmare stories from her childhood were only stories. The Herbal Man didn't really steal children, or boil them in a vat. There really wasn't a cave of horrors beneath his tumble-down hut. Her brother had been healed by him. Her parents wouldn't send her on an errand up the mountain if the stories were true. She tried to laugh to hide her nervousness but couldn't. She scolded herself for being so silly. Yet still a feeling that all was not right in that place pervaded her thoughts.

The door to the hut was closed. She hesitated to summon her courage and then knocked. She waited. No-one came to the door. She shuffled her feet and knocked again. Still no-one answered. Perhaps the Herbal Man wasn't in. She thought of trying the door to see if it was locked but decided against that in case the Herbal Man was inside and mistook her entrance for rudeness. Instead, she ventured to a tiny window on the near side of the hut that was partly obscured by creepers. When she tried to peer through the gaps in the rickety shutters she could hardly see, it was so dark inside. She moved to a second window. The new angle presented her with more darkness, but some thin rays of light filtered into the dusty interior. She could make out a table, and part of a chair, but that was all. The hut appeared to be empty. The Herbal Man wasn't home.

She shrugged her shoulders and retraced her steps across the clearing. Her father would not be happy to learn that the Herbal Man did not accompany her. At the clearing's edge she halted and considered whether it would be prudent to wait a while longer, in case the old man was simply off somewhere collecting herbs. Just then she heard a noise. In the foliage to her left, someone or something groaned. A sharp rush of adrenalin pumped through her. She wanted to run, but hesitated, straining for any further sound. There was another groan.

Curiosity overcame her fear. She cautiously picked her way through the huge tree ferns until she came to a gap where a small stream cascaded along a rough pebble bed between two large trunks. A human foot poked out from behind one tree. Her fear and curiosity doubled. She crept to the opposite side of the moss-covered trunk and peered around. Lying spread-eagled on his back, on the tiny bank of the stream, his white hair flowing in the water, was the Herbal Man. The unexpected discovery startled Tam, but when she looked closer she saw that the old man's head rested against a large rock. There was dried blood caked on the rock and in the old man's hair. She slipped down beside him and bent to check the extent of his injury. The back of his head had apparently struck the rock quite fiercely. The Herbal Man groaned again and rolled his face into the water. She reached across and gently lifted his head out of the stream, and as she did, the old man opened his eyes.

'It's all right,' she said softly. 'You're all right. I'll get you out of this.'

The old man's eyes widened and Tam saw the intense grey colour within. Then they creased into a painful smile. He tried to speak, but all that issued from his lips was a dry hiss.

'Don't talk,' Tam whispered gently. 'I'll need any strength you have to help me get you out of here.'

Chapter Five

The Dragon Head strode across the open ground separating the Warriors' Hall and the Long Hall. Those who saw him pass knew he was very angry.

'Eesa,' warned Janys, who was sitting at the door to the Long Hall mending a rush basket. 'Your husband is coming and he looks displeased.'

'Men,' cursed Eesa. She put down the length of sailcloth she was sewing and moved to meet Kevan at the doorway. Her husband stood glowering like a storm-cloud.

'Where is that girl?' he demanded.

'I take it she's not brought the Herbal Man yet,' Eesa said, knowing full well that was the reason for Kevan's dark mood.

'No, she has not,' he growled. 'And the day is slipping by.'

Eesa glanced up at the sun. It was lower in the western sky than she had realised. 'Perhaps he had a task to complete and she has been made to wait,' she suggested.

'When I give an order I expect it to be obeyed,' he stated bluntly. 'If the Herbal Man disobeys me that is one thing, but if the girl does not come back down in good time then that is entirely different.'

'There is still time in the day,' Eesa responded, trying to placate her husband. 'Tamesan will be here soon with the Herbal Man.'

'If he comes,' grumbled Kevan. 'But I will speak with the girl when she returns.' So saying, he grunted a greeting to Janys, turned on his heel and stalked back towards the Warriors' Hall where the men were busy cleaning their weapons and armour after the summer's long journey. Eesa watched her husband's back until he disappeared into the Warriors' Hall, then she let out a deep sigh.

'Ten weeks is not nearly enough sometimes,' Janys remarked sardonically.

'That girl will drive me to madness,' said Eesa as she squatted beside Janys. 'No matter what I get her to do she finds a way to annoy her father.'

'Isn't that the way of girls?' Janys grinned. 'They drive their fathers to distraction until they find a husband. My husband could not marry our Margret off to Heron's son quickly enough. All I remember at Procra's Feast was him saying how delighted he was to have her off his hands.'

Eesa laughed. She could see Kevan talking like Janys' husband, but marrying Tamesan off was not going to be as easy as that. She was certainly growing into an uncommonly pretty girl, with her green eyes and flowing mane of red-gold hair. She would turn many a man's head. But she lacked a woman's grace. Her spirit was too flighty, too irresponsible, too fiery to make a man happy. Yet it appeared Trask's lad, Marron, had a keen interest in her. Even Kevan had noticed as much. Perhaps Kevan and Trask had already discussed the matter. It was not uncommon for fathers to arrange pairings, and a liaison between Kevan and Trask through the matching of their children would strengthen Harbin. Marron was a strong, determined youth, and Eesa knew only a strong man could curb her daughter's fanciful ideas and wandering ways. It would not be a happy pairing for a while. But Tamesan would learn to adjust. All women did. It was how things went.

'Tamesan will be back shortly, Eesa, you'll see. It's a long walk up and down the mountain for a girl,' said Janys.

Eesa studied the sun's angle again. The girl was later than she expected. If she was foolishly wasting time gazing into the distance, or chasing birds and rabbits through the forest, as she too often did, she would be sorely punished by Kevan, of that much Eesa was certain. Her husband held the highest rank in Harbin. He could ill afford people talking about his daughter's lack of respect for her father and his weak discipline. The gossip would undermine his position. Besides, Tamesan was nearing her coming of age. Within two years she could be chosen to be a dragon-warrior's wife. She would be accorded the status of a woman. It was time she started to act like one.

Getting the old man to his hut was not easy. Tam dragged him carefully up the tiny slope between the two trees, and then made him lean on her shoulder as she half-carried him into the clearing. Fortunately he was not much taller than her, and surprisingly frail.

When she reached the hut she discovered that the door was unlocked after all. She opened it and steered the old man inside. Her eyes quickly adjusted to the gloom. A dishevelled bed stood in the furthest corner of the single-roomed hut, so she manoeuvred the Herbal Man towards it and eased him onto it. He groaned and moved his lips painfully, trying to mouth something. She bent and put her ear close to his mouth.

'Water,' he gasped.

There were no water jugs in the room, but she located a dusty bowl and returned to the stream. As she dipped the bowl into the water, she noticed broken pottery shards scattered along the bottom of the stream. The old man must have been fetching water when he slipped and hit his head. She scooped up a bowlful of water and hurried back.

In the hut again, she gently held his head so that he could sip a little water. 'Better,' he gasped, and lay back down. 'Thank you.'

'You have a nasty gash on the back of your head,' she informed him. The old man was silent. 'Were you just getting water?' she asked.

'Yesterday—evening,' he whispered. 'I think—I— slipped.'

72

She was astounded. He had lain beside the stream for a day without help. 'You should have that wound cleaned and bandaged,' she said. The old man did not answer.

Tam pulled the door wide open to let light into the interior. Then she searched through the dust-covered and oddly useless collection of articles jumbled on rickety wooden shelves until she found a flint and a rusty, battered old lantern. She found a near-empty container of paraffin and topped up the lantern. Then she lit the lantern and placed it closer to the old man's bed so she could study his head wound. Because it had been immersed in the stream water it was relatively clean, although strands of hair were caught in the congealed mess surrounding the cut. She searched for some rag and a knife. On a low shelf that also apparently served as a bench, she found an old hunting knife, but she couldn't find much in the way of rags. Finally she tore a strip from her skirt that, with some cleaning, would serve as a bandage. She found a larger pot in which she could boil water, and there was a small pile of wood beside a cold hearth in the corner of the hut. Tam set to organising a fire, although it was awkward arranging the wood in the hearth because a vertical hole sat at the back in line with the chimney. By carefully stacking the wood so it would not spill into the hole, she was finally able to start a fire. Then she went outside to fill the pot.

As she crossed the clearing she realised it was late in the afternoon, but she figured she would still have sufficient time to tend the old man's injury and get back down the mountain before darkness settled. She certainly couldn't leave him lying hurt and uncared for alone up here. It was sheer good fortune that her father had decided to send for him, otherwise no-one might have stumbled upon him in the stream bed. She laughed at herself for being so afraid of an old man. The terrible childhood tales of the poor hermit were cruel lies. He was no different to poor old Asmae, or even Gramma Harmi. He just needed someone to care for him.

When she returned to the hut, lugging the heavy water pot, she was shocked to find the Herbal Man lying on the floor beside his bed, breathing hard and sweating profusely.

'What are you doing?' she cried, and put the pot down.

'Have to—have to get—medicines,' he gasped. 'Down there.' He pointed vaguely at the floor near the small hearth. All Tam could see was a dirty mat covering the floorboards. 'Down—there,' he repeated slowly, and collapsed.

Tam hoisted him back onto the bed. She had forgotten his clothes were damp from lying beside the stream all night and all day. She pulled a musty blanket over him to keep him warm. Then she studied the mat. He had been intensely focussed on it. Why? It was so faded and dirty and worn that its original weave and colours were indistinguishable. And what did he mean by 'down there?' Tam nudged the mat aside with her foot. Beneath it she discovered a metal pull-ring and a faint square outline in the wooden planks. A trapdoor. She hesitated, remembering all the childhood horror stories about the cave beneath the Herbal Man's hut where he kept terrible beasts to gobble up naughty children. Then she steeled her nerves and pulled on the ring. The trapdoor was surprisingly light and fluid to open. A neat set of wooden stairs disappeared into the darkness. She retrieved the lantern from beside the bed and, caught between curiosity and fear of what she might discover, she gingerly descended into what had to be a cellar.

The lantern light revealed a space much larger than the cramped, dusty confines of the hovel. The room was like a cross between a natural cave and a man-made cellar carved out of the earth and rock. A large bench occupied the centre. Two walls filled with shelves displayed myriad jars and containers. A third wall had a hearth built into it with a chimney hole leading upwards and freshly split wood piled neatly before it. No doubt the hole was the same one that had hampered her efforts to build a fire upstairs— sparks and embers from her fire were dropping infrequently into this fireplace. The fourth wall was basically bare rock with bunches of drying and dried plants and flowers hanging upside down from wooden hooks in the wall. A simply carved wooden door sat to the left of the hearth. Three lanterns hung from the ceiling above the bench. In the shadows under the bench were dozens of urns. The entire place had an atmosphere of organisation and cleanliness in marked contrast to the dingy hut above ground. The Herbal Man had suddenly become a deep mystery for Tam.

She took a few moments to look over the collection of jars and urns. They were all marked with strange scratchings. Some contained powders. Others held liquids. The whole room was filled with a variety of strong and subtle fragrances, and the scents teased her as she moved around. Finally she reached the wooden door. It was solid, smooth, and polished, unlike any door in her village, and the handle was made from a shiny white substance that was cool and silky smooth to touch. When she turned the handle and pushed, the door opened.

Her lantern revealed a second chamber, slightly smaller than the first. It also had lanterns hanging from the ceiling, but here the natural cavern shape was allowed to dominate. If it wasn't for the furniture it could easily have been just a cave. Carefully carved into the walls were more shelves containing strange rectangular bundles, and rolled portions of thin yellow material. A dwarf table with a single chair sat beside a bed—a tidy bed, with a large quilted covering, maroon in colour, with a fine gold filigree pattern worked through the fabric, more elegant than any in her own home. On the table, one of the unusual rectangular bundles lay open. Beside it were a large feather, a small container of dark liquid, and a squat candle. Animal skins and rugs were scattered comfortably over the floor, giving the room a warm, homely, welcoming air.

Two more doors led from the room. The one directly opposite the entry was locked. Tam moved to the second door. It was unlocked and opened onto a storeroom. The Herbal Man obviously kept his winter food supplies there. She returned to the first door and tried it again, but it was definitely locked. Further exploration would have to wait. She withdrew to the first room and climbed the stairs.

The Herbal Man had not moved. Tam checked and saw that he was asleep again, so she placed the water pot over the tiny fire to boil. She hoped the pot had been fire-hardened. Then she sat on the floor and waited. She understood now why so much dust permeated the Herbal Man's hut. It wasn't really his home. It was a ruse, a facade. She wondered why he went to so much trouble to make it appear as if he was a poor hermit, though she couldn't think of any possibilities, except that he didn't want anyone to know how comfortably he really lived. The idea was absurd. The mystery puzzled her.

The water soon boiled—though Tam quickly discovered that lifting the pot off the hearth wasn't going to be all that simple because it was too hot for her bare hands. She descended to the lower chamber and found a large, rough piece of green cloth hanging near the downstairs hearth, obviously left there for exactly the purpose she had in mind. Back in the hut, she lifted the pot from the fire and poured water into the smaller bowl she had used earlier. Then she dropped the strip of cloth she had torn from her skirt into the water and cleaned it. When it had cooled a little, she used it to dab at the congealed blood on the back of the old man's head, until the blood gradually loosened. The cut was not long but it was deep enough for Tam to believe she could see a white sliver of skull. She used the hunting knife to carefully trim the old man's hair from around the injury. He groaned and woke when she was halfway through.

'Hold still,' she said gently. 'I'm cleaning your wound.'

'Where—am I?' he breathed. He seemed confused.

'In your old hut,' she informed him, and cut away another hunk of hair.

The old man squinted in the flickering lantern light. 'Who—?' he half-asked weakly.

'Tamesan,' the girl replied, hesitated, and then added, 'Daughter of Kevan.'

The Herbal Man didn't seem to understand. 'Downstairs,' he said. 'My medicines.'

'I've seen,' said Tam. She used the cloth to clean the outer edges of the wound.

'You must get me downstairs. I need medicines,' the old man rasped. She could hear the note of insistence in his voice.

'When I have finished cleaning away the mess here,' she replied. The old man sighed.

Getting the Herbal Man down to the lower level was just as difficult as dragging him from the stream bed, but Tam struggled gamely until she had him lying on his own bed in the second chamber. The old man really needed to get out of his dirty and damp garments. Tam had dressed and undressed Gramma Harmi and Jaysin at home many times, but the old man was a stranger and she was embarrassed to do what she knew needed to be done for his health. She went to the storeroom and dragged out another set of clothes—a tunic, a pullover, a cloak, breeches— and laid them on the end of the bed. 'You can't stay in the clothes you're wearing,' she said hesitantly.

'I need—medicine—first,' the old man slowly replied. 'In—the other—room. Bring me some water—some callania herb, some dewdrop essence, and—the red jenna berry powder.'

Tam stared at him. She had no idea what he meant. 'I'll go and look,' she promised lamely, and left the room.

The shelves and containers in the first chamber were an infuriating puzzle to her. She found a host of jars containing red powders, but nothing that looked like the blue dewdrop flowers she sometimes picked early in the morning on the mountain. She felt helpless. She returned to confess that she couldn't find what he wanted, and found him struggling feebly to change out of his damp clothes. There was no longer time for social propriety. She simply helped the old man get into drier things.

He was exhausted by the time she had him dressed again. He collapsed back into the bed and looked as if he was going to drift into sleep again. But he grimaced and forced himself to remain conscious.

'Can you read?' he suddenly queried.

'What do you mean?' she asked.

'I thought not,' the old man said, shaking his head sadly. 'No-one in your village can.' He sighed heavily. Then he took another deep, shuddering breath and said, 'I want you—to bring some—things—for me. Listen very carefully.' He stopped as though he was going to pass out, but she realised he was merely thinking.

Tam diligently followed each laborious instruction. Still, she had to bring five different jars containing red powder to the Herbal Man before she found the right one containing jenna berry powder. The dewdrop essence was less difficult to find. He drank a mouthful mixed with water and had a violent coughing fit immediately after.

'Nasty,' he sputtered with a distasteful expression, 'but necessary.' Then he described a crucible dish and a pair of tongs to hold it which Tam found under the long bench. She lit the fat candle beside the Herbal Man's bed, and mixed the other two ingredients with water in the crucible over the candle flame as he instructed, taking special care not to let the mixture boil. The Herbal Man slipped in and out of consciousness at times during this exercise, but he appeared to have an iron will to see that Tam did exactly as he required. Eventually she had a thick mauve paste in the crucible. It smelt terrible.

'Let—it cool,' the old man wheezed. He was succumbing to his exhaustion. Sweat beaded on his brow and he was shaking violently. 'You must—smooth it—over—the wound,' he stammered and crumpled onto his pillow.

Tam panicked. She waved the crucible in the air to cool the paste as rapidly as possible. She stuck a finger in to test its temperature and nearly burnt herself. She blew on the paste but it was still several minutes before it was cool enough to touch. As soon as she could, she scooped a gob of the mauve mixture out of the crucible and spread it over the back of the old man's head, covering the gash with a thick layer. No doubt it would be smeared all over his pillow while he slept, but she hoped she had spread it thickly enough to keep the injury covered. She rinsed the residue from her hands and pulled the quilted cover over the old man's sleeping form. There was nothing else she could do. She had to get home to tell her father the Herbal Man was ill. Perhaps tomorrow her mother would let her return to see how the old man had fared during the night. A shiver ran down her spine. What if he died? What if she came back and found his corpse? She pushed the morbid thought from her mind, picked up the low-burning lantern, and headed for the stairs in the adjoining chamber.

The interior of the upstairs hut was darker than ever. She realised why. Time had escaped her while she was helping the old man. It was already evening. She walked outside into the clearing and looked up at the sky. Stars twinkled in the deepening darkness. The mountain and forest were settling into the night. What should she do? She considered taking her chances and heading down the mountain, moving quickly so nothing ferocious could catch her. Her father and mother would be furious. She had not done what they had asked. Perhaps Kevan was already on his way up the mountain, coming to drag his failure of a daughter home. She listened, straining for any approaching sound, but all she heard were rustlings and whisperings amongst the ferns and trees. What if she slipped in the darkness on the steeper section of the path? What if a bear stumbled across her? Caught by indecision, she stood in the cold night air and gazed at the stars for a long time. Whatever she did would be wrong. Perhaps it would be better to wait for her father to come. At least his anger was something she understood. It was the least risk. Tam crept back into the hut.

The little hearth fire had long since burned out. She glanced at the trapdoor. She could light a fire in the lower hearth and sleep by it. She was sure the Herbal Man wouldn't mind her using his wood. With the paraffin lantern close to dying, she organised a fire in the first chamber. She marvelled at how the Herbal Man had constructed a chimney that rose through the fireplace in the hut above. It would give the impression he had a fire going in the hut without disclosing his downstairs secret. Once she stabilised the fire, she climbed back up into the hut and retrieved the musty bedding she had found there. She hastily arranged the tattered blankets in front of the downstairs hearth, then curled up to sleep, trying to ignore the gnawing hunger in her belly and overbearing guilt plaguing her mind. It was a long time before the comfort of sleep enfolded her.

Chapter Six

She stood before a door, an old chipped and cracked wooden door. It hung on one hinge at a crazy angle, threatening to fall. As she extended her fingers to grasp the shattered handle, the door swung open as freely and as quietly as a new door might. Blackness lay beyond. A breath of hot air rushed out of the darkness and washed over her. Now she was inside, in the inky dark. The warmth was smothering. She was in some kind of danger, a terrible invisible danger, and the fear of it clawed at her gut. She wanted to run out, but she knew without turning that the door she'd entered by no longer existed. She was trapped in the darkness with an unnameable horror. Fear froze in her throat. She could not scream. Something with talons gripped her shoulder.

Tam started suddenly. 'So you're awake,' said a man's voice. 'Are you hungry?'

She rubbed her eyes and stared blearily up at the Herbal Man. His hair was secured in a loose ponytail and he wore a large black cloak that looked too big for his frame. A steaming bowl was in his out-stretched hands.

'Gruel,' he announced. 'Hot and healthy.' She accepted his offering and, after a moment's hesitation, during which the old man moved away to another part of the chamber, she ate greedily. Behind her, the hearth flames burned brightly, illuminating the room and warming her back.

'I owe you a big thankyou for helping me yesterday,' the Herbal Man said as he approached her again. 'If you hadn't found me and stayed to mix the healing paste, I don't think I would be feeling very well at all today. You did an excellent job on the wound.' He lifted his hand and gingerly patted the back of his head, where the wound, and the hair she had cut, were hidden by the ponytail.

Tam swallowed the last mouthful of her breakfast and said, 'My father sent me to fetch you to the village. The dragonship is back. Except now he'll be angry with me for not going home last night.'

'No doubt he will be,' the old man agreed. 'But I will explain the circumstances, Tamesan, and he will appreciate what you have done.'

'You remember my name?' she asked.

The Herbal Man smiled. 'You have a brother Chasse and a little brother Jaysin. Your mother is Eesa, and you look after your grandmother Harmi. I know the names of everyone in your village, Tamesan.'

'How?' she blurted, and then blushed for responding so rudely.

'Names are important things. I might not come

down to the village more than a dozen times in a year—often less—but I like to know who is there. You could call me nosy, perhaps, but when you have lived in this world as long as I have, some things just come naturally to you. Names and people in my case.'

'I didn't mean to be so rude,' she said apologetically.

'It is not rude to ask questions,' the old man reassured her. 'If you do not ask, you might never know.'

Tam was surprised by his response. Her mother would have warned her to be less inquisitive and to accept what is. She felt she had to ask another question, one that had plagued her since discovering the old man's underground home.

'Why do you live down here?'

The old man coughed and said, 'I was hoping we would get to that point. You see, I have a very important favour to ask of you.'

'What?'

'I would very much appreciate it if you said nothing about these lower chambers to anyone. You see, no-one else in your village knows about them, and I would prefer to keep it that way.'

'Why?' she inquired.

'You do like to ask questions, don't you?' he noted with a frown, and then grinned. Tam feared she had overstepped the bounds of decency, but before she could attempt another apology, the old man went on.

'I can't explain it without telling you a very long story, Tamesan,' he said. 'And unfortunately I don't have time to tell it to you now. Perhaps another time. Your father and brother are already on their way here to fetch you. We should leave and meet them on the way down the mountain.'

That was it. The matter was closed, it seemed. But the old man had left her yet another question—how did he know her father was coming? She wanted an answer but she held her tongue. She stood and shook out the makeshift bedding she had slept in, and set to straightening her long red hair with her fingers.

'You don't have a brush, do you?' she asked, as her fingers caught in a mass of tangles. The Herbal Man went to his bedroom chamber and returned with a brush which he handed to her. She was astonished by its ornate beauty. The handle was carved from an unusual soft white wood and covered with delicate reliefs of exotic birds and plants. She had never seen a hairbrush so exquisite.

'Thank you,' she said, and set to work on the heavier tangles in her hair.

'You can wash your face and hands in the water bowl if you wish,' the Herbal Man offered. 'Then we really must go. The sun is about to rise.'

Tam watched the old man busy himself selecting certain containers from his shelves and placing them in pockets within his heavy cloak while she finished brushing her hair. She rinsed her face in the cold water which rudely awakened her senses, and then handed the brush to the old man as he went to climb the stairs to the hut.

He waved his hand and shook his head. 'No. You may keep it,' he said.

'But it's yours,' Tam insisted.

'Call it part of a small gift for helping me yesterday,' he replied. 'And perhaps a bribe to remind you not to tell anyone about this place,' he added with a sweep of his hand to indicate the lower level. 'As far as people should know, I live in this unworthy little hut, please.'

'I won't tell anyone,' she promised. She clutched her new brush in her hands. 'I wouldn't have anyway because you asked me not to,' she stressed. The old man smiled appreciatively and led her upstairs.

The world was waking when they entered the forest. Birds chorused their dawn song, and the sky was engaged in its ritual metamorphosis from black to grey to blue. Tam followed the Herbal Man's dark back along the path, and marvelled at the speedy recovery the old man had made overnight. He walked slowly, though, and tentatively, as if he was uncertain of his steps, which also made her wonder just how much illness still remained.

When they reached the downward path on the steeper slope of the mountain the old man paused. 'Look,' he said, and pointed towards the peak of Dragon Mountain. Tam gazed up and saw the first rays of the morning sun spreading across the sky. They added a yellow hue to the air and transformed the snow-capped peak into a golden mantle.

'Te-Amen-San,' the Herbal Man whispered.

Tam shivered when she heard the old words that formed her name. She had heard them spoken by the Dragon Heart priest, and by her mother, but they rolled from the old man's tongue so fluently it was as if his voice resonated in the very core of her being. She stared at the widening glow in the eastern sky, caught for a moment in the childhood rapture that had often drawn her onto the roof to watch the sunrise. Then she turned to ask the old man if he knew what the words meant, but he was already descending the path. She caught up and fell into silent step behind.

The old man rested three times on the steepest section. Tam expressed her concern but he pushed it aside, promising that he would take time to rest and recuperate in the village. At the third stop he reached inside his cloak and withdrew a phial of blue liquid. Tam guessed it was more dewdrop elixir. He uncorked it and took a mouthful. The taste made him screw up his face and he coughed involuntarily.

'Is it really *that* bad?' she asked.

The old man grimaced. 'It is. I have been trying to find a way to make it taste less foul for several years, but every time I do the mixture loses most of its potency as a curative.'

'What is it supposed to do?'

'Clears out infection in the lungs, mainly,' he explained. 'Sometimes it reduces a fever if it isn't too far advanced. I was told once it was good for curing boils if it's applied hot, but I doubt that.'

'Why?'

The old man cocked a bushy white eyebrow and looked up at her. 'It would take too long to explain. Let's just say there's a flaw in the logic of it.'

'Could you teach me about it?' she asked.

The old man's stare hardened. He was searching her face for something, though she had no idea what. It made her feel horribly uncomfortable. But then he smiled and said, 'Perhaps I could. If you were really willing.'

Before she could declare that she would really like to learn the old man's craft, without thinking seriously about what she was going to say, she heard her father's familiar voice booming from below.

'Tamesan!' He emerged from amongst the rocks and trees with Chasse in tow.

'Now we meet with Kevan, the Dragon Head of Harbin,' the Herbal Man said, more to himself than to her, she observed.

Kevan climbed the short distance to confront the Herbal Man and Tam. He dwarfed the old man with his presence and he glared at Tamesan.

'Where in Shaddho's name have you been, child?' he demanded.

'Your daughter has been caring for me,' the Herbal Man interrupted before Tam could respond. 'Thanks to her, I am alive.'

Kevan's anger was replaced by astonishment. 'What do you mean?' he asked warily. Chasse drew alongside and he grinned at Tam.

'I fell gathering water two days ago,' the old man began. He went on to tell Kevan how Tam had found him and taken him to his hut to heal him. As he completed his explanation he loosened his ponytail and bent forward to show Kevan the evidence of the injury to his head.

Tam's father studied the paste-covered wound and glanced at her. 'Why didn't you come back down the mountain and get help?' he asked. She recognised the tone of frustration. He had come ready to vent his anger, and now he had no justifiable reason for doing so.

'If she had left me, I would almost certainly have died,' the Herbal Man announced. 'By the time she had done as I asked it was dark and the mountain is not a place for people at night.' The Herbal Man had dissolved Kevan's last reason for maintaining his anger. Reluctantly, he would have to admit the girl had acted properly in the situation.

Kevan led the group down the mountain, travelling slowly to accommodate the Herbal Man's weakened condition. Chasse dropped back with Tam and the pair chatted.

'I saw the dragon's horde yesterday,' he said enthusiastically.

'Much?' she asked.

'No. Some gold coins, a handful of gems and a collection of shields, swords, spears and armour. Most of the armour was damaged. The men were disappointed. The dragon they killed was a small one. It hadn't acquired a true treasure.'

'I wonder how many dragons are left?' Tam asked, and then added, 'I would love to see a dragon.'

'Next summer I will,' Chasse declared.

'Yes, *you* will. But *I* won't,' she reminded him petulantly.

'I'll tell you all about him when we return, Tam. Promise.'

'That's not the same,' she complained.

'I doubt you would really want to see a dragon,' interrupted Kevan sternly, having overheard their conversation. 'They are ugly, greedy creatures that fly in the night, breathe fire, and delight in eating girls.'

Tam felt like saying, 'So what has that to do with me seeing a dragon?' but she thought better of it and kept quiet as usual. She had learnt in the past from her father that girls weren't supposed to have opinions, especially about dragons. What she did notice, however, was the strange, questioning look the Herbal Man gave her father while he was speaking to her, a look that her father did not see but which seemed to query his words. What did the Herbal Man find wrong with what her father said? she wondered.

They entered Harbin mid-morning. Kevan directed Tam to go straight home while he took the Herbal Man and Chasse to the Warriors' Hall. Tam knew her mother would be waiting, and no doubt she would receive a scalding reprimand no matter what the reason for her not returning the previous afternoon. As she passed a pair of villagers she felt them staring at her, so she hurried towards the bridge over

Watersdrop. Before she reached it, however, someone called her. She turned and saw Katris and three other girls approaching. What did they want?

'Your mother wants you in the Long Hall,' Katris announced. Her three companions giggled.

'What's so funny?' Tam asked. Katris sent her companions a sly look, whispered and laughed. 'I asked you a question, Katris,' Tam said, annoyance rising in her throat.

Katris stepped forward and said provocatively, 'We were just wondering what he's like.'

'Who?'

'Your man.'

'I don't have a man.' Tam was puzzled and irritated by Katris' absurd notion. The girls broke into a bigger fit of laughter. Tam could not be bothered remaining a figure for their obscure ridicule so she started to walk away.

'We mean the dirty old Herbal Man you stayed with last night,' Katris called after her.

Her taunt halted Tam. She spun around, fighting the seething anger that welled within, and responded as calmly as she could, 'He is not a "dirty old man".'

'Oh,' said Katris with mock apology, 'of course not. At least not to you. But then,' she added derisively, 'he *is* the only man in this village you're likely to get, so you wouldn't think of him as being dirty, would you?'

Her sarcasm cut deep. Tam struggled with blind rage and for the briefest instant she nearly charged at

Katris. But she fought her compulsion. Fighting proved nothing. She had come to that conclusion through watching the boys brawl over almost every issue. She bit her lip and turned away.

Katris, though, kept up her venomous attack. 'You're not even denying it, are you?' she sneered. 'You really do like him, don't you? Don't you, Tamesan of the dawn light? Oh, how disgusting!'

Tam increased her pace to leave the girls behind, but she heard them laugh as they followed. For once she would be glad to be with her mother in the Long Hall. Why was Katris so intent on teasing her? When she reached the Hall she rushed inside. Her mother looked up, startled by her sudden entrance.

'Where in Procra's name have you been, child?' Eesa demanded. She dropped the rush basket she was weaving and stood to meet her daughter. Tam caught her breath as Katris and her friends walked calmly into the Hall as if nothing had been said. They didn't even look in Tam's direction.

'Helping the Herbal Man,' she replied.

'*All night?*' Eesa asked. Someone sniggered, but when she glanced irritably at the girls, they were all intent on their weaving.

'He was hurt,' Tam explained, and then she briefly outlined the previous day's events for her mother's benefit. Eesa asked the expected questions. Why hadn't she come for help? Why didn't she come home before it got dark? Then she reminded Tam of her responsibilities to her father, and Gramma Harmi's needs, and how little Jaysin fretted for her. Tam wanted to argue that the Herbal Man's life was more important under the circumstances, but she knew that would be pointless, and she certainly didn't want to give Katris any more fuel for teasing. Instead she took the scolding. When it was over, Eesa set her to work smoothing rough edges off the unfired pots the women had made during summer. Tam avoided the other girls while she worked, although when they all stopped to share the midday meal she noticed them whispering and giggling, and she was certain it was at her expense. After Tam had eaten, Eesa sent her home to feed Gramma Harmi. Then she was to take a bowl of food to the Warriors' Hall where the men were working.

Tam was relieved to be rid of the Long Hall. She walked quickly home through the village. At her door, though, she paused. There were voices inside the cottage. At first she thought her grandmother was simply talking to herself. The old lady sometimes did that, though her one-sided conversations seldom made sense. But this time the old woman was talking clearly and sensibly. Then a quieter, deeper voice responded. Gramma Harmi was talking to someone— a man. Tam didn't know what to do, so she listened, curious.

'That was a long time ago,' Gramma said.

'It was only yesterday,' the man replied.

'To you, Eric, to you,' the old lady sighed. Tam heard a deep sadness in her grandmother's voice.

'When I saw her early this morning, I thought it

was you,' the man said. 'The same hair, her eyes lit by the morning sun. You haven't changed that much, Harmi. I can still see you.'

The man's voice was very familiar. Then Tam realised who was speaking—the Herbal Man. She missed part of her grandmother's response and only caught '——as much any more. It fades. Everything is fading.' She thought she heard her grandmother sob. Tam coughed and opened the door.

In the half-lit room she saw her grandmother hunched in her chair and the dark figure of the Herbal Man kneeling before her, holding her hand. Tam's entrance made him release his hold. He stood slowly. Partly obscured in shadow, she thought the Herbal Man appeared very old and very tired.

'Sorry,' she apologised. 'Mother sent me to feed Gramma. I thought I heard you talking.'

'We were,' the Herbal Man replied quietly. 'But Harmi is very tired.' He looked down at the old lady. Her eyes were closed. 'I think she is asleep,' he confided gently.

Tam walked past the Herbal Man and bent down beside her grandmother. Harmi was fast asleep. As Tam smoothed a loose strand of the old lady's white hair, she noticed a tiny teardrop sitting in the corner of one closed eye. It sparkled like a tiny jewel. She turned her head in time to see the door close. The Herbal Man had gone.

Chapter Seven

The Herbal Man stayed in Harbin for four days. It was rare for him to spend so long there except in cases of extreme sickness, but he remained this time because he was still recovering from his own illness. He spent the nights on the shoreline in an abandoned fishing hut used to store tackle. Kevan offered him the right to sleep in the Warriors' Hall as a mark of respect, but the Herbal Man declined, saying simply that he preferred solitude. Chasse told Tam that her father's offer had met with significant dissension amongst the warriors. Many were reluctant to share their sleeping quarters with the Herbal Man because he had never earned the formal status of manhood. Trask had especially criticised their father's gesture.

Each day the Herbal Man treated a handful of people who suffered from minor ailments, and worked on the more serious injuries brought home by the dragonwarriors. He attended the ceremonial gathering at Watersdrop when the Dragon Heart sang the Words of Passage for Jared, Banni's dead warrior husband, to speed his soul safely to Varst's Eternal Paradise. Tam observed that the Herbal Man stood apart from the crowd throughout the ceremony. Long-established rumours and lies made people shun him even when they needed and made use of his help, and he maintained a distance in accordance with their distrust. He was very much an outsider. So often she felt like that. Only Banni's grief kept her in the village crowd this time. She cried for Banni, and for Jared, and strangely she also cried for the Herbal Man, though she did not fully understand why.

The Herbal Man visited Gramma Harmi every day. He gave her small doses of herbal medicines and instructed Tam how and when to administer them during the coming winter months when he would not be able to journey down the mountain. Whenever the Herbal Man touched Gramma Harmi's hand or arm, she suddenly seemed to light up with a smile which remained for quite some time after he had left, but Tam did not catch the two old people speaking again as she had the first day.

The mystery of that moment gnawed at her. Several times she considered just asking the Herbal Man straight out what had happened, why Gramma Harmi had suddenly seemed to be herself again, why she responded as she did to his touch, but her questions remained unasked. No opportunity arose to ask them. The Herbal Man was always busily attending to someone, or other people were present when Tam was with him. The only time he was alone was at night in his temporary quarters, when she had to be at home helping her mother.

Tam was kept busy by Eesa throughout the days. The short autumn season was approaching, and with it came two of the village's important annual festivals. In one week's time, the people would hold Procra's Dance, a fertility celebration in honour of Varst's goddess wife, Procra. On that night the single dragonwarriors had the right to choose a partner from the village maidens. It was a night of dressing up, of dancing, drinking and singing. It heralded the end of summer, and for some young women the start of womanhood. Women were already sewing new garments for themselves and for the eligible young maidens. The Long Hall was full of gossip about who would be chosen and by whom, and speculation, and knowing smiles at the mention of names. Tam was still two summers from being eligible to be chosen, and for that she was glad. To know that the rest of her life would be devoted to one man, to answering his beck and call, satisfying his whims and lust, frightened her. But she listened on the outer edges to the idle chatter of the girls who were of age, and those who would be old enough next summer, and learned the gossipy details surrounding the coming festival.

The most popular young men in the village were Kerik, Aaron and Sawl. Kerik had just been initiated into manhood that summer. He had dark piercing eyes that several of the young women found hauntingly attractive. Aaron had not chosen a wife despite entering manhood three summers ago, much to the immense disappointment of many girls because he was tall, handsome, and strong. Sawl was an older dragonwarrior whose first wife had died six summers past of the strange disease brought back on the dragonship. Of the three, he was considered the least handsome, but his maturity, and the fact that he already owned a well-kept cottage, made him an attractive prospective partner.

Tam estimated there were eleven single warriors in the village, four of them young men for the first time. There were only six eligible maidens. She knew there were also four single women who had lost husbands, though they were not invited to dance in the celebration. If they chose to pair again it would be discreetly, at another time, and village life would continue as if the pairing had always existed. The right to refuse a man's advances was confined only to those women who had already been chosen once before. For any village maiden, it was a tragedy not to be chosen by a man, and it was a severe social disgrace to refuse any man's offer. Old Asmae's isolated existence was proof enough of that. It was generally agreed that all six maidens would be husbanded this Procra's Dance. The odds, and the gods, for that matter, were in their favour.

Tam persevered with cutting out and sewing, though she found no pleasure in the task. She was creating a garment from dark green material her father had given her from the Etkuan dragon's bounty. Chasse suggested it would look good on her, matching the green of her eyes and complementing her golden-red hair. She teased him playfully for making judgments about women's dresses, but she also told him how much she sincerely appreciated his comment and warned him never to forget it.

When they found a spare moment together before one evening meal, Chasse proudly showed his sister the new fighting techniques he was being taught by the dragonwarriors. She initially pretended to be interested only out of love for her brother, but eventually her interest became genuine when Chasse involved her in the action. They finally became embroiled in a rough-and-tumble play brawl.

'Easy, Tam,' Chasse laughed as he disentangled himself. 'You're stronger than you think.'

'Girls can fight if they have to,' Tam asserted indignantly.

'Not most girls,' Chasse corrected. 'I think you and I played too many games together. None of the other girls in the village would ever dare do this.'

'Have you asked any of them?' she teased and grinned.

'Not yet,' he replied and mirrored her grin. 'But I don't think I'd want to fight with any of them,' he jested.

Tam flicked back her tousled mass of red hair and sat cross-legged on the ground. 'Who will you choose?' she suddenly asked.

Chasse stared open-mouthed at her. 'What?'

'When it comes your time for choosing at Procra's Dance, who will you choose?' she repeated.

'I don't have to choose this time,' he said. 'I'm too young, remember?' He gave her a glance that suggested he thought she had lost her senses.

'Not this time. Next time.'

'I don't know. No-one, probably.'

'You must like at least one of the girls in the village. They're not all ugly,' she argued.

'Why do you want to know, Tamesan?' he asked. Her questions were irritating him. He turned this one back on her. 'Who do you hope will choose you?'

'No-one,' she answered flatly.

'You don't get a choice,' he said.

'That's just it,' she said, fixing him with a determined gaze. 'I won't get a choice. That's why I hope no-one will choose me. Because I won't choose them.'

'What about Marron?' Chasse asked. He had seen the youth study his sister. All of the boys knew Marron wanted Tamesan. Of the girls in her age group, she was considered the prettiest, but most thought she was too aloof, too headstrong. And Marron was interested in her, which meant no-one else should be unless they were willing to fight him first.

'What has he said to you?' she demanded.

'Nothing, Tam,' he replied hurriedly, aware his sister was becoming very annoyed. 'Just some boys' talk. That's all. I just wondered what you thought of him.'

'He's rude, arrogant, self-centred, and a bully,' Tam announced. 'I wouldn't have him if he was the only boy left in Harbin.' She kicked a clump of grass out of the ground and walked towards the cliff top that overlooked Watersdrop and Harbin Bay.

Chasse watched her. He felt sorry for his sister. If Marron waited, and still chose her when she came of age in two summers' time, she would have no option but to accept him. That was how things went. Every girl knew that. Every boy knew that. It seemed Tam was the only one who didn't want to be like everyone else. By the end of next summer Chasse himself would be a man and have the right to choose a girl if he wanted one. To be honest, he hadn't even thought about a choice. He liked Katris. So did several other boys. Blonde-haired Kerryn, daughter of dragonwarrior Trent, was also a nice girl, and she was the same age as Chasse. But choosing to live his life with a woman didn't seem important yet. First he had a winter of training to prepare for next summer's dragon hunt and his initiation. That was what mattered most to him. He really couldn't understand why Tam had even brought up the subject.

Tam caught the Herbal Man crossing the bridge. He was dressed in his dark cloak, and carrying a bundle of items he had bartered for or been given as payment for his healing work during the past four days.

'You're leaving?' she asked.

'I am, Tamesan. I feel stronger, and I am not needed here any longer.'

'Did you see Gramma?'

The Herbal Man smiled when he heard the note of curiosity in Tam's voice. 'Yes, I saw Harmi. She is looking a little better today.'

'Did you talk with her again?'

The Herbal Man's eyes flickered slightly at her question. He seemed to peer closer, though the friendly smile never wavered. 'I always talk to Harmi when I visit. She is a dear old friend of mine. We've known each other for a long time, Tamesan, longer than most would remember in this village.'

Tam wanted to say 'I heard you talking together on the first day. I heard you *really* talking,' but she held back. Something indefinable in the way the old man was looking at her warned her not to pursue the matter. 'Can I come and visit you sometime?' she asked.

The old man's face registered genuine surprise. 'You are more than welcome, Tamesan. It would be an honour to have you visit,' and then he added, 'As long as your father and mother approve.'

She wished he hadn't said that. He probably already knew they wouldn't let her go traipsing up the mountain whenever she wanted. Her mother would always find some menial task to keep her tied to the village.

'Remember what you said about teaching me more about your herbs and things? I would like to learn about them,' she said.

'If you visit, I will teach you,' the Herbal Man promised. 'But now I must go home. There are important things to be done, even for an old man like me, Tamesan.'

'Don't go falling in any creeks,' she joked. 'And just call me Tam.'

The old man smiled. 'May the child of the dawn light be blessed by the dragon,' he said, and walked away.

As she watched the old man leave, she considered his unusual parting words. She understood them clearly enough, but the blessing itself seemed to be much older in meaning, as if the Herbal Man had dragged it out of an ancient world. The words haunted Tam.

That evening as she fed Gramma Harmi, she watched her grandmother for any glimmer that might reveal she was thinking clearly, or was able to remember the Herbal Man's visit that afternoon. Harmi gave Tam no clues. She babbled once about collecting small buds of the snowpea plant, and then she had an imaginary conversation with someone named Claryssa. She called Tam 'child' as always. Tam began to doubt whether she really had overheard the conversation she stumbled upon the first after-noon the Herbal Man visited. She cleaned the old lady's chin and wondered if, when she got old, she would have tufts of white hair growing on her face like her grandmother had. She tucked Gramma Harmi into bed, said her goodnights to everyone, and went to the room she shared with Jaysin and Chasse.

Chasse was in the main room with his father, dis-cussing alternative methods for honing a blade. Since last summer, he always went to bed after Tam so she could undress without him being there. It wasn't because of any embarrassment between them, just tacit politeness. She appreciated her brother's gesture. Her younger brother, however, was still awake. His eyes shone in the semi-darkness.

'Close your eyes, Jaysin,' she said softly. 'I want to get into bed.' The little boy rolled over. Tam quickly slid off her dress and over-tunic and put on her nightdress. She crossed to Jaysin's cramped bed-space and bent over to kiss her little brother goodnight.

'Tam?' he asked.

'What?'

'Are the stories about the Herbal Man true?'

'What stories?'

'You know. About him taking little children away?'

Tam gently ruffled her brother's hair. 'No, little fieldmouse. They're not,' she laughed softly.

'Gramma says there's a dragon on the mountain,' he whispered.

'Gramma says lots of things. It's only called Dragon Mountain. There isn't a real dragon up there.'

'She says the Herbal Man keeps it.'

'Then it must be a very tiny dragon. He only has a very tiny hut to live in,' Tam informed him.

'Gramma said she saw it once, when she was a little girl,' he persisted.

'It's just a story, Jaysin. Gramma tells lots of stories. Now you go to sleep. I'm tired.'

Jaysin fell silent. Tam climbed under the skins and rough quilting of her bed and wriggled to get comfortable. She was tired, but she did not sleep. She could hear the murmur of voices in the main room where

Chasse and her father were involved in their talk. She heard her mother go to bed. Later, Chasse came into the room and went to bed in silence, thinking Tam was asleep. She could not sleep. Her mind was full of images of the Herbal Man's underground chambers, and the conversation she'd overheard between Harmi and the Herbal Man. His name was Eric. The words of his blessing repeated themselves over and over in her head. She could hear her father snoring, and Harmi mumbling in her sleep. Tam strained to listen, but the words were garbled nonsense. There was a dragon on the mountain. More nonsense. Jaysin listened too closely to Gramma's ravings.

When sleep finally came to Tam, she dreamed. She stood on a mountain top, dressed in the green garment she was sewing for Procra's Dance. The sun was rising far off in the east, throwing the light of dawn across the sky in an arc of gold. Gramma Harmi was looking up at her and waggling her finger as if she was trying to warn Tam about something. The Herbal Man stood beside Harmi, smiling. She could hear Jaysin shouting to her, but that couldn't be right—his voice was coming from overhead. When she did look up into the deepening blue sky, she saw a dragon, or at least she thought it was a dragon, flying towards her out of the east. Jaysin was clinging to its back and he was laughing, really laughing like he had never laughed before. He was calling to Tam but she couldn't understand his words. All she could see was that he was deliriously happy.

Chapter Eight

Her period started the morning of Procra's Dance. Tam woke feeling cramped and sore. She stayed in bed until Chasse and Jaysin had left, and waited until Eesa came looking for her. Her mother simply shook her head and said, 'There's nothing for it. This is what being a woman brings. Blood and tears. And work. You will learn to live with it, child. Clean up your bedding. There is little point you coming down to help prepare the Long Hall today. I will send one of the girls here with something for you to do.'

'Not Katris,' Tam entreated.

Eesa frowned. 'All right,' she agreed. 'I will send another girl. Whatever is your reason, though?'

'I just don't want her to come here today,' Tam answered sullenly.

'Procra knows the mind of a girl,' Eesa sighed as she gathered a pile of bedding from the boys' beds. 'And I was one once, Varst forbid. You and Katris used to be as close as fleas on a dog.' She carried her bundle away but kept talking from the next room. 'There's no point lying about in there feeling sorry for yourself, Tamesan. You know what you have to do. There are clean cloths beside my bed, and plenty of water to boil to wash and keep yourself fresh, child. Hang the bedding outside to air, and make sure Gramma is comfortable and fed. You can sweep the floor through, and by then someone will have brought you some work from the Long Hall for tonight. Procra knows there's enough to do as it is.' Her mother shuffled around in the main room while Tam climbed out of her bedding. Then Eesa appeared in the doorway with a concerned expression. She held out her arms and pulled Tam close.

'I'm sorry for you girl,' she said. 'You don't need your bleeding on this day of all days. Let's hope the cycle of things will turn your way when your time for choosing comes.' Tam knew her mother was trying to show sympathy, but it only made the circumstance seem more awkward than it was. For one thing, Tam didn't want to be ready for Procra's Dance in two summers' time. She didn't want to be 'chosen', like a sacrificial goat for Varst's Great Feast. For another, she was so much taller than Eesa, and being hugged like a small child felt utterly absurd. Everything about the moment irritated her.

When her mother released her, Tam smiled weakly and said, 'I have to clean myself up first. I'll be fine.' Eesa replied with an understanding smile, and let Tam pass through to the main room. Eesa collected a woven basket of items for her work in the Long Hall, then hurried out of the cottage, leaving her daughter alone.

When Tam had organised herself, she crept in to check on Gramma Harmi. The old woman slept in the same room as Kevan and Eesa, and this morning it stank of stale urine, which meant the old lady had wet her bed again. She did most nights. She was still fast asleep. Her bedding would have to be changed, but Tam decided to let her sleep a little longer before tackling that task. Instead, she took the pile of bedding Eesa had collected outside to hang on the honeynut tree beside the cottage.

A fresh westerly breeze carried the smell of brine to her. The weather was changing. She finished hanging the bedclothes on the tree and made her way to the top of the cliff a few metres away. To her right Watersdrop rushed over the cliff and thundered into the ocean twenty metres below. The stream started deep in the mountains beyond Dragon Mountain, and wound a narrow, tortuous course through gorges and over cataracts before sluicing out onto the narrow strip of land at Harbin. It made Tam suddenly think of a dragonwarrior's life—rough, violent, short. That was what could lie ahead for her brother—a few short journeys into wild adventure and then death. She corrected herself. That wasn't entirely true. Her father had lived a relatively long time, all of thirty-six summers. He bore several scars, earnt on his annual journeys, but he had survived the violence and the danger. It was likely Chasse would, too.

Dark grey clouds were massing further out over the great western ocean. A small storm was coming.

Tam was no weather expert, but she guessed it would only be a brief one. Winter was still two moon cycles away. But it did look as if the Procra's Dance celebrations might have to be held in the Long Hall instead of around a village bonfire. It didn't matter. She knew she could still go to the celebration if she really wanted to, but her period gave her an excuse not to go now if she chose to use it. It was a rare moment in her life when she really did have a choice of action.

She sat on the cliff and stared at the heaving ocean. Waves surged against the base of the cliff, gentle but powerful. She felt the thud of each wave through the earth beneath her as it broke against the rocks below. For every wave that rose and dissolved against the impassive cliff, another replaced it, time after time, day after day, year after year. The cliff hadn't appeared to have changed in her short lifetime, but Tam marvelled at the blind persistence and determination of the waves, trying to break it down. She felt an affinity with the ocean. Like it, she wanted to grow, expand, do more, see more. But there were cliffs all around her life, holding her in the one place. She was too restless to accept the cliffs. She had to keep pressing outward, pushing, moving, until the cliff barriers eroded, until there were no more barriers. Lost in her thoughts, Tam sat and watched the grey ocean swell for a long time.

'Tamesan?' The voice called to her like the cry of a gull. Her reverie broken, she turned and saw a younger girl, Alys, standing near the honeynut tree. Alys cradled a huge bundle of flowers in her arms. Tam got to her feet, brushed down her long skirt, and approached the girl.

'Your mother asked you to weave these into necklets and headbands for tonight,' Alys said.

Tam took the bundle and thanked her. The girl smiled shyly and then ran towards the bridge. Tam watched her retreat, thinking how lucky Alys was to be only ten summers old and happy. So much was going to change for her.

Inside the cottage, Tam spread the flowers on the floor and regarded them. Five colours. Her mother had sent yellow summerflowers, a host of purple frostpaws, large orange field banners, white dragonspears, and a sprinkling of tiny blue maidenbells. She loved the colour show. It was a pity to destroy them for one night of celebration. As she bent to begin sorting the flowers into smaller bunches for weaving, she heard Gramma Harmi coughing. She remembered she had yet to change the old woman's bedding, and feed her. She sighed.

It took a large portion of the morning to deal with her grandmother's needs. When she was finished, she had Harmi propped in the rickety old chair her grandmother favoured, rugged up against the cold air that was settling over the village as the change in the weather approached, so the old lady could watch her arrange the flowers if she wanted. But as she expected, Harmi drifted in and out of sleep, blissfully ignorant of her granddaughter's work. Tam dutifully weaved colourful necklets and headbands. She held one up for Gramma's approval. The old lady waggled her head and mumbled something incomprehensible but Tam seriously doubted her grandmother even knew what was going on in front of her.

Thunder rumbled across the bay and reverberated against the mountain. The light inside the cottage darkened, and Tam had to find a lamp to continue her work. The storm was sweeping in faster than she predicted. A flash of lightning startled Gramma, who sat bolt upright and stared at the window.

'It's all right, Gramma,' Tam said soothingly. 'It's just a little storm.'

'Where's Eric?' she asked. 'Is he here?'

'Who?' Tam inquired, perplexed by her grandmother's question.

'A bolt of light. There's a dragon there you know,' the old lady said and closed her eyes.

Her grandmother was obsessed with dragons, thought Tam. She kept talking to Claryssa and Eric as well. She had no idea who Claryssa was, but the name Eric jogged her memory. Wasn't it the name Gramma used the afternoon Tam had stumbled in on her conversation with the Herbal Man? She hadn't imagined the conversation, had she? The wind outside had a sudden, brief burst of fury. Heavy raindrops clunked on the shingle roof, heralding the coming downpour, then the hissing rain set in.

Tam abandoned the flowers and ran through the

cottage, closing the four sets of window shutters. Then she collected all the available pots she could muster and placed them strategically to catch the drips that would inevitably fall from the roof. Her father, and her mother, and even Chasse had used buckets of pitch to seal the leaks, but every downpour exposed new weaknesses, new holes and gaps, so she was well used to the ritual of shifting pots.

Then she remembered the bedding. In a panic she raced outside and salvaged the bedclothes from the honeynut tree. The whole world was watery grey, but she took little notice in her frenzy. Back inside she threw the bedding down and checked how wet it was. Sodden. Her mother would be angry. Tam cursed under her breath and set to stoking the hearth. Once she had the fire blazing she dragged the table and chairs in front of it and hung the bedding on them to dry. Finally she returned to her flower weaving. Gramma was snoring again. The musty smell of drying bedclothes slowly permeated the room.

The storm was brief. No sooner had it passed than Chasse blustered through the door. He was muddied and his nose was bleeding.

'What's happened?' Tam cried, jumping up to meet her brother.

'Nothing,' he muttered sullenly as he pushed past her to the bedroom. Tam grabbed a damp rag and followed.

'Chasse,' she demanded. 'Tell me.'

'I had a fight, that's all,' he said. He took the rag

she proffered and dabbed at his nose to wipe away the blood.

'Who with?' she inquired. Chasse remained silent. 'Who with?' she repeated with greater insistence.

Her brother flinched and lifted his head. He had been crying. 'Marron,' he muttered.

'Why?'

'Because he says things that aren't true.'

'Like what?' She squatted beside her brother.

He hit his clenched fist against the floor and swallowed as if what he was going to say tasted sour in his mouth. 'He said Father is too afraid to fight the dragons any more. He said that on the last trip his own father led the dragonwarriors. He said our father stayed back on the ship. Like an old woman.'

'But that's not true. We know that it's not. We've heard the stories since the men returned,' Tam argued.

'Marron says it's just our father's friends lying to cover up what really happened. There are others who say differently.'

'Have you heard them say anything different?' she asked. This time Chasse's face clouded with anger. He seemed even less willing to answer. 'Chasse?' she prompted. 'Did they?'

'Yes,' he whispered hoarsely. 'I've overheard them in the Warriors' Hall.'

Tam rocked back on her heels. Her father was Dragon Head, the most respected warrior in Harbin. No-one dared suggest he was anything but the bravest. Her brother's news astounded her. She put a hand on his shoulder and said quietly, 'It's just gossip. See? Even men gossip.'

'It's not just gossip!' Chasse shouted. He flung away the damp cloth. 'I've heard what they say.' He buried his face in his hands and shrugged off her hand.

'I'll get you a drink,' she offered. She retreated into the main room to give Chasse a few moments alone.

As she filled a wooden goblet with water, she heard Gramma Harmi cough. The old lady was looking straight at her.

'A man is a man,' she rasped, and waggled her head wisely.

Tam stared at her grandmother, surprised by the old woman's statement. 'What do you mean?'

'They all come to that,' Harmi announced. 'Eric showed me that once.'

'Gramma?' Tam appealed, moving towards the old lady's chair. 'What do you mean?'

'A dragon knows such things.'

Until that remark, Tam thought Gramma had understood what Chasse was saying. Now she was on about the dragon again, it seemed. She patted her grandmother's hand and asked if she wanted something to eat. Harmi simply closed her eyes and went to sleep. Tam straightened the old lady's blanket and took the water to Chasse. He was standing, staring at the flames in the hearth.

'Here,' she said, offering him the goblet.

'Thanks.' He drank it in one gulp, and started for the door.

'Where are you going now?'

'Back to the Warriors' Hall.'

'Didn't you just come from there? Won't Marron still be there?'

'No,' he declared. 'We fought by the goat yards.'

'What if he's gone to the Warriors' Hall too?' she asked, but Chasse was already gone.

Marron watched her carry the flower arrangements to the Long Hall that afternoon between rain showers. She noticed him watching her after she crossed the bridge. He was lounging against his father's hut, lazily twisting an old sword handle in his hands and drawing lines in the rain-softened earth. She was surprised to see him on his own. He nearly always had two or three youths with him for company. As soon as she noticed him, she made a sustained effort not to acknowledge him or look in his direction, but she felt his eyes following her down the path. He had a predatory air, a hunter's presence, and that made her avoid him. She was relieved to reach the door of the Long Hall.

The interior was awash with colour and light. The women arranged to hold Procra's Dance inside because of the change in weather. Freshly cut flowers and streamers of vividly dyed material festooned the wooden beams and walls, and bright lanterns were hung at regular intervals, just high enough to avoid the head of the tallest man in Harbin. A bonfire-size hearth, more like the one traditionally lit for the Mad Wizards' Dance in mid-winter, was being organised in the centre of the hall.

Eesa hurried to meet her daughter. She scooped up the colourful headbands and necklaces Tam had crafted into her own arms and complimented her daughter's handiwork, saying, 'Beautiful work, my girl. The girls will be very proud to wear these tonight. You have done well.' Tam was pleased to receive her mother's praise for a change, and smiled. 'How are you feeling?' Eesa inquired.

'A little better,' Tam replied, 'but the cramping is still there.'

Eesa wrinkled her brow with concern and said, 'It would be a shame to miss the night's celebration.'

'I know,' Tam agreed, feigning disappointment, 'But it hurts too much still. I would only be a burden to you.' She quickly glanced around, anxious to change the subject. 'Where are the girls?' she asked.

'It's getting late and it will be dark quickly in this poor weather, Tamesan. They have gone to Emma's hut to prepare. I will take these flowers to them now.'

Tam saw Amarti and old Sharmine staring. She smiled weakly at them, feigning illness for their benefit, and said to her mother, 'Then I will go back and feed Gramma and Jaysin. That will save you time.'

'Thank you, child,' said Eesa, and dismissed her daughter.

She watched Tamesan turn and leave the Hall. Her daughter had grown so tall, and so quickly. The girl has so much potential, she thought. She would make a wonderful wife for any man in this village if she only realised how much she had to offer. She was just so frustrating at times, so unwilling to accept what was, what really had to be. She shrugged her shoulders, sighed, and wondered if her own mother had ever worried about her future as much as she worried about Tamesan's. Perhaps that maternal concern, that frustration, was also a part of what had to be in the scheme plotted by Varst and Procra in their eternal wisdom.

Chapter Nine

Tam relaxed in the warm water and let it swirl around her, easing away the week's grime and weariness. Bathing in the steaming hot springs was always a pleasure. Normally she would be in the company of other girls or women, but this past summer and autumn she had started to come alone. The springs were trapped in a jumble of rocks a short distance up the mountain. Villagers called them the Dragon's Cauldron and legend claimed they were formed when the great silver dragon Nakiades fought spat at its foe and missed. Its vile fire had cracked the rocks, and water gushed out to fill the hollows, but the heat of the dragon's spittle was so fierce that the rocks it covered would never cool. There were other places on the mountain where steam escaped from the heart of the rock, but the Dragon's Cauldron was the only known hot springs.

Tam had missed Procra's Dance, but she did not regret it. All six maidens were chosen as everyone expected, and the night's revelry was happy and long. Her father, Kevan, had spent most of the following day in his bed, sleeping off the effects of excessive mead-drinking, and her mother had been unusually quiet and sedate. Chasse, however, was energetic the morning after Procra's Dance. He had bounced out of bed and left the cottage without sharing details of the night's events with Tam, much to her annoyance. She pinned him down the following evening, so he told her most of what had happened, especially who paired with whom, but she knew he was also deliberately concealing something. He did not even mention his fight with Marron. When she pressed him about whether or not he had danced with any girls, he laughed and changed the subject. She suspected why.

Two days later she spied her brother walking through the trees on the outskirts of the village with Kerryn. They held hands. Tam smiled, and then was stung with a sudden pang of jealousy. Her emotional reaction was absurd. She chided herself for feeling so possessive of her brother. He was nearly a man. He had the right to choose any girl in the village when he was of age. Kerryn was attractive and friendly. She would be a good match for him. But Tam could not entirely free herself of her irritating jealousy. It ate at her fiercely for the rest of the day, and she struggled to sleep that night, arguing with herself that Chasse's choice of a woman was not for her to deny.

As she lolled in the warm spring she reflected on the change in her brother's mood. Since pairing with Kerryn he was more secretive, yet also more confident. Tam ached to talk with him about his new relationship but he seemed determined not to share his thoughts with her. She was being carefully shut out of his life, and that was what hurt most. She knew he was not deliberately trying to hurt her. He was just so engrossed in getting to know Kerryn, and coming to terms with what that meant for him, that he had no time to spare for his sister. Perhaps he was simply too embarrassed to talk to her, she reasoned. But she did not have the courage to force him to discuss it—not yet. She loved him too much to bully him. When Chasse was ready, she knew he would talk. She simply had to be patient.

The morning air was cool when she emerged from the water. She quickly towelled herself and dressed. Eesa wanted her help at home before midday. But there was enough time to spare to walk through the woods, perhaps even to watch the world from her favourite lookout. Time alone, without all the responsibilities her mother forced onto her, was exceedingly precious.

The mountain forest was readying for winter. The leaves on the deciduous trees were changing hue, washing the mountain slopes with shades of yellow, orange and brown. Some trees had already shed their foliage, exposing stark limbs in mute warning that Blitzart would soon spread his cold breath over the world. Tam spotted a fuzzy-tailed squirrel scampering across the ground, carrying a nut between its teeth. Like the squirrel, the villagers in Harbin were preparing for winter. The last celebration of the Harbin year was in three weeks. Called Procra's Feast, it was a time when all the village met to share and store the food that would tide them through the winter weeks. Each family would be invited to take its portion from the collective produce, and an additional portion was then stored in the Long Hall for emergency use, and for the mid-winter Mad Wizards' Dance, or Blitzart's Feast, as it was traditionally called. The mid-winter feast brought everyone together to break the boredom that winter forced on them.

Tam crossed the path that led up to the Herbal Man's residence and slipped between the trunks of a stand of saplings. As she entered a small clearing further in, she heard a snorting sound to her left. The bushes rustled. She turned to see what had caused the disturbance. A furry grey muzzle emerged. Black eyes stared at her. Then the bushes parted and a mountain bear lumbered into full view. Tam froze. What should she do? The bear took a hesitant step towards her, then sat back on its haunches, as if it, too, wasn't sure what should happen next. Even on its haunches the bear was as tall as Tamesan. She recalled all the horror stories about bears. No-one she knew had been attacked by one, but there were village tales of how unfortunate people had wandered onto a bear's territory and been torn apart by the angry creatures.

She watched the bear. It was studying her, tilting its heavy head to left and right as if analysing what it had found. Tam considered making a dash into the trees. Or she could climb a large rock to her left.

The bear opened its mouth and growled. Large white teeth glistened with saliva. How hungry could this bear be? She tried to remain calm as she eased one foot to the left towards the rock. The bear tilted its head again and leant forward. Tam eased her other foot towards the rock. The bear sniffed the air and grunted. Then she moved another step. The bear rocked forward onto all fours and padded towards her.

Tam made her choice. She bolted for the rock and clambered up, desperately hoping the bear could not reach her. It didn't. She scrambled to safety and spun around, panting, to peer back down at the creature. It was at the base of the rock, sniffing the ground. Then it reared up on its hind legs and lifted its muzzle towards her. If she put out her hand she could touch it. She didn't. The bear growled and its teeth flashed. Great claws scratched against the surface of the rock. Tam screamed.

'Don't do that,' commanded a human voice. 'You will scare the poor animal.'

A dark-robed figure stepped out of the undergrowth into the clearing. The bear turned towards the sound of the voice just as Tam recognised the old Herbal Man, who began speaking in a language she did not understand. The grey bear cocked its head as if listening. Then it dropped to all fours and ambled away into the trees.

'There,' said the Herbal Man as he approached the base of the rock, 'he's gone. He wasn't going to eat you. He was just curious. In fact he was probably just as nervous about meeting you as you were at meeting him.'

'But,' Tam argued, staring at the claw marks scratched onto the rock, 'he might have eaten me. I've heard how bears have attacked people.'

'Wouldn't you, if some stranger, carrying spears, intruded into your home?'

'Well, yes, but this is my home.'

'Your home is the village,' the Herbal Man corrected. 'This forest is the bear's home. We are the intruders here. It's up to us to respect his ways in his home.'

Tam slid down from the rock. 'What did you say to the bear then?' she asked.

'A simple "thank you" would suffice,' the Herbal Man said, ignoring her question and pretending to be offended by her lack of manners.

'Oh, I'm sorry. I meant to say thank you,' she apologised hurriedly. 'I was just surprised by it all.'

'No injuries?' the Herbal Man inquired.

'None.'

'Then we'd best be moving on,' the old man said, and he turned to leave.

'Where are you going?' she asked.

'I'm stocking up on some herbs. It will snow before the end of this week.' He glanced up at the grey clouds hanging overhead.

'Do you mind if I come along?' she asked. 'For a little while. My mother doesn't expect me back home just yet.'

The Herbal Man considered her request for a moment, then said, 'I see no harm in that. You are welcome to accompany me, Tamesan.' So saying, he led her out of the clearing.

Every so often the Herbal Man stooped to study a flower, or a plant, or a growth on a rock or a tree. Sometimes he deviated from a narrow run he was following to collect samples of plants he spotted. Tam was fascinated by the methodical manner in which the Herbal Man worked his way across the mountain slope, choosing certain growths and rejecting others. All the while he talked to her, telling her precisely about everything he found and what he was doing.

'Do you know what this flower is?' he asked, holding up a clutch of red blooms.

'Seleserin's sorrow,' Tam answered, recognising them.

'Very good,' he declared. 'The flower is pretty but not much use except as a component for a dye. But the ragged leaves on the stalk can be boiled to make an elixir that eats away warts on the skin, and it makes a useful component of other elixirs used for curing skin ailments.' A moment later he was scraping pale yellow fungus from the base of a clump of rocks. 'Excellent,' he chortled, like a happy child. 'Rock mould. There's very little of it around this time of year. Soon there will be none.' He packed the sample into a small leather bag and hung it on his laden leather belt. 'It can be worked into a paste that draws poison from the blood. There's not much call for it here, but I always have some on hand just in case.'

As they walked, he began to teach Tam the essence of his trade. He explained how he searched the mountainside and the valleys and the narrow strip of earth that nestled at the mountain's foot for an enormous variety of plants. Spring to early summer was the best period. Growth of plants was luxurious and fresh, and he worked hardest then, collecting what he needed. But even in the dead heart of mid-winter there were tiny fungi and bitter little plants that battled for existence in the snow and ice, and he sought them because they had greater qualities of strength and endurance than any other plant life. He began to explain the processes of drying and distillation and powdering and liquefying, but Tam found she was becoming overloaded with information.

He led her down into the gorge where Watersdrop streamed towards her village and showed her the location of his favourite herb.

'Mountain blossom, this is called,' he said as he held up a small damp white flower. 'It sometimes has red flowers as well.' Tam had seen an occasional bloom drifting in Watersdrop near her home, but she had never seen the plant itself. 'It only grows here, in this part of the gorge,' the old man explained, as if he guessed her thought. 'I don't know why. There are other parts of the gorge, deeper in the mountains, that have exactly the same soil and water conditions, but there are no mountain blossoms there. Only here.' He turned the thin-leaved, delicate flower in his fingertips, studying it closely. 'I only ever pick a dozen or so when I come here. I'm afraid if I pick more the plants won't reproduce and then they'll die out. Collecting herbs isn't just a case of ripping up whatever you need. You have to understand the balance of things here, the way everything is bound together.'

'But why is this flower so special?' she asked.

The Herbal Man sat on a rock just above the thundering water of the cataract and looked directly at her with his piercing grey eyes. 'Every part of the mountain blossom is useful. The flower can be dried and crushed into a dye powder. It can also be mixed in water to make a tonic which will help someone suffering from a fever, or tight chest complaints. If it is boiled in water, the vapours alleviate breathing difficulties. The leaves, eaten raw, are good for food. Dried, the leaves can be burned, and the aromatics they exude are very relaxing.'

She listened as the Herbal Man described the variety of ways the mysterious little plant could be applied for herbal treatments. The roar of the angry water churning between the cliffs and over the rocks slipped into the background as he spoke. He wasn't even shouting. She was mildly surprised at how she could hear him so easily in the situation. He was describing a world of things she had never heard of, and it kept her interest as the sun climbed through the morning sky.

The Herbal Man's prediction of early snow was correct. The first light fall spiralled out of the low grey clouds at the end of the week and sent Harbin into restless activity. Eesa coordinated the girls and women in filling food pots with grains and nuts and seeds, and preparing cooked breads and cakes. The herdsmen mustered the goat flock and selected the beasts to be slaughtered for meat. Plump chickens were rounded up. The warriors forayed onto the mountain to hunt, and they brought back more meat for storage. The plans for Procra's Feast were brought forward to just a week away. The village rumour-mongers were already predicting a long and bitter winter.

Chasse shifted his few possessions into the Warriors' Hall. Along with the four other boys who were approaching manhood, it was expected that he winter with the men. During the coming months he would receive his formal training that culminated in the dragonship journey. Tam helped her brother carry his gear, and she felt his excitement. For the first time in several days, he was openly chatting to her.

'One last winter as a boy!' he shouted. 'This time next year I will be a man!'

She smiled, but made no response. What could she say? She was never going to be a man. Never going to have the same sense of exhilaration and impending freedom her brother was experiencing now. Next year she was still going to be a girl, and the year after, a woman. There was no freedom in either position.

When her mother and father stopped bossing her around, a husband would take their place. She would rather be like the Herbal Man. He came and went as he pleased. The whole mountain was his home. If only she could choose to do something like that.

Tam left Chasse at the door to the Warriors' Hall. Women never entered unless invited, and then it was merely to clean, or take food to the men. Several times she had been seized with a desire to just burst into the Warriors' Hall unannounced, simply to break the traditional law. She always resisted this urge, though. Her father would be so dishonoured by such an irresponsible act he would be forced to treat her very harshly. She hardly needed that.

Trapped in duties set by Eesa, Tam carried pots and kept the smaller village children amused while their mothers worked. Nevertheless, she managed to spend early morning hours on the mountain, where she walked with the Herbal Man as he continued to hunt for the last blooms and growths of the dying autumn. Each morning she learnt more of the old man's art and listened to his wisdom: how each plant and each creature on the mountain were interdependent, working in harmony and balance.

'Men have too little respect for these things,' he told her. 'They fail to see beyond their own greedy needs. The whole world is our garden to tend and nurture.' The underlying passion in his voice, the words clearly coming from the old man's heart, struck a resonant chord in her. She had felt these things herself, alone on the mountain, and for the first time she was hearing someone else confirm what she believed.

'Can you remember this one?' he asked her one morning. He held a small, prickly plant in his gnarled hand.

'Dogweed,' she answered.

'Very good,' he said. 'Does it have any uses?'

Tam racked her brains. 'Only the roots,' she answered. 'You have to dry them, boil them, and then distil the liquid until there is a white—no, green—residue. That has to be mixed with—' She paused, having forgotten what he had told her the previous day.

'With snowbud juice,' the old man prompted.

'Of course,' she said quickly, 'snowbud juice. And it's good for wind in the body and headaches, isn't it?'

'Flatulence,' the old man grinned. 'That is correct, Tamesan. You do learn very quickly.'

'What are you collecting tomorrow?' she asked.

The old man heaved his sack onto his shoulder before answering. 'I won't be coming down the mountain tomorrow, Tamesan.' He looked up at the sky. The peak of Dragon Mountain was shrouded in heavy grey cloud. 'The full winter snows will fall tonight.'

Tam was suddenly depressed. She was enjoying learning the Herbal Man's trade. It was certainly more interesting than learning how to be a good village girl. Now the old man was leaving and he would not return until the winter snows released their grip on the mountain. The same empty feeling she had had escorting Chasse to the Warriors' Hall washed over her. She did not know what to say. The old man broke the silence for her.

'I have a favour to ask,' he said. He put down his sack and rummaged inside his cloak. Finally, he produced a tiny drawstring pouch and handed it gently to Tam. 'I would like you to give this to Harmi.'

'What is it?' she asked as she accepted the small pouch.

'Just something. A ring. She will understand when you give it to her,' he answered. 'Give it to her on the night of Blitzart's Feast. Not before. And not while anyone else is near.'

'Why?' she asked. The gift was becoming a rather complex mystery.

'There are very special reasons why, but I cannot explain them to you. It is not that simple. I'm asking you to trust me. All I can tell you is that it is very important that Harmi has this gift that night. Will you do this for me?'

Tam cupped the tiny pouch in her hand. She had kept the secret of the old man's hut and his underground chambers. This would be no different, although her curiosity about the relationship between the Herbal Man and Gramma Harmi flared yet again.

'I'll keep it safe and give it to her as you ask. It's the least I can do for you teaching me about the herbs,' she promised, and smiled.

The old man bowed his head in an unusual mark of respect. He shouldered his sack again. 'I have enjoyed your company these last few days, young Tamesan. If you are willing to keep learning, I will see you after winter has passed. Perhaps you could even learn to read and write.'

She appreciated the sincerity of the old man's offer, though she had no idea what he meant by learning to read and write.

'I will be waiting,' she said.

'May the dragon warm your winter,' the Herbal Man declared, and then he turned and trudged into the trees. Tam watched him go, then descended the path to Harbin. That night, just as the Herbal Man had forecast, the snow-white hand of true winter closed over Harbin.

Chapter Ten

'Are you coming, Tam?' Chasse called.

'Yes!' she yelled. She grabbed a coarse string bag Eesa had asked her to bring, and a plate overloaded with steaming scones, kissed Gramma Harmi on the forehead, and closed the cottage door. Chasse was waiting outside, stamping his feet on the cold earth in a vain effort to drive the biting cold out of his toes. His breath escaped in cloudy vapours.

'I'm ready,' she announced.

Brother and sister trudged along the snow-covered path over the bridge into the village. The snowfall had forced the villagers to hold Procra's Feast much earlier than planned. The whole world was coated with a white mantle, and the heavy clouds hanging overhead threatened to lay down more snow. Tam saw her little brother Jaysin standing alone near the Long Hall, watching a group of children throwing snowballs at each other. It was clear to Tam that he desperately wanted to be included, but he made no attempt to join in. She wondered how she could help without interfering too much, but couldn't come up with an answer. Jaysin's social isolation seemed as complete as if he was an injured gull trapped on an islet in the bay. Forcing her attention away from her little brother, she noticed people moving towards the Long Hall from all directions, each carrying a bundle of goods: foodstuffs to be shared with the rest of the population at Procra's Feast. Her eyes were drawn to a familiar figure, the young widow Banni, bearing a platter of food and dragging a sack of goods behind her in the snow.

'Here, you lazy Chasse,' Tam said, shoving the scones and string bag into his arms. 'You carry these. I'm going to help Banni.' Before he could protest, she had bounded away across the snow.

'I'll carry the sack,' Tam offered as she reached the young woman. Banni gratefully let her take hold of the drawstring, and they walked on together.

Inside the Long Hall, people busily milled about. Eesa and several friends were receiving the food from those who entered, and had already started the slow task of sorting the goods into household piles. On a row of low trestle tables in the centre of the hall, food for the feast had also been laid out. Two fires were alight, one at either end of the Hall, warming the interior against the icy winter, and the sweet aroma of roasting meat filled the air. Eesa immediately directed Tam to help with the sharing out of the food into household lots, and Tam busied herself accordingly. This was one village tradition she saw as important. Winters were always long and bitter beneath Dragon Mountain. Sharing food ensured that no-one starved.

A commotion at the entrance captured everyone's attention and halted the activity. The Dragon Fang entered, led by Tam's father. Their arrival signalled the opening of the Feast. Eesa immediately made the girls and women clear spaces for the Dragon Fang at the central table, and the warriors moved to their seats. The dragonwarriors with wives left a space to their left for their women. Next, the eldest village boys were called to take their places at the central tables. Then Eesa sat beside Kevan, and the dragonwarrior wives followed suit. Only men who were not dragonwarriors, unmarried women, widows and girls remained. The men took places closest to the door. The women and girls would sit wherever there was spare room, but first their duty was to serve the people at the central table.

As everyone settled, the door to the Long Hall opened again, and the Dragon Heart priest stepped in, wearing his finest grey bear cloak with an ornate ceremonial headdress representing a dragon's claw. Village children swirled around him as he entered, but they were shooed aside by old Sharmine and Amarti. The Dragon Heart paraded in a slow circle around the central table, shaking a handful of dried reeds rhythmically and chanting a traditional song to begin Procra's Feast. Tam listened to the words, even mouthed some, having heard them every year. Every child in Harbin knew them. They sang them playing games, and parents sang them to babies to calm them during the dark nights. The song spoke of the seasonal cycles, the coming of winter and the ascent of Blitzart, of warm fires and ice-covered water, of contrasts in the world of Harbin.

When the priest finished, he stood at the head of the table with Kevan to his left and Trask seated on his right. He cast a discerning eye over the food and nodded appreciatively. Then he selected a leg of roasted pigeon and pronounced in a loud voice, 'Almighty Varst himself would be greatly pleased with gentle Procra's offering set today before the children of Nakiades. Eat well, my children.' The formal blessing given, he bit into the pigeon leg to signal the men to take their first portion of food.

Tam brought drinks to those who requested them. She filled Kevan's goblet with mulled mead first, as a mark of respect for her father. He smiled and, surprisingly, broke with convention by handing her a slice of roasted meat to eat while she was still serving. Eesa glared at him, but knew better than to make an issue of his impropriety.

As Tam moved further along the table, she heard someone call. She turned to discover Marron's dark eyes focused on her. He was holding out his goblet.

'Tamesan, fetch me some mead,' he said. She reached for his goblet, but as she grasped it Marron deliberately stroked her fingers. She quickly pulled her hand away and retreated towards the hearth where a jug of mead was being warmed over the coals. As she stooped to pour mead into Marron's goblet, she heard another voice address her.

'Give me the goblet, Tamesan,' the voice ordered. 'I'll take it back to Marron.'

She turned to find Katris glaring at her and holding out a hand to take the goblet. Tam shrugged and passed it to the dark-haired girl without comment.

Katris' eyes narrowed, however, and she said spitefully, 'Don't think you have any chance with Marron, because you don't.' Then she whirled around, and carried the drink towards Marron's place at the table. Despite Katris' threatening manner, Tam was grateful not to have to serve Marron. His constant staring, his unwanted attention, were making her increasingly uncomfortable. Katris could have him.

Tam took drink and then sweetmeats to the men. She served Chasse and laughed at his attempts to act like a man. He was miffed at first, but then he relaxed and teased her in turn. As the feast wore on, the single women and girls found places at the tables and shared in the meal, only rising to fetch things on request. Tam squeezed between Banni and a girl one summer older called Fay. She even got pleasantly involved in idle chatter about weaving, and babies, and cooking. Then Banni told her she was pregnant. Her admission caught Tam unprepared. She didn't know whether to be happy for Banni because of the coming child, or sad because Banni had lost her husband Jared and would have to raise the baby alone.

'Aren't you happy for me?' Banni asked when she saw Tam's bewilderment.

'Yes,' Tam blurted trying to mask her confused thoughts, 'of course I am. It's just—' she started to explain and then thought better of it.

'I know what you are thinking,' Banni said. Her smile tightened. 'But it means I haven't really lost Jared, Tamesan. I have a part of him here,' she said, pointing to her belly, 'within me. This will be our son. And I will name him after his father.'

Tam smiled. Then she hugged Banni. Perhaps it wouldn't be so hard for the young woman after all. She had a purpose, a link with her husband. She let her happiness for Banni take over her mood and helped her friend share the news around the table. The only aspect of Banni's news she hadn't resolved was whether Banni had considered the possibility that the coming baby could be a girl.

The afternoon's feasting was full of warmth and happiness. The people were content to face the approaching winter given the plentiful stores they had come to share. Word began to spread that the snow was falling again and was getting heavier. The news prompted families to take their leave. They collected their allotted portion of food, and paid their respects to the Dragon Head as they departed. Slowly the numbers at the feast diminished, but the warm atmosphere continued to spread the feeling of comfort through those who remained in the Long Hall, eating and drinking and talking.

An unexpected outburst of angry voices at the head of the tables caught everyone sitting near Tam by complete surprise. When she stood, she saw her father and Trask facing each other across the table.

'Take back your words!' Kevan roared.

'Not unless you admit what everyone knows to be true!' shouted Trask.

'I have nothing to admit! I am the Dragon Head!'

Trask put both fists on the table and leant forward, closer to Kevan. 'I say you are unfit to hold that title any longer. I say it is time for a stronger leader, a real man who is not afraid to fight!'

Kevan's face reddened with fury. 'You are a fool, Trask!' he growled. 'I am the leader of this village and my word is law. You mock the traditions with this outburst.'

'You mock our traditions with your cowardice!' Trask spat. Kevan's right arm shot out and he grabbed Trask firmly by the throat. Trask retaliated by grappling with Kevan's arm.

'Stop this!' bellowed the Dragon Heart. 'You desecrate Procra's sacred feast!' but the two men continued to wrestle, ignoring the priest's plea for order. Already some of the Dragon Fang were on their feet to watch the action. Five older warriors pushed forward and tore Kevan and Trask apart.

'Enough!' cried Theo, holding one of Kevan's arms. 'This is neither the time nor place to dispute such matters. You are squabbling like little boys.'

Trask strained against the arms that pinned him, then relaxed, realising the futility of his action. Kevan, however, shrugged aside those who were loosely holding him, and stormed from the Long Hall.

'See?' Trask shouted after Kevan, 'You want him as your leader? You want someone who runs from a fight to lead the Dragon Fang?'

'Enough of your mouth, Trask!' growled Theo.

Trask gave the warrior a piercing look of hatred. Then he spat on the floor and resumed his seat, lifting his mead goblet as he did so. 'I say here's to the Dragon Head,' he proposed sarcastically. 'May he live long and prosper.' Then he downed the contents of his goblet before his stunned audience.

Eesa tried to remain calm despite the circumstances. She rose from the table and crossed to where family groups waited to collect their food. Tam watched her mother at first, and then went to help her. Banni and Fay and several women followed. A handful of men remained at the tables, drinking with Trask, after the last of the family groups withdrew. Eesa dismissed the girls.

Tam waited outside the Hall for her mother. The snow was falling quite steadily and the afternoon light had all but faded. It was getting very cold. Chasse had already entered the Warriors' Hall. She would only see him now on rare occasions during winter. She presumed her father had gone home. The confrontation between her father and Trask had shocked her. She remembered what Chasse had disclosed after his fight with Marron, so she already knew there was ill-feeling between the two men, but she had not imagined it to be as bitter as it appeared in the Long Hall. She was astonished to see it flare so openly. The

Dragon Head was the most powerful person in the village. Anyone who defied his law under any circumstances was liable to harsh judgment and punishment. Yet Trask was obviously undeterred by that traditional threat. He seemed determined to publicly oppose her father. Why? What so rankled Trask that he was willing to risk public humiliation to oppose Kevan?

Eesa appeared in the doorway and closed the door behind her. She was carrying a bundle of goods. 'There was no need to wait, girl,' she said as she handed the bundle to Tam. 'I hoped you would go home and see to Gramma.'

'I wanted to make sure you were all right,' Tam replied.

Eesa stared at her daughter. 'Whatever in Procra's name do you mean by that?' she asked.

'I mean with Trask and Father arguing.'

'Tsh!' Eesa exclaimed. 'They're men. They argue all the time.'

'About father's right to be Dragon Head?'

'About *everything*,' said Eesa. 'They argue about who has the quickest hand, the sharpest spear, the biggest nose. They spend all their lives trying to prove that one is better than the other. That's men all over.'

'But it seemed so serious,' Tam insisted. Her mother's explanation wasn't convincing her.

'Men think everything they do is serious, my girl,' Eesa announced. 'And the argument you saw probably was serious. But it was a mead argument. Trask had drunk too much. Men say stupid things when they are drunk. They say they love you forever, swear they killed a dragon bare-handed, and claim they can tame the oceans. Tomorrow it will be forgotten. Believe me, I have seen it all before. Now let's get home before this snow buries us where we stand.' The discussion was at an end. Eesa had said so.

Tam hoisted her burden and trudged through the snow beside her mother. Eesa had emphasised the incident was nothing out of the ordinary, but Tam was not so sure. It was the first time she had witnessed two important dragonwarriors clash in the village and she was unaware of any similar incidents. That alone made the argument everyone had witnessed out of the ordinary in Harbin. Something in her mother's tone also lacked credibility. She was more friendly than usual, as if she wanted Tam to accept her word regardless of whatever else she had seen and heard. So Tam reached her home less convinced than ever that things in her village were normal.

The snow fell unabated for five days. It wasn't an unusual length of time for snow to fall in Harbin, but it came a fortnight earlier than usual, and fell heavily enough and constantly enough to keep people indoors. The temperature remained bitterly cold, day and night. When Tam took opportunities to peer through the window shutters, she saw the world she knew rapidly disappearing under the swirling snow. Huts were half-buried in drifts that reached the height of window ledges. Doors were blocked. Even the acute angle of the shingled roofs did not prevent snow from making many huts and cottages appear to be nothing more than little hillocks in the general countryside. Only the larger structures of the Long Hall and the Warriors' Hall retained any semblance of their former selves.

Locked in their cottage, Eesa gave Tam a variety of jobs to occupy the long hours. There were clothes to sew, baskets to weave, utensils to make and repair, foodstuffs to bake, Gramma to care for, the fire to tend. Eesa usually set her daughter to work and then found a separate task to do herself to while away the time. Kevan merely sat and whittled wood into animal shapes, or honed his great axe, or slept. Trapped with his family by the excessive and sudden snowfall, unable to rejoin the men in the Warriors' Hall, he was morose. He tried to teach Jaysin the art of whittling but the boy was too young to stay interested for very long, and he had a strange aversion to sharp things like the whittling knife. The latter only served to irritate Kevan further.

'The child is a changeling,' he complained to his wife on the third afternoon he had unsuccessfully tried to encourage Jaysin to whittle.

'Patience, husband,' Eesa soothed. 'Patience. He will learn when he is ready.'

'Varst's wrath he will!' snarled Kevan. He threw

the whittling knife at a nog of wood near the hearth. It buried its point in the wood, and stuck. 'He will never learn. The boy is too weak. He's nothing like the other boys.' Jaysin skulked away into his bedroom to escape his father's ridicule. Tam rose from feeding Gramma Harmi and followed him. 'And don't you go mothering him any more!' Kevan warned. 'He has too much girl in him already.' She ignored her father's scathing remark and left the room.

Jaysin lay face down on his bedding. At first Tam thought he was crying, but when she put her hand on his shoulder he merely sighed.

'I think Father is just bored, Jaysin. You know how he gets,' she said softly.

'What's a changeling?' he asked.

'I—don't know. It doesn't mean anything.'

'Yes it does,' he persisted. 'I heard an old lady use it behind my back once. She said I had to be a changeling. Father says it, too. I want to know what it means.'

Tam knew what it meant but she didn't have the heart to tell her little brother how cruel her father was being. Legends and folk tales sometimes had changelings in them—fairy children swapped for human children. A changeling was usually strange and mysterious, and always brought disaster to the unfortunate family who received it.

'It doesn't matter what it means,' she reassured him.

'Tam?'

'Yes, Jaysin?'

'Why am I so different?'

His candid question touched her heart. 'You're not different, Jaysin,' she said awkwardly.

'Yes, I am. I know I am.'

'How?'

'I don't know,' he murmured into his bedclothes. Then he turned his head to stare at her. His big eyes were full of appeal and sorrow. 'You know how,' he said quietly. 'I don't do what the other children do. I'd like to sometimes but then it just doesn't interest me. I don't like how everything is about fighting and chasing. Why are all the games like that, Tam?'

'I don't know. That's just how games are,' she replied.

'But they don't have to be, do they? Aren't there other things we could do? Things that don't hurt anybody?'

'Are you worried about the others teasing you?' she asked.

'No,' Jaysin said. 'A little,' he corrected. 'But I don't really care about that. I mean, it's not only me they pick on. They pick on others as well. That's why I don't want to play. They have to always be picking on someone. They always have to be hurting someone.'

Eesa called Tam from the main room. 'Mother wants me, Jaysin. Are you coming out?' she asked.

'No. He'll only give me dirty looks,' Jaysin sighed. He buried his head back in his bedclothes.

Eesa had potatoes for Tam to peel. Her father was

peering anxiously out of a window at the falling snow. All he really wanted to do was to retreat to the safe haven of the Warriors' Hall, to be among the men in an environment he understood, thought Tam as she glanced at him. He was never comfortable in his home. He always acted as if he felt under threat there, as if he was afraid his family would all stop obeying him. She rinsed the potatoes in a jug of cold water and set to scraping the skin from them. Her little brother's dilemma sat in her mind. He *was* so different from the other children, even, she thought, from herself. He was a misfit. He had a distaste for violence. He would never be a dragonwarrior of Harbin. And she knew he wanted it that way already, even though he was the second son of the Dragon Head. There was no logical reason why he thought the way he did. Perhaps, just perhaps, she mused as she started slicing the potatoes into a bowl, he was a changeling after all. Then she scolded herself for thinking so cruelly. Jaysin was Jaysin. She loved him all the more for being so different.

Chapter Eleven

When a break in the snowfall finally came, Harbin was buried. Families clambered through windows to clear the snowdrifts from their doorways and scrape the weight from their roofs. The dragonwarriors and the next summer's initiates emerged from the Warriors' Hall, and helped where help was needed. The last place to be cleared was Asmae's hut on the furthest outskirts. It was totally buried beneath the snow, but the old woman had survived.

Chasse returned to help his family and Tam was glad to see him. 'So what is it like in the Hall with the other men?' she asked as they scooped snow from below the lip of a window. 'What do you do all day?'

'There's no fun in it, Tam,' he replied. 'All we seem to do is clean and polish things. We have to polish every link in the chain-mail corslets, sharpen every blade, and work oil into every scrap of leather the men can find.'

'What else?' she asked.

'There is nothing else.' Chasse flicked a scoopful of snow over his shoulder. 'Oh, except for learning the legends and the stories. We have to sit every night and learn verses from the old legends about Nakiades and the dragons, and we have to memorise the stories about different dragon adventures. It's all boring stuff.'

'It must be important, though, otherwise you wouldn't have to do it.'

'I think they make us do it because there's nothing else to do. No-one's done a thing about teaching us how to hunt or kill a dragon yet. No-one's even mentioned it. It's probably more exciting here.'

Tam snorted with contempt. 'I hardly think so, brother,' she said. 'Nothing changes. I have to look after Gramma and do everything Mother tells me to do. Father whittles wooden figures and mopes about like a bear in a cage and Jaysin just mopes. I miss having you at least to talk to or fight with.'

Chasse scooped a handful of snow and tipped it on her head. 'So you miss that, do you?' he grinned.

'Yes!' she laughed and retaliated in kind. Within moments they were pitching snowballs at each other, using the honeynut tree as a shield, until Eesa intervened and made them get on with the task at hand.

The following day patches of blue appeared in the sky. Tam worked quickly to complete her morning's list of duties, and once she had Gramma comfortably dressed and seated, she quietly left the cottage. She headed for the hot springs, hoping no-one else was foolish enough to bathe in the Dragon's Cauldron on so cold a day. The confining space of the cottage, and the sweaty work shifting snow the previous day, made her long for a chance to take a dip in the soothingly warm spring waters.

There were no footprints in the snow which confirmed no-one had gone ahead of her. When she reached the springs, she stood silently, watching the spiralling steam. Winter had its own fascination in this place. The thermal rocks kept the snow several metres from the water's edge, and she admired the cold beauty of the ice-covered trees and rocks surrounding the Dragon's Cauldron. Providing the weather was suitable, the women and girls would bathe here on the morning before Blitzart's Feast. Tam intended to bathe that day no matter what the weather was like, and she would come early to be alone again. That way she wouldn't have to weather Katris' snide comments. She stood on the lip of the larger pool, stripped off her clothes, and slipped into the water. The rush of warmth over her skin was wonderful. After she adjusted to the temperature, she shifted to the very centre of the pool and savoured the serenity of the moment.

Her mind drifted. Katris was incredibly jealous of Marron's attention towards Tam. Perhaps that was the main reason Katris no longer liked her. Perhaps she should tell Katris that she could have Marron all to herself. That might change her attitude. Maybe. Maybe.

Chasse was going to choose Kerryn after he earned the status of dragonwarrior next summer. He had hinted as much to Tam yesterday while he was helping to shift snow. They both came of age next summer. It wasn't unusual for a warrior to choose a woman his own age. Some even chose women older than themselves, though mostly there were three or four summers difference between partners. Chasse would be a good husband. He was sensible. And caring. He would treat Kerryn with respect, and, as a consequence, she would have more freedom than most women. If Tam decided to accept a husband, he would have to be like her brother. But there was no-one else quite like Chasse in her village—no-one that she knew of, anyway.

She wondered what the Herbal Man was doing. Then she remembered the ring she was meant to pass to her grandmother on the evening of Blitzart's Feast. She had carefully stored the ring in a crack in the wall of her bedroom where no-one would find it. Why was it so important? What was the connection between her grandmother and the Herbal Man? He was becoming more and more mysterious.

'Hello, Tamesan.' The intruding voice startled her. She faltered in the water and looked around to her left to discover a youth sitting on a rock at the edge of the pool. Three more boys stood behind him, grinning and staring. She recognised Marron immediately. 'Isn't it a bit too cold to be swimming today?' he asked. He framed his face with a serious expression of concern, but the boys behind him sniggered.

'Would you mind going away?' she requested calmly, although she glanced uncomfortably across the pool to where her clothes were strewn.

'Why?' Marron asked. 'We were just admiring the view. It is quite beautiful,' he said and smiled.

Tam shifted her arms in the water to cover her nakedness. 'Please, Marron. You know it's not right to be here when a girl is bathing,' she tried to reason with him.

'We're just as surprised as you are,' he replied to the delight of his appreciative audience.

'Marron,' she said. Her tone shifted from polite pleading to a warning.

Marron's eyebrows rose, but his dark eyes remained fixed squarely on her. 'I will go,' he said. 'But only if you tell me how much you want me.'

'I don't want you,' she snapped. Her green eyes flashed angrily.

'Then I have to stay here,' he declared, and he pretended to make himself more comfortable on his rock.

'Marron!' she snarled.

'Your eyes flare when you get angry,' he said. 'They look prettier like that.'

The watching boys laughed and began to mock him, but politely, in case he took offence. Marron was not a boy they were foolish enough to rouse to anger. They had already seen him win too many fights.

Tam turned her back and drifted closer to the opposite bank, nearer her clothes. She was deciding whether or not it was worth just simply getting out, getting dressed, and ignoring the ogling boys. Or she could try to wait them out. The water was pleasantly warm and it was still quite cold in the open air. They might give up and move on.

'All you have to do is admit you want me, Tamesan. Then we will go away and let you get out,' Marron offered again.

'I don't want you, Marron,' she repeated.

'But next summer I can choose to have you.'

'I won't be old enough!'

'Then the summer after that. I can wait. I want you.'

Tam felt increasingly frustrated. She was trapped. Marron had her trapped. 'Wait all you want,' she retorted. 'I couldn't care if you were the only man left in Harbin, I wouldn't have you. I don't want you.'

'You won't get a choice, Tamesan. I choose because I will be a man,' he said arrogantly. 'And I will choose you.'

'Why don't you choose someone else? Like Katris? She wants you. She wants you badly. Choose her,' she entreated.

Marron smiled, but it was a malicious smile, one that made Tam suddenly feel more vulnerable than ever. 'I know Katris wants me,' he admitted. 'That's why I don't want her. She's too eager, too easy. You are different. You're beautiful. Your father is head of the village. You are the most desirable girl in Harbin. Every dragonwarrior says so. But only I will have you. I will choose you.'

'You won't!' Tam cried vehemently. 'I won't go with you. Hear me? Now take your creepy friends with you and go away!'

'Not until you say you want me,' Marron reasserted calmly.

'Marron!' Chasse appeared out of the trees, in the company of two more village youths. He started to speak but hesitated when he noticed Tam in the pool. His eyes registered surprise. 'What are you doing here?' he asked.

'I was bathing,' his sister explained. 'At least until these boys barged in.'

Chasse looked at Marron for an explanation. The latter shrugged and said, 'Your sister was just telling us how she was waiting for me to choose her as my woman in two summers' time.'

'I was not,' Tam countered. 'I asked him to go away and he won't.'

'If she's bathing we shouldn't even be here,' Chasse affirmed. 'I've been sent by Theo to fetch you back to the Warriors' Hall. We'll leave you to yourself, Tam,' he added with a smile.

'I haven't got an answer to my request yet,' Marron objected. 'I'm not leaving until I have.'

'What request?' Chasse asked.

'None of your business,' Marron replied. 'Run back to Theo.'

'I think you can leave my sister alone,' Chasse warned.

Marron stood on his rock. 'Who's going to make me do that? You?'

'If I have to,' Chasse replied.

'Chasse, don't,' Tam pleaded. She could see the violence brewing, and she didn't want her brother to get hurt the way he had the last time he fought Marron.

'Better listen to your sister,' Marron teased. 'She knows you shouldn't fight with her man.' He swaggered around the edge of the hot springs towards Chasse.

'I'm not looking for a fight, Marron,' Chasse stated calmly. 'I just don't think it's right to be at the Dragon's Cauldron when a girl is there.'

Marron came within an arm's length of Chasse. 'You mean you don't want a fight because you're as gutless as your old man,' he sneered. Tam went to protest, but Chasse leapt, taking Marron down in a heap in the snow. The other boys raced forward for a better view.

'Stop them!' Tam screamed but she knew her words were futile. The boys always loved to watch a fight. They were urging on the two combatants. Marron and Chasse wrestled violently for a moment, then fell apart. Marron was the first to his feet.

'When you're ready to fight like a man,' he taunted.

Chasse struggled out of the snow. He already had a small cut above his eye. 'Try me, dog breath,' he snarled.

Marron lunged. His first move was too confident. Chasse read it easily and dodged. He brought his arm out and caught Marron across the back of the head.

154

The youth sprawled face forward. He rolled and kicked to his feet.

'Lucky hit!' Marron spat. 'Now we get serious.'

Tam watched them circle clumsily in the snow. Marron feinted but Chasse anticipated what was coming and ducked a swinging right hand. As he side-stepped, he caught Marron a stinging blow across the left ear. The youth roared and charged. Chasse back-stepped to fend off the uncontrolled attack but his ankles sank in a small snowdrift, tripping him. The pair collapsed in a flurry of arms, legs, and spraying snow. In the confusion, Marron used his greater bulk and strength to lever his way onto Chasse's back. Then to Tam's horror, he pushed her brother's face into a pile of soft snow.

'Stop that!' she screamed. 'You'll smother him!'

Marron laughed. Then he looked at her and said, 'Tell me you want me.'

'No!' she yelled defiantly. Marron pressed down harder on Chasse's head. 'Don't!' she screamed. She started to stumble out of the water.

'I'll let him up,' Marron offered, 'If you admit in front of everyone here that you want to be my woman.' Tam felt her rage rising again. She wished she was strong enough to leap out of the water and save her brother from further humiliation. Marron wrenched Chasse's head up and let him suck in a mouthful of air. Then he pushed his face back into the icy snow. 'That's his last gasp unless you admit what you really feel for me, Tamesan,' he said coldly.

She looked in vain to the five boys watching the proceedings for assistance, but although their distaste for the situation was evident on the faces of Chasse's companions, the others relished the incident as much as Marron. Chasse struggled against the weight on his back, but to no avail.

'All right,' Tam capitulated. Her brother's life was more important than a handful of words.

'All right what?' Marron asked.

She hesitated again. She could still rush Marron. She could not hope to overpower him but it might make him release Chasse long enough to alter the situation. 'What you said,' she muttered reluctantly, trying to avoid making an open declaration accepting Marron.

Marron shook his head and pressed harder on Chasse. 'You have to say you want me.'

'I want you,' she announced hurriedly, in the foolish hope that saying it quickly would lessen the effect of the words. 'Now let my brother go.'

Marron lifted Chasse's head again to let the youth gasp another breath. 'Tam——' he sputtered, but Marron forced his face back into the snow before he could finish what he tried to say.

'Let him up!' she demanded. 'I've said it.'

'Just one more thing,' Marron said. He glanced at the small audience who were waiting to see what else he had in mind. 'Come out of the water.'

Despite the heat in the springs, she felt like someone had suddenly trickled ice down her spine. 'That wasn't part of it,' she objected.

'Your poor brother is feeling very cold around his head,' Marron taunted.

Tam cast an appealing look at the other boys. They were watching her like hungry dogs outside the Long Hall on a feast night. 'Are you all just going to stand there and let him do this?' she implored, searching for their sympathy. None of them moved. Chasse started to kick violently without any effect on Marron's hold. She took a deep breath, braced herself, and climbed out of the pool as quickly as she could, shielding her body with her arms.

'Lift your arms up,' Marron ordered. She glared at him but obeyed. Chasse needed her. 'Now that is very pretty,' Marron declared, and wrenched Chasse's head out of the hollow in the snow. 'Look at how pretty your sister really is. See now why she has to be mine and no-one else's?' He looked around at the other boys. They were staring at her naked form exactly as he expected. 'You heard her say she wants only me, didn't you?' he asked. His three friends nodded. The other two looked away. 'Good.' He turned to study Tam again and said, 'Remember it, Tamesan. You belong to me. You are Marron's woman. Everyone in the village will know that from today onwards. And don't worry. I will treat you as kindly as any great warrior should treat a good woman.'

'Let my brother up,' she insisted. She was shivering.

'After you get dressed,' he replied. He glared at the other youths and said, 'Have you no manners? My woman is dressing. Go back to the village.' Obedient to Marron's will, all five slunk into the trees. 'And you shouldn't be looking either,' he added, and pressed Chasse's face back into the hollow his face had formed in the snow. 'Don't worry,' he assured Tam, seeing she was about to protest, 'I'm not holding his head all the way down. He can breathe.'

'Do you have to do this?' she asked as she quickly towelled her limbs. She was starting to freeze.

'My pleasure,' Marron replied casually.

She dressed as rapidly as she could, refusing to look at Marron. As soon as she finished, she demanded he release Chasse.

'Of course,' he acceded.

He pushed up from Chasse, but kept sufficient pressure on him to prevent Chasse rising quickly. Then, as Chasse tried to stand, Marron kicked him solidly in the ribs, sending him sprawling again.

Tam knelt to help her gasping brother and yelled, 'You had no need to do that!'

'If I didn't, he might stupidly try to attack me as I walk away,' Marron explained nonchalantly. 'A great warrior never lets his enemy have any chance at all. And you wouldn't want any harm to come to your man, Tamesan,' he added with a smirk. He brushed snow from his leggings and sauntered away through the trees towards the village. Tam heard him laughing as he disappeared.

Chapter Twelve

Chasse begged Tam not to speak to anyone about the incident at the Dragon's Cauldron. She was so infuriated by Marron's attack on him, and Marron's humiliation of her, that she wanted to tell her father at once, but Chasse warned her that it would be dangerous to say anything.

'But why?' she asked when he refused to go with her to find Kevan.

'It won't change anything,' he muttered.

'Chasse, he can't just go around doing what he's doing.'

'Tam, you don't understand,' he sighed.

'What don't I understand? That he bullies people?'

'It's not bullying people. It was a fight. He won. I lost. That's all anyone will see.'

'He could have killed you, Chasse.'

'But he didn't, Tam,' he replied. 'Look, it's no good you trying to say anything about it. How am I supposed to hold my head up as a man if you run around trying to protect me, or if you get Father to do that? I have to face Marron on my own. You know that's how it is.'

Tam suddenly understood what was eating at her brother, why he didn't want to make an issue of the incident. Marron had challenged his manhood. He had denigrated Chasse in front of five other boys. Now Chasse believed he had to prove his inner strength by accepting Marron's challenge. It was a stupid attitude. She knew that. But it was driven by Chasse's sense of honour.

'Then what about what he did to me?' she pleaded, trying a different tack to spur him into action.

Chasse lifted his face. His pale blue eyes caught her steady gaze for an instant, but then turned away. 'He had no cause to do that,' he mumbled.

'Then at least let me tell Father what happened to me,' she implored.

Chasse did not answer. He kept his eyes fixed on a point just in front of his feet.

'Chasse?'

'Tam—I can't,' he answered reluctantly, and swallowed, as if the words were a bitter herb.

'Why not?'

He stood and glared at her. 'See? You don't understand. It's not that simple any more.' She opened her mouth to argue but he turned and sprinted towards the centre of the village.

She let him go. He was heading for the Warriors' Hall. What choice had he left her? If she didn't say anything about the incident, Marron would get away with the injustices he had committed. If she did talk, she risked humiliating her brother further, and it seemed he had already suffered enough to make him question his place in the ranks of men. She couldn't bear the thought of Marron gloating in triumph over them. He had forced her to say she wanted him, but that was the least of her concerns. Her words meant absolutely nothing to her. She loathed Marron. If it came to him choosing her, she would refuse him. There would be an uproar. No doubt her mother and father would be furious with her for denying tradition and law, but even enforced, marriageless isolation, like the kind old Asmae endured, would be preferable to being Marron's wife. She knew he would treat her with less respect than the herdsmen treated their goats. What most frustrated her was that he had attacked them so cruelly and now nothing was going to be done about it. There was no justice. Chasse was caught by his principles—principles the men had forged for themselves for centuries. If she related what had happened, even if she attempted to keep the focus on what Marron had specifically done to her, the whole incident would be exposed by Marron and Chasse's humiliation would be complete. He had asked her not to let that happen. How could she do otherwise, under the circumstances? Tam kicked her foot through a small mound of snow, making it puff out in an angry cloud, and headed home.

The temporary break in the weather freed Kevan from the isolation of his home. He spent every possible moment in the Warriors' Hall, and he stayed there overnight three nights that week. Chasse avoided Tam. She was employed mending and making, but for once she appreciated the work. It kept her from dwelling constantly on Marron's attack. Sometimes, to break the monotony, she silently recited the information the Herbal Man had taught her. She had enjoyed learning the various uses of the plants she had taken for granted, or ignored, or never even realised existed.

Three days after the hot springs incident, Eesa took Tam to the Long Hall. The women were meeting to clean, prepare and smoke a haul of fish caught by a stroke of good fortune during the lull in the wintry weather. By working together quickly they could share the spoils with their families. Tam saw Banni busy at one basket, so she found a long scaling knife and sat down to help her. The pair chatted as they worked, mainly about Banni's coming child and the clothing she was making for its arrival. Tam enjoyed the company. For the first time in a long while she was actually coping with the menial role women were expected to fill in Harbin.

She was made aware of Katris' presence when the dark-haired girl slapped a half-gutted fish on the bench before her and said, 'You didn't scale this one right.'

Tam looked up. Katris' dark eyes narrowed. 'Then I'll do it now,' Tam conceded and reached for the fish.

'Don't touch my fish!' Katris snarled and snatched it away.

'Then why put it down in front of me?' Tam asked. She noticed people were staring at them.

'You take everything that isn't yours!' Katris snarled spitefully.

Tam straightened, a puzzled expression on her face. 'What is your problem, Katris?'

Katris slapped the fish down in Tam's lap. 'You!' she snapped. 'You think because you're the Dragon Head's daughter you can have anything you want!'

'Katris, get on with your work,' Banni said.

'You shut up!' Katris warned her. 'This is nothing to do with you.'

Tam heard several sharp intakes of breath. It was unacceptable for a girl who had not yet come of age to speak so rudely to a woman in public. Banni, however, seemed unperturbed by Katris' rudeness.

'If I have something to say to a girl, I will say it,' she said firmly. 'You remember who and where you are.'

Katris pulled a face at her, then suddenly spat at Tam. Tam stood, seething with anger. One of Katris' companions grabbed Katris' arm and said, 'Come on, Katris, that's enough. Everyone is watching you. Even Eesa.'

'Good,' Katris declared brazenly. 'Let them.' She raised her voice and said, 'Let everyone know that Tamesan thinks that she is so much better than all of us that she even takes a man before it's her time of choosing.'

Tam was stunned by Katris' announcement. She was only vaguely aware of a startled gasp from one woman and the murmur of amazed voices in the Long Hall. She saw Eesa stand and come towards her.

'Don't deny it, Tamesan,' Katris challenged. 'All the men know already. Why shouldn't we?'

'You don't know what you're talking about,' Tam replied.

'Yes I do!' Katris screamed. 'I know because it's Marron you're taking! You're stealing Marron from me!' She suddenly grabbed Tam's tunic and went to slap her face. At least that was what Tam thought Katris intended. Before the dark-haired girl could move quickly enough, though, Tam lashed out defensively and knocked Katris backwards. The girl collapsed amid a collection of buckets. Fish heads and fish guts cascaded over her. Some women and girls were shocked by the accident. A few, Banni among them, grinned at Katris' misfortune.

Several women went to help Katris out of the muck. Before Tam could apologise, Eesa grabbed her hands and whirled her around.

'You, girl, get to your home at once!' she ordered. Tam tried to object, but Eesa cut her short and started to drag her towards the door. Humiliated by her mother's action, she shook free of Eesa's grip and marched out in disgust. She heard Katris sobbing and babbling, but she didn't look back, and ignored the stares of the women she passed on her way to the door.

Once outside, she clenched her fists in rage and screamed at the grey sky. Katris could only have heard about the incident at the Dragon's Cauldron from Marron. He would have gone out of his way to ensure she knew what had transpired—at least his version of it. He had broken through Tam's defences, wounded her dignity with his actions at the Dragon's Cauldron, and now he was simply, deliberately, twisting the knife. He had no heart. He was using Tam to torment Katris, and forcing his will on Tam at the same time. She hated him!

She kicked the snow at her feet and headed home. No doubt Eesa would listen to Katris' side of the story now. What chance did she have? If she told the truth, Eesa would demand to know why Tam hadn't told her about the incident straightaway, and Chasse would never forgive her for exposing his own humiliation at Marron's hands. If she didn't, her mother would, at best, see her as a presumptuous child meddling too early with boys; at worst, as a slut interfering with Katris' chances of pairing with Marron. In the end, she would have to endure the harsh attitude the entire village would adopt towards her. It was becoming so unfair.

'Look who's here,' a voice said as she passed the Warriors' Hall. She knew it was Marron. How could she forget the sound of his voice? She ignored him and walked on, but he thrust out his hand and caught her arm. 'Tamesan, why do you ignore me?' he asked in a frighteningly gentle manner.

'Let go of me!' she yelled. She wrenched her arm free and glared at him. His face wore a reproachful expression that might have disarmed her if it had been anyone else. On Marron, though, it looked vulgar.

'Gloat and tell lies if you want, but I'm telling everyone what you really did,' she threatened.

Marron shrugged. 'Tell people what you want, Tamesan. It's your word against mine.' His eyes narrowed and he leaned closer. 'But don't expect me to feel sorry for your big brother when I make him look a complete idiot because of his sister's stories.'

'It's not a story, Marron, and you know it!'

'Do I?' he asked, with a feigned look of surprise. 'I can ask Aaron, or Hale, or Jared. They'll say it happened exactly like I say it happened. They were there.'

'So were Tass and Evan,' she reminded him.

'Were they?' He flexed his biceps and cracked a knuckle in his fingers as he pressed one fist into the palm of his other hand. 'I think you'll discover they weren't anywhere near the place. That's what they'll say if you ask them. Even your brother doesn't know about the incident. You seem to be making it all up, Tamesan.'

She was overwhelmed by the enormity of his lie. She stood, staring at the wall behind his shoulder for what felt like an eternity, unwilling to move, unable to move. He had trapped her again. Then the blind fury that was welling in her exploded. She lashed out, swinging her arms, kicking wildly. All feeling, all sense of control, was lost. She hit and kicked until someone pinned her arms and pulled her away. Big hands gripped her like iron manacles. A man's voice ordered her to stop but she could not. Only when she heard her mother's angry voice did she snap back into awareness.

'You have a hell-cat for a daughter,' the man who held her was saying. 'The lad is lucky she is not a boy.'

'I sometimes wish she was a boy,' Eesa replied bitterly. 'She would be less of a problem that way.'

Tam felt the heavy hands release her. She focussed on Marron. He was leaning against the Warriors' Hall with his hand against the side of his mouth. A tiny trickle of red ran over his fingers, but he forced a smile at her despite his hurt. She flinched.

'You, child,' Eesa demanded. Tam shifted her attention to her mother's bulky figure. 'I told you to get to your home. Now do as I say.' Tam glanced around and saw three warriors gazing at her. The man who had pulled her away from Marron was Theo, her father's friend. He was studying her with a serious expression.

'Go!' Eesa growled.

Tam turned on her heel and stalked away, her angry mother following resolutely.

The storm that swept over Harbin that night could not match the storm in Tam's house. She weathered Eesa's diatribe about public behaviour, a woman's manners, the rights of girls, bathing alone, fighting. It seemed her mother would never let up. When Tam was allowed to speak, she told Eesa that she knew Katris was jealous, but that nothing existed between herself and Marron. The latter statement did not appear to appease her mother. She ordered Tam to explain what Katris meant about Tam having pledged herself to Marron. Tam denied it emphatically. Eesa then lectured her anyway about the correct way young women behaved around young men. Forced to listen, Tam was grateful for the driving wind that carried sleet and snow in from the western ocean, keeping Kevan and Chasse locked away in the Warriors' Hall. She felt pity, not for herself, but for Jaysin, who was almost certainly lying awake in the adjoining bedroom listening to Eesa's incessant castigation of his sister. He was frightened whenever people raised their voices. Gramma Harmi, on the other hand, in Eesa's room, was probably oblivious to the whole affair.

When Eesa tired of upbraiding her errant daughter, Tam retreated to her bedroom. She dragged on her bedclothes and climbed into her bedding but she could not sleep. She listened to the sounds of her mother readying for bed until the cottage quietened, and only the whistling of the swirling storm winds outside remained. In the embracing darkness she thought she heard another, softer sound. It came from Jaysin's bed. She crawled across to investigate, and found her little brother whimpering.

'What's wrong?' she whispered. He did not answer her, just kept sobbing quietly. Finally she reached out and cradled the boy in her arms. 'It's all right,' she crooned as she rocked him gently. 'It's all right.' Outside, the storm winds rose, hammering against the walls of Harbin's homes.

Chapter Thirteen

Men and boys were gathering at the jetty. Storms had come and gone for three weeks, but the last had damaged the dragonship and now the men were taking advantage of the break in the weather to repair what they could. The sky was still burdened with heavy clouds, warning that yet another storm was brewing and heavier snowfalls were coming. People moved through the village on their various errands, driven by chilling urgency.

On the outer edge of Harbin, herdsmen were bracing the roofs and walls of the animal shelters against the coming mid-winter storms. Eesa sent Tam and three girls with Banni to assist the herdsmen. They raked out the shelters and packed the manure in small bricks. Later, when the bricks dried out, they would be used to fuel hearth fires. Galt, Derin's father, sent two girls back to the village to borrow grain containers from the Long Hall's store. The containers would bolster the animal feed bins. He asked Banni to organise a meal for himself and the other two goat herders. Then he instructed Tam and the remaining girl to fetch armfuls of twigs from the forest which he would then use as fresh flooring for the shelters.

169

The girl accompanying Tam was called Serene. She was three summers younger and a chatterbox. All the way to the edge of the forest she talked about different wild animals she had seen, and how frightened she was during the last storm. Tam didn't mind her company, but she wondered if Serene ever tired of talking. Once they entered the forest, however, the younger girl became unusually quiet. Tam didn't notice at first. She was simply pleased to be able to walk through the trees away from the bustling village. When she realised Serene was silent, she turned and saw the young girl's wide brown eyes staring nervously. She appeared to be afraid.

'What's the matter?' Tam asked.

'I don't like it here,' Serene whispered.

'Why? Nothing is going to hurt you.'

'Are you sure?'

'Of course. What can hurt you here?'

'What about the wolves?'

Tam laughed. 'The wolves are probably more scared of you,' she assured the girl, remembering the Herbal Man's words after she screamed at the mountain bear.

'I just don't like it,' Serene insisted. 'I never come up here.'

Tam sighed. 'How about I load you up with wood and you go back with it? I'll go on a bit further and find some more after you've gone.'

'Aren't you scared?' the girl asked.

'Of the forest? No,' said Tam and she smiled. 'I love coming up here.'

She collected handfuls of twigs protruding from the snow and hanging from the tree branches and piled them in Serene's trembling arms. The girl watched her as if Tam was suddenly someone very strange and incredibly brave because the forest didn't frighten her. When it appeared she might pile so much wood on the girl that she would collapse, Tam stopped and sent Serene back down towards Harbin. Then she climbed higher on the slope and started gathering more wood.

It was good to be alone for a change, and she took her time. She had been cooped up in the cottage with Eesa, Jaysin and Gramma Harmi far too long, and she was glad of the fresh air and exercise that wood-gathering offered. Even the cold air was refreshing, though she rubbed her hands constantly to keep her blood circulating. As she stooped and tugged at small sticks, she imagined how the Herbal Man found his herbs at this time of year in thick snow. He had said he searched during mid-winter for the hardiest plants of all, but she could see nothing living in the bleak spaces between the trees. Then she laid down her bundle of twigs and decided to experiment. She scraped away the powdery snow at the base of an old tree. In other seasons of the year, plants grew in the shelter of large tree roots. Perhaps winter plants also survived like that, clustering between the tree roots for protection, beneath the snowy mantle.

The scrunch of approaching footsteps through the snow froze her. When she turned, she discovered

Marron staring at her. He held a spear in one hand and a brown leather bag in the other.

'What are you doing here?' she asked, her mind full of suspicion.

'I was just going to ask you the same question,' he replied. 'I'm hunting squirrels, although this looks far more interesting,' he added, studying her closely. Then he glanced at the dishevelled pile of sticks at her side. 'It can't be firewood,' he said.

'No,' she answered. She gathered the wood and stood to leave.

'You aren't going?' He took a step towards her and cut off her path downhill.

Tam glared fiercely at him. 'I have to take this back to Galt. I've already been up here too long.'

'A little longer won't hurt,' he said, and grinned. 'You wouldn't disappoint your man.' He closed the gap separating them.

She instinctively stepped backwards, simultaneously searching the surrounding landscape for Marron's friends. She couldn't see anyone. Anywhere.

'You know better than that,' she warned when she realised he was alone. 'I already told you I don't want you. Don't you understand what I'm saying? I don't want you.'

Marron was bouncing the spear in his hand. His eyes glinted in the weak daylight. He wore the supercilious, overconfident smile he always wore when he was certain he was in total control of a situation. His whole presence was menacing.

'All I want is a kiss,' he announced.

The air on the mountainside seemed suddenly very chilly. Yielding a kiss to Marron was fraught with danger. It had too much finality. Tam knew it would only be a prelude to an even greater demand, and he would see it as full confirmation of her subservience. She weighed up her chances of escape.

'No,' she said.

'A kiss, Tamesan. One kiss,' Marron appealed. 'Even you can do that much for me.' He reached out to catch hold of her shoulders, but she flung her armful of twigs in his face and bolted into the trees. When Marron gathered his senses, he dropped his spear and sprinted after her.

Her first reaction was simply to run. After a few metres, she realised she was heading straight up the mountain. There was no sure safety in that direction. Her only hope was to reach Galt or another of the herdsmen. She veered left, and bounded across the face of the slope, dodging trees and skirting the rocky outcrops that protruded from the snow. She could hear Marron pursuing but she didn't dare look around, not now. The snow underfoot hid treacherous obstacles. She had to concentrate on running. She crossed her earlier tracks, paused, then thought better of following them—she had meandered erratically as she collected wood. She deviated right and scrambled over a low snow-ridge. Marron was calling her. She shut out his voice with the wind in her ears and dashed across a tiny clearing into the thicker forest.

If she could make it to the pasture she would be safe. The herdsmen would see and hear her, and even Marron wouldn't be arrogant enough to pursue her that far.

She turned at a copse and headed straight down the slope. As she did, she chanced a glance over her shoulder to see how close Marron was. She couldn't see him. It didn't matter. She had probably lost him but she wasn't slowing down until she reached the open pasture. Then her heart sank. Between her and the edge of the forest, a figure moved. Marron. He had second-guessed her escape plan. Now he cut off the direct route out of the forest. She considered her options. Marron had spotted her and was running up the hill. She decided. She knew the quick paths and short cuts better on the slope nearer her hideaway. If she could beat Marron to the rocks there, she was sure she could lose him and make it safely to the village. She sucked in a deep breath and doubled back on her tracks.

She had the initial advantage, running across the slope while Marron had to climb, but her advantage quickly diminished. Her legs were tiring. She wasn't prepared for running like this. The snow hindered her. Marron closed the distance. She could hear him panting. Then she could hear his feet crushing the snow. But she could also see the rocks just ahead. A few more metres and she would have a real chance. She pushed herself.

Too late. Marron caught her quicker than she

anticipated. She dodged his clumsy lunge, but his hands caught the hem of her skirt and he dragged her down into the snow. She screamed and kicked, and heard Marron grunt as her foot connected, but he didn't release his hold. She struggled as she felt Marron's arms pin her legs, and then he clambered onto her and sat astride her stomach. He pushed her thrashing arms into the cold wet snow. She screamed again.

'Stop that!' he demanded.

She screamed louder. Her voice echoed across the mountain. Then she winced as Marron's hand caught her with a stinging slap across her cheek.

'I said stop it!' he yelled.

The slap shocked her into silence. She stared up at him. His weight was starting to hurt.

'That's better,' he murmured softly. 'Now we can share that kiss you promised me.' She was about to protest that she hadn't promised anything when she saw he was leaning forward to kiss her. With the hand he had released when he slapped her, she lashed up and dug her fingers into his face. Her rough nails cut. Marron howled and clutched at his cheek with both hands. Seizing her opportunity, she overbalanced the youth by rolling to the left, and as he toppled awkwardly into the snow, she scrambled to her feet and ran. Whether or not he pursued her any further, she did not know. He yelled as she fled, but she didn't understand the words. She only wanted the safety of her home. She forced herself to forget her throbbing legs, and ran on sheer fear down the mountainside.

'I want the truth, girl. I don't want any foolish lies.'

Tam stared at her father. Kevan was observing her closely, awaiting her reply. Eesa stood at his back. She looked tired.

'What I said is what happened,' Tam explained resolutely. 'Marron chased me and attacked me. I got away.'

'And the cuts on his face?'

'I scratched him to get him off me.' She watched her father's reaction. He shook his head slightly. 'It's true, Father,' she insisted. 'I swear it's true.'

'That's not what he said happened,' Kevan replied. 'He said you attacked him.'

'No!' she cried. 'Why would I attack him? He's lying to you.'

'Why did you go off alone?'

'Serene was too scared to go into the woods to fetch wood, so I sent her back. I went to get wood by myself.'

Kevan rubbed his hand across his grey beard. 'Why were you so long about it?'

She knew she had to be truthful. She also knew her father didn't approve of her wasting time day-dreaming, but that wasn't the issue here. 'I like walking in the forest,' she confessed.

'But you were supposed to be gathering wood for Galt,' her father growled.

'I did.'

'What happened to it?'

She was becoming irritated by his barrage of questions. The fate of the wood was irrelevant, but he was treating it as if it was an important mistake she had made. 'I dropped it when Marron attacked me.'

'He said you threw it at him.'

'I did.' It was true. It was the only defence she had on the spur of the moment. 'But only because he tried to grab me.'

'Marron says that's how you cut his face.'

She was stunned by her father's accusation. Marron had twisted the story into something very different in the Warriors' Hall. He was trying to lie his way out of the circumstances. 'No. That's not how it happened,' she objected. 'I scratched him with my nails.'

'So you did attack him?' Kevan declared.

'No!' she cried in utter frustration. Her father was making her into the guilty one. He wasn't being fair. 'Don't you listen to me?' she implored. 'He attacked me.'

'Did he hurt you?'

'Yes.'

'Show me where.'

'He didn't put any marks on me.'

'You just said he hurt you,' he reminded her. He lifted one grey eyebrow, having spotted a discrepancy in her story.

'He did,' she insisted. Her father's questions were confusing her.

'How?' Kevan asked, then added before she could answer, 'He's the one with all the cuts. What did he do to you?'

'He chased me,' she replied, then realised how weak that sounded. 'He tried to kiss me.'

Her father shook his head and said, 'He says you walked up to him and threw the sticks in his face and said you hated him for looking at Katris.'

'Not true!' Tam shouted defiantly.

'Then you didn't throw the sticks in his face?'

'Yes I did!' she screamed. 'But not for the reason he says I did!'

Kevan let out a heavy sigh and ran a hand through his mass of hair. 'Make up your mind, girl. Either you attacked him or you didn't.'

Tam felt as trapped in her father's words as she had on the hillside with Marron breathing hungrily over her. She threw up her hands in absolute despair. 'You're turning it all around. Why? What do you want me to say? I'm telling the truth and you're not even listening.'

'Talking to me like that isn't going to help, Tamesan,' her father warned.

'But you're making me sound like a liar and I'm not.'

'Why did you attack Katris in the Long Hall?'

His new question made Tam catch her breath. She glanced at Eesa and said, 'She accused me of taking Marron from her.'

'I thought Marron wanted you.'

'He does,' she said. Perhaps there was a chance to make her father see sense after all. 'At least he keeps telling everyone he does. But I don't want him.'

'Why not?'

'Because he is so cruel. He's always bragging and fighting.'

'He's a strong young man,' Kevan reasoned. 'Trask's son can be no different.'

Her father's defence of Marron angered her. 'He's a liar. And he bullies people. He won't leave me alone.'

'All young men are persistent when they think they have found the woman they want,' Eesa remarked as she shifted to stand beside Kevan.

'You should be honoured he has chosen you,' added Kevan. 'All you have done so far is humiliate him.'

'Humiliate *him*?' Tam gasped. 'That's all he ever does to everyone else. Ask the other boys what he does to them. Ask Derin.'

'They all respect him, Tamesan,' said her father. 'Every boy in the village listens to what he has to say. He will be a leader one day.'

'He terrorises them. They don't respect him, they fear him!' she insisted. She couldn't believe her father was so naive about Marron's ways.

'A leader has to be strong,' Kevan stated. 'He will be a fine young dragonwarrior next summer. You are privileged to be sought after by the finest and newest young warrior in Harbin.'

'Why do you think Katris and the others envy you so much?' asked Eesa.

'They don't have to envy me. They can have him!' Tam declared.

'If you keep treating him like this they may well end up with him. And it will be your loss, girl,' her mother cautioned.

'My loss?' sputtered Tam, exasperated. 'How can I lose what I don't want? I hate him! Hear me? I hate him!'

'If the son of Trask chooses to pair with my daughter you will accept him and do so with good grace,' Kevan pronounced with all the authority he could muster. It had no effect.

'No!' Tam screeched. 'I would rather be paired with a goat than with Marron!'

Kevan glared at her. His face held the fierce determination she imagined he might have when he faced a dragon. It was the look of a man who would kill to get what he wanted. It was an expression she rarely saw on her father, but one she sensed wisely would be better to obey than oppose.

'You *will* do as your father and Dragon Head of Harbin orders, child! Do you hear me?' he snarled. She remained silent, hoping to avoid further confrontation. Kevan, though, was not satisfied. 'Answer me respectfully!' he demanded.

Tam took a short breath and muttered, 'Yes, Father.'

'By Varst's eternal fires I want it clearer than that, girl!' he roared. 'Say it louder!'

'Yes, Father,' she repeated. Her heart was filled with rage and defiance and fear, but she lowered her eyes so he would not see how she felt. She hated him immensely for beating her down like that.

'Good. That is the last I want to hear of it. Now see to Harmi,' he ordered. 'Eesa, I have work for you in the Warriors' Hall before it gets dark. There is a storm coming so we must do it now.'

Tam waited in obedient silence for her parents to leave. When the door closed, she slumped to the floor, totally desolate, and burst into tears. It was all so wrong, so terribly wrong. Marron had caused all the trouble and yet she was getting all the blame. He was arrogant and ruthless, but everyone else saw those faults as his strongest qualities. She had come home for help and been made to look like the troublemaker. Why? Why couldn't her parents see what was happening? Why were they forcing her to accept things that just weren't right? Now, the worst of it was that both her father and her mother believed Marron should be her husband when she came of age. They had already decided. They were going to make her accept him, going to force her to live with the person she most hated. Why? Why wouldn't they listen to her? It should be her choice, not theirs.

A sudden gust of wind hit the cottage and the door swung open. Tam wiped her eyes and stood to shut the door. She heard her grandmother stir in the adjoining bedroom where Kevan had placed her before all the questions began about Marron's injury.

She crossed to the doorway and stuck her head around the corner.

'What is it, Gramma?' she asked, not really expecting the old woman to answer. Poor Gramma seemed to be lost deeper and deeper inside herself. Tam had overheard Eesa telling Amarti in the Long Hall that this winter would probably be Gramma's last. The thought made her feel uneasy. She couldn't imagine the cottage without Gramma in it. She had been there all of Tam's life.

'I thought I heard Eric,' Gramma said. 'Tell him I'll be ready soon.'

'Eric isn't here, Gramma. It was the wind.' Tam explained gently. She pulled a shawl over the old lady's shoulders.

'He will be here. I heard the dragon.'

Tam shook her head in despair. Gramma, Eric, dragons. Her grandmother lived in another world. Perhaps she was lucky. There were no Marrons or parents there, no menial tasks, no barriers. Why were her parents so determined to make her do the things she just didn't want to do? She was never going to accept Marron. She refused to be just another woman serving the warriors of Harbin. There had to be more to living than that. Choices. Where were the choices? Another gust of wind shook the cottage. It was getting darker. The storm was coming. Eesa would be back from the Long Hall very soon, and then Tam would be trapped again inside the cottage. Jaysin would also return soon. She wondered where her little brother disappeared to when her father had started in on her. He had his own special hiding place even Tam hadn't discovered. Everything was so cruel. No-one accepted Jaysin either because he didn't do what the other little boys did. What would her parents do to him when he reached his coming of age? He was never going to be a dragonwarrior. He hated violence.

She found a cloak and wrapped it around herself. She would never marry Marron. Never. If her parents were going to force her to do that she had to make a choice of her own. She rummaged through the pots in the main room and filled a small bag with foodstuffs. Then she grabbed another cloak, made of leather, and pulled that over the top. She checked outside. No-one was on the bridge, and she couldn't see Eesa coming up the path from the Long Hall yet. She could slip away unnoticed before the storm settled and find shelter on the mountain. She could even go to the Herbal Man.

Then she remembered her promise. The mid-winter feast was due in less than a fortnight. She darted into her room and fossicked until she found the small pouch that held the ring the Herbal Man wanted given to her grandmother. She carried it into Gramma's room, loosened the drawstring, and gently shook the pouch. A spiderweb-thin band of glittering metal fell into her palm. It looked so fragile she was afraid she would crush it, but when she put experimental pressure on the band it felt stronger than any ring she had ever held. She had never seen anything in her life as exquisitely delicate. She carefully lifted her grandmother's hand and brought the ring towards the old lady's middle finger. The wind outside the cottage suddenly whipped into a brief frenzy and rattled the wooden shutters. Tam hesitated and glanced apprehensively at the window in Gramma's room.

'Eric?' the old lady rasped. Her eyes snapped open, startling Tam. Harmi's gaze was fixed on the window. 'Eric?' she repeated, 'is that you?'

'It's just me, Gramma,' Tam said soothingly, pressing her grandmother's hand. 'Just me and the wind.'

Harmi's eyes shifted to focus on Tam. The old lady smiled. 'Tamesan,' she whispered. 'Sweet Tamesan.' Then she closed her eyes. Tam glanced once more at the ring she held poised before Harmi's finger. In her memory she could hear the Herbal Man's voice, reminding her. *'Give it to Harmi only on the night of Blitzart's Feast. Not before.'* The words suddenly seemed to carry special meaning, a warning. What would happen to Harmi if she was given the ring ahead of time? Why should it matter? Circumstances had changed. She couldn't be here for Blitzart's Feast, not any more. She brought the ring closer. The wind surged briefly again and howled around the cottage. Suddenly the front door flew open and a cloud of snowflakes swirled in. In the doorway stood Jaysin, peering at Tam.

'What are you doing, Tamesan?' he asked in his soft piping voice.

She instinctively cupped the ring in her palm and replied, 'Talking to Gramma. Where have you been?'

'Out.' Jaysin stepped closer. 'What's in your hand?'

'Nothing.'

'Yes, there is. You had something, Tamesan. You were holding a ring or something.'

She was caught, but she knew she could bluff her way out. Jaysin seldom dared to argue with anyone. Then another possibility presented itself. It was a risk. But then she didn't have time for alternatives with the storm sweeping in.

'It's a ring,' she confessed and opened her hand. 'It's a gift for Gramma, a very special gift.'

Jaysin stared solemnly at the thin gold band in his sister's palm. 'Are you giving it to Gramma?'

'I am—or rather I was,' Tam replied, correcting herself as she weighed up her plan.

'Why?'

'Because the Herbal Man asked me to give it to Gramma.'

'Why?'

'Why doesn't matter, Jaysin. It's just, well, I was going to give it to her, but then I remembered that the Herbal Man said I wasn't supposed to give it to her until Blitzart's Feast.'

'Why does she have to have it then?'

So many questions, thought Tam. Am I this painful? 'I don't know,' she said. 'All I do know is she has to have it only on that night. She can't have it before then. Only I mightn't be able to give it to her now the way I promised the Herbal Man I would.'

'Why not?'

Questions. She had to think quickly. 'Um—because Mother said she wants me to help prepare the feast and clean up after it. I won't get a chance to spend any time with Gramma.'

'How will you give her the ring?'

'That's what I was going to ask you,' Tam quickly proposed. 'Would you give the ring to Gramma on Blitzart's Feast if I forget—or if I'm too busy?'

Jaysin's eyes lit up with fervent hope. 'Can I?' he asked. 'I mean, if you're working? You'd let me?'

'Of course I'd let you,' Tam assured him. 'But you have to be able to remember that it's a very, very special secret. You can't say anything to anyone else about it, not even Mother or Father. Can you keep that kind of secret?'

'I can do it,' Jaysin confirmed eagerly. 'That's easy.'

Tam fingered the ring. She hoped the Herbal Man would approve of her decision. She didn't understand the ring's purpose at all, just the promise she had made, and promises had to be kept.

'Here,' she said suddenly. She slipped the ring back into its pouch and pressed it into Jaysin's tiny hand. 'You have to promise to keep this safe and tell no-one else about it. If I can't give it to Gramma on the feast night you have to. You mustn't ever forget this. Promise?'

'I promise,' Jaysin said, with all of his serious six year old's conviction.

'This is very important. You mustn't forget,' Tam repeated.

'I won't forget,' Jaysin insisted.

'Good.' She ruffled her little brother's mop of auburn hair and asked him to go and hide the ring securely in his bedroom. As he left the room, Tam bent towards Harmi and whispered, 'The Herbal Man said the ring was for you Gramma. I was meant to give it to you at a different time, but I can't any more. Jaysin will do it. I know he will.'

She wondered if her grandmother understood what was happening. The old lady just seemed to be dozing. But then Harmi opened her eyes and muttered, 'I knew he would come this time. She made him promise. Dragons never forget.'

Tam straightened up in surprise and stared at her grandmother. Harmi's head nodded slightly and her eyes closed. Tam hesitated, expecting her to speak again, but the old lady had silently fallen asleep once more. Tam lifted Harmi's hand and kissed it, and backed out of the room. She felt sorry to be leaving Gramma Harmi like this. It might be the last time they would see each other. She wanted to go back, to give her grandmother a cuddle, but if she didn't hurry Eesa would return, and then she could never leave.

She picked up the gear she had dropped at the door and stepped outside. Jaysin called, 'Where are you going, Tamesan?'

'Mother wants me to take this to the Hall,' she said, holding up her food bag for him to see.

'But there's a big storm coming.'

'I know,' she replied. 'That's why you have to go inside. I'll be back quickly with Mother. You can warm up the hearth. Can you do that for me?' Jaysin nodded. Tam scuffed his hair again and urged him back into the cottage.

A final glance towards the Long Hall revealed that people were filing out. She had to hurry. Pulling her leather cloak tighter, she jogged across the bridge. Rather than follow the regular path which would take her closer to the Long Hall, she cut past several buildings and followed the lip of the gorge that enclosed Watersdrop until she reached the forest. As she climbed the lower slopes, the first flakes of the impending snowstorm spiralled to earth.

Chapter Fourteen

She was dreaming. There was a halo of white light. It expanded until it filled the whole world. Coming towards her out of the centre of the light was a man. She thought she knew him. He had white hair and a long white beard. He walked with a staff in his left hand. He was smiling at her.

She opened her eyes. Everything was white. Then she remembered. Snow. She was face down in the snow. The strangest sensation was that the snow she lay in felt warm and dry. Had she lost all sense of feeling?

The storm had swept in quicker than she anticipated. She had followed Watersdrop gorge as far as she could from the village and then cut back across the face of the mountain to find the path to the Herbal Man's home. As she traversed the mountain the wind whipped at the trees and the sleet and snow swirled with increasing menace. Soon she could barely see a dozen steps ahead. She struggled through the mounting snow. Just as she reached the path, the world was swallowed in darkness and the wind howled over the mountain like a tortured soul. Even with two cloaks wrapped over her winter clothing she felt bitterly cold. She sweated from the exertion of fighting against the wind and staggering through the ever-increasing snow, and the sweat froze on her brow and the tip of her nose. She was cold, so very, very cold.

'You will be all right,' a voice whispered. 'Drink this.' She was locked in darkness like ice. The gentle voice, a familiar voice, came and went. She swore she had her eyes open, but she couldn't see. She didn't even feel the vessel that was held to her lips. Only knew the liquid trickling down her throat. She was cold, oh so cold, but the liquid spread through her veins like fire.

'Where are you going?' someone called. Marron's face appeared. He was laughing. 'I'm going to have you,' he grinned. He reached towards her. She tried to scream 'No!' but her mouth would not form the word. She tried to run but fear rooted her legs to the spot. Marron's hands reached out to encircle her and her heart pounded with terror.

'It's all right,' crooned the other voice, the man's voice, 'you will be all right.'

The mountain was invisible in the darkness. She bent forward, feeling the rocks and snow with her hands, trying to decipher where she was in relation to the path. But it was too difficult. She was lost. She was cold, so very, very cold. The freezing storm was burying her. She was overwhelmed by a desire to lie down in the darkness and sleep.

'Te-Amen-San; the dawn's light,' whispered the voice. She felt the cold fading. The pain was easing. Her fingers, her feet, her hands, her arms were numb. She was losing all feeling to the darkness. 'Te-Amen-San,' said the voice. And then the dot of light appeared, far away at first, and faint. But it grew, it grew until it was washing over her, enfolding her in its radiance, and then the man's voice called to her, called her by her real name, the name she had been given at birth.

Her only hope was to go up. If she went up she would at least be heading in the right direction. She had to climb. It was the only way out of all this confusion. She had to climb.

Tam slowly opened her eyes. Her first impressions were of white fabric and warmth. She blinked. She heard a voice. 'How are you feeling?' She turned her face up from the pillow and saw the Herbal Man leaning over her. A lantern flickered on a small table to her right.

'Where am I?' she asked groggily.

'In my home,' the old man replied. 'Are you hungry?'

She considered his question. She recognised the room. It was the Herbal Man's bedroom. She was in his bed. A faint voice inside her asked how she had come to be there, but its call was distant and weak. She had no interest in the answer yet. 'Yes,' she said sleepily.

'Good,' he acknowledged. 'I'll bring you some warm broth.' With that he stood and left the room.

She had no energy. The bed was so big, so warm, so comfortable. She lay on her side, listening to the Herbal Man's activities in the adjoining room, and stared at the lantern's flickering yellow flame until she heard his returning footsteps.

'Here,' he said as he knelt beside the bed. He held a steaming bowl of broth. Tam rolled over and very unsteadily sat up.

'I feel so weak,' she confessed.

'I can feed you if you want,' the old man kindly offered.

'Thank you, but I'll try first.' She took the bowl and wrapped her hands around its warmth. The pale green broth smelt enticing, and she lifted it to her lips. 'What is it made from?'

'Various legumes,' said the old man. 'Mountain potato mainly.'

'It tastes good,' she breathed after sampling her first mouthful. She blew on the surface of the broth to cool it a little, and slowly drank. Between mouthfuls she asked, 'How did I get here?'

'By luck,' the Herbal Man replied.

'I can't remember,' she said hesitantly. 'There was a light.'

'I found you,' the old man explained. 'You were lying in the snow.'

'There was a storm,' she said.

'There still is a storm. A big one. It has been blowing in from the north for five days.'

She paused and stared at him in astonishment when she realised what he'd said. 'Have I been asleep for five days?'

'Mainly,' he replied. 'You were very sick, Tamesan.'

When she finished the broth, the Herbal Man took the empty bowl. He returned moments later with a small cup. 'Drink this,' he instructed. The cup contained blue liquid.

'Is this dewdrop elixir?' she asked, recognising the colour.

'Yes.'

Tam screwed up her nose in disgust. She remembered all too well his own reaction when he had had to take this medicine. 'Do I *have* to drink this?'

'It will make you feel better, Tamesan.'

She took another look at the blue elixir in the cup. She had never tasted the medicine herself. Perhaps it wasn't quite as bad as it appeared when the old man took it. She braced herself and drank. It was awful! The instant the elixir ran down her tongue she wanted to spit it all out. She had never imagined anything could taste so foul. She gagged and coughed.

'Procra's mercy!' she swore. 'It's horrible!' She pushed the half-empty cup away and then realised the Herbal Man was laughing. She was shocked to see him laughing at her. She was about to complain when the absurdity of the moment struck her and she started laughing as well. 'It really is *so* horrible,' she sputtered as she tried to regain her breath and composure.

The Herbal Man nodded in agreement. 'It has to be the worst remedy I've ever discovered,' he admitted. 'It's really such a shame that it works so effectively.' He pushed the cup back towards Tam. She suddenly realised what he meant.

'You don't mean I have to finish it?'

'It won't be effective otherwise.'

'*All* of it?'

'All of it.'

She grimaced. It would be better to be sick. The Herbal Man was watching her with his sharp eyes. No. She had to do it. She took a deep breath, lifted the cup, and quickly drained the remaining contents. Goat dung would taste sweeter, she decided.

The Herbal Man came and went while Tam drifted from wakefulness to sleep. He brought her drink and a little food, broth mainly, and her strength quickly returned. When she finally asked if she could get up, the Herbal Man brought her fresh clothing and a cloak, and left her in peace to dress. She was amazed by the intricacy and delicacy of the robe he provided. It was maroon in colour, with silver and gold thread woven through it forming what could only be a dragon motif that ran across the back and extended over the left shoulder. The cuffs and collar were embroidered with patterns symbolising flames. She had never seen such craft, nor held material so soft, almost liquid, to the touch. When she slipped it on it raised goose bumps on her skin, and it fitted her exceedingly well, almost as if it had been tailored to her measurements. The cloak was equally unusual. Unlike the rustic animal skin cloaks or rough weave commonly worn in Harbin, this cloak was made from soft, thick grey thread that was lightweight and tightly woven. The Herbal Man had also left her a pair of boots, goatskin turned inside out, like the traditional ones the dragonwarriors wore in wintertime. She slipped them on and then dutifully tidied the bed's quilt cover before leaving the room.

She found the Herbal Man hunched over the bench at the centre of the main room. He held a candle and was etching coloured dye into the wax surface, forming a series of equidistant rings along the candle's length. A similarly-marked candle burned nearby on the cluttered benchtop.

'What are you doing?' she asked, studying his handiwork.

'Creating a clock,' he replied without raising his eyes. 'Do the clothes fit?'

'Perfectly,' she responded. 'What is the robe made from?'

'Silk.' He glanced up and noticed Tam's puzzled expression. 'It's a very special thread made from a very special insect.'

'Oh,' she said, no less confused by his explanation. 'What's a clock?' she asked. The Herbal Man completed colouring the final ring and held up the candle for Tam's inspection. 'That is a clock,' he announced. 'See each of the rings? When the candle burns, the wax melts down in roughly the same amount of time to each ring. It has to be kept out of any breeze to be reasonably accurate. I've measured how long it takes for these candles to burn down to this bottom line and that is the length of half a day. When the candle reaches here,' he said, and pointed to a line part-way down the candle, 'I know it is the middle of the day or the middle of the night. Two candles burned down means a whole day has passed.'

'Why do you need a—clock?' she asked hesitantly.

The old man smiled and crossed the room to stir a mixture in a pot bubbling over another candle as he answered her question. 'Many things I do must be done in a specific time. A clock helps me break the day into parts, not just morning, midday, afternoon. Each candle has ten rings, so each day has twenty candle rings to it. If something I need to do takes two candle rings to do, I can measure it exactly.' He smiled and lifted the steaming jar from over the candle.

'What's that?' she asked.

'A special herbal mixture. I've boiled the leaves and roots of a goatnut plant. The liquid is an essential ingredient in an elixir called Arthur's cure. It's supposed to soothe sore throats and bad tempers according to the *Apothecary's Compendium*, but its real use is as a drying agent on festering wounds. I only found that out by accident when I spilt some once on a bad cut I had on my finger.' He lifted his finger and stared at it as if he could still see the wound. 'That was a very long time ago, of course,' he added. Then he pointed to another object on a shelf behind her.

'See that?' She looked at the strange device he indicated. It was shaped like a parody of a woman's figure, going from a large bowl at the top, to a very skinny middle, to a large bowl again at the bottom. It was made of a clear substance that glistened like polished pottery, but she could see straight through it. Heaped in the bottom bowl was clean yellow sand. Two smaller versions of the same object sat beside the first. 'They're called timing glasses. Some people call them hourglasses. They're clocks, like the candles, only they measure time in short amounts and it doesn't matter what time of day you use them.'

She listened patiently to the Herbal Man's lecture on clocks and their functions. He obviously needed them for his work, but she couldn't see an application for them in her village. Perhaps the candles could measure the days for people who were trapped inside during winter storms. She found she was tiring quickly, but she forced herself to listen simply because the Herbal Man was an enigma. He described things she had never heard of, and mentioned places that existed in the greater world beyond Harbin, a world Tam had only glimpsed in the ballads and tales the dragonwarriors shared after their summer journeys.

'Where is Ilyastral?' she interrupted at one point.

'Was,' the old man corrected. 'It was a city built in the forests of Janiya, but it doesn't exist any more.'

'Why not?'

'Barbarians found their way there and destroyed it all.'

'Why?'

'Greed, mainly. Ilyastral had a great culture, fine artists, musicians, poets, philosophers—but it also had a lot of gold, and that attracted the wrong people. One day an army came and burnt down the city, killed the people and took the gold. Then they torched the forest and nothing was left of Ilyastral but ashes and legends.'

'But that's wrong,' she complained. Tam didn't know what poets and philosophers were, but the wanton destruction of a fine city did not meet with her sense of justice.

'It may be wrong, Tamesan,' he agreed, 'but sadly that's the way of things in the world. The greedy and the powerful prey on the weak. It happens even in your own village.'

'What do you mean?' she asked.

The Herbal Man checked himself and mumbled, 'That's how some things are. But now it's time for sleeping.' He indicated she should return to the bedroom, and concluded by saying, 'Tomorrow we will see what the weather brings. For now you still need to rest.'

She let herself be bundled back to the bed, but she wanted to know why he didn't complete his explanation of who was greedy and preying on whom in her village. He avoided the topic when she broached it again by stating adamantly, 'Some things are best left alone,' and then offered to let her have a candle clock in her room. She accepted his offer but she was dissatisfied that he had evaded her question.

When he left her to undress and climb into bed, she speculated on who in Harbin could be a 'barbarian', the unusual name he had applied to those who pillaged Ilyastral. Her first choice was Marron. He had all the potential to burn and destroy beautiful things, but she doubted the old man was referring to him. He probably didn't even know half of what Marron had done. So who in Harbin would prey on the weak or seek gold? Only the Dragon Fang, Harbin's warriors, retrieved gold and riches from dragon treasure-troves. What they did was honourable beyond measure. Who could the old man mean? The puzzle teased her as she snuggled into bed. The Herbal Man was full of puzzles, more puzzles than answers. She needed answers. She tried to reason through all the possibilities as she lay staring at the flame on the candle clock, but the combination of her exhaustion, the fluid candle flame, and the bed's comfort, rapidly drew her into a deep and restful sleep.

Chapter Fifteen

'This is the writing symbol for the sound "ah",' the Herbal Man carefully demonstrated. 'If the sound "ah" has to be written as part of a word, this is how it is written. If you see this symbol you know how it should be said.' He wrote the symbol again, slowly so Tam could grasp the pattern and process, and then he handed her the quill. 'Now practise,' he instructed. He watched her stumble over her first effort with the new symbol, gave her advice on how to improve the shape, and then moved away to work on his own project.

Tam hunched over the parchment and scratched at it, copying the flow and curl of the 'ah' letter with painstaking care. This was the eighteenth symbol he had shown her. Five a day so far. She was already memorising whole words from labels affixed to the abundant pots and jars on his shelves. He called the main room his study. She had to remember that. Just as she had to remember other facts, such as the order of the symbols in something he called an alphabet.

She was caught in a dilemma. No-one in Harbin could read or write. Learning the skills intrigued her, although, like the clocks, she couldn't imagine how they were going to be of much use. And learning them was so tedious, so repetitive. It was as bad as her mother teaching her how to weave, how to gut fish, how to lay out the bedding in the Warriors' Hall. Writing was boring. If it wasn't so different from anything she, or anyone else she knew, had learnt before, she would simply tell the Herbal Man she wasn't interested. That's if she wasn't trapped in his home.

The storm was still raging after nine days. The Herbal Man informed her the weather had deteriorated since her arrival, and she gathered from his unspoken emotion that the storm was worse than even he was used to. She also wondered how he knew what the conditions were like outside when he apparently never left his underground shelter. He had already warned her that there was no use attempting to leave via the trapdoor into the old hut above ground, because snowdrifts had buried the building, and its roof had partially collapsed under the excessive weight, thereby sealing the trapdoor.

'Which isn't a major problem,' he reassured her. 'There are other ways out of here.'

Tam hadn't seen any, unless they lay beyond the locked doors she had yet to explore. The only compensation in being confined was that the Herbal Man's home was constantly warm, tolerable even when the fire wasn't burning. If she had been weathering this storm in her own home, she would be huddling together with her mother and Jaysin, rugged up under several worn blankets to keep out the bitter cold. Their hearth was not as large as the Herbal Man's fireplace, and the cottage, despite its abundance of animal skin rugs, could not keep in the warmth as efficiently as this underground hideaway.

'Tomorrow night is Blitzart's Feast,' announced the Herbal Man as he returned to see how Tam was progressing with her writing. He paused at her side, critically examining the letters she was forming on the parchment. 'What did you do with the ring I gave you?' he asked.

Tam looked up from her work. She saw the shadow of concern on the old man's brow. 'I gave it to Jaysin. I made him promise he would give it to Gramma if I couldn't,' she explained tentatively.

The Herbal Man frowned. 'When did you give it to Jaysin?'

'Just before I left. I didn't know what else to do. I wasn't sure what I was going to do or where I was going to be. I didn't want to break your promise.'

The Herbal Man straightened up and moved away a couple of paces, scratching his beard meditatively. 'Are you certain Jaysin will remember?' he asked after a moment.

'I made him promise,' was all Tam could offer in reply. She suddenly felt very annoyed with herself for running away from home and leaving such an important responsibility in the hands of her little brother. Her decision had been too hasty, too selfish. 'I nearly put the ring on her finger before—before I came here,' she muttered.

The Herbal Man turned to her with a stern expression. 'I'm glad you didn't,' he said firmly. 'It would not have been the right time. These things can only be done when the time is right.'

'I don't understand,' Tam responded. The old man was talking in a confusing manner. He had already hinted at the ring's importance, but why was it so important? Why did Harmi need it?

'How was Harmi before you left?' he asked, changing the topic. The tone of his voice had softened.

'She was sleeping,' Tam replied. 'Although she woke when a gust of wind rattled everything.'

'Ah,' nodded the Herbal Man, 'Did she say anything to you?'

Tam shook her head. Gramma seldom said anything sensible.

'Nothing at all?' the Herbal Man persisted.

She wondered why he was suddenly so concerned with what her grandmother might have said. She was embarrassed to repeat the last words she had heard the old lady utter. 'She only mumbled something about dragons never forgetting,' she confessed shyly, and then quickly qualified it with, 'But she always babbles about dragons and things.'

'Does she?' A faint smile flitted across his face, but then he became more solemn. 'I wish you had told me this before.'

'You didn't ask.' She wondered what she had done

wrong. The Herbal Man dropped the subject, though, and showed her the next writing symbol he wanted her to learn. She sighed and returned to her lessons, but the mystery of the ring plagued her throughout the afternoon and well into the evening until she drifted to sleep.

The following day the Herbal Man seemed chirpier than usual when Tam woke. He was singing a ballad in the study as she dressed in yet another silk robe he provided, this one silver, and when she emerged from the bedroom he was dancing around the bench with a couple of jars in his hands.

'Good morning, Tamesan!' he sang as she entered the room. 'Breakfast is waiting in the cooking pot. Eat up. I have work for you this morning.' He danced past her into the bedroom. She heard a door open and close as she scooped a bowl of warm cereal from the cooking pot. As she ate she tried to guess why the old man was so happy. Perhaps the storm had finally ended.

He returned just as she finished eating, carrying a wooden pail. 'Eaten?' he inquired, and answered his own question, 'Good.' He produced a set of keys on a large key ring. 'Take this key,' he said, singling out a copper-coloured one, 'and go through the door in the bedroom. This key opens the door on the left side of the corridor. Fetch back a fresh bucket of goat's milk, will you?' He smiled and handed her the pail. She hesitated, surprised by the request and his jocular mood. 'Well, go on,' he prompted. 'If we're going to celebrate Blitzart's Feast we might as well do it in style. Oh, and take a lantern with you. To see,' he added, as an afterthought. Tam hooked the keys on a cord around her waist, and, carrying both lantern and pail, left the study.

She had always wondered what lay beyond the locked door in the bedroom. Now she was going to find out. Goat's milk? The door must lead outside in that case. She hadn't even considered that the old man might keep his own animals. The storm must have stopped if she was supposed to milk goats. She opened the door leading from the bed chamber and discovered a narrow corridor just as the Herbal Man described, cutting deeper into the mountain rock. She walked several metres before she reached an end-point. However, there were three doors. One door was on the left wall as the Herbal Man promised, but there was also one leading directly ahead, and another to the right. She paused.

Curiosity got the better of her. She tried the handles of both the right and central doors. They were locked. She had the keys. She could take just a little peek. Milking goats was not going to be a quick task so the Herbal Man wouldn't expect her back too soon. She checked in case the old man was following, but no-one was in the corridor. Then she fumbled with the keys and tried the central lock. None fitted. Odd. She repeated her check of the keys in the right door and found one that fitted. She unlocked the door. She opened it carefully and lifted the lantern.

As she leant into the room, the feeble yellow lantern light suddenly leapt into a life of its own. It splashed across the chamber, exploding into a rainbow of colours as it touched and radiated from a myriad of multifaceted crystals embedded in the walls and ceiling. Greens and blues and golds and reds illuminated the chamber. Tam was so dazzled by the light display that she almost dropped the lantern. She steadied and squinted until her eyes adjusted to the varicoloured light.

The entire ceiling was a mass of crystals, as was the wall to her right. The wall's crystals were smooth, almost flat. Those in the ceiling were harsh and jagged. The wall directly opposite was very unusual, though the light didn't throw up a lot of detail. It was a dark golden hue, curved along its length, with a tessellated texture, like the rock platform at the base of the cliffs near Watersdrop. The wall to her left was full of volumes of the things the Herbal Man called books; hundreds, all neatly stacked in shelves. The centre of the chamber was occupied by a pedestal and a large circular mat.

She crept a few tentative steps forward until she could see the top of the pedestal. It was hollowed into a bowl and contained a shimmering liquid. Then the mat caught her eye. It was woven in a pattern that so perfectly imitated the light and face of a full moon that Tam gasped with astonishment. It was as if the moon itself had fallen from the sky onto the floor in this strange room. As she stared at the mat, she sensed something else. She glanced in the direction of the golden wall. A shiver thrilled through her spine. She was not supposed to be in here, she reminded herself. Very cautiously, she backed out of the room, gently closed the door, locked it, and breathed a grateful sigh of relief.

The notion was absurd, she told herself. Her fear made her imagine it. Yet in that brief instant, staring at the moon mat in the centre of the chamber, she thought she saw the golden wall move—as if it breathed! She trembled again at the notion and chided herself for being a fool. It was the effect of the crystal light in the chamber. It shimmered so erratically anything would look like it was moving.

'Walls don't breathe,' she whispered, and grinned nervously at her childish notion. Then she examined the keys and found the copper one to unlock the left door.

The chamber she entered had a low ceiling and reeked of goat. Her lantern cast twisted shadows on the rough cavern walls, giving the place an eerie aspect. Eyes glittered at the edge of the light. Three animals took a wary step towards her. One bleated. It was part anticipation, part timidity.

'Come on,' Tam crooned. 'Come on, scruffy goats.' Reassured by her voice, the lead animals approached, noses raised expectantly for a morsel. She had no food, but she rubbed their proffered muzzles as she moved amongst them searching for nannies with swollen udders. As soon as she found one she squatted to milking. She was pleased at how readily the nanny accepted her touch. In Harbin, all the girls knew how to milk. It was part of growing into womanhood, as important as sewing and cooking. Tam considered it one of the more pleasurable tasks she was forced to perform. Once her hands got accustomed to the cramping action, she found milking a relaxing way to spend work time.

As she milked the Herbal Man's goats, she became aware of the faint presence of a cold breeze. She finished milking the third animal, her pail nearly brimming, so she lifted the heavy container onto a ledge out of the reach of the wandering goats, and traced the source of the breeze. She found a narrow tunnel hidden behind a heavy stack of stalactites. The tunnel was low-ceilinged, forcing her to stoop to peer in, and the air in it was bitterly cold. She guessed it led outside.

On hands and knees she crawled along, following the downward slope and feeling the increasing rush of wind. Then her lantern flickered violently and died. She pushed it aside to retrieve on her return journey, and continued in darkness. A little further on, the tunnel levelled out, and Tam's fingers sank into freezing wet snow. She had reached the entrance. The world was dark and wild. The winter storm was as ferocious as ever and showed no signs of abating. Lashed by the vicious wind, she started shivering uncontrollably. She retreated along the tunnel, collecting the lantern as she crawled, and was grateful to make it back to the warmth of the goat cavern. The animals had a wonderful shelter from the storm, certainly better than the shelters their kin shared at the base of the mountain outside Harbin. Without any way to rekindle the lantern, she stumbled in the darkness, feeling for the pail of goat's milk on the ledge. Finally, she found it. After several more moments of blind fumbling, she also found the exit into the corridor. She hurried towards the comforting light of the Herbal Man's chambers.

'Wonderful,' the Herbal Man cried as she entered his study. He took the pail and then instructed her to wash. 'Today there will be no formal reading or writing lessons, Tamesan. Today we cook and prepare dishes for Blitzart's Feast,' he declared.

'Why do they also call it the Mad Wizards' Dance?' she asked as she boiled water over the hearth.

The Herbal Man stopped and stared at her for a moment as if considering a range of answers. Then he smiled and replied, 'A long time ago, Tamesan, there lived people who were called wizards. They always held an annual meeting this time of the year and all the wizards would journey from their homes to attend. At the meeting, after all the formal business was attended to, they would challenge each other to out-trick one another, and so their meetings were mostly a time of laughter and practical jokes. People who didn't understand them called them mad, of course, and the meeting day was called the Mad

Wizards' Dance. Actually, the meeting used to go on for a fortnight sometimes.'

'I thought the day was Blitzart's Feast first?'

'Dragon's fire no!' the Herbal Man exclaimed. 'It has always been called the Mad Wizards' Dance. Your ancestors renamed it when they settled in Harbin. You see they had no wizards, and Blitzart seems to breathe his frigid vapours heaviest in this part of the land, so they changed the name.'

Tam dipped her hands in the warm water and began to wash her forearms.

'Can you tell me about wizards?' she asked.

'Ah,' sputtered the Herbal Man. 'Wizards. Well, that's not an easy story to tell. When you learn to read you can find out a lot about them.'

'But what did they do?' she asked.

The old man shuffled through a handful of parchments on the bench top. 'Wizards studied, mainly,' he said. 'They studied the stars, the earth, animals, plants, people, water. They studied laws and philosophies and ideas. What they didn't already know they wanted to learn. They met and shared ideas and parted and met again. They wanted to know everything about everything.'

Tam listened to the old man while she finished bathing her feet. He explained how wizards travelled, and acquired mysterious arts and knowledge, and how great kings sought them, and employed them, and even bowed to them at times, because they knew more than any living man. He seemed so involved in the telling of his story that Tam thought he was in a trance. She let his words wash over her as she organised cooking utensils on her own initiative, but she interrupted when he mentioned dragons.

'What did you say?' she asked.

The Herbal Man blinked and repeated, 'They were dependent on them.'

'Before that,' she said.

The old man scratched his head. 'Each one had a dragon, but they're all gone now?'

'Yes,' she said. 'What do you mean "they're all gone"?'

'What I said,' he replied nonplussed.

'Do you mean there are no more wizards, or no more dragons?' she asked, seeking clarification.

'There are no more of either,' he replied. 'Dragons and wizards were mutually dependent on each other. What one thought, so did the other. What one felt, so did his companion. Two lives; one essence. So when the last wizard died, so too did the last dragon.'

'But there *are* dragons.' she contended.

'Not in this world.' Then he seemed to realise where he was and sucked in his breath. 'So that's the story about wizards, Tamesan. It's a legend, nothing more, but that's why we call the feast the Mad Wizards' Dance,' he concluded and immediately changed the topic. 'Have you ever cooked with exotic herbs?'

The day became a mad flurry of cooking activity,

211

burying Tam's inquisitiveness and opportunities to pursue questions about wizards and dragons. Normally she found cooking a bore with Eesa or the village women, but the Herbal Man introduced her to a fascinating range of sweetmeat and herbal recipes she had never heard of. Every time he returned from his storeroom he carried a new culinary wonder, an ingredient to alter the flavour, the smell, the colour of the foods. Amongst all the food, she noted with curiosity, not one shred of meat appeared. Meat from goats and poultry, and forest-dwelling creatures, formed the centre of Harbin feasts, but the Herbal Man kept no such fare in his larder. When Tam mentioned this, he laughed and said, 'The forest garden provides all the food I ever need. It provides all every living creature should need. Why kill just to eat meat?' The idea fascinated her and she dwelt on the idea of a meatless feast while they worked. They snacked throughout the day as they baked, and by evening, according to a candle clock, the preparation was complete. The hearth fire was roaring. Spread across the Herbal Man's bench was a feast worthy of three times as many people.

'To the feast!' he cried after they had cleaned away all the cutlery and dishes they had used. 'Let the madmen dance away the night!'

Tam was worried that working with food all day had destroyed her appetite, but the moment she tasted the first dish the Herbal Man offered, her appetite returned with a vengeance, and she ate heartily.

When they had eaten their fill, the Herbal Man

excused himself briefly and returned carrying two large goblets. He used the sleeve of his robe to polish the goblets until they shone with a golden lustre.

'Real dragon's gold,' he grinned with pride as he passed one goblet to Tam. Then he went to the hearth and lifted a pot that had been mulling on the edge. He poured a white liquid into Tam's goblet and then filled his own. 'Honey milk,' he announced as she sniffed the sweet aroma. 'In the kingdom of Hatua it is called the nectar of the gods, fit only for royalty to drink. Poor caught drinking it are beheaded in the marketplace.' So saying, he sipped a mouthful and indicated Tam should join him and do the same.

Her stomach full, a warm fire raging in the hearth, her head fuzzy with honey milk, Tam found herself struggling to stay awake. She drifted to the floor on a rug spread before the hearth, and listened to the Herbal Man's voice fade in and out as he told her yet another story about a young wizard who had an equally young dragon. The pair were notorious throughout the land for constantly getting into unlikely scrapes. There may have been an ending to the tale. She did not care. Somewhere along the journey she slipped into another realm, a world full of soft edges and warmth and contentment, and the comfortable darkness of sleep.

When she awoke, the world was glowing red. She started, confused by the strange hue, and then realised the light was only the glow of dying red embers. She was still lying on the hearth rug. The lanterns were out. A solitary clock candle burned in the far corner.

She shivered as she sat up, although the room was still quite cosy. There was no sign of the Herbal Man. He wasn't in his temporary bed in the study. She wondered if he had decided to sleep in his own bed. She crept in to check, but he wasn't there, either. She felt enormously tired but a buzzing curiosity infested her thoughts now that she couldn't find the old man.

She crossed to the door that led deeper into the mountain, feeling her way in the semi-darkness until she caught the handle. She carefully turned it and eased the door ajar. Light spilled into the corridor from the far door on the right-hand side, the door that led into the chamber with the weird crystals and the wall she imagined had moved. A sudden chill knifed through her. She shook her head. Perhaps this was one of those really vivid dreams she sometimes had, when everything seemed so much more real than it was. She summoned her courage and crept towards the light.

As she approached, she could hear a voice—no, two voices. One was the Herbal Man. The other was a woman. Her voice was uncannily familiar.

'And then you wouldn't believe it,' the Herbal Man said, and he laughed. So did the woman.

'Eric, you teased me until I cried,' she replied. '"There's no such thing," I said. "No such thing."'

'Claryssa was most upset by that. Dragons have intense pride, you know,' the Herbal Man declared.

'So I've learnt,' admitted the woman. 'Procra bless her.'

The woman was Harmi. It was her voice just as Tam had heard it the day the Herbal Man visited her in the village. Her grandmother was in the cave. Tam was suddenly filled with excitement. She rushed forward and burst into the chamber. It didn't matter how Gramma had got here through the storm. She was here and Tam was overjoyed at the prospect of seeing her. The light in the chamber was more intense than she anticipated. It momentarily blinded her as she blundered out of the corridor's darkness.

'Gramma!' she cried.

In the centre of the light she saw a figure bending over the pedestal, staring into the shining water. He was dressed in flowing white robes that glowed in the bright light radiating from the surrounding crystal. He seemed to be one with the light, as if it flowed through him and he through it. Her cry made him lift his head and he stared at her, at first with surprise, and then from the depths of a very great sadness. She was pierced by his shining eyes. She gasped, astounded by the vision in the chamber, and felt her knees weaken. As she stumbled forward, the last image that filled her mind was of a great golden eye watching her from the far wall.

Chapter Sixteen

The Herbal Man made Tam memorise words and read short passages to him every afternoon. Every morning he encouraged her to laboriously transcribe texts while he worked with his herbs and chemicals, or read texts from his library. His teachings had held her interest originally because they were something new, but now she was bored. The only compensation was that the Herbal Man seemed to sense exactly when she was reaching the point of telling him she no longer wanted to do the lessons. At those moments he would interrupt and give her an entirely different task, like marking candle clocks, or mixing a herbal elixir. She resented the fact that he left all the tidying and cleaning jobs for her. She made the beds, and washed the cooking and experiment utensils every day. She brought in the fresh goats' milk in the morning, and fed the goats from the store each night. She felt as trapped in mundane work with the Herbal Man as she did in her own home. She had no free time to herself except when she fed or milked the goats.

The memory of the crystal chamber haunted her. Every time she entered the corridor to go to the goat cave she had to pass the right-hand door that led to it. She planned to unlock the door the evening after Blitzart's Feast, but the Herbal Man removed the key from the key ring. She was unsure what she had actually witnessed on Blitzart's Feast night. It all seemed indistinct, like a half-remembered dream. She'd heard her grandmother's voice. Or at least she thought she had. There was a great deal of bright light surrounding the Herbal Man. Or was that what she dreamt when he found her in the snow? Her memories were confused. But she clearly remembered a golden eye staring at her. Because everything was so confused, so hazy, so dream-like, she held back from asking the Herbal Man anything about that night. She hoped he would mention it, even by accident, so that she could begin her questions, but he didn't. The morning after, when she finally woke, with a vague headache and dizziness, all he asked was whether she had enjoyed the meal. He also indicated she had fallen asleep on the hearth rug and he had carried her to her bed with a great deal of exertion. No mention was made of the crystal room. Only the key's disappearance gave her any clue that what she thought she had witnessed might in fact have happened.

Eight days after Blitzart's Feast, the Herbal Man woke Tam with the news that the storm was over. 'Put on some warm clothing and come outside,' he invited. 'We can take in some fresh air.' She dressed and followed him into the corridor. They were obviously going outside via the goat cave. At the end of the corridor, though, the old man pulled a tiny key ring from his pocket. It had six keys. One looked very much like the key to the crystal room. The Herbal Man bent and unlocked the central door, the door Tam had never entered. He swung it open and held up the lantern.

'Through you go,' he said, and followed after.

Beyond the door the corridor widened, and branched into three arched openings. The Herbal Man directed her to the left arch. The lantern light exposed an array of intricate carvings decorating the portals, twisted goblin faces that leered down at those who entered. She glimpsed enough of the other archways to learn that the central one led straight on into the heart of the mountain, whilst the one on the right plunged into its depths. The portal she entered had a stone stairway that rose steeply.

'Where do the other tunnels go?' she inquired as the Herbal Man led the ascent.

'Down and in,' he replied cryptically.

His inadequate answer annoyed her. She was growing tired of having more mysteries than facts. 'Exactly where?' she persisted.

She thought she heard the old man chuckle to himself. Then he said, 'Ask me your questions when we get outside, young Tamesan. I'll answer what I can answer then.'

She wanted to protest but the old man's tone sounded sincere enough. She wouldn't forget to ask, though. He wasn't going to avoid the questions that were gnawing at her. And she would ask the other ones, too, the important ones about the crystal cave.

The stairway zigzagged up four flights before it levelled into a large oval cavern. The Herbal Man's lantern revealed that the entire cavern had been worn smooth somehow, so smooth that the walls and ceiling glistened in the light. Tam noticed a portion of the rear wall was blackened by soot and she saw a hollow in the floor where countless fires had been lit. Other sections of the wall were marked with dim lines and drawings. She approached one drawing and discovered that it represented a bear and another animal with horns near its mouth. Smaller figures of people carrying spears clustered around the horned animal.

'Interesting, aren't they?' the Herbal Man observed as he joined her. 'These pictures are older than anyone knows.'

'Who drew them?' she asked.

'Probably a tribal arm of the first people. They are given different names in different places but mostly they are called the Dawn People. I was surprised to find their artwork in this cave when I first came here. It's too far north for them. They preferred warmer regions. But perhaps this area was once warmer than it is now.'

'It's always been cold,' Tam asserted.

'In your time, and even in Nakiades' time,' agreed the old man. 'Perhaps even a long time before that. But not always, Tamesan. Nothing is for always. Except universal laws, and that's one of them. Some philosophers argue that may be the *only* universal law in the end.'

He was rambling about philosophers and laws again. He frequently drifted into ideas she could not even imagine, always giving her more questions than answers, and the questions constantly plagued her. She was considering what he meant by a 'universal law' when she felt him tug at her arm.

'Come on,' he urged gently. 'There's sunshine outside, and we should be in it.' She followed him through the large cavern, past a pile of discarded bones in one section, until he led her through another short tunnel into the fresh air.

The daylight dazzled her eyes. She had become so used to the underground gloom and lantern light in the Herbal Man's retreat that it took her several minutes to adjust to the outside glare. The sky was bright blue, dotted with puffy white clouds, and, at its heart, the sun shone with bright defiance. She stood on a broad ledge on the face of Dragon Mountain, higher than even she had ever ventured. From this vantage point she could see right out to the far reaches of the great western ocean. The world was a vista of white and blue—water, air, snow and clouds. She gazed down at the base of the mountain but could not see her home. Harbin was buried beneath the white mantle of winter. Only a tiny dot, which had to be the dragonship at the jetty, was distinguishable from this height. She sucked in the brittle, fresh air. It stung her throat with its purity.

'It's beautiful,' she breathed.

'A rare morning,' the old man agreed. 'If I was religious I would be praising the gods for this moment.'

'What do you mean, "if you were religious"?' she asked.

The Herbal Man chuckled and scratched his head. 'Do you know what a religion is?' he quizzed. She shook her head. 'Ah,' the old man exhaled. 'How do I explain this?' The question was self-directed. 'Religion is to do with gods and goddesses,' he began.

'Do you mean you don't believe in Varst or Procra?' she ventured.

The Herbal Man smiled. 'In a way I do, and then again I don't,' he replied.

Tam shuffled her feet with annoyance. The old man was still playing his word games. 'How can you do both things?' she asked.

'It's not as silly as it might sound,' he proposed. 'You see, I don't believe there are beings like Varst or Procra. There simply isn't any logic to their existence. The old wizards studied and researched and argued over that concept for thousands of years but none of them could prove what they believed.'

'But Procra made all this.' Tam spread her arms grandly to embrace the world. 'And great Varst breathed life into everything. He brought the mighty dragons into existence.'

'That is what you believe, Tamesan?' he asked. She nodded affirmation. 'Ah,' he breathed again and continued. 'Then for you, Varst is real. Procra is real. You believe in them. The gods exist for you because you believe they exist.'

'Then why don't you believe in them if they exist?'

'Tamesan, do you believe in The One Eternal Being?'

She shook her head and squinted at him with a puzzled expression. 'Who?' she asked.

'The people of the Karmin Empire believe in The One Eternal Being. He or she—no-one knows for sure which, if either—is their god. The One Eternal Being creates all and destroys all: Maker and Unmaker. Do you believe in The One Eternal Being?'

'I've never heard of it,' she declared.

'And the people of Karmin have never heard of Varst or Procra. Just as the Weremouth Tribes with their two thousand gods and goddesses have never heard of The One Eternal Being.'

'That's ridiculous,' she exclaimed. 'How can there be two thousand gods and goddesses?'

'Why not? Who is to say your belief is any more right than theirs? Have you ever seen Varst?'

She hesitated. 'No,' she reluctantly confessed, then quickly added, 'But I know he is real.'

'You have faith, as most religions would call it,' said the old man softly. 'That is the basis of all religions. You believe in something so it must be true.'

'Then why don't you believe?' she asked.

'What you believe is true for you. What I believe is true for me. The universe is full of such truths.'

She was confused again. The old man talked in constant riddles, and about things she had never heard of. 'Are they the "universal truths" you mentioned before?' she asked hesitantly.

The Herbal Man became enigmatic and replied, 'Some say they are, some say they aren't.'

'And you?' she pressed, determined to get a straight answer.

The Herbal Man squatted on a rock jutting from the snow and stared into the middle distance. 'I think the gods, whoever believes in them, have their uses: some good, some bad. I believe in the belief in gods, Tamesan, but I do not believe in the gods themselves. They are a universal truth with no truth within them.'

His answer was no answer for Tam. She stared into the hazy blue distance trying to see if he was studying anything in particular but the world was void of anything except light, colour and the cold. Silence settled between the pair for quite some time. Tam finally broke it by asserting, 'You said you would answer my questions when we got outside.'

The Herbal Man turned his head and replied, 'I did. What do you want to ask?'

She was quiet for a moment. So many unanswered questions, so many puzzles to solve since meeting the Herbal Man. Which should she ask first? She didn't want to offend the old man. Whenever she asked important questions at home her mother scolded her. Her father would inform her it wasn't important. The

Herbal Man always answered in confusing riddles. All she wanted were plain answers.

'Were you talking with Gramma Harmi on Blitzart's Feast?' she asked quietly.

The Herbal Man stared at her in silence, his grey eyes shining in the brittle daylight, his face emotionless. Tam suddenly felt she had asked a foolish, perhaps an inappropriate, question. She knew she had worded it badly. She'd meant to qualify it by admitting she thought she had dreamt it, but her words had come out wrong. She began to apologise, but even as the words formed in her throat, the Herbal Man said solemnly, 'Yes. I spoke with Harmi.'

His admission startled her, not only because it confirmed what she believed she had heard, but also because it opened the path to a lot more questions, a lot more possibilities concerning what she thought she had seen and heard in the crystal cave.

'Do you want to know how I could do that?' he queried. 'How I could speak with Harmi when she is in Harbin and we are here?' Tam, still sorting through her flood of thoughts, merely nodded. 'The ring,' he revealed. 'The ring and the Seeing Waters. The ring I asked you to give Harmi was a link. You'll be pleased to know that Jaysin kept his promise to you and gave Harmi the ring. He is a rare child.'

Tam's mind whirled. What were the Seeing Waters? How could a ring make it possible for the Herbal Man and Harmi to talk to each other? Every answer merely raised a host of fresh questions. Where could she start?

'You told me there used to be wizards. Why aren't there any left?'

The old man cocked his left eyebrow as if he hadn't expected that particular question. He cleared his throat and said, 'People grew suspicious and envious of them. Kings and emperors were threatened by their power. Religious leaders were angered by their lack of belief. Ordinary people were frightened by their dragons. So laws were passed to prevent wizards living in the great cities. That way they couldn't influence masses of people and they were forced to take a low profile. Their universities were either pulled down or turned into barracks for soldiers.'

'Why didn't they protest?'

'Some did,' he replied. 'Some petitioned the rulers. Some marched through the streets. Some even barricaded themselves in the universities and libraries and refused to leave. The irony was that most wizards actually preferred to live in isolation outside the cities. Only a minority ever really exerted power and influence in the cities. They were the hungry ones, the ones whose research led them into the Dark Arts. They believed in gods and goddesses, and demons and devils. They tried to make them real in different, bad ways. Their interests were ultimately financial or political. They were the ones who protested against the new laws, and they plotted, and sometimes carried out, evil acts against other people, especially influential people who stood in their way. But their actions only really served to make wizards more hated than ever. New laws were issued in many countries banning wizardry altogether. Wizards were outlawed, hunted down, and hanged or burned. It didn't matter whether they were innocent or guilty of anything.'

'Didn't they fight?'

'Some did. There were several wars and battles in different places. One that was decisive was the Massacre of Dragons in the Hayge Valley. It was a long and bloody battle with both sides evenly matched. In the end, the wizards were betrayed by one of their own kind who was offered freedom and glory if he helped Emperor Jorg defeat the dragons.'

'What did he do?' She was becoming fascinated by this tale of old intrigues.

'Ethan—he was the traitor—gave the other wizards and their dragons a potion at dinnertime to put them into a deep sleep. Emperor Jorg's men crept up in the early hours of the morning and cut all their head's off.'

'What happened to Ethan?'

The Herbal Man snorted contemptuously. 'Jorg let him and his dragon live in the Imperial City for a year and a day after the Massacre, and then he had them killed in exactly the same way. It was a crude kind of justice, really.'

'What about the ones who didn't fight?'

'They fled into the wildernesses. Many were hunted down and slain in the early years. Those who found isolated strongholds and refuges outlived several generations of their enemies, but they eventually grew old and died.'

'What happened to their dragons?'

'Remember what I told you?' the old man prompted. 'Wizards and dragons are one essence. When a wizard dies so does his dragon.'

Tam took a deep breath. The Herbal Man's answer had given her a chance. This was one of the questions she had been waiting to ask. 'But how come there still are dragons?'

'There are no more dragons, Tamesan,' the old man replied. 'The last dragon disappeared almost two hundred years ago.'

'I know that's not true, and so do you,' she argued. 'The dragonwarriors hunt dragons every summer. There are lots of dragons left.'

The Herbal Man shook his head sadly, and stared into the horizon. 'Some things are best left alone, Tamesan. If you believe there are dragons still to be hunted, then there are dragons.'

'What is that supposed to mean?' she demanded.

'I have told you what I know. It is the truth as I believe it to be. I know there are no more wizards, and without wizards there cannot be dragons. Amongst wizards that was a kind of universal law. Perhaps it was wrong. Perhaps it is only true for me because I believe it.'

'Like I believe that Varst exists?'

The old man nodded appreciatively. 'You are learning quickly, Tamesan.'

'But I know that there *are* dragons,' she insisted.

'Have you seen one?'

'No,' she admitted, 'But my father has. And so have the dragonwarriors. They've all seen dragons.'

'Then we believe different truths, Tamesan. Some argue that truth is indisputable but I have always held that truth is a matter of perception. That is not necessarily a bad thing. Remember I think religious beliefs have much good, even if I do not hold them as true for me. I guess you must say dragons still exist. For you,' the old man concluded.

'Have you seen a dragon?' she asked.

The Herbal Man let a wry smile play across his mouth. 'I have,' he replied. Then he shook his hands and clasped his arms as he stood. 'It is getting too cold to be sitting out here discussing philosophy and history and religion. I think some warm broth is in order, and then I will take you outside again to help me find a batch of important herbs while the weather remains so pleasant. You have a lot to learn yet, my young friend, and this winter is nearly over.'

Chapter Seventeen

Chasse caught his balance. His spear was point-heavy. He adjusted his grip, keeping his eyes on Derin's hips and his blunted weapon.

'Watch his left shoulder, boy,' Theo growled.

'Be patient,' another voice warned.

Both youths circled, heeding the advice. Other voices urged them on. 'Come on. This isn't a festival dance.'

'Take him, Derin! Take him now!'

'Hit low, Chasse! Hit low!'

Chasse enjoyed fighting when it was a game. This was a game in a way, but it was more, much more, for the initiate youths. Winter's hard training was coming to a close. The spring melt was underway. Soon it would be summer, and the dragonship would carry them south to adventure, to manhood. All winter the initiate youths had lived in the Warriors' Hall, learning how to care for their weapons and armour, learning how to fight, learning how to obey the experienced warriors like Theo or Trask, or Kevan, Dragon Head of Harbin.

They were also learning how to earn status

amongst the dragonwarriors. The better the fighter, the higher the status. Marron established himself as the foremost of the five initiates. He fought hardest and best. What he lacked in technical skill with weapons at times, he made up for with sheer blood-lust and strength. He acquitted himself more than admirably in mock fights with the younger dragon-warriors. Only Chasse had come close to beating him. Marron fostered a different emotion in Chasse during their mock fights. Chasse tasted the incentive of hatred whenever he faced Trask's son, because of Marron's deliberate humiliation of both Chasse and his sister. One day he would turn the tables and humiliate Marron.

Inspired by the thought, Chasse feinted forward and low, then swung his spear high towards Derin's left shoulder. Derin dodged, stepped right and brought the shaft of his spear across the unprotected back of Chasse's legs with a resounding whack. Chasse yelped and leapt aside, barely escaping Derin's second swing. The spear shaft whistled past his left ear. He spun to meet the stabbing attack he antici-pated would follow, only to see Derin roll right and come up with his spear point dangerously close to Chasse's throat. A deft defensive swing knocked that threat aside, but Derin surprised him by viciously kicking his knee. Knocked off-balance again, Chasse could only manage to block a flurry of attacking blows. Then Derin made as if to swing high and instead stabbed under Chasse's attempted block, catching the youth smack on the sternum. The painful blow sent Chasse reeling into the circle of spectators amidst a rousing cheer.

'Derin is the victor!' Theo announced. He stepped forward to clap his big hand on the youth's shoulder. The herdsman's son grinned with pride and offered his hand to help Chasse to his feet. Chasse accepted it graciously. The painful bruise forming on his chest made it difficult to smile. It was embarrassing to lose, but Derin was a good opponent and Chasse considered him a friend.

Two more combatants stepped into the circle. They were older dragonwarriors, eager to hone their skills. Chasse was about to settle against the wall with Derin to watch the fight when the door burst open and a young boy came running in. He went straight to Kevan. The reaction on his father's weathered face told Chasse something was amiss. He pushed himself to his feet, still rubbing the bruising from the spear on his chest, as Kevan spoke to Theo. Then Kevan strode towards the door, following the boy. As he passed Chasse he ordered, 'Come with me.' Chasse obediently followed.

Kevan walked so fast towards home that Chasse had to half-jog to keep pace. He had no opportunity to ask what had happened, and a dozen wild possibilities ran through his mind. They crossed the surging waters of Watersdrop, freshly fed by the melting snow off Dragon Mountain, and were met at the cottage door by Eesa. A tacit message passed between the adults before Chasse followed his father inside. The unexpected sight of his sister Tamesan standing by the table in the main room stunned him. Kevan also seemed unable to decide what to do. Like Chasse, he stared as if he did not believe what he saw. Finally he swallowed and asked, 'Where have you been?'

'With the Herbal Man,' she replied.

Movement in the darker corner of the room caught Chasse's attention. Sitting in the old chair that had been Gramma Harmi's favourite was a familiar white-haired, dark-robed figure. Kevan, aware of his presence as well, turned to the Herbal Man, seeking confirmation of Tam's answer.

The Herbal Man rose and said, 'I found her in the snow on the mountain. It was just lucky that I was caught out late by the incoming storm or else she might not have been so fortunate. As it was, she nearly died from exposure to the cold.'

'Why didn't you let us know?' Kevan demanded, but he already knew the obvious answer. The first storm had buried the mountain and the village beneath snow so thick it was impassable. He waved aside the Herbal Man's reply before the old man could give it, saying, 'It is a foolish question. I apologise—but this vision of a daughter we all thought had been devoured by Blitzart's cold maw overwhelms me. I—am caught between joy and astonishment. I should be making you welcome.'

Tam watched as her father stumbled through his

emotions. She had never seen him so confused. She came forward impulsively and embraced him. He winced at first, but it was a fleeting reaction and he softened, enfolding her in his arms.

'Procra has indeed blessed this child,' he said and glanced at his wife. Eesa was leaning against the door jamb, crying softly.

The Herbal Man refused to stay in Harbin. He made brief visits to individuals who requested minor treatments, and then left on the pretext of being very busy. Tam heard later that he had been seen briefly near the jetty in the company of her little brother Jaysin. The last time she saw him, he was speaking with her father on the village outskirts. Then he left.

Tam spent most of the day with Chasse. He listened eagerly to her tale of adventure, of being lost in the storm, of her rescue and the hazy memories of a shining light. She tried to explain what she had learned from the Herbal Man about herbalist medicines, and she scratched some words in the earth to demonstrate her budding writing skills. Chasse was overawed by his sister's newly acquired skill, although he failed to see the significance of it. She didn't tell him about the Herbal Man's underground home or the tunnels. The Herbal Man had requested she not tell anyone the truth about his life on the mountain. When she'd pressed him for his reason he answered with, 'I am a simple hermit and herbalist, Tamesan.

That is how your world knows me and that is how it should stay. It is the only thing I ask from you in exchange for teaching you my trade.' She respected his request then, reminding herself that he was a good man and a healer, if a little eccentric in his ways and ideas. Only her knowledge of the ring, and the obscure and incomplete explanation the Herbal Man had offered for it, made her cautious about trusting him completely. It also fuelled her curiosity to unravel the mysteries surrounding the old man on the mountain.

Tam noticed changes in her older brother. In the wintry weeks since he entered the Warriors' Hall he had put on body bulk. He was a little taller, and his arm and chest muscles had greater definition. She could see the man emerging from the gangly blond youth her brother had been, and because of that he was a partial stranger to her. He described the exercises and training he was undergoing, and the traditions he was learning. He explained how Marron had risen in status, and how there was still constant bickering between their father and Marron's father over the leadership of the Dragon Fang. He gave her sketchy details of the struggles the villagers had endured because of the excessive snowfalls and constant storms, and how Sharmine and her crones predicted the return of Blitzart to wreak revenge on Nakiades' descendants. It had been a hard, cruel winter.

There were other changes to her family. Gramma Harmi was gone. The old lady had died in her sleep in the middle of Blitzart's Feast. Constant storms prevented the whole village from meeting in the Long Hall for the mid-winter celebration, so families huddled in their isolated homes and celebrated as best as they could. Chasse and Kevan were trapped with the dragonwarriors in the Warriors' Hall, leaving Eesa, Jaysin and Harmi to celebrate alone. Chasse told Tam he heard from their mother that Gramma was happier than usual that evening, brighter than she had been for many years. Later in the night, Eesa swore Gramma was talking to someone in the main room, long after they had all supposedly gone to sleep. Tam immediately remembered her vision in the Herbal Man's crystal chamber that same night, but said nothing to Chasse. When curiosity drove Eesa from the warmth of her bed to check on the old lady, she found her sitting in her favourite chair, quite dead. A ceremony for Harmi was held at Watersdrop when the weather calmed. Chasse described how Jaysin had gone into mourning after Harmi's death, refusing to speak to anyone, or eat for almost a week, until Eesa coaxed him back to more sensible behaviour. Ever since, however, the younger boy had withdrawn even deeper into himself.

There were other Words of Passage sung that past winter. A stillborn baby and an older man, Marc, a dragonwarrior until he had been injured on one journey, were buried in the bitter earth. And old Asmae, alone and isolated at the edge of the village, also perished in the freezing storms.

Chasse also told Tam about her own funeral. When she disappeared into the teeth of the first vicious winter storm and did not return, everyone believed she had frozen to death on the mountain. Kevan and a handful of the Dragon Fang searched the lower mountain in the foul weather to no avail, and they returned knowing that no-one could survive more than half a day anywhere out in the storm. Yet Eesa refused to let the Dragon Heart priest sing the Words of Passage for Tam's spirit. As weeks slipped by, and the hope of Tam's return became impossible even for Eesa to maintain, a small memorial was held at Watersdrop.

'Even Katris cried,' he said. She smiled at that piece of irony. 'The only people who didn't seem to believe you were dead were Jaysin and Gramma. Mother said Gramma just kept mumbling that you were safe with Eric and Claryssa and that was how it was meant to be—?

Tam's eyes widened. 'And I was!' she declared before Chasse could finish.

'Pardon?' her brother queried. Her sudden enthusiastic response confused him.

'Eric,' Tam explained. 'That's the Herbal Man's name. His name is Eric.'

Chasse could not hide his astonishment. 'Are you trying to say Gramma knew where you were?'

She hesitated. The idea was impossible—wasn't it? 'No,' she muttered, and then corrected herself, 'I mean, yes. I know it doesn't make any sense, but Gramma was right.'

'But how could she know? Did you tell her you were going to the Herbal Man?'

'I don't think I told her anything. It was probably a wild coincidence. She was always talking about Eric and Claryssa. I didn't meet anyone called Claryssa anyway, so perhaps it was just Gramma being Gramma,' she suggested.

Chasse accepted her explanation because the alternative made no sense to him at all, but it plagued Tam long after their conversation. Why had she forgotten to ask the Herbal Man about his relationship with her grandmother? The coincidences and fragments collecting in her mind concerning the Herbal Man and Gramma were forming a vivid picture with endless possibilities.

Late in the afternoon Chasse returned to the Warriors' Hall, and Tam was left to help Eesa prepare food. Eesa could not contain her joy at her daughter's miraculous return. She told Tam that Kevan was organising a feast that evening to celebrate her return, which the entire village would attend. At the mention of the feast Tam felt embarrassed. She protested that she didn't want a feast in her honour, but Eesa cheerfully ignored her. Jaysin kept coming up to her and clinging to her arm as if he never wanted to let her go.

'I missed you, Tamesan,' he said at one stage when Eesa had gone out to collect eggs. 'I was scared, but I gave Gramma the ring like you asked and she told me you were safe.'

Tam hugged her brother and said, 'I missed you too, Jaysin, but Gramma was right, wasn't she?'

The boy nodded and looked up at her with his sad dark eyes. She felt as if her little brother knew Harmi better than anyone in her family did. She guessed at her grandmother's secrets, but Jaysin almost knew them for what they were.

'I miss Gramma,' he muttered. Whether it was the sorrowful expression on Jaysin's face, or whether her own loss suddenly surfaced, she could not tell. Tears welled in her eyes. Gramma Harmi was gone. A piece of her life had been snatched away by the Death Dragon, Shaddho. Unable to hold back her grief any longer, she hugged Jaysin to her chest and cried.

The people of Harbin flocked to the Long Hall. Denied Blitzart's Feast by the bitter winter, this early spring celebration announced by the Dragon Head was warmly welcomed. Harbin normally opened the new season with the Celebration of Fler, and preparations were already underway for it to be held in five days, but no-one complained when Kevan ordered the celebration brought forward, especially after they received the news that his daughter Tamesan had miraculously returned from the dead. Fler was the goddess daughter of Procra, the symbol of rebirth and growth. How fitting, many thought, that Kevan's daughter should return at that time. It was a sign from almighty Varst that the people of Harbin were blessed and that they would prosper.

Tam felt terribly self-conscious being made to sit at the head table in the Long Hall between her father and the Dragon Heart priest. People entered and stared at her as if she was a spirit, a ghost. She wanted them to speak to her, to show her that nothing had changed, but no-one came close enough to do that, and she was not allowed to leave her seat. She made a minor protest when she saw Banni enter and stare. Banni was a good friend. Tam didn't want to be kept at a distance from her. But the Dragon Heart restrained Tam in her seat until Banni took her place with the other single women at the furthest table from the front.

He said quietly, 'Patience, child. Tonight you must keep your place. You are a gift from the gods, a symbol of their power and their presence. The people can see this and know you for that. It would be wrong if you trivialised this moment with womanly emotions. Be the moment. Be what it is ordained by Varst and Procra that you should be. You will make your father and your mother proud.' Held by his hands and his words, she acquiesced, reluctantly.

The Hall quickly filled and the women presented the warm meal from stock that had been kept in storage throughout the winter. Dressed in his best chain mail, Kevan rose as Dragon Head and welcomed everyone to the Celebration of Fler. Then he called on the Dragon Heart to give the traditional blessings.

The priest stood, regaled in his green, yellow and white robe, wearing the ceremonial goat's horn and feather headdress, and began the formalities. When he finished the introductory vows, he laid a hand on Tam's shoulder and motioned for her to stand beside him. He smiled at her and bowed his head, an act of obeisance normally reserved for her father on very important occasions. Then he opened his speech with inspired passion.

'It has been a bitter winter. Great Blitzart's icy breath blew longer and more fiercely than ever anyone can remember. The land lay frozen, and some were called to journey across the great darkness to Varst's Eternal Paradise. This we have all seen and shared. Perhaps it is punishment for some wrong we have done unwittingly. Perhaps it was Blitzart's futile attempt to be avenged on the children of Nakiades. It has been a trial for us all, and the sorest trial has been inflicted on the family of the Dragon Head. We have sung the Words of Passage for both the daughter and the grandmother of Kevan this past winter, and great sorrow has lingered in the Dragon Head's home.

'But the gods are just. Harmi lived long, longer than any, a full seventy summers and then some. She was blessed by Procra, who gives birth to all life, and taken mercifully by Shaddho without pain or struggle. The gods are just. And the gods are merciful beyond all measure. For although it seemed that they were cruel and vindictive in leading the girl Tamesan from her home into the teeth of Blitzart's storm, they were orchestrating something far greater, more miraculous than we could ever begin to comprehend. For here is Kevan's daughter among us again, brought back alive from the Winter Dragon's clutches, delivered to us as a gift of trust, a sign that we, the children of Nakiades, the people of Harbin, are many times blessed by great Varst, by Procra, by their children. We have seen death and we have seen rebirth. It is the eternal cycle, the mystery of life, the beauty in the terror. Praise be to Varst. Praise be to Procra, to Ecg and to Fler. They have led us through the bitter winter of death and shown us the promise of life eternal. Let us accept their gifts of food tonight, their promise through the return of Tamesan, the child who is the Dawn's Light, and know in our hearts that we are truly blessed.'

Chapter Eighteen

Tam was furious. The Celebration of Fler had been a total disaster. The Dragon Heart and her father made her appear to be something greater than she really was. They had lied. To everyone. She had not been saved or delivered by the gods. The Herbal Man had found her. He kept her safe through the winter. He taught her new skills. He deserved the accolades for saving her, not Varst or Procra. Yet when she said as much at home, Eesa told her to keep the truth to herself. Kevan simply refused to discuss it.

The priest did, though. He took her aside when she told him the following day that she was not happy to be set up as a gift from the gods, and said, 'You are more than a gift from the gods, Tamesan. You are an inspiration and a strengthener.'

'How?' she asked.

'The people of Harbin believe Varst is their protector. They are happier because of it. Didn't you see their faces last night? Couldn't you see what the story of your amazing survival did for them?'

'All I saw was my friends staring at me as if I was something strange. No-one spoke to me after the feast. Now I feel as if I can't see anyone because of it.'

'It is because you are something very special now,' he asserted gently.

'A lie isn't being special,' she argued.

The priest leaned closer. 'Sometimes a lie is more special than the truth, Tamesan. Can you tell me you have never lied?'

She hesitated. How could she argue with that? She had lied. Many times. 'No,' she admitted. 'But never like this.'

'No,' agreed the priest. 'Never like this. Because this is a special truth, a truth that will bring the people of Harbin together. They not only see Varst's hand protecting them, they also see your father as a blessed warrior, the man chosen by Varst as their Dragon Head, chosen to lead them again this summer against the dragons. That strengthens all of Harbin. It makes the Dragon Fang mighty again.'

'But I know the truth,' she objected desperately.

'And what truth is that, Tamesan?'

'I was rescued by the Herbal Man. He cared for me and brought me home again,' she replied.

The priest shook his head. 'He may have done that, Tamesan, but he was merely acting as an instrument of Varst's wishes,' he stressed. 'Tell me how he managed to stumble upon you in the middle of a howling snowstorm. It could not have been by accident. Think, girl. An old man in that storm would have perished as easily as you almost did. So what protected him from the icy breath of the dragon Blitzart, if not the gods themselves? It was Varst himself who saved you. Almighty Varst took pity and led the old man to you, and kept both of you safe from harm until you returned to the old man's hut. That is the truth.'

'But—' she started to object and stopped. The priest was arguing with her just like the Herbal Man did on Dragon Mountain. She knew the truth. Or at least she thought she did, but the priest's interpretation of events made her even less sure of what had really happened on the mountain during the first storm. How did the Herbal Man find her? How had he managed to carry her to his hut? He was not a tall strong man, but old, bent and skinny. She doubted he would have the strength to carry her very far at all, and yet, if he did rescue her, he must have carried her halfway up the mountain through a raging storm. What was the truth, then?

'The gods have blessed you, child,' reassured the priest with a kindly touch on her shoulder. 'You are alive when you should be dead. You are tall and beautiful and the daughter of the Dragon Head of Harbin. When it comes to the time of your choosing in one more summer, what warrior would not give everything he has to call you his wife? Few women in Harbin have been blessed with so much, and none returned to their family as you have been so mercifully been returned to yours. Be thankful to the gods for what you have been given, and trust what is happening. It is not only for you but for the good of all

Harbin, of that I am certain.' And the matter was ended. The priest left to attend to other matters in the village. She had no choice, it seemed, other than to accept what was being said about her.

She expected her mother to set her to work in the village almost immediately, yet all that first day after the Celebration of Fler, Eesa made no demands of her. She went to the Long Hall to help clean up after the night's feast and was told she did not need to help. She walked down to the fishermen's tables where Eesa sat with Amarti and several other women, cleaning the morning's catch. They greeted her with a great deal of fuss, and she had to answer questions about the Herbal Man's home, and what the winter was like on the mountain, and they all commented on how blessed she was to have been rescued, but there was an emptiness in their welcome. She felt as if she was outside the moment, a stranger among them. She sat to help with the scaling, but Eesa informed her she did not have to stay if she chose not to. Tam waited for a while, at a loss what to do, and then asked if anyone had seen Banni. Eesa told her that Banni and several younger women were bathing at the Dragon's Cauldron. Tam dallied a little longer and then excused herself. She walked quickly through the village and headed towards the hot springs.

She found Banni and four others soaking in the springs. They greeted her happily and invited her to join them, but she remained on the rocks. She had to answer the usual questions about her wondrous adventure. The only question she noticed no-one asked was her reason for running away into the storm in the first place. Her return, not her motivation in going, was all that mattered to everyone. Then conversation swung to Banni's approaching baby. Her abdomen was swelling noticeably, though Banni said it was almost two more months before the baby was due. Tam was happy for Banni, but she felt as distanced from the young women as she did from those working with her mother. When they began to emerge from the pool, Tam left and returned to the outer edges of the village.

She paused in a stand of trees near the goat pasture to watch the dragonwarriors training. They were practising a manoeuvre which required them to keep in a tight defensive bunch as selected warriors harassed them with wooden spears and swords. She saw Chasse's blond hair in the group, and Marron's dark, athletic figure at the centre. Her father stood apart with Theo, observing the action. Theo pointed and issued instructions, and the younger warriors separated. They fell into a melee amongst themselves. She waited to see if Marron and Chasse were going to confront each other, but they were separated by three other pairs and seemed ignorant of each other's presence. The rules for the mock battle were not readily understood by her so she studied her brother and realised how much he really had changed. He fought gracefully and confidently, beating down his opponents as they appeared, including Theo, who stepped into the fray when the energy started to wane. He was fast becoming a dragonwarrior. She watched Marron fighting as well. He moved with the same fluid efficiency as her brother, but there was something deadlier in the way he hit out at his opponents with his wooden sword. Three opponents retreated holding their arms in genuine pain after Marron had ruthlessly attacked them. Whereas her brother had the style of a warrior who was doing what he had been trained to do, and doing it well, Marron was revelling in the fight, enjoying every blow he dealt out, delighting in every howl of pain he drew from his foes. The bully in him was growing hungrier.

She avoided Katris and her peers when she entered the village. She imagined her public elevation at the Celebration of Fler would only make Katris hate her more. Chasse's news that Katris had cried when the Dragon Heart sang the Words of Passage for Tam's spirit did not really surprise her, but she sincerely doubted her return would make the dark-haired girl happy. Moreover, she had seen Marron studying her all through the night of the feast, and Katris eyeing them both. She knew, more than ever, just as the priest's words all too accurately predicted, that she would be sought after by the warriors as a prize, and that would make Marron even more determined that she should be his. In turn, Katris would be even more jealous. It seemed so ironic that what she had tried to run away from was made worse by her return.

She wandered the village outskirts, and filled some of her spare time herding goats with Derin's father. She climbed the lower slope of the mountain to her favourite retreat and sat on the rock, staring over the bay. Alone, she had time to think over what had happened, and to ponder the mysteries the Herbal Man had unfolded to her. She had come home, yet she felt further from it than ever.

When she descended towards dusk she was surprised to find her father waiting outside the cottage. He ushered her inside, where her mother Eesa sat waiting at the table. A lantern burned in the table's centre. Kevan sent Jaysin to his bedroom and then indicated for Tam to sit down.

'Are you happy to be home?' he asked. He remained standing. It made him appear more imposing in the low-ceilinged room.

'Yes, Father,' she replied, wondering what he was leading up to. After a brief exchange of common pleasantries, Kevan coughed. Tam knew the signal. He was about to make a statement he considered important.

'We know why you ran away, Tamesan,' he said.

'We are also glad that you have been returned to us, more than you could understand,' added Eesa.

'It is not easy to be a woman,' said Kevan. He glanced at Eesa. She nodded. 'You already know more about that than I do,' he conceded. 'A woman's lot is work and more work. A woman must not only bear her own burdens but also the burdens of her husband and her children, too. Even as a man I know this much. It has always been so.'

'Your father understands the importance we women play in this village,' Eesa affirmed. 'The women of Harbin are its backbone and its soul.' She looked up at her husband and added, 'No man will deny that.'

'It is true,' he agreed. 'The women of Harbin are its strength. Without them there would be no Harbin, no home for the Dragon Fang, no sons to become dragonwarriors, no future, no memory of Nakiades.' He paused and ran his hand through his long mane of greying hair. Then he leant forward and said, 'I have been thrice-blessed in my daughter. First in that she is a beauty like her mother. Second in that she is strong and healthy. And now third because she has seen the face of Blitzart's fury and returned unharmed. When you come of age in one more summer you will be the rarest of women for all of these reasons.'

Tam heard the echo of the priest's words in her father's voice. She had already guessed what he was leading up to. She kept an outward show of respect but her heart sank. She was caught in a web spun well before winter and nothing had changed. If anything, it had worsened.

'The daughter of the Dragon Head has more responsibility than most girls,' Kevan was saying as she returned her attention to her father. 'You were born into a position of highest honour, a position every other girl in Harbin would gladly have. It is time for you to accept that responsibility, to be ready for what your future holds for you.'

'The son of Trask is a handsome young man,' Eesa offered gently.

'His interest in you has been inexperienced,' her father admitted, 'but he is merely learning what is right and what is wrong for a man to do. If he does choose you in one summer's time you will also do what is right for a woman, exactly as you will if you are chosen by another.'

'Your father's words are not meant to be unkind, child,' Eesa intervened. 'He only wants you to understand what is right and to be happy in doing it.'

'There are traditions,' Kevan reminded her. 'Each of us is bound by them. Coming of age is not just a measure of how many summers we have lived. It is also measured by what we understand and what we do.'

'We want you to have the honour and the respect you deserve when you are received as a woman,' said Eesa.

'Do you understand?' Kevan asked.

The silence anticipating Tam's answer hung over her like the sharp blade of an axe. What choice did she have when all was said and done?

'Can I have time to visit the Herbal Man?' she inquired.

Her question was not what her parents had expected. Kevan shot Eesa a precautionary glance and scratched his chin.

'That is another matter,' he replied.

'But what is the answer?' Tam asked.

Kevan shifted his weight and moved around the table. Then he leaned forward and put both hands on the table top so that he was staring straight into Tam's eyes. 'Has he asked you to be his—what was his word?'

'Apprentice,' suggested Eesa.

Tam shook her head. 'No.' She was puzzled by her father's line of inquiry. The term 'apprentice' had never passed the Herbal Man's lips.

'Perhaps not,' Kevan acceded. 'Which is just as well. What he proposed to me when you were brought back down the mountain would not be appropriate for you.'

She did not understand. 'What did the Herbal Man say?' she asked.

Kevan threw another look at Eesa before he replied. 'I see no harm in you knowing, because you will understand why the idea is foolish,' he began. 'When we last spoke, he offered to teach you his skills in herbs and healing. It was a kind gesture, one I am sure was meant in good faith, but it is not something for a Harbin woman to contemplate. Not when she is young and close to coming of age. There are more pressing things to learn. I thanked him, but told him it was not a suitable thing for you to consider.'

'There will be too little time for the learning he would want you to have,' claimed Eesa. 'A husband would not want his young wife dallying around the mountain with an old man.'

'It is not a young woman's place,' Kevan asserted. 'Perhaps an older one, or one without a husband or children would suit the Herbal Man's needs better,' he suggested. 'You understand?'

'Can I still visit him?' Tam persisted.

Kevan's eyes widened as if he did not believe he had heard the question again. When he saw she was awaiting an answer he straightened and threw his arms up in exasperation. 'By Varst's Holy Fires, I have tried!' he moaned.

'Be patient, husband,' Eesa said placatingly. 'The girl's question is not that difficult to answer.' He glared at her but Tam's mother ignored him and turned to her daughter. 'Why would a young woman want to share her time with an old man?' she asked with a bemused expression on her face.

'He teaches me,' Tam replied.

'See?' growled Kevan. 'Already he meddles.'

'Hush,' warned Eesa. 'What does he teach you?'

'How to read and write. How to recognise which plants are useful for healing and what has to be done to them to make them useful.'

Kevan shook his head in disapproval. 'These things are wasted on you. What use are they to you?'

'I could learn to do what he does for the village. I could teach others.'

'No,' declared her father. 'My daughter will not be led away from her responsibilities. You will not be his apprentice and that is final.'

'Can I still visit him?' she repeated doggedly.

Kevan swore another oath and smashed his fist on the table. 'Is my child deaf after all? What have I said?' he demanded.

Tam's own frustration threatened to overwhelm her, but she held back her tears and anger, and calmly replied, 'You said I cannot be the Herbal Man's apprentice. I accept what you have said, Father. All I ask is that I can visit him sometimes, when there is time. That is the least I can do to honour him for saving my life. I thought it would please you that I am willing to meet my responsibilities to those to whom life is owed.'

Kevan sucked in his breath. His daughter had called his bluff. Honour was a foremost principle in the Dragon Fang's code. Warriors were willing to die for honour. Did she know what she had done? He looked at Eesa. She was nodding very slowly. So it was decided. Tamesan could visit the Herbal Man. When it was convenient. Briefly. She was correct. It would be seen as an act of honour, a sign to everyone in the village that the Dragon Head and his family respected debts owed to others regardless of their rank. But that was an end to it. There would be no apprenticeship with the Herbal Man. The daughter of the Dragon Head would accept her village responsibilities exactly as any young woman should.

Chapter Nineteen

The days of spring swung through passing rains and streaming sunshine. The snow blanket quickly melted, sending fresh streams cascading down the mountain gorges. The men hauled the great dragonship from the water to scrape barnacles from the hull and re-caulk its leaking seams. The women repaired the dragonship's red sail and renewed the ropes. Fishermen drifted on the bountiful spring oceans, and the herdsmen managed their flocks. Village children revelled in their release from winter's white prison, playing and exploring the world of Harbin.

For Tam, as the Celebration of Fler faded, life settled into its traditional cycle. Eesa kept her washing, mending, supervising children, cleaning fish. She accepted her duties, and made herself do them well. She listened politely to the conversations of the women she worked with, and even tolerated Katris' presence, though Katris made no attempt to communicate. Tam felt the brewing enmity between them, but what could she do? She knew it would be futile if she tried to appease Katris. Neither of them had any control over Marron's desires. When it came to choosing, Marron would choose whomever he wanted. There was no guarantee, for that matter, that either girl would be his choice. He could well become infatuated with someone else in the intervening months and overlook them both. Because they were girls it was something they could not determine.

Whenever Tam had time, she put into practice the knowledge and skills the Herbal Man had revealed to her. She wandered the forest edge and searched for herbs, identifying them as best as she could. She searched for a quill and parchment in the village but no-one understood what she was looking for. She found seagull feathers and tried to fashion her own quill. She tried using tar, and fluids squeezed from bloodberries, as ink, with limited success, but she did not find a substitute for parchment. Finally she gave up, and resorted to using a stick to scratch letters and words into the earth. When she had to supervise the smaller children she amused them by teaching them how to draw a letter from the Herbal Man's alphabet. In a spare moment with Jaysin she also taught him what she knew of writing. To her surprise and pleasure, he was instantly keen to learn, and within a few sessions he knew as much as she did. He was disappointed when she admitted she didn't know any more. It was the first time she had ever really observed a sense of hunger, a longing in her little brother, a happiness. But he withdrew even further from the company of other people to practise writing the letters of his name and the Herbal Man's alphabet. He became obsessed with the new skill.

The village was also organising the next festival—the Feast of Ecg—when initiate dragonwarriors were presented with their armour and weapons. Tam assisted in decorating the Warriors' Hall, which involved cleaning it thoroughly and hanging armour and weapons on the walls. She longed to see Chasse initiated, but the Feast of Ecg was an all-male affair. The only exception was for the initiates' mothers, who were invited to lay out the food for the men at the start of the festival. Then they, too, had to leave.

On the night of the feast, Eesa returned to the cottage after she had finished serving food, and boasted to Tam how fine Chasse appeared, seated with the men at the long table in the Hall. She was pleased to see father and son together, the men in her life looking handsome and strong. It reassured her that her world in Harbin was prosperous and in balance.

A week after the Feast of Ecg, the dragonwarrior Symon was killed. As the men were hauling the dragonship back into the water, a log used to roll the ship forward jammed on a small rock. The hull heeled over, and Symon wasn't quick enough to scramble to safety. He was crushed beneath the ship's great weight. By the time the men lifted the ship off the trapped man, he was dead. The subdued warriors carried Symon's body to his wife, Ashlee. Then they withdrew to the Warriors' Hall to mourn their dead comrade.

Eesa and Amarti were summoned to Ashlee's hut to prepare the dead man's corpse, and Eesa insisted Tam accompany her. 'There is a time for everything, Tamesan,' she explained as they walked along the narrow path. 'You know more about the living than the dead, but now it is time you learned about the dead as well. This is something women do better than men.'

Banni and several other women were waiting outside Ashlee's hut. 'Ashlee will not see us,' Banni informed Eesa. 'She says she wants to be left alone.'

Eesa put a gentle hand on Banni's shoulder and said, 'Then do as she wishes, Banni. You also wanted to be alone when you lost Jared. She will be wanting someone to talk to in time, but for now you will all do best for her by going back to your work.'

Banni and her companions accepted Eesa's wisdom. They asked her to tell Ashlee how sorry they were to hear of her loss, then they withdrew, leaving Eesa, Amarti and Tam to enter the hut. Eesa paused as she put her hand on the doorhandle and said, 'I think it might be best if I go in alone first. This is not easy for Ashlee.'

'That would be wise,' Amarti agreed. 'The girl and I will wait until you call.' Eesa entered then and closed the door.

Tam and Amarti waited outside the hut for a long time. They heard Ashlee sobbing, and once she screamed, 'Get out and leave me alone!', a cry that startled Tam. She looked at Amarti.

'She does not mean that, girl,' said the fisherwoman. 'It is the anger and the fear she is feeling. It will pass.'

'Perhaps we should leave her alone for now, like mother said,' Tam suggested.

'No,' Amarti quickly replied. 'No. Grief is needed, but it is something we must not let overwhelm us. Death is a part of life. That's what my old mother used to say, Procra guard her spirit. When my father drowned, I was no older than eight summers, and my mother missed him deeply. But she told me then that it was how the world went. She said, "Remember we are blessed with every moment of happiness, and it is those living moments we should remember when we lose a friend or a husband or a child to Shaddho's dark passing." I have never forgotten that. When she died, Varst keep her, twelve summers ago I think it was now, I said those words over her burial mound and at Watersdrop. When I think of her, or even what little I can remember of my father, I remember only the happy moments, the living moments. They keep the dragon grief in its place.'

Tam reflected on Amarti's advice. The woman surprised her. She had always thought of Amarti as the tough little crab her name implied. She was tough. She had to be as a fisherman's wife, used to hauling in fish whenever her husband needed help. But she was someone else inside her shell—someone softer, wiser, than Tam had imagined. The good thing about her advice was that it was true. When Tam thought of Gramma Harmi, she could only picture the good moments, the living moments, as Amarti's mother had called them.

The hut was deathly quiet for some time before Eesa opened the door and beckoned for Amarti and Tam to enter. Tam followed Amarti, remembering the woman's advice, but once inside she felt increasing trepidation, not knowing what to expect. The window shutters were closed and the main room dark. There was only sufficient light to reveal that some furniture had been overturned. Symon's corpse lay on the floor in the centre of the room. Tam glimpsed movement out of the corner of her eye. When she turned her head she spied a woman huddled against the wall. It was Ashlee. She was staring blindly into empty space as if she was totally unaware of her three visitors.

'We'll need more light,' Eesa said quietly. 'Tamesan, will you kindle the hearth?'

Tam was relieved to have something to do straightaway. She walked through the hut and out the rear door where a small lean-to housed a supply of firewood. She gathered an armful and carried it back to the hearth in the main room. Amarti had found and lit a lamp. A glance at Ashlee revealed the young woman hadn't moved. Within a few moments Tam had the fire alight.

'Good,' said Eesa. She and Amarti were kneeling beside the corpse. 'Now warm some water. There's a bowl to your right.' Tam found the bowl of water and placed it on a crude metal stand designed to suspend containers above the fire.

When the water began to steam she lifted it from

the fire, using a heavy piece of cloth to avoid burning her hands, and carried it to Eesa. Her mother and Amarti stripped Symon of his clothing. They dipped cloths in the water and began to gently sponge the body, cleaning away the dirt and blood. Tam stared at Symon's face. Mercifully he had no head injury. He looked as if he was merely sleeping, and the care both women applied to cleaning him enhanced the illusion.

Ashlee started sobbing. Eesa looked at her as if gauging her mood and then said, 'It might be time she got some fresh air. Tamesan?'

Tam crossed slowly to Ashlee and squatted before her, but she was at a loss what to say. Finally she put a hand on the woman's arm and gently asked, 'Do you want to come outside?'

The woman did not answer and Tam sat waiting for what seemed a long and awkward moment. Then Ashlee wiped her arm across her face and staggered to her feet. Without acknowledging anyone, she stumbled across the room and out the door.

'Go after her, child,' Eesa instructed.

Once outside, Ashlee turned and headed along the path towards the northern end of the village. Tam caught up and walked beside her, but Ashlee made no attempt to talk as they walked. Tam respected her wish for silence. The pair followed the curve of Harbin Bay until they reached the second of the mountain streams that ran into the bay, the stream called Meltsparkle. Unlike Watersdrop, which plummeted into the bay as a waterfall, Meltsparkle cascaded over and through a conglomeration of boulders on a gentler slope into the ocean. The mountain that reared above it was called Varst's Bluff. Its sheer cliffs and steep slopes made it virtually impossible to climb except from the leg called Nakiades' Watch that jutted into the bay.

At Meltsparkle Ashlee scrambled across a narrow channel of rushing water onto a large boulder. She sat there, knees tucked under her chin, and stared across the bay's dark blue water. Tam stood uncertainly on the stream's bank. There was easily enough room on the boulder for two to sit safely, but she was certain Ashlee did not want her company. She even considered returning to the hut, but she finally plucked up her courage and climbed across the slippery boulders to sit beside the grieving woman.

They sat in silence for a long time. Tam patiently watched the ocean rise and fall, waiting for a sign from Ashlee that it was all right to talk. Sea birds wheeled around the cliffs and over the ocean swell, circling in the ever-changing spring air currents. The sun drifted in and out of the clouds, sending shadows scampering across water and land in an endless game of chasey. Tam remembered sharing this strange emptiness with Banni the night the dragonship returned the previous summer. She thought she understood how Ashlee felt now. The beauty of the spring day surrounded her, but, with Symon dead, Ashlee gazed upon an empty world.

'He wanted a son,' she murmured. She kept staring

straight out to sea. 'I could only give him two girls. He wanted a son and I gave him girls. Two dead girls.' She fought back a sob and it came out as a choking sound above the rushing water. 'He wanted a son and now he has nothing.' She hit her fist hard against the rock, but she did not cry. Tam gently touched Ashlee's fist to offer her comfort, but the grief-stricken woman turned swollen eyes on her and sneered, 'Why are you here, daughter of Eesa? What was my husband to you?'

Ashlee's anguish unsettled Tam. She started to say, 'A dragonwarrior—' as testimony to Symon's exalted status in Harbin, but Ashlee cut across her angrily.

'A pillager! A rapist! A slayer of children!' she screamed vehemently. 'A killer and a coward!' She burst into a flood of tears. 'All wasted!'

Tam was shocked by her passionate outburst. She didn't understand why Ashlee was so bitter towards Symon. She tried again to coax the woman into a calmer emotional state by saying, 'Your husband was a dragon slayer. Everyone in Harbin knows that.'

'No-one knows that!' Ashlee howled. 'No-one! It's all a lie, one horrible big lie! And it killed my husband. It killed him as sure as that stupid ship. They say they go to hunt dragons! There are no dragons!' Ashlee's final revelation stunned Tam. The woman stared at her through tear-stained eyes, still sobbing, trying to catch her breath. Her mouth twisted in utter contempt and she snarled, 'Be as sorry for me as you like, little girl. It doesn't matter. I don't care any more. Nothing matters. Just leave me alone. Hear me? *Leave me alone!*'

Tam needed no further prompting. The fierce expression in Ashlee's eyes was murderous. She scrambled off the rock and walked away from the bank. A few paces on she stopped and looked back. Ashlee was staring out to sea again. The sea breezes toyed with her mass of dark hair but she seemed oblivious to the external world. Tam so much wanted to help, wanted to take away the pain, but Ashlee denied her that. She had never seen anyone look so maddened. She shivered, clutched her arms to her breast, and slowly walked back to the hut where Eesa and Amarti were still attending to Symon's corpse.

That night, and several nights thereafter, Tam struggled to get a restful sleep. Ashlee haunted her dreams. Sometimes she dreamt she stood on Nakiades' Watch looking into the bay, watching the dragonship drifting on the ocean. She could see Symon, clean and silent, standing on the prow of the dragonship, the way her father normally did. And then a creature, a dragon, would sweep out of the sky with a screaming banshee wail and breathe a ball of fire over the ship, engulfing it all. Every time the dragon creature turned its head towards Tam its face changed and became Ashlee's face, a strangely twisted reptilian version of it, with one big golden eye staring at her. And the dragon face would scream, 'It's all a lie! A lie! There are no dragons!' before it vanished. At other times she dreamed Chasse stood on the ship. Tam was beside him, on the deck, and Symon too, though he lay under a white shroud. And then Ashlee would appear. 'Killer!' she would scream. 'Child-slayer!' Tam could see it was Ashlee but Chasse always declared she was a dragon and he would throw his spear at her just as she screamed her haunting words, 'It's a lie. All a lie!' And Tam could do nothing but watch in horror.

The Words of Passage for Symon were sung five days after his burial. Ashlee stood silently staring over Watersdrop throughout the ceremony, spoke to no-one, and went home alone, refusing visitors. A week later, on the eve of Varst's Great Feast, which heralded the start of summer and the departure of the dragonship on its annual quest, Ashlee's body was discovered by a fisherman, washed up amongst the rocks at the base of Watersdrop. Kevan postponed the Feast for one day while the villagers mourned the tragedy.

Chapter Twenty

Varst's Great Feast was the highest event of the year. Fresh spring berries and nuts were gathered and made into sweetmeats, bread and cakes baked and decorated, and fattened young goats and chickens slaughtered for the feast. The Long Hall was furnished with a central table for the Dragon Fang, embellished to represent the dragonship, and surrounding tables were set up for the common folk. Eesa directed a group of younger women, Tam included, in the construction of a pseudo dragon from goatskins, feathers, and dried grass. The dragon would be paraded before the village assembly in the Long Hall and then 'killed' in a ritual battle by the initiate warriors. The young warriors took the entire day to attire themselves in their new armour. This was their last appearance before they departed on the summer journey into manhood, and they wanted to look as handsome as possible.

Tam enjoyed the busy time preparing for the feast, and the night's celebration buoyed her spirit. There was an enormous bounty of food and mead, and endless dancing and singing. The women and girls laughed uproariously at the young men parading before a very drunken dragon carried by Theo and four senior warriors. When the initiates finally moved in for the ceremonial kill, the disoriented dragon lost its balance and collapsed in a chaotic heap. There were promises made, oaths sworn, and the Dragon Heart priest offered up a series of prayers to Varst the Almighty, to his bountiful wife Procra, to their warrior son Ecg, and to their beautiful daughter Fler. The villagers broke into traditional ballads about the voyage of Nakiades and the summer journeys of the great dragon Arkamroth. Tam was swept along by all the merriment, and enjoyed herself far more than she had for a long time.

When the night wore on, and the warriors made their ceremonial farewell, Tam was overcome by a deep sadness that brought her to tears. Her brother Chasse, so tall and so handsome in his shining armour, was going away. The brother she loved was leaving and would never return. In his place would be a new Chasse, a stranger she had already glimpsed in the moments since winter's end. He would be a young man, a man who had travelled on the dragon-ship and seen the glory of battle with a dragon. She cried, and then looked around shamefully, fearing others had seen her crying when there was so much pride and happiness in the celebration. But she saw she was not alone in her sadness. Other women were crying, too—mothers, daughters, sisters—all feeling their impending loss, sharing their fears and hopes for the men who were sailing away. Tam felt a hand on her shoulder and turned to find her mother beside her. Eesa smiled and hugged her as the men marched out of the Long Hall.

The tide and breeze called the Dragon Fang to their ship well before the sun rose above the mountains. The womenfolk of those who were leaving huddled on the jetty in the dull grey pre-dawn light, along with a handful of children and onlookers. Some villagers were still asleep, warm in their beds or unable to stir from the after-effects of the previous night's long festivities. Farewells were shared; hugs, kisses, promises and tears exchanged.

Kevan reminded Tam to look after her mother. Then he hugged Eesa. 'Do not worry,' he said gruffly. 'How many summers now have I done this?'

'Too many,' Eesa replied and laughed softly. 'You just be careful.'

'There isn't a dragon smart enough to better me,' Kevan boasted.

'It is just as well dragons aren't very smart,' quipped Theo as he leant over Kevan's shoulder and winked at Tam. The men laughed.

Chasse kissed his mother and then stood before Tam. 'How do I look?'

'Handsome,' she replied. They stared at each other awkwardly while others bustled around them. Then Tam bent forward and kissed her brother's cheek.

'Take care,' she said. He grinned sheepishly and nodded. Then he turned and climbed aboard the ship.

Theo gave the order to cast off. Kevan mounted the prow as always, and fixed his eyes squarely on the distant dark gap between Nakiades' Watch and White Eagle Ledge. The Dragon Head of Harbin was proudly leading the Dragon Fang. Tam searched for Chasse amongst the dark mass of figures in the ship. He was waving, but to someone else in the crowd. Probably Kerryn. Would he choose her as his wife when he returned? Theo gave the order to row, and the oars slid noisily over the gunwales into the dark water. It was then that Tam noticed Marron. He was looking up at her. The semi-darkness hid his expression, but his eyes glittered, reflecting the light from a lantern hung on the jetty. She looked away. His attention was the last thing she wanted. Instead, she focussed on the figure of her father, tall and solid, as the ship slid away from the jetty. The summer journey had begun.

At the top of the steepest climb, where the mountain path levelled onto the plateau, Tam halted to catch her breath. She took in the magnificent view of Harbin Bay with its deep blue harbour and mountain sentinels. Far out on the western ocean a small rain squall scudded southwards. She wondered if it would reach the dragonship. The sky closer to Harbin, though, was clear blue, as if the gods were keeping the early summer rain away.

Eesa had relented and finally allowed Tam to visit the Herbal Man. With her father gone three days on the dragonship, her mother was more relaxed in her mood, at least towards Tam. Eesa was in fact too busy overseeing the affairs of the village in Kevan's stead to be overly watchful of her daughter. She reluctantly agreed that there wasn't any important work for her to complete that morning. So Tam made certain Jaysin was out and about, doing whatever it was the boy liked to do, before she climbed the mountain alone. She found him tracing alphabet letters in the earth behind their cottage. She informed him she was going up the mountain and that if he needed anyone their mother was instructing a group of girls on basket weaving in the Long Hall. Then she left.

She wanted to see the Herbal Man. He had not visited the village since the beginning of spring when he had brought her back down. She wondered whether it was because her father had told him she could not be his apprentice. That decision made her intensely angry. Thereafter, she had deliberately gone out of her way to appear to be the dutiful daughter while her father was home, but at every opportunity she revised the skills the Herbal Man had already taught her. She was finding it frustrating to practise writing or reading without writing tools, parchment or texts. And she wanted to learn more. As boring as the Herbal Man's lessons sometimes had been during the long winter, she nevertheless appreciated how different those things were from anything she could learn in the village. If she persevered, she could have skills no-one else even understood. She could be useful to the village, helping to heal and teach. After all, who would do those things after the Herbal Man was gone? He was an old man, possibly even older than Harmi. He was fortunate to have lived so long. But he had no children to inherit his skills or knowledge. It made sense that someone should learn from him, be his 'apprentice' as he called it. Why shouldn't it be her? If the Herbal Man could lend her writing parchment and some of his texts, she could continue to learn. Perhaps she could even convince him to visit the village more often and teach her there, if her mother and father were unwilling to let her visit him.

She had other important reasons for seeking him. More questions plagued her thoughts. What was really in the crystal chamber? Why did Ashlee echo the Herbal Man's belief that there were no dragons? Why had the Dragon Heart priest called Harmi her father's grandmother, for that matter? Questions. Questions without answers. She knew instinctively the Herbal Man held those answers. She needed to know to put her own mind at ease.

She wound through the fresh, rich forest that covered the plateau. The first time she passed through, she had been amazed how this portion of Dragon Mountain seemed to be a world of its own, a little paradise. Only in mid-winter, when everything was buried beneath the crushing weight of the heavy snow, did it not look any different from the rest of the mountain.

Otherwise it was full of greater life and vitality than any other area around Harbin. It had an air of mystery that pervaded everything about the Herbal Man.

As she entered the small clearing where the Herbal Man's hut lay, she was astounded to discover the hut looking relatively secure and tidy. When the Herbal Man had brought her down from the mountain, the hut had partially collapsed under the weight of the winter snow. Because it was merely a blind to the Herbal Man's underground living quarters, she assumed he would only partially restore the old hut, but the closer she approached the more she realised how much work he had obviously put into rebuilding the entire structure. It still retained its rustic appearance, a building poorly constructed by a layman, but it looked more homely, more lived in than previously. There was a bundle of kindling against the front door. Smoke drifted lazily from the hut's stone chimney, the only unchanged feature Tam recognised. She knocked, half-expecting an answer, although she wasn't surprised when no-one appeared. She wondered how the Herbal Man actually knew he had visitors if he didn't spend time in the makeshift hut. She tried the door. It was locked. She went to a side window. The shutters were partly open, so she peered in. The interior was also tidier than she remembered. The bed was made. The only aberration was the smoke drifting from the hearth—there was no fire visible. The actual fire, as she knew, burned in the Herbal Man's underground study.

She considered her options. Perhaps he was already on the mountain searching for herbs. She hadn't seen any sign of him during her ascent, but that meant little, as the mountain was so vast. She could search for the entrance to the goat cave and enter that way. Or she could climb in the window and go through the trapdoor. She decided on the last choice. If he was home, she was certain he wouldn't mind her inviting herself in.

She forced the wooden shutters wider and squeezed through. The floor of the hut had even been swept. The decrepit rug was clean, too—though it was very faded, and the design still incomprehensible. She edged it aside and uncovered the trapdoor pull-ring. It would be more polite to knock, she decided. She knocked on the wooden floorboards and waited. There was no answer. She knocked again. Still no answer. Perhaps the Herbal Man was out on the mountain after all. If he was, then there was every possibility she wouldn't be able to find him. Or he could be deeper in the hideaway and simply hadn't heard her knocking. She lifted the trapdoor.

The Herbal Man wasn't in his study or his bedroom. A candle clock burned in the study and a lantern lit the bedroom area. The customary books lay open on the bench top. Tam guessed the Herbal Man wasn't far away since he had left a lantern alight. She checked the storeroom without success, then noticed that the door leading to the inner corridor was slightly ajar. Perhaps he was with the goats, or up on the higher mountain ledge overlooking Harbin. She opened the door and stepped through.

As she approached the three doors at the end of the corridor a thrill of fear whipped along her spine. The door to the crystal room was open. She hesitated, unsure what she might find, remembering flashes of her last experience on the night of Blitzart's Feast. Then she took a deep breath and entered.

The crystal chamber was dark, but a pale orange glow filled the far wall. Except there was no far wall. The golden tessellated structure she had seen the last time she entered the crystal chamber simply wasn't there. Her curiosity aroused, she walked cautiously around the pedestal that held the shallow bowl of water. The glow from the space that had previously been a wall barely touched the crystalline structures in the chamber, but it revealed that a great emptiness lay beyond. She approached it nervously. Nothing was what it seemed in this strange chamber. When she reached the gap, she peered into a massive space. What she saw made her gasp.

Beyond the missing wall lay a chamber, wider and deeper than Tam would have believed possible. The floor she stood on dropped several metres to a lower level. The new space was curved and smooth, like the cave the Herbal Man had shown her where the Dawn People lived, but this one was so much larger, and the walls were stained with streams of multicoloured rock. The soft glow in the giant chamber radiated from a ball of apricot light floating a metre below the ceiling. She saw the Herbal Man, too, standing near the centre of the chamber, dressed in white and gold robes, his long white hair flowing grandly about his shoulders. But what amazed her most of all, was the creature curled before him. It was huge and scaly, its skin like that of a snake, but its body was more like a four-legged creature, a lizard almost, with a long raking tail that curled around it and along the edge of the chamber. A pair of delicate bat-like wings lay folded along its back. In the apricot glow, its scales were russet-coloured, and in patches under its belly and along its muzzle, the darker colour faded into golden hues. The creature lay before the Herbal Man expectantly, obediently, its great golden eyes fixed on him in adoration.

Tam had never seen a dragon. She had heard the warriors tell tales of the dark—or red, or green—winged creatures that swept through the sky, breathing fire on unfortunate victims, ripping apart villages with their sharp talons and teeth like spears. They were mindless, voracious reptiles that struck fear into hearts, and ignited vengeance in the minds of the dragonwarriors. But now she was sure she was gazing down on a dragon, a creature from Nakiades' legends. Her fear struggled with fascination as she stared. She was rooted to the spot, unable to run, unable to speak, caught like a mesmerised mouse under the stare of a death cat, so awesome was the vision before her. There was a dragon. It lived in the mountain above her home. And the Herbal Man was talking to it as if it was nothing more than one of Galt's goats. And it was so terrifyingly beautiful.

She lost all sense of time. She didn't know how long she stood staring into the great chamber. Her mind was full of confusion and wonder. She realised why the wall had disappeared. There never had been a wall on this side of the crystal chamber. What she had seen, the tessellated pattern, the oddly curved wall, was the dragon's flank, pressed against the chamber. The great golden eye she glimpsed on Blitzart's Feast was the dragon's eye. She shivered. It had seen her that night! The dragon had stared straight at her. She felt a spinning touch of vertigo and fought to refocus her mind. This was no dream. There *was* a dragon. And it was looking up at her now with those great golden eyes. They were so deep, so liquid. The Herbal Man was staring at her, too. He started to walk towards her. Terror outstripped her fascination. She was suddenly seized with an irresistible desire to run, to run home to safety, to escape this instant of living nightmare.

'Te-Amen-San,' a deep voice whispered. '*Eswyllyion fay Te-Amen-San. Ilya ta'est.*'

She felt her fear melting, smoothed away by the voice. The words were strange, but she heard her name in them. The voice was speaking in the old language, the language of ancient Nakiades' homeland, the words only the Dragon Heart knew.

'*Eswyllyion fay Te-Amen-San.* Do not be afraid.' The dragon stared up at her with eyes like languid pools of fire and she was not afraid any more.

Chapter Twenty-One

'She won't hurt you, Tamesan,' promised the Herbal Man. Tam wasn't so sure. She eyed the dragon's protruding fangs. A golden eye blinked. Even though she was standing in the upper chamber with the Herbal Man beside her, the presence of the dragon was unnerving. 'Perhaps you will feel better if we go back to the study,' he suggested.

'No,' she replied, getting enough courage to take her eyes off the dragon. 'Here is fine.'

'As you wish,' the old man said. 'Watch your eyes a moment.' He passed his hand over a small crystal embedded in the wall. It instantly gave a pulse of brilliant white that set every other crystal in the ceiling aflame. The chamber burst into light. It initially hurt Tam's eyes, but she rubbed them until they adjusted to the luminosity.

'How—how did you do that?' she asked.

'It's simple art,' explained the Herbal Man. 'The ignis crystal in the wall there has a self-generating energy structure that responds to touch because it's so unstable, and the light it gives off when it's activated is reflected in the crystal structures of all the other lumin gems in the ceiling.'

She nodded wisely, but had not understood the old man's explanation, although the concept fascinated her. Light without the need to strike a tinder, or suffer smoke, was a miracle.

'I didn't mean to sneak in like this,' she began to apologise. 'I only came up to visit—'

The Herbal Man waved aside her apology, saying, 'It doesn't matter, Tamesan. What has happened has happened, and I am not concerned that it has. In fact,' he added with a smile, 'I think it is the right time for it to happen.'

She looked at him with a bewildered expression. 'For what to happen?'

'This,' he said. 'You learning about Claryssa and me.'

Tam turned to stare at the dragon. 'The dragon is Claryssa?' she blurted in astonishment.

'Yes,' he replied. 'At least that's her pet name. Her real name is Ke-Ly'aar-Ees-Ar-Shem-Var-Del. It means "She Who Shines Like Gold". Claryssa is simpler to say, but not as beautiful.'

'You mean Gramma Harmi really did know about you and—and Claryssa?' she exclaimed.

The Herbal Man grinned. 'Of course Harmi knew about us. She even used to come and visit us.'

'How?' she asked. 'She could hardly get around the cottage at home.'

'It was a long time ago,' he answered sadly. 'A very long time ago. In fact Harmi wasn't much older than you are now when she first came here.'

'Harmi wasn't really my grandmother, was she?' Tam stated, remembering one of the puzzles she wanted answered. 'She was my great-grandmother, my father's grandmother.'

'She was,' he replied. 'I thought you knew that.'

'No. I only ever called her Gramma. Chasse and Jaysin and I always thought she was our grandmother. Father and Mother never ever said anything about it.'

The old man nodded as if her explanation made sense to him. 'Harmi brought your father up from when he was very young.' he explained. 'His mother and father both died when he was only about three or four summers old, if I remember correctly. That's why you never knew your father's parents—your grandparents.'

'How did they die?'

'There was a fever in the village. Almost half the people came down sick. Some got over it, and others died. Your father's parents were amongst those who did not recover. So was Harmi's husband, Leith. It upset Harmi very badly. She took a long time to get over her sadness, but she took in Kevan as if he was her own son and raised him alone. I think very few people in Harbin now would remember or even know the truth.'

'Why is it a secret?'

'It isn't a secret,' the Herbal Man corrected. 'Just a sadness.'

'How did Gramma meet you and Claryssa?' Tam cast another sidelong glance at the dragon.

The Herbal Man smiled faintly as if recalling a fond moment before he replied. 'Much as I met you, Tamesan. Very much like you. She loved to walk on the mountain just the way you do. You both look so much alike. She had long red hair like you, and the same green eyes. When I saw you for the first time I thought Harmi had come back again. It was uncanny. She was always in trouble for avoiding women's work. She stole away from the village to be on the mountain so many times that her father threatened to chain her up in the Long Hall so she couldn't get away.'

'Did he?'

'No,' answered the old man, and he shook his head gently. 'Not quite. Although he eventually banned her from coming here.'

'So how did you meet her?'

'By accident the first time.' He turned to stare into the dragon's chamber. 'You see no-one in Harbin knew I lived up here then. People sometimes climbed the mountain, warriors mainly, but I had no hut here then, only the caves, and no-one could find them. It was what I wanted, what Claryssa and I both wanted. Peace. Security. The world of people had been too cruel to us and we were getting older, too old to be concerned with the petty day-to-day routines of people. So I never revealed I lived on the mountain to anyone. But Harmi was different. The first time I saw her she did not see me. She was so beautiful you see, and I was struck by that. I must have watched her a dozen times without her knowing. She was the most beautiful girl I had ever seen.'

'Why didn't you just introduce yourself to her?' Tam suggested.

'I couldn't. Not at first.' The Herbal Man turned to face her, and she thought he looked unhappy. 'You see, Tamesan, I was already an old man, even then. A girl as young and as pretty as your great-grandmother was, wouldn't want to know a strange old man like me. And I was afraid that if I spoke to her she would tell others that I lived on the mountain, and then Claryssa and I wouldn't be safe any more. We would have to move on.'

'So how did you meet?'

'By accident as I said. I was careless.' He coughed, and said candidly, 'I was careless this morning, too, wasn't I? It will be our undoing one day I am sure.' Then he returned his gaze to the dragon's chamber, but his eyes seemed to be focussing on a scene Tam could not see. 'It was such a beautiful, warm summer's morning, not cold at all, so I crept down to bathe in a pool in Watersdrop. There's one trapped further up the gorge, further up than any people from Harbin ever venture. I went there because I thought it was far enough away to be safe. I was wrong, of course. While I was bathing I heard a voice. When I looked up it was your great-grandmother. She was standing on a rock, laughing at me.'

'Why?' asked Tam, surprised by Harmi's unusual reaction. 'What was so funny?'

'She wasn't laughing in that way,' explained the Herbal Man. 'Harmi was always happy, always smiling and laughing. She loved being alive. On the mountain she was happy and carefree. That was why she came here.'

'That's why I come,' Tam admitted. 'It's the only place I can go to be just me. I don't have to be a girl or a daughter of the Dragon Head or anything like that. I can just be myself.'

'You are Harmi's great-granddaughter without doubt,' the old man chuckled. 'Ah, but I miss her.'

'So what did she do after she saw you?'

'It was all rather embarrassing, really,' he confessed. Tam noticed his sadness had evaporated. If anything, she could almost see him blushing. 'You see I was, well, undressed. And where I had come from it was impolite to be seen undressed by anyone else, especially by a woman. But Harmi didn't seem the least bit offended by my—how shall I say—my indecency. And I wasn't coming out of the water. So she just sat down as comfortably as you like, as if she had always known me, and asked me to introduce myself. I had no choice.'

Tam could picture the moment. She would probably do exactly the same as Harmi had done. But she stifled her laughter for fear of offending the Herbal Man, and persisted with her questions. 'How did she meet Claryssa?'

The Herbal Man stroked his beard before answering. 'I took a chance, as I have with you. Harmi kept my secret as I asked her to, and she kept coming to visit me. I realised how lonely a life I was living here. Not that Claryssa isn't good company,' he said and gave the dragon an apologetic smile. The dragon blinked, and the end of her tail twitched. 'But you see, we think the same things. Our lives are inextricably bound together, and we have lived together for a very long time. It was nice to have someone else to talk to.'

'You talk to the dragon?' she asked, amazed by the idea.

'Of course,' he asserted indignantly. 'Why not?'

'I didn't mean to be rude. It's just, well, I mean I thought dragons were—'

'Animals?' he interrupted. She nodded. 'Far from it, Tamesan. All things considered, a dragon is the wisest and most intelligent being in the world. They know things human minds barely guess at.'

'Do you use the ancient language to talk?'

'We don't really use any language, Tamesan. Claryssa and I share our thoughts. If she wants me to know something she thinks it into my mind.'

'In words?'

'No. That would be too complicated. It's more like a mixture of pictures and feelings. It's the one thing wizards have tried to describe to each other for a long time, but really no-one has explained it successfully. It just exists, I think because it is something dragons know better than we do.'

'How did Harmi meet Claryssa?' She was determined to get all her answers now that the Herbal

Man was so open and so talkative. She might not get a similar opportunity.

'I brought her here,' he confided. 'That was the chance I took. Somehow I knew I could trust her. She was the first person in a very long time that I found I could trust. And I knew time for me was growing shorter. One day I would need an apprentice, someone to inherit from me.'

'Why didn't you choose a wife?' she asked. 'You could have had a son of your own to inherit your skills.'

'A son isn't necessary to inherit. A daughter would do as well,' the old man stated. 'Besides, I did marry, Tamesan. Twice. The first time I was very young. I was living in Yssaria. It's a long way from here. It may not even exist any more. The world changes so much in a wizard's lifetime. Eunice was her name. She wasn't much older than you, but in Yssaria a man did not choose a wife like your men in Harbin do. The parents of the girl selected a husband for their daughter. The man could only refuse if he was a soldier, or if he was of higher birth than the girl. Eunice was higher in rank than I, so when her parents told my master that she had chosen me I had to accept. Not that I minded. I was young, and a pretty woman's interest in me was almost a dream come true. We had seven children.'

'What happened to them?'

'War. Yssaria was invaded by the Empire of Asharkaan. While I was away, serving Prince Alund, the Asharkaan cavalry pillaged my family's town of Gathis and put every person to death, even babies.'

Tam suddenly felt she had asked too much. 'I'm sorry. I didn't mean to pry.'

'I do not mind, Tamesan,' the old man reassured her quietly. 'Although I still grieve for them, it was a long time ago, and I know grieving does not change things.' He paused as if thinking deeply. Then he said, 'My second marriage came when I was made High Wizard to the Queen of Marigan. I was a much older man by then, and I had seen the Asharkaan Empire rise and fall. The Queen insisted her High Wizard be married to an important lady, so she arranged a wedding with Lady Elisabet. There was no courtship, no sharing of vows before the ceremony. I hardly knew the woman. She told me on the night of our wedding that she did not want to live with an old man. I told her I was sorry and that it was not my choice. I should never have said that. It made her all the more bitter.'

'That must have been terrible for you,' said Tam, imagining what it would be like to be forced to accept Marron if he didn't like her as much as she didn't like him.

'It was terrible for us both,' the old man conceded. 'We kept up a public facade for the Queen, but we went our separate ways whenever we could. She spent all her time with her court friends, and I, well I was studying too much. Claryssa and I had so much to teach other.' He paused again, recalling a moment in his life, and a wry grin appeared on his face. 'It was almost amusing that Elisabet became jealous of Claryssa.'

'And you had no children,' concluded Tam.

'We did, actually,' he admitted, and shook his head. 'Don't ask me to explain how these things happen. It would be improper of me. But Elisabet and I had two children, a boy and a girl. The boy, Mark, grew up to be a soldier I think. I never saw him after he turned eight. You see, in Marigan, boys born into the middle class, and some higher social ranks, are taken from their parents at eight and trained in the public barracks to be soldiers. Mark was taken away according to the law. I thought it was a barbaric practice, I still do, but Elisabet was proud to mother a soldier for the kingdom.'

'What happened to the girl?'

'Jennett was sacrificed on the Holy Altar to the Goddess Ite.' There was more than a hint of bitterness in his words.

Tam was shocked. 'Sacrificed? You mean like the goats at Varst's Great Feast?'

'Probably. Elisabet arranged it all.' The old man shuffled his feet and shifted to stare into the shimmering water in the top of the pedestal. 'To be chosen as a sacrificial virgin for the annual ceremony was to be accorded the highest honour in Marigan,' he continued. 'The families of the sacrificial virgins were feted throughout the kingdom and given a new social rank, second only to the Werelords, who owned enormous tracts of land. It meant a lifetime annuity that enabled the parents and the remaining family to live very comfortably.'

'Couldn't you stop it?' she asked. She felt so sorry for him now. She wished she hadn't pried. The world had not been kind to the old man.

'I tried, Tamesan. But it wasn't that easy,' he said, and shrugged his shoulders. 'You see I wasn't just fighting the Queen or Elisabet. I was fighting a whole social order, and a history. People in Marigan believe sacrificial virgins enter the Eternal Realm of Ite's Paradise, and serve the Goddess herself as handmaidens. Even Jennett believed it. She didn't want me to interfere. I couldn't stop the thing from happening.'

'What happened to Elisabet?'

'I outlived her,' he replied soberly. 'After Jennett's sacrifice, she had the status and freedom to do whatever she pleased. We saw very little of each other. I went to her funeral. Then the world changed, as I told you once before, and wizards were outlawed. I had to leave the kingdom. I spent many years moving around, searching for somewhere for Claryssa and me to settle. Finally we came here.'

'Did you ask Harmi to be your apprentice?' she asked.

The Herbal Man chuckled again, and said, 'Almost. But I knew the time wasn't right. Something else happened as well, something I only found out about by chance. It's not relevant you should know, only that in answer to your question it changed everything, and I didn't ask her.'

'Did she tell the others about you? Is that what happened?'

The Herbal Man laughed. 'No. Well, not exactly. Circumstances made us break our secret. Harmi's mother, your great-great-grandmother, became very ill, so ill that everybody in the village believed she was going to die. Harmi was very upset. As much as she fought with her mother, she loved her dearly all the same. She came to me and asked if I knew any remedies to help. She felt ashamed to ask, because she knew if I helped it would give away my secret existence here. What could I do?' he asked and lifted his eyebrows in mock exasperation. 'I loved your great-grandmother. I couldn't stand back and let her watch her mother die, especially when I might be able to prevent it. So I went down to the village with her, and I attended her mother. She had a fever I recognised. With Harmi's help, I found the herbs I needed to make up an elixir that would bring down her temperature and improve her chances of survival. Anyway, it worked.'

'But what did the people in the village say?'

'Most of them were amazed. A few were suspicious. Then Harmi concocted this story that I had been washed ashore from a shipwreck out on the western ocean, and had trekked across the mountains around Harbin Bay, searching for help, when she found me wandering on Dragon Mountain. It was an utterly absurd story, but no-one doubted it. I was even invited by the Dragon Head of the time to live in the village. Naturally, because of my hideaway, and Claryssa, I declined, and kept up the charade that I was a grumpy old man who preferred a hermit's life. I had to build the hut on the plateau as a result, and pretend it was my home. That's how things have stayed ever since.'

'And Gramma?'

'She visited when she could. But, because I'd helped during her mother's sickness, people knew who I was, so she couldn't come as often as she wanted. Then her father intervened and she stopped coming altogether.'

'But you had helped to save her mother's life. Her father even offered you a place to live in the village,' Tam pointed out.

'He was not being ungrateful, Tamesan. That was what I meant when I said the circumstances changed. Harmi had come of age. She was chosen by Leith to be his wife and it was no longer right for her to come here.'

'But why not? You were friends.'

The Herbal Man shook his head and said, 'People gossip. They spread rumours when an old man is seen with a woman who already has a husband. They say cruel things. I could not let that happen to Harmi. Or Leith.'

She understood what he meant. Katris' barbs had struck deep even though they were lies. 'So Gramma never came here again?'

The Herbal Man shifted his weight onto his other foot. 'No,' he said. 'Not here. We saw each other when I visited the village, when I needed supplies or was asked to tend the ill. I was with her when Leith was sick with the plague. It was a terribly sad time.'

Tam heard the catch in his voice. Tears pooled in the wrinkled corners of his grey eyes. He raised his hand slowly to wipe the moisture away, and the awkward moment of silence that hung in the chamber made Tam regret asking questions. She was about to apologise when the Herbal Man slumped forward and just managed to catch his balance on the lip of the pedestal. The dragon's scales scraped against the rock, and Tam saw the creature's yellow eyes peer into the crystal chamber.

'Are you all right?' she asked, and moved towards the old man.

'I am just weary, Tamesan,' he explained as he straightened up. She saw how tired he really was when the crystal light lit his face. 'It's Claryssa who is unwell. I have been up with her most of the night.'

'What's wrong with her?' she asked.

'She's old, Tamesan, old and tired,' he replied. 'Dragons live a very long time, longer than most humans can imagine, but even their clocks burn out in the end. Age is her illness.'

'Do you mean she is dying?' she half-whispered, in case the dragon overheard.

'We are all dying,' the Herbal Man answered in his cryptic way, and then he said, without pausing,

'You have asked all the questions this morning. Before I ask you to return to the village, so I can continue attending to Claryssa, and perhaps catch up on some sleep, I have a question to ask you. Are you willing to be my apprentice?'

The question caught her unprepared. She knew he had already asked her father the very same question and her father's answer had been an emphatic no. 'Why do you ask me?' she inquired cautiously.

'Because Claryssa chose you,' he informed her. Tam turned to stare at the dragon. The golden eyes stared back at her. 'And I agree with her choice,' the old man added. 'You are intelligent, willing to learn, and a free spirit. You have all the right qualities.'

'But you've already asked my father,' she reminded him. 'He told me he said no to it.' She knew she was willing to defy her father's word, especially given a chance to do something she desperately wanted to do, but no-one else in Harbin dared oppose a decision by the Dragon Head. Was the old man any different?

'It is not your father I am asking, Tamesan,' the Herbal Man stressed. 'It is you. You must make the decision. No-one else can.'

'But what must I do?' she asked, still overwhelmed by the turn of events.

'What you are already doing now,' he replied. 'Learn. Ask. Try. Claryssa has accepted you. Dragons understand humans far better than humans often understand themselves. We have not chosen to offer you this burden lightly. It is a gift of our total lives' work.'

Tam looked from the Herbal Man to the dragon and back again. She was standing in a crystal chamber of light unlike anything she had ever dreamed could exist. She was standing so close to a real dragon she could hear its scales shifting as it breathed. She was talking to a wizard who made light appear from gems with a simple touch, a man who had lived longer than any person could possibly live, travelled further than any person could ever hope to travel, and seen more than anyone would want to see. A dragon had chosen her to be the wizard's apprentice, the same dragon Gramma Harmi had babbled about for years without anyone understanding what the old lady was saying. But she had known. She had known all along. It was everyone else, not Harmi, who was mad. And now the wizard wanted Tam to learn all he knew, wanted her to take his inheritance.

What choice did she have? What answer could she offer that wouldn't offend her father or the Herbal Man? Yet she realised she was being offered one chance at freedom from the monotony of Harbin and the slavery of being a dragonwarrior's woman. If she accepted, she might be able to break free of her shackles, and be what she dreamed she could be. One chance. And it was offered by a dragon.

Chapter Twenty-Two

The warm summer weeks drifted through their cycles. The mornings were crisp and fresh, the days full of blue sky and bright sunshine, the nights cool and calm. Just as Harbin had endured the harshest winter anyone could remember, so now it enjoyed a stable summer, punctuated only twice by passing rains. The fishermen slept away most of the days, their work confined to early mornings before dawn and late afternoons until just after dusk. The women and children, and the handful of men who remained in Harbin, constantly found time on their hands, despite Eesa's best efforts to create work to keep them occupied.

The relaxed lifestyle was a blessing for Tam. It gave her ample opportunity to spend valuable time in the Herbal Man's company, continuing her apprenticeship in earnest. To allay Eesa's mistrust, the Herbal Man visited the village more often than Tam went up the mountain. Nevertheless, Eesa confronted the old man the first time he visited.

'By Procra, you have a cheek interfering like this!' she snarled as she stepped in his path.

In return, he bowed his head respectfully and replied, 'I mean no-one harm.'

'You know very well what my husband's answer to your proposal was. The decision of the Dragon Head is law in this village,' she warned. She placed both hands on her hips to emphasise her determination.

'Young Tamesan is a very talented girl,' the Herbal Man answered politely. 'And I am a very old man. I am nearly too old to be doing what I do best. It would be a shame for me to die and not leave someone here in Harbin to do my healing work. Your daughter would be an excellent herbal healer. She has a rare feeling for the art.'

'That does not dismiss my husband's decision,' Eesa persisted.

'No,' he agreed. 'It does not. Kevan is the wise and rightful leader of Harbin. His word is law. But what harm can come of your daughter learning from me while the Dragon Fang are away? Kevan need not know, and by the time he returns much of what I want to teach Tamesan will be done for this year. Perhaps when he sees what she has learned in his absence he will rethink his answer.'

'You are asking me to let my daughter lie to her father,' she accused flatly.

'Who is lying?' he calmly challenged. 'I am only teaching Tamesan. She will not be my apprentice in the true meaning of the word. She does not have to come and live with me as her master. I will come to Harbin. I will make sure she does not shirk the work you require of her. The discipline will be good for her. Even you must agree with that.'

The Herbal Man's offer appealed to Eesa. Tamesan was certainly not the most disciplined girl in the village. The lazy summer weather only exacerbated the problem. But her husband had said no to the idea. What was she to do?

'I cannot go against the word of my husband,' she argued.

'Who is Dragon Head of Harbin while Kevan travels on the dragonship?'

Eesa's eyes narrowed with suspicion. The old man was playing games now. 'Kevan is,' she answered.

'On the ship with the Dragon Fang,' the old man agreed. 'But what about in the village? Who is in charge while he is away?'

'I am.'

'Can you make decisions in his absence?' he asked.

'Yes.'

'Then you can decide whether or not Tamesan may learn from me,' he concluded. 'Kevan said she may not be my apprentice. That is his word and you and I must abide by that. But he did not say I could not visit Tam or teach her what I know. That is a decision for you in Kevan's absence. Is that not true?'

Eesa was caught. The Herbal Man's argument made too much sense. She was in charge. He hadn't asked her if Tamesan could be his apprentice. He was not really going against her husband's order. Perhaps there was no harm in what he was offering.

'I will allow Tamesan to learn from you,' she decided reluctantly, but qualified her answer with, 'Only if you visit Harbin. And only if she does her other duties first before she wastes time with you. Am I understood?'

'The woman is the true leader in Harbin,' he announced with a gracious smile.

Eesa blushed momentarily at the undisguised flattery and then checked herself and added, 'When Kevan returns the matter is ended unless he is willing to change his mind. I am only acting as he would.'

'I understand,' the Herbal Man replied with a sober expression. When Eesa excused herself and walked away, he smiled and went to find Tam.

So Tam continued to learn how to read and write. The Herbal Man insisted those skills were the most important of all. 'If you can read, Tamesan,' he told her, 'every mystery, every truth that anyone has ever recorded, will open up to you. Reading is the secret to all magic, all power. Most people learn about the world through their own experiences, and that is all they ever truly know about the world, but reading gives you access to knowledge of other people's experiences. It lets you see the world through other people's eyes, through the words, to see things you might never experience for yourself.' He also expanded her knowledge of herbalism whenever they walked on the mountainside, showing her the plants that grew or bloomed in summer, and describing their uses as medicines.

While the Herbal Man visited, Tam found a third party seeking their company. Jaysin followed them everywhere.

'He wants to learn about reading and writing,' she explained after Jaysin refused to go and play as Tam had asked.

The Herbal Man's eyebrows lifted and he bent to speak to Jaysin. 'Has Tamesan shown you any of the alphabet?' he inquired. Jaysin nodded slowly. The Herbal Man handed the boy a stick, and asked him to scratch in the earth what he knew. With painstaking accuracy, Jaysin drew every letter Tam had taught him. The Herbal Man nodded appreciatively and said, 'Very good. It seems there are two of you who learn quickly, Tamesan.' He squatted and studied the boy's forlorn face. Dark eyes stared back at him. 'Do you want to learn more?' he asked. Jaysin nodded. The Herbal Man rubbed his beard as if deciding, and then informed Jaysin he could stay while there were writing lessons to be done. 'But you must practise everything, and you must listen to what your sister tells you to do when I am not here,' he ordered, a serious frown creasing his brows. Jaysin nodded emphatically, as if he was making sure the Herbal Man clearly understood that he would do anything to be involved in the lessons, and Tam witnessed a faint smile creep across her little brother's face.

The Herbal Man's agreement with Eesa restricted Tam to four visits up the mountain. He assured Tam it was a small price to pay in exchange for the opportunity to keep learning. She also had a new reason for wanting to climb the mountain—Claryssa. After her first encounter with the Herbal Man's secret dragon, fascination overcame her ancestral fear of the ancient enemy of Nakiades. Although the Herbal Man insisted her visits were to attend specific lessons based on how to use the equipment for his experiments, she wheedled opportunities to sit in the crystal chamber and study Claryssa's golden form while the dragon slept in the larger cavern. The dragon almost always slept, it seemed.

'Her age,' the Herbal Man informed Tam. 'It's the weight of all those years. She is so tired now. Dragons spend a lot of their time sleeping when they are young, but they sleep then because they want to. Claryssa sleeps now because she has to. There is so little energy left in her body.'

'How much longer will she live?' she asked.

'I don't know, Tamesan. But I fear her time is growing very short. She knows that herself. There's a wizard's legend that says dragons know exactly when they are going to die. Claryssa hasn't revealed anything like that to me, but she knows her time is coming. She feels it.'

There was so much melancholy in the old man's voice: too much. Tam avoided questions about Claryssa's health after that. In the back of her mind she remembered that the lives of wizards and dragons were inseparably bound. What would happen to the Herbal Man when the dragon died?

The summer lessons became more complex as the weeks passed. She tried to take in everything the Herbal Man shared with her, but it seemed too much in such a short time. Summer was quickly coming to a close. The dragonship would return within days, and her father would be home. Without doubt he would be angry when he discovered that Eesa had been so lenient concerning the Herbal Man's influence on Tam. Eesa kept saying as much to her in the evenings. She had never known her father to change his mind once he had made a decision. He believed only weak men backed down from what they said, and applied that philosophy to every decision he made. His justification was that a man worthy of respect never made stupid decisions in the first place. Tam and Chasse had both received that lecture enough times to memorise it. So Tam forced herself to learn as efficiently as she could while there was time.

Her fourth visit prompted her to ask the Herbal Man how he controlled the dragon. 'I wondered how long it would take you to ask that question,' he laughed.

'What's so funny?' she queried, annoyed that he found her straightforward question so amusing.

The Herbal Man saw her irritation and ceased laughing. 'I'm sorry, Tamesan. The question is a fair one, a good one. I only laughed because it's the question that leads to the answer all apprentices want from their wizard masters.'

'And what's that?' she asked. She had no idea what the old man was babbling about now.

He peered at her in disbelief, as if he distrusted her mood. His intense scrutiny unnerved her. Then he shook his head and settled on a stool at the bench in his study. 'Sit down, Tamesan,' he instructed quietly. Bewildered by his sudden serious change of mood, she sat.

The old man fixed his gaze squarely on her and asked, 'Do you know what magic is?' She shook her head. She had never heard of it. Her response appeared to surprise the Herbal Man even further because he hesitated before he continued. 'I had forgotten how isolated the world of Harbin is,' he began, and tapped the bench top with his fingertips. Tam noticed how long his fingernails had grown. 'Tamesan, in the world beyond Harbin, a long time ago, perhaps even before Nakiades led his people to settle in this wilderness, wizards were revered as powerful and sought by kings and queens and emperors to solve their problems. I told you all this.'

'I remember,' she replied.

'Good,' he said. 'But when I told you, I omitted a detail which I took for granted you would already know. Under the circumstances it might be well that I did.' He ceased drumming his fingers and squinted. 'I told you why wizards fell from favour.'

'Because people feared their dragons and the kings and queens thought they were becoming too powerful.'

'Correct.' He smiled approvingly. 'A wizard's

power is twofold, Tamesan. A wizard has the power of knowledge. I have given you the key to that part. But there is a second factor. It is called magic.'

'What is magic?' she asked.

'It's a force, an energy, an ability, and a burden, all wrapped up in one thing. It's the power to do almost anything.'

'Like what?' she asked. The Herbal Man was still making no sense.

'Like this.' He snapped his fingers. Instantly, a small green flame appeared, and danced on the old man's fingertips.

Tam gasped in wonder. 'How?' she squeaked.

'Magic,' he replied. 'Wizards could fly, make themselves invisible, heal with a touch, tear down walls, stop whole armies. With the right knowledge, and a dragon, nothing was more powerful than a wizard.'

'But where does the magic come from?'

'That is an excellent question, Tamesan,' the old man said. 'Most apprentices only want to know how they can use magic straightaway, and they are disappointed when they are told they must learn about the source of magic first before they can ever hope to use it. You see, to understand a thing you must first know its source.' He blew on his fingers and the flame disappeared. 'Wizards have studied the source of magic for as long as there have been dragons. What they discovered, much too late in the end, was that magic is a gift from the dragons. No,' he corrected himself, 'that's not entirely true. It's a burden.' He rose from his stool and paced the floor of the study as he continued his explanation. 'You see, there is something that makes dragons different from every other creature. Somehow their bodies and psyches create vast energy fields. These energy fields are wild forces that dragons have learned to control to enable them to fly, or breathe fire, or cast spells. At least that's how a wizard called Tarran once described it. When a dragon chooses a human to become its attendant wizard, the two meld as one being, and the dragon both gives the wizard access to its energy as well as activating the wizard's own mental and physical energy at the same time. A wizard then has to learn how to tap into that vast energy store, and direct it, without losing control of it.'

'But why would a wizard want to use a dragon's energy field?' Tam was already becoming bewildered by the Herbal Man's theory.

'To create magic,' he replied.

'But how, though?'

'Ah.' He paused and pulled at his beard. 'That is not a simple question. You see, dragons and wizards aren't the only things that have energy fields. Everything in this world has a personal field of energy, or an aura, as certain of my colleagues used to call the phenomenon. The art of magic is to identify and harness energy fields. Some, like those that surround most people, are weak. Others, like the four elements of earth—water, fire, and air—are vast repositories of energy. Alone, no wizard is capable of working anything but minor magic.

Even the most potent human energy fields lack the power to do more than work hypnotic spells, trivial illusions, and minor healings. A dragon's energy source, however, is infinitely greater. It provides potency, and the wizard provides control, as I said before. Magic is created when a wizard and a dragon combine their energies to alter the energy state of some other being or thing.'

Tam's mind was swimming in confusion again. Why did the Herbal Man always make everything seem so complicated? 'What would happen if the wizard lost control?' she asked, uncertain whether or not she should even ask such a question.

'He would destroy both himself and the dragon,' said the Herbal Man. 'At the very least he would bring a great deal of harm to them both. Dragons usually won't let that happen, though. They interrupt any outpouring of magic that can potentially put themselves in jeopardy.'

'Always?'

The Herbal Man kept his gaze firmly on Tam as he replied. 'No. Not always. Sometimes there is a need to take a risk. I've heard of it happening.'

'What happened?'

'I know too little of the details to describe it, Tamesan. Perhaps you will find it recorded in one of the texts in my library.'

She swallowed. Her mouth felt unnaturally dry. She summoned her courage and asked, 'Will you teach me how to use magic?'

The old man shook his head and said, 'No. I cannot. I will teach you all I know *about* it, but you will have to learn how to use it for yourself. You see, without a dragon of your own, there will be no magic for you to use.'

Each day thereafter, she contemplated the Herbal Man's theory of magic. Combined, a wizard and a dragon were able to generate magical power, and do wondrous deeds. But wizards were only created when a dragon chose them to be wizards. Claryssa had chosen her to become the Herbal Man's apprentice, but what did that mean? Claryssa was the Herbal Man's dragon. They were paired for life, according to everything the Herbal Man had taught Tam. So Claryssa could never be her source of magic. The Dragon Fang and her father never mentioned wizards or magic in their dragon-hunting adventures during the summer journeys. Perhaps the dragons further south were searching for wizards to adopt. If she could travel south on the dragonship next summer she might find a dragon willing to accept her as its partner. She laughed. The whole idea was absurd. Even if her father agreed to let her travel on the ship—and that would never happen in his lifetime—and even if she actually did manage to find a dragon, chances are it would eat her before she could introduce herself.

The Herbal Man's offer was a simple one. He wanted her to learn how to heal and teach the people in Harbin. The magic he spoke of was something else, something beyond her reach. It was a talent she might aspire to under different circumstances, but the limitations of her world were far greater than even the wise old Herbal Man could comprehend. She would have to be content with learning to be a very good healer and herbalist. Yet at least it was a better alternative than the Harbin lifestyle offered every other girl.

The sea-watcher's horn echoed from White Eagle's Ledge across Harbin Bay late one summer afternoon, its familiar resonance calling everyone. The dragonship was coming home. Tam put down the scrap of weaving she was adjusting for Banni, and followed the women, her mother included, out of the Long Hall. Outside, she stood with everyone and strained to see the blood red sail at the bay's entrance. A stiff sea breeze blew from the west, one that would carry the dragonship swiftly to its mooring. Eesa immediately issued orders to prepare for the ship's arrival. The dragonwarriors were coming home—the heroes—the husbands, fathers, brothers and sons of Harbin. Tam savoured the anticipation and swelling excitement in the village.

Eesa sent her down to the shore to help Amarti clean fish for the homecoming banquet. Last summer, the very same job had been set as punishment for Tam's tardiness. This time she accepted it as a sign of her mother's trust. Eesa knew she could rely on her daughter to help her old friend Amarti do the job properly. The summer, and the Herbal Man's lessons, had altered their relationship for the better. Tam knew that. She was confident now that her mother understood her ideas and attitude. In turn, she also felt she understood Eesa better. Perhaps that was part of the secret of reaching adulthood—learning to understand each other's point of view. Enthused by the bustling activity sparked by the dragonship's return, she sang a Harbin fishing ballad as she walked down the slope towards the fishermen's huts.

The dragonship swept across the harbour quicker than anyone predicted. Tam and Amarti stopped cleaning fish and watched its approach. The great red sail was fully rigged, and the ship raced towards the shore. As the distance closed, Tam noticed disconcerting discrepancies in what she expected to see. Although the wind blew from the dragonship's stern, the vessel heeled to port far more than it normally would. Then she noticed the sail's tattered condition. It had worked itself partially loose from the upper spar, and there were tears and rents across its face. A flicker of fear touched her mind. She turned to Amarti, only to discover the old woman's face mirrored her concern. Wordless, they left their tables and headed towards the jetty. Other villagers were already gravitating towards the shore. The three village herdsmen were running down from the pasture.

Clustered on the jetty, the people of Harbin watched with increasing trepidation as the dragonship bore down on them. At the last moment a warrior's voice shouted, the red sail dropped with a clatter, and the ship swung to run beside the jetty. Before the belaying ropes were tossed out, everyone saw the reason for the dragonship's hurried approach. A mournful cry rose. One woman screamed. Tam, momentarily caught at the back of the crowd, pushed through to see what caused the sudden ripple of anguish. She gaped in astonishment at the scene. The ship's watery bilge held the motionless corpses of dragonwarriors, their bodies and limbs caked with blood. Her father, Kevan, sat amongst them, cradling Theo's shaggy blond head, and weeping. Half the Dragon Fang had not come home this summer.

Chapter Twenty-Three

'Amarti, I want all the clean cloth you can find. Banni, take five girls and clean a bedding space in the Long Hall. Galt, find poles or some oars and make at least a couple of stretchers to carry the badly injured. Don't stand there! These men need our help!' Eesa stirred the stunned villagers into action. She boarded the listing dragonship and clambered towards her husband.

Kevan lifted sorrowful eyes and stared blankly. 'Theo walks the shadowed path,' he murmured. 'I could do nothing.' Eesa kneeled, and put both arms around her husband to share his loss.

Tam spied Chasse at the rear of the ship. He was staring into the water. At first she feared her brother was badly hurt in some way, he was so still, but before she could respond to her fear, he climbed out of the ship onto the jetty unaided. She pushed past people to reach him as he straightened.

'Thank Procra you're safe,' she whispered. She hugged him and was surprised how his body stiffened at her touch. 'What's wrong?' she asked, as she released him and stepped back to study his face.

'Nothing,' he grunted. 'I have to help the others.' So saying, he climbed back into the ship and started tying down ropes as if they had suddenly assumed great importance.

Tam remained on the jetty, watching her brother. What had changed him like that? Her attention passed to her father. He was being helped to stand by Eesa and Jon. A bloodied bandage covered his left shoulder, another masked part of his head, and yet another was wrapped around his left calf. It had been a terrible and costly fight whatever dragon they had found.

Eesa was signalling her. 'Fetch the Herbal Man, child,' she ordered. 'I don't want any of his excuses. Tell him what you have seen here and bring him back, even if you have to carry him.' Tam hesitated. 'Go at once!' Eesa yelled. She ran.

By the time she reached the Herbal Man's abode the sun had slipped below the western horizon and Dragon Mountain was swathed in grey tones. She was exhausted by the rapid climb. After she caught her breath, she knocked at the hut. As usual there was no answer, so she slipped in through the window and opened the hidden trapdoor. The Herbal Man was in his study. Tam apologised for her rude intrusion, and hurriedly informed him of the tragedy that had befallen the Dragon Fang. He agreed to come to the village, and then instructed her to collect certain containers and other items while he organised himself. Within a short time, they were both heading across the plateau.

The overcast sky hid what fragment of moon there

was. When it was obvious the descent would be dangerous without light, the Herbal Man produced a short walking staff and muttered a dozen words in the ancient language. An instant later a bright glow radiated from the staff. Tam could not contain her wonder. Then she recognised the glow.

'That's the light you used when you found me in the snowstorm,' she gasped.

'It has its uses,' the old man replied. 'In a storm, it's not affected at all by wind or rain. Quite practical, really.'

'Is this part of your magic?'

'A part. A very small part,' he sighed. 'Unfortunately it's all I have left.'

'What do you mean?'

'No time for talking, Tamesan. There are men dying,' he reminded her, and led the way briskly down the mountain path.

At the perimeter of the village, the Herbal Man extinguished the staff light and exchanged it for a small lantern he produced from under his cloak. 'We'll need to use this now. It would be difficult to explain the staff to anyone else.' He fumbled with a tinderbox until he lit the lantern, and then the pair crossed the goat pasture into Harbin.

The Long Hall was lit by a dozen lanterns and torches. Eesa, Banni and several other women knelt beside individual warriors, attending to their injuries. Tam led the Herbal Man straight to Eesa. She straightened up as they approached and frowned.

'You took too long. Vetch has died,' she announced.

'I am sorry to hear that news,' the Herbal Man replied, and bowed his head. 'I will look to where I am needed most.'

'See to Kevan,' Eesa said. Her tone was caught between an order and request. Then she turned to Tam and said, 'Amarti is preparing a small meal in the Warriors' Hall for the men who are not hurt. Go and give her your help.'

Tam was about to obey her mother's wishes when the Herbal Man stopped her. He spoke to Eesa. 'With your permission, Eesa, I would rather Tamesan remained here. She knows enough about the healing process to be useful, and I need someone to help mix pastes and apply poultices.'

Eesa glared at him, then at Tam. She shrugged her shoulders and declared, 'As you wish. I put what happens here in your hands, Herbal Man. I will help Amarti myself.'

'Thank you,' the old man responded. Then he beckoned Tam to join him.

As Eesa had asked, the Herbal Man went to inspect Kevan's wounds first, but the Dragon Head ordered him aside. 'My wounds need little attention,' he said. 'There are others more in need of your healing than me, Herbal Man. See to them.' The Herbal Man heeded Kevan's direction, but as he went to turn away, the Dragon Head grabbed his arm and held it tight. 'You have the life of the Dragon Fang in your hands tonight, Herbal Man. Do not fail them.'

Tam saw the Herbal Man glance down at the hand her father had placed on his arm, and then lift his eyes to gaze straight at Kevan. 'I will do all that can be done,' he said firmly. 'That is all I can promise.' He maintained his steady gaze until the warrior released his grip. Then he walked away with Tam in tow.

Kevan included, Tam counted fifteen dragonwarriors in need of healing. Most, like her father, had injuries that looked ugly but would heal with care. Ion had a nasty gash running across his upper cheek to his brow, and the cut had taken his right eye. Keegan's chest had a hole punched through it, but the gods had spared him major damage inside and, miraculously, the wound had not become infected. Four dragonwarriors were not so lucky. An older man, Frankton, had lost too much blood. He was already pale and unconscious and, according to Jon, had been that way for four days on the dragonship. Adrian had received a horrible blow which left a dent in the top right-hand side of his head. The wound was infected, and he drooled and babbled incomprehensibly. The men had tied him up to stop him hurting himself or anyone else. Fallan was in his death throes. His wound, only a small puncture below his left knee, was so badly infected the poison was already all through his body. He would be dead before the night was half over.

And there was Marron. Despite her dislike for the young man, Tam was shocked to find him lying amongst the seriously injured. His right arm was fractured in three places. A jagged bone pierced the skin just below the elbow. His father, Trask, had tried to keep the injury clean on the homeward journey. After the Herbal Man inspected the arm, he stepped back and shook his head very slowly.

'What is wrong, Herbal Man?' Trask growled suspiciously. 'You will make my son well again.'

'It is a bad break,' the Herbal Man conceded. 'And there is already poison in his arm. I cannot promise it will mend.'

Trask grabbed the Herbal Man's cloak in both hands and wrenched the old man closer. He scowled and said, 'He is my only son! Understand me? My only son! And you will make him better again. You *will* make him better. Or I will kill you!'

Tam reached for Trask's arm, but she was stopped by Jon, who pulled her gently aside before putting his free hand on Trask's shoulder. 'Let the old man do what he has been called here to do,' he said calmly. 'He will do what he can for Marron. He has promised that much. But Marron's life is not in the Herbal Man's hands. It is in Varst's. He, not the Herbal Man, will judge whether your son lives or dies.'

Trask gave Jon a murderous stare. He grunted to show his frustration, then released the old man's cloak. 'Be sure you do all you can, old man,' he warned before he stalked away. The Herbal Man thanked Jon for intervening. Then he set Tam to cleaning Marron's arm with a strong-smelling disinfectant while he went to inspect Frankton again.

Marron was asleep, but the instant Tam touched his arm with the damp cloth he jerked awake and screamed. She cringed as he turned his eyes on her. They were dark, wide, and wild.

'Make him drink this,' said the Herbal Man as he crossed the hall to help her. He handed Tam a goblet containing a watery green liquid. She took it, and offered it to Marron. Trask's son kept his eyes fixed on her and refused the goblet.

'You must drink this,' she coaxed, 'It will help.' Marron ignored her plea. Instead he made the error of moving his injured right arm and cried out in pain. She grabbed his left hand and squeezed it. 'Please drink this, Marron,' she begged. 'It will ease the pain.' With reluctance, he accepted the goblet and drank.

'It will put him to sleep,' the Herbal Man explained. 'The drink is called Jasmin's green cloud. It's made from the powder of a plant that does not grow locally, Tamesan. I've always kept a large supply. Lucky I did.' Marron's wide eyes stayed fixed on Tam for several moments. Then they glazed over as the youth slipped into unconsciousness. 'That will make the next part much easier,' murmured the Herbal Man.

'What next part?' Tam asked as she tentatively recommenced bathing Marron's relaxed arm. The sight of the protruding bone made her queasy.

'I have to reset the bones. If they're left like this he will have no arm worth using,' he explained.

'Make sure you wash every scrap of dried blood and dirt away from the bone, especially the infected area. And put a smear of Becchrin's cure over every section of broken skin,' he added. 'I will see to some of the others while you do that.'

Tam carefully cleansed Marron's arm. She wondered how he had received so brutal an injury—how, for that matter, the Dragon Fang had come to be so badly defeated. Perhaps the dragon ambushed them. Perhaps it had been harder to kill than any before. Perhaps it was bigger. She pictured a creature like Claryssa lurking in wait. She was a big beast, but lethargic. For all her size, Tam couldn't imagine the old dragon faring very well at all against the Dragon Fang. But Claryssa was old. Perhaps younger dragons were more ferocious. Perhaps the dragonwarriors had stumbled upon more than one dragon.

By the time the Herbal Man returned, she had done as he instructed. He asked if she wanted to watch him reset the bones or if she would prefer to do something else. She opted to watch.

'It is not a pleasant business. If you feel you do not want to watch at any stage, just go. I will understand,' he told her. Then he began his mending.

Tam winced for Marron several times as the old man probed and twisted the young warrior's arm. She nearly passed out when he forced the broken bone back beneath the skin, but she watched the entire operation, and helped him tightly bind the arm at the end.

'You are very brave,' the Herbal Man announced as they finished. 'The first time I ever saw this done I ran from the tent to be sick. You have more stomach for this work than I do.'

She accepted his compliment silently, but it did not quell her hidden distress. She took several deep breaths when the arm was finally bound, and then offered to attend to another warrior's wounds to escape the scene. The Herbal Man directed her to her father.

Kevan watched her approach. She read a measure of questioning distrust in her father's eyes, an emotion bordering on anger, but she pushed her own feelings aside to avoid conflict with him. When she reached him, she smiled, and asked to see the wound on his head.

'I take it my daughter disobeyed my instructions,' he muttered as he bent forward.

'You have been bathing these wounds in seawater, Father?' she inquired. She was not going to argue with him now.

'Yes,' he answered. He did not pursue his query.

She was relieved he acquiesced so easily, though she was curious why. He was tired and sore. Perhaps that quietened him. She unwrapped the bandage and checked his wound. Something had taken a chunk of flesh from the top of his head. His greying hair was matted with dried blood.

'I must clean this wound first, Father,' she informed him. 'Then I will do the same for the others. You have kept it from becoming infected.'

315

She attended her father's wounds efficiently, bathing them, applying ointment, bandaging them again. All the while, Kevan sat patiently and let her do as she needed. They exchanged very few words other than those necessary for dressing the wounds. Tam sensed her father's uneasy mood, though. Later there would be time to argue over her lessons with the Herbal Man. Later. When she finished, she noticed a change in her father's demeanour. He was very tired, exhausted, but he was looking at his daughter with a faint glimmer of acceptance, akin to pride.

'Thank you, Tamesan,' he mumbled. 'It feels better.'

'You need sleep, Father. There is a bed beside you. Sleep here tonight,' she replied. She helped him lie down and made him comfortable. In a matter of moments, Kevan fell asleep.

Tam assisted the Herbal Man throughout the night. When Eesa returned, she made warm broth for the Herbal Man and Tam to drink, and helped where she was most needed. At times during the night a sleeping warrior would cry out in fear.

'Why do they do that?' Tam asked the Herbal Man after one warrior howled in anguish, then immediately fell silent.

'They have seen things more terrible than they wished to see,' he replied. 'This summer's journey has cost the Dragon Fang dearly.'

Fallan died in the middle of the night. Frankton died just before dawn. Eesa sat beside Kevan's bed during the early morning hours and refused to sleep.

Tam battled her own fatigue. The Herbal Man told her she should rest but she insisted on remaining awake in case he needed her help. She moved amongst the sleeping warriors, mopping perspiration from brows, checking they were comfortable. She stayed with Marron when his sleep became unsettled. He moaned and writhed, caught for a long time in the grip of a terrible nightmare, and his condition filled Tam with pity for the young man. Eventually he drifted into a calmer slumber, and she moved on to comfort others. When the last lantern burned out, a sickly grey dawn light was already filtering through the shutters. The Herbal Man, exhausted by the night's long battle, shuffled between the makeshift beds, checking each patient as he passed, and found Tam curled up on a spare blanket at the foot of her father's bed, fast asleep.

Chapter Twenty-Four

Harbin was in mourning. It had not suffered so great a tragedy since the plague, and that was before most people were born. The Dragon Fang, pride and heart of the village, was torn apart. Of fifty-three warriors, including five initiate youths, only thirty-five returned home. Two, Theo and Vetch, had died on the return journey. Several were still perilously close to walking the path of shadows. Sixteen Harbin dragonwarriors, three of them on their first summer journey, lay dead in a strange land to the south. Only twenty-two had escaped relatively unscathed, and many of them carried minor wounds and bruises to show that the adventure's encounter had been fierce and bloody.

The women bore the greatest impact. Mothers, wives, sisters, and daughters were caught in the numbing web of loss. Those whose men had returned, and Eesa was among the luckiest, did what they could to comfort the families that had been devastated. Everyone's heart went out to Carmel. She had lost her husband, a brother, and her son. All three had not returned. News of her personal tragedy quickly spread, and women came to her hut to be with her, even some with their own sorrow to endure. The Dragon Heart priest sat with the mourners throughout the first morning after the ship's return, helping them pray for their men's spirits to find the path to Varst's Eternal Paradise.

Tam woke late in the morning, cold and stiff from lying on the Long Hall's floor. The Herbal Man knelt beside her holding a steaming cup of warm goat's milk.

'Energy,' he smiled. 'Drink it. You worked hard last night.'

She looked around guiltily. She had fallen asleep and slept half the morning away. The Herbal Man read her thoughts and said, 'Relax and drink, Tamesan. Your mother and I let you sleep. You sleep when you have to.'

'But what about you?' she asked with concern. 'Have you had any sleep yet?'

The Herbal Man waggled his head and smiled. 'The older you get the less sleep you need,' he said. 'I am so old, I doubt I will ever need to sleep again.' He pulled a silly face which made her laugh. She caught her breath and sipped at the warm milk.

A little later, after she had helped the Herbal Man tighten bandages and clean weeping wounds, she asked if she could find her brother Chasse.

'Of course, Tamesan.' the Herbal Man agreed. 'Find your brother. But be careful what you say to him,' he warned gently. 'What all these men experienced, he has been through as well. He may not want to tell you anything about it.' She nodded, and promised to return as soon as she could. Before leaving, she crossed to see how her father was faring. He was still asleep. So too was Marron.

Chasse was not at the Warriors' Hall. Jon met her at the door and told her Chasse had gone home. The news raised her hopes that her brother was all right. She headed for the bridge over Watersdrop and home, only to find that Chasse wasn't there, either. Neither were Eesa or Jaysin. She wondered where her brother could have gone.

As she considered her options, she walked to the side of the cottage, and stood under the honeynut tree. Chasse was sitting at the edge of the cliff overlooking Watersdrop. Jaysin sat beside him. Both were silently staring across the dark blue ocean towards the bay's mouth. She pulled a twig from the tree and joined her brothers.

She stood beside Chasse for quite a while, respecting his brooding silence. Then Jaysin suddenly got up and ran towards the village. His unexpected departure startled Tam, but Chasse remained rigidly staring out to sea.

'Father is sleeping,' she said. Chasse did not answer. 'The Herbal Man fixed Marron's arm last night as well,' she added. Chasse still did not respond, but she felt she had to talk, if only to keep away the dreadful silence. 'I cleaned and dressed Father's wounds. I think he was surprised I could do it. The Herbal Man taught me over summer. I am learning his healing skills.'

'Did anyone die last night?'

Chasse's blunt question stunned her. She hesitated, hoping he would say something else to divert her answer, but he remained silently staring across the bay. She swallowed and said, 'Fallan. And Frankton. Nothing could be done for them.'

'No,' he muttered. 'Nothing.'

She was at a loss. Her brother's mood reminded her so much of Ashlee's despair on the rocks at Meltsparkle. Suddenly feeling very afraid for him, she reached across and put her hand on his shoulder. He flinched at her touch, but he still said nothing. Encouraged by his passive acceptance, she moved closer, and put her arm around his shoulders. He was so much broader than she remembered. Then she felt his shoulders shake. He pushed her arm away.

'Don't mother me, Tam,' he insisted.

She was hurt and puzzled by his rejection. What little remained of their bond of affection was being deliberately severed by her brother on the cliffs above Watersdrop, and his strange coldness deepened her concern for him.

Chasse returned to the Warriors' Hall later in the afternoon. He told Tam he wanted to walk alone on the mountain, and then left without telling her anything more about the summer journey or disaster. Despite her expression of concern and love, he kept whatever secrets and sorrows were hurting him locked inside. Tam stood on the edge of Watersdrop for a long time, contemplating the veil of sorrow that had fallen across her village. Then she returned to the Long Hall to help the Herbal Man care for his patients.

There were several women there, relatives of the injured men. Marron's father was at the young man's bed. Marron was awake. The Herbal Man was asleep in the corner, but he woke when Tam leant over to check on him.

'I'm sorry,' she whispered hurriedly, 'I didn't mean to disturb you.'

'No harm, Tamesan,' he replied and stretched his arms. 'I've lain here too long as it is. There is work to do.' So saying he stood up slowly, stretching as he rose. 'The man Edgar is suffering from a strange ailment he must have caught on the homeward journey. I need some handfuls of the purple fungi your people call Seleserin's table. Can you find some and bring it to me?'

'I know where there's some,' she replied.

'Good,' he said. 'When you return I will show you how to make an elixir called Danso's breathing drink. Hurry, though. The quicker Edgar can have it the easier it will be to make him well again.' Tam nodded and headed out of the Hall.

It took her very little time to find the purple fungi the Herbal Man required. On her way back into the village she met her mother.

'Where are you going?' Eesa queried. Tam explained, then Eesa said, 'When the Herbal Man has shown you what is needed, can you go home and prepare a meal for us? I will get some of the others to cook food for the men in the Warriors' Hall, and for the sick in the Long Hall. I am going to spend a little time with your father.' Tam said that she would do as Eesa requested, and the two parted.

The Herbal Man's preparation of the medicinal elixir from the fungi was quite quick and easy. After he administered it to Edgar, Tam explained her mother's request and excused herself from the Long Hall.

Evening was settling across Harbin, painting the western sky pastel shades of apricot, grey and dark blue. Tam hurried. Little brother Jaysin would be hungry, and irritable because of it. Her mother had not yet arrived at the Long Hall, so she had time to organise the meal. As she reached the bridge over Watersdrop, she turned to look over the village. Her mother's familiar figure was entering the Long Hall. She knew how concerned Eesa was for Kevan. Despite their faults, her parents loved each other. Tam possessed an inner warmth knowing that. She shifted her gaze to encompass the rest of Harbin. Children were playing in the twilight at the water's edge, near the jetty where the forlorn wreck of the dragonship swayed idly. A solitary woman sat on the end of the jetty staring out to sea. From where she stood, Tam could not identify the mourner, but her heart went out to the lonely woman. So much heartache burdened the people. It would take a long time for their scars to heal. No-one else moved in the village. The paths were empty, silent. There weren't even any fishing boats bobbing in the bay. Only a string of grazing goats dotted the outer pasture near the forest fringe, oblivious to their masters' sorrow. Harbin was melting into the darkness.

The Dragon Heart held a long ceremony at Watersdrop to sing the Words of Passage for Harbin's twenty-three dead dragonwarriors. In the five days since the dragonship's return, five of the seriously injured had died. Frankton and Fallan were first. Then Denys, Patrik and Adrian succumbed to infections that were too far advanced to cure. Each new death tightened the grip of sorrow on the village.

Tam helped in the Long Hall as often as she could, and she saw the impact each death had on the Herbal Man. He worked tirelessly, desperately, to save the chronically ill warriors, and when one died he seemed stunned and exhausted by the loss, as if he truly believed he had the power to save them. She also heard the whispering discontent brewing in the village. People were suggesting the Herbal Man was to blame for the deaths. They whispered that he was a servant of Shaddho, that he was cursed, and that the men he touched were marked for death. The lies and accusations riled her, but since they were only whispered insinuations, she knew there was nothing she could say or do, except to be his friend and work with him. Distrust for the Herbal Man ran too deep in Harbin. It was a tradition.

Kevan was able to leave the Long Hall by the fourth day. Like six other patients, his injuries healed very quickly. Treatment the Herbal Man and Tam applied, with the help of the Harbin women who took turns working in the Long Hall, brought most of the men to rapid recoveries and made a mockery of the doubters. Although they were still bandaged, and limping or bruised, they attended the ceremony to honour their dead companions, and then they returned to the care of their families. Kevan insisted on speaking briefly at the ceremony. He paid his final respects to the memory of his lost companion, Theo, before exhaustion forced him to accept the help of others to bear him away to his cottage.

After ten days only one warrior remained critically ill: Marron. For four days after the Herbal Man had reset the young man's arm, he appeared to grow stronger and healthier. Even Trask's distrust lessened. But on the day of the singing of the Words of Passage, the Herbal Man and Tam returned to the Long Hall to find Marron groaning and sweating profusely. A quick inspection of the injury confirmed the Herbal Man's worst fear.

'There is a deep infection,' he concluded. There was bitterness in his voice.

'What happens now?' Tam asked.

'We have to work quickly and get him drinking draughts of Acton's curative. If the poison is too deep it will not be good for the boy.'

'Will he die?' she asked tentatively. Whatever

residue of hatred she retained towards Marron was subsumed by her concern for his life.

The Herbal Man frowned and replied, 'No, Tamesan. I will not let that happen. But we must stop the infection spreading. Fetch boiling water, please.'

The Herbal Man applied all of his attention to Trask's son, but when Trask visited, and learned that Marron's condition had worsened, the warrior was infuriated. He confronted the Herbal Man, as he had on the day the dragonship returned, and threatened to kill him if Marron died. Then he stormed out of the Long Hall, condemning anyone who trusted the words of foolish old men who thought sucking on plant juice would cure everything.

Marron's condition rapidly worsened, and word of the setback quickly spread through Harbin. Just before dawn the following day, Tam discovered the Herbal Man sitting beside Marron's bed, shaking his head slowly. Marron was still groaning, though weakly. His body was dehydrating because of the rivers of perspiration pouring from him.

'What's happening to him?' she asked as she crouched beside the old man.

'The infection in his arm is too deep. It's spreading through his whole body. The curative isn't working where it's needed.'

Tam sucked in her breath. 'Is he dying?'

Her question made the Herbal Man lift his face. He was drawn and tired. His grey eyes were sad beyond measure, and he looked older than ever. 'He will,' he answered slowly. 'Unless I remove the source of infection. If I do that, there is a chance he will live.' Before she could ask what he meant to do, he stood and spoke grimly. 'Bring your father here. There must be no excuses. Bring him at once. Every moment wasted now is a step closer to death for Marron.' Tam leapt to her feet, bolted from the Long Hall, and sprinted up the slope towards her home as the first morning rays set fire to the snow-capped peak of Dragon Mountain.

Kevan's injured leg hampered his speed but Tam had him at the Long Hall in a relatively short time.

'The girl tells me I am needed here,' he puffed as he entered. The Herbal Man steered him towards Marron's bed, describing the extent of the young warrior's infection as they walked. 'But how can I help?' Kevan asked when they reached the bed.

'There is only one thing I can do now to save the boy's life,' the Herbal Man explained. 'And even if I do what I think must be done, there is still a chance the boy will die. I need you to speak to his father.'

'But what is it you intend to do?' Kevan asked.

'I must amputate his arm.'

Trask burst through the doors into the Long Hall carrying a spear. Five men followed in his wake, looking as if they were trying to gather enough courage to grab the enraged warrior. A woman washing bandaging cloth for the Herbal Man near the door, screamed at the unexpectedly violent intrusion. Tam looked up and saw Trask's twisted mask of hatred as he raised his spear. She turned to warn the Herbal Man, but the old man was already at Marron's bed, facing the angry father.

'Get your Varst-forsaken filthy hands away from my son!' Trask bellowed. Kevan's bulk appeared in the doorway behind the gathering crowd.

'Put down the spear,' the Herbal Man very calmly requested.

'In Varst's hell I will!' Trask roared. He bent his arm to hurl the missile, but as he went to throw it, Kevan caught the tail end and held on. Trask whirled to see who dared to interfere. When he realised it was the Dragon Head, he swore and snarled, 'This does not concern you! Your son is whole! Go back to your home where you belong, and let this meddling fool who wants to hack up my son learn what it feels like to be struck by a warrior's wrath!'

'You are the fool,' Kevan said in a level tone. 'This is not how a warrior behaves. You lack courage.'

'*Courage?*' howled Trask. 'Courage? To do what? Stand aside while a doddering old man maims my only son? You call that courage?' He spat at Kevan's feet. 'Your kind of courage can rot in the eternal fires!' He spun and strode towards the Herbal Man. He grabbed the old man's cloak and threw him roughly against the wall. The old man grunted as the breath was knocked from his frail body, and he crumpled like a rag doll to the floor. Then Trask hauled him back to his feet, lifted him fully off the floor, and pinned him against the wall. 'Forget the butchering, you worthless bag of dragon dung!' he growled. 'When I've finished with you there won't even be enough left to feed to the fish.' Trask then raised his heavy fist. Something thwacked across the back of his wrist and stung his attention away from the old man. He turned to find Tam holding a broom handle. 'Back in your place, girl!' he jeered, and made a back-handed swipe at her. She ducked and rapped the broom handle smartly across his nose. This time the warrior howled with pain and released the Herbal Man. He spun to face Tam but met Kevan instead who had crossed the room with the other warriors.

'Enough, Trask,' the Dragon Head warned. 'Act like a man. You are a dragonwarrior, a member of the Dragon Fang—' he started to say to calm Trask's temper, but Trask cut through his words.

'A plague on your stinking words! No-one will butcher my son!'

'Then your son will die,' Tam said in a thin voice.

Trask's defiant eyes rested on her. 'He will die if I let that piece of dragon dung touch him!' he rasped and pointed at the Herbal Man who was fumbling to his feet.

'The Herbal Man is doing more for Marron than you are,' she retorted.

Trask's eyes flared with rage. He took a menacing step towards her, but Kevan stood in his path.

'Touch my daughter, Trask—' he growled and left

his threat unfinished. Several dragonwarriors closed in. Trask clenched his fists and spun to face the Herbal Man.

The old man bowed his head respectfully. 'The girl is right,' he said politely. 'Your son is dying and he will die. There is nothing that will save him now. The infection is too deep. And you are right. What I offer is not without a great risk. But it is all I have.'

'You wretched butcher!' Trask roared. He lunged. Other hands grappled with the warrior this time, pulling him away before he could catch hold of the Herbal Man again.

'Take him to the Warriors' Hall,' Kevan ordered. 'Keep him there.' He waited for Trask's head to be lifted so that he could look him in the face. Trask's eyes burned with hatred. 'If you have to use ropes to keep him there do so,' he instructed while he maintained a steady gaze on Trask. 'But if he is man enough, you won't need them. Now take him.' The five warriors restraining Trask escorted him, struggling, from the hall.

As he was dragged out, he screamed. 'You are dead, old man! Dead! No man harms my son and lives! No man! You are dead!'

Kevan waited until Trask's cries subsided before he turned to the onlookers who had witnessed the confrontation and said, 'Go back to your chores and do whatever you must do. The Long Hall is closed. The Herbal Man has important work to undertake. Leave us to help with what must be done.' The crowd of warriors and women and children shuffled out. Kevan shut the door behind them, leaving only himself, Tam, the Herbal Man, the woman who had been washing bandages, and the Dragon Heart priest in the Hall. He cast a cautionary glance at his daughter before he addressed the Herbal Man. 'Jon is coming soon. He has what you asked for.'

'Thank you,' the old man replied. 'This is not something I want to do.'

'We understand,' said the priest, who was staring at the pale, sweat-soaked youth stretched out on his bed of pain. 'Too often Varst directs us to do things we do not want to do. We are merely his servants.'

The Herbal Man smiled thinly, and then turned to Tam. 'I need a lot of boiling water, as much as you can make. And I need one lot beside the bed in a large container, large enough to fit an axe head into.' As she prepared to start her work, Kevan spoke urgently in a low voice to the Herbal Man. The old man nodded and beckoned to Tam.

'The last time I said this to you I was setting the lad's arm. This time I have to take his arm away,' he explained, making absolutely certain she understood what was happening. 'This is a terrible thing I have to do. But I have to do it. There is no need for you to be here. If you want to go, say so. There is no shame in not wanting to see this, Tamesan. Everyone here will understand.'

She looked straight at her father. His craggy face was as tired and drawn as the Herbal Man's. His eyes were asking her to leave. Perhaps it was because he believed it wasn't the right place for a girl. Perhaps he was just concerned for her. Perhaps both. What was about to happen to Marron was terrifying to imagine. She had seen as much fear as anger in Trask's eyes as he was dragged out. Grown men were afraid of the thing she would witness if she stayed. But it was her decision. She also knew that. She would be responsible for what she chose to do. Her father was even prepared to let her make that choice. She was ready to do that. She looked back at the Herbal Man and shook her head.

'I will stay,' she announced quietly.

Chapter Twenty-Five

'He took his arm, didn't he?'

Tam studied Chasse before she answered. Her brother's face was hard, angry. 'He had to,' she said. 'Marron would have died otherwise.' But she sensed the familiar air of ingratitude in her brother's mood that was infecting others in Harbin against the Herbal Man for cutting off Marron's arm, and it disappointed her.

'I'd rather be dead than left with one arm,' Chasse muttered.

'Don't say that. Being dead is forever. Nothing is as bad as being dead.'

'Being useless is worse than being dead,' he retorted. 'What's Marron going to do with one arm? He can't be a warrior any more.'

'He could become a fisherman,' she suggested.

'How's he going to pull the lines or nets in when they're heavy and full and slippery, with one arm?'

'He could be a herdsman, or a sea-watcher on White Eagle Ledge.'

'Marron?' snorted Chasse. 'Marron lives to be a dragonwarrior. He won't accept anything less than that.'

Tam considered his statement. It was true. Marron would not cope. His whole life had been dedicated to becoming a dragonwarrior. 'He proved himself, at least,' she offered. 'At least he fought the dragon. It took his arm, but he faced it.'

An ironic snigger escaped Chasse's lips. The sound drew her attention back to his face, but his eyes stared up at the mountain. Since returning, Chasse's mood had been negative, sour. The happy youth who had been her brother and friend had sailed away. The young man who returned was bitter and secretive. The change in her brother had been far worse than she had expected. 'Why did you laugh like that?' she asked.

'It is nothing, Tamesan,' he replied.

'No,' she countered. 'It wasn't nothing. Why did you do it?'

'Because I felt like it,' he snapped and glared at her. 'Do I have to explain everything I do to you?'

His angry reaction startled her, but she recovered her nerve. He had been constantly avoiding the issue since coming home. Now he roused her determination. 'I want to know what's going on, Chasse. I want to know why you've changed.'

'There's nothing to talk about. I haven't changed,' he said sulkily.

'Were you there when Marron was injured?'

Her change of tack momentarily caught him off guard. 'Yes,' he answered, then scrambled to correct himself, 'I mean no.'

'You didn't see the dragon?'

'Of course I saw the dragon.'

'What did it look like?'

'Why do you want to know?'

'I've never seen a dragon,' she explained. 'I've only heard the stories and legends. I want to know what they're really like.'

Chasse appeared confused. He knitted his eyebrows and seemed reluctant to answer her. He took a deep breath and said, 'It was big and, er, sort of,—oh, I don't know, sort of black. It breathed lots of fire.'

'Anything else?'

'What do you mean?' he asked.

'I mean did it have scales, or large golden eyes, or wings?'

'Yes. All of that.'

'Oh.' She was disappointed by her brother's lack of interest in describing the dragon. He seemed unsure of what he was saying. 'Were you scared?' she asked.

He glared at her angrily. 'Of course I was scared, Tamesan. You would be too if you saw a dragon.'

She smiled inwardly. Yes, she had been terrified when she first saw Claryssa. If only Chasse knew. 'Why didn't you see what happened to Marron?' she asked.

'Because it was dark and there was a lot of fighting and noise and confusion.' he replied irritably.

'Did the dragon surprise-attack the Dragon Fang?'

Chasse hesitated before answering. 'Yes. It wasn't

where we expected it to be. No-one expected it. All of a sudden there was a lot of noise and fighting and we had to get back to the ship. That's why I didn't see how Marron broke his arm. Now do you understand?'

She nodded. It explained why Chasse was so moody. He had not really had a chance to fight the dragon. Perhaps he didn't feel as though he was a true dragonwarrior because of it. 'You don't have to actually fight the dragon to be a brave warrior,' she offered in consolation. 'I think you are very brave.'

Her brother's eyes widened and then narrowed in suspicion. 'What do you mean?' he asked.

'What I said,' she replied. 'You've been on a dragon hunt. That makes you a dragonwarrior just like Marron, and even like Father. And there will be next time.'

'I'm not going any more.'

Chasse's blunt statement stunned her. She studied his face, but his eyes were staring into the middle distance again. Once again she couldn't help but recognise the same faraway sorrow she had seen in Ashlee's eyes. It worried her. There was a greater secret to unravel. She had to know the truth, whatever the cost. She couldn't bear to see her brother so tormented.

'Why not?' she asked gently.

Chasse muttered, 'I have my reasons,' and began to stand.

'Where are you going?'

'For a walk.'

'I'll come.'

'No!' he snarled. 'I want to walk alone.'

'You haven't told me everything,' she argued. 'You haven't told me why you don't want to go next summer.'

'Leave it, Tam,' he warned. His eyes glittered with anger.

'I won't leave it, as you put it,' she declared defiantly. 'I want the truth. What really happened, Chasse?'

'Leave me alone, will you?' he begged in exasperation. 'I want to be left alone.' He turned and ran towards the hillside. Tam was frustrated by his departure. Then a picture of Ashlee came into her mind. She chased Tam away when Tam had asked her to talk. Ashlee killed herself. Tam wasn't going to let that happen to her brother. Spurred by fear, she ran after him.

She caught up with him on the forested slope above Watersdrop gorge. He slowed and was climbing onto a rock perch, but when he saw his sister following he started to slide off.

'No!' she yelled. 'Don't run away. I'll just run after you.'

He swore and cried, 'I don't want to talk about it any more. Do you hear me? It's nothing to do with you.'

'It's everything to do with me,' she argued as she approached. 'You're my brother. That makes it to do with me.'

'Tamesan, you don't understand.'

'I want to understand!' she implored. 'You have to tell me.' Chasse moved to the edge of the gorge and gazed into its depths. Watersdrop churned through the gorge, swirling and foaming between and over the rocks. It mirrored the swollen torrent of confusion in his mind. Tam stood beside him and saw what he saw. She felt pity and love for her brother. She had to know what was eating at him.

'Talk to me, Chasse,' she pleaded.

'I can't, Tamesan,' he replied. His face was scarred with frustration.

'It's all right. I'll listen.'

'No. You don't understand,' he said. 'I know you'll listen. It's not that. I'm not allowed to talk to you.'

'What do you mean?'

'I can't tell you the truth. It's the Dragonwarriors' Oath. They make us swear it on the ship once we're at sea. We promise not to say anything about the journeys to anyone else in the village.'

Now she was even more confused. 'I don't understand,' she admitted. 'You mean it's a secret?'

'Yes,' he answered and shook his head despondently. 'A terrible secret. A lie.'

'But the men share all the stories at the feasts,' she argued. 'What's the secret?' Chasse cursed and kicked a loose stone into the gorge. It rattled against the rocks and didn't make it to the water. 'What's the secret?' she persisted.

'The lie,' Chasse replied reluctantly. 'The secret is the lie.'

Now her brother was starting to sound like the Herbal Man. He was talking in riddles. The secret was the lie. What did he mean?

'I don't understand,' she repeated.

'I told you you wouldn't understand.'

'Explain it to me.'

'I'm not allowed to.'

'I won't tell anyone else, Chasse. You know I won't,' she promised, hoping he would open his heart to her.

'But I can't, Tamesan. I really can't. I've sworn the Oath. I'll be punished if I tell,' he emphasised passionately.

'Punished? By whom?'

'The Dragon's Wrath.'

Tam knew what that was. Matters of law or dispute in the village were discussed and resolved by the Dragon's Wrath. It was a very special meeting between her father as Dragon Head, the Dragon Heart priest, and three older men chosen from the Dragon Fang. No women were ever involved, only men.

'How would they punish you?' she asked.

'I don't know. It's not been explained.'

'Chasse, I promise you I won't tell anyone,' she reasserted. 'You can't keep this locked inside. It's not good for you. Believe me, I know. You've got to tell me.'

Chasse ran a hand through his blond hair and sighed. He turned away, and took three steps along the edge of the gorge. She was afraid he had decided not to talk. She had failed to get him to open up. Then he turned. His face was twisted with anger and sorrow. Tears glittered in his blue eyes.

'They lied to us, Tam. They lied to us!' he cried. 'Even Father. They lied!' A wrenching sob burst from his chest. Tam was stung with compassion and moved towards him, but he suddenly thrust away from her and scrambled up the rocks.

'Chasse!' she screamed. 'Chasse, come back! Chasse!' but her brother climbed until he cleared the rocks, and then he disappeared into the forest, leaving Tam standing alone above the thundering gorge.

'He said they lied. What did he mean?'

The Herbal Man studied Tam's face intently as he always did when he was contemplating an extremely important answer. Then he stroked his beard and cleared his throat.

'You are right to be concerned for your brother. He carries an enormous burden. Perhaps,' he said, and then faltered as if uncertain of his thoughts, 'perhaps it is time you knew.'

'Knew what?' she asked. More riddles.

'Come with me, Tamesan,' the Herbal Man instructed.

'Where are we going?'

'No more questions. It's time to watch and listen only. You can ask your questions afterwards.'

He ushered her into his hut, down the trapdoor ladder, and through to the crystal chamber. Light flooded the space at a wave of his hand. It reflected off Claryssa's golden scales. The dragon filled the space that opened into the dragon's chamber beyond. The crystal chamber looked much as it did the first time she ever stumbled into it. Then she had presumed that the dragon's flank was an unusual wall. If she had only known the truth! The Herbal Man called for her attention.

'Stand at the Seeing Waters,' he ordered, indicating the central pedestal.

She approached and looked into the shallow pool in the circular head of the pedestal. A rainbow of colours danced in the watery reflection. 'I must have Claryssa's help with this,' the old man said, and he began to chant. His words were ancient, unfamiliar to Tam, the old words of magic. Only when he used Claryssa's full title—Ke-Ly'aar-Ees-Ar-Shem-Var-Del—was anything remotely comprehensible to her. She heard a gigantic intake of breath, and the dragon's scales heaved and shuddered. Claryssa shifted her bulk until she could bring her massive head and great golden eyes around to peer into the crystal chamber. The Herbal Man spoke very softly to the dragon, still using the old tongue. Then he turned to Tam. 'Claryssa agrees that I should show you the truth. She says you are ready.'

Tam looked at the dragon. It was impossible to read the expression in the creature's reptilian face, although the Herbal Man obviously could. 'I will stand with you, Tamesan,' the old man said. 'Claryssa and I will bring the Seeing Waters to life for you. What you will witness in them is the truth. The Waters cannot lie. Remember that. What you see has happened, exactly as you see it. Understand also, Tamesan, that the truth is often more painful than we would like it to be.' She went to ask a question, but the Herbal Man put his finger to his lips and shook his head. 'Later,' he whispered. 'Watch.'

As Tam watched, the colours in the still water began to shimmer, then fade. She was aware that her surroundings were dimming, growing darker. It seemed as if every source of light at the periphery of her vision was extinguished, so that she stood beside the Herbal Man in a circle of light. Everything beyond that light vanished. The water lost all its pale luminosity, becoming a well of emptiness; black, forbidding. Then it changed. Movement. Grey. It was dark. Shadows flitted across it, shadows of figures, a line of figures. Men. Warriors. They were creeping through a forest. It was night-time. The figures were familiar. One was solid and tall. It reminded her of her father. Another beside him could have been Theo. They were crouching in bushes, watching a fire. The fire threw its flickering light over shadowy buildings. People were gathering around the fire. Strangers. Some were eating, some talking, some singing. There were men, women and children of all ages. Families celebrating around a communal fire. They were happy. The scene made Tam feel content. It reminded her of Harbin feasts. Until a woman screamed. She was pointing at a man beside her, probably her husband. A spear jutted from his chest at a crazy angle. He staggered like a drunken man at Varst's Great Feast. Then he pitched, face forward, into the fire. As the sparks erupted and others screamed, the warriors in the bushes charged into the midst of the scene, flailing their swords and axes with bloody abandon. The men at the fire tried to fend them off with their own swords, or with burning brands, but the attacking horde swept over them, hacking indiscriminately at whoever got in their way. There were faces everywhere, strangely familiar faces distorted by masks of anger and the flames of the dying bonfire. Even as the fire itself threatened to die, the surrounding buildings suddenly erupted in flames, setting the night alight. Dark figures ran to and fro carrying torches, touching them to anything flammable. Then men with bloodied faces and weapons dragged the mutilated bodies of their victims onto the bonfire. The blaze grew, higher, brighter, spreading its light across the scene of carnage. A man stood apart, directing the ravaging warriors. His beard and hair shone like burnished gold in the light of the funeral pyre. He was a big man, strong, determined. The firelight expanded until it lit his face and Tam could clearly see his features. It was her father.

Around Kevan, the Dragon Fang was completing its butchery and destruction.

'It's not true!' she protested. 'It can't be true.'

'The Seeing Waters never lie, Tamesan. I told you that,' explained the Herbal Man gently. 'Besides, Claryssa and I have no reason to lie to you.'

'But they were killing people. *People*,' she repeated, as if she was trying to make herself believe what she had seen. 'Why would they do that? Why? They're supposed to be hunting dragons.'

The Herbal Man shook his head sadly. 'Would hunting dragons make it any different?'

'Yes. It would. That's what they're supposed to do. That's why the legend of Nakiades is so important. The dragons have to be hunted,' she exclaimed.

'Why, Tamesan? For vengeance? Is that what makes dragon-hunting so important? The men of Harbin sail away every year because they're trying to exact revenge for someone who died four hundred years ago? Isn't that rather stupid?'

'No!' she cried. Then she stopped. It was all so confusing. Every belief her village was built on, every value of Harbin, was being brought into question. Hunting dragons because a legend says it should be done seemed suddenly very stupid to her. But her father, and his father, and now Chasse, belonged to that. It was what made boys in Harbin into men. 'But why people?' she asked in exasperation. 'What did they do wrong? Were they hiding a dragon or something?'

'Those people did nothing wrong, Tamesan. At least nothing more than you or your people do in Harbin. They certainly weren't hiding a dragon. They just happened to be in the wrong place when the Dragon Fang came.'

'But *why* people? Why kill the little children?'

'Because there are no dragons left, Tamesan,' the Herbal Man said. 'There haven't been any dragons for more than a hundred years. Men wiped them out. They killed every wizard and every dragon.'

'But you're a wizard,' she pointed out. 'And there's Claryssa.'

'Yes,' he agreed. 'We are still here. But we have been very lucky. That's all. We ran away when the wars and the huntings started. We are the last of our kind. The last dragon and the last wizard,' he said with a hint of pride, but then he faltered and added, 'Except we are both so old now we are only shadows of what we were.'

'But there could be others,' she suggested.

'No, Tamesan. There are no others. The Seeing Waters showed Claryssa and me what happened a long time ago. All our friends and colleagues are dead. There are no more wizards and no more dragons. The Dragon Fang of Harbin haven't even seen a dragon since before your great-great-great-grandfather sailed on the dragonship. And it's likely even his generation didn't really hunt dragons either.'

Tam looked up and her eyes caught Claryssa's. The dragon looked immensely sad. Was she imagining the expression on its face? 'Then what Ashlee said was true,' she muttered. 'And Chasse. Chasse knows it's all a big lie. That's what he was trying to say. It's a lie. Every summer is a lie.' She hung her head and stared at the crystal water on the pedestal.

The Herbal Man put his hand very gently on her shoulder. 'I'm sorry it is like this,' he said, 'But I think you would have found out very soon anyway.'

'Do you know what happened to the Dragon Fang this summer?' she asked despondently.

The old man nodded. 'Yes,' he said. 'We have seen.'

'What?'

'Do you want to see?'

Tam shook her head. 'No,' she whispered. 'Just tell me.' She had seen enough bloodshed and brutality.

The old man cleared his throat and said, 'The Dragon Fang of Harbin have become too well-known to the villagers who live further south. Your people have preyed on them for too long. The southern people united and complained to their Empress many times. She finally accepted that the Dragon Fang's annual intrusions were a nuisance to her Empire's stability and its economy. So for the past five summers, with the assistance of Imperial soldiers, they have laid traps to catch the Dragon Fang. Sheer luck protected them from blundering into one of the traps until this summer. But this time, as your father and the dragonwarriors attacked what they thought was another unprotected village, they were ambushed by Imperial soldiers. The Dragon Fang was fortunate to escape so lightly under the circumstances. The men of Harbin are brave, but they are no match for Imperial soldiers.'

'I don't understand why my father and the others would want to attack people. It doesn't make any sense,' Tam muttered disconsolately. Too much had changed with the Herbal Man's revelation. What was right, had always been right, was now wrong, terribly wrong.

'They have their reasons, Tamesan,' the Herbal Man replied. 'All men have reasons for what they do, no matter how senseless their actions might seem to others. The men of Harbin need to prove their manhood. They need to feel they are the descendants of Nakiades—brave, strong, adventurous. They see nothing like Nakiades' fabled adventure in fishing, or herding goats, or doing the mundane matters of village life. They are victims of Nakiades' legacy. They have to prove themselves. And since there are no dragons left to fight, which would be the ultimate adventure for them, they make do with a lesser enemy. Other people. It satisfies their need.'

'But surely they know what they are doing is wrong?'

'Of course they do, Tamesan. At least most do. That's why they never tell anyone who is not a dragonwarrior what they are really doing. They all carry the guilt in one way or another. Young Marron will carry it with him all his life. A dragon didn't maul his arm. It was crushed during the Dragon Fang's retreat to the ship. The men will never tell anyone what really happened. Neither will Chasse. Your brother was made to swear an oath in order that he will keep what he now knows a secret. And he will. His hands have been marked with blood. He won't like what it means, but he won't break the oath. To do so would be to sacrifice the very title of manhood he has been waiting for so eagerly all his life. Keeping the secret, living the lie; that is what being a man means in Harbin. It is all part of the tradition.'

'Chasse said he won't go next summer,' she announced in his defence.

'He will,' the Herbal Man replied in a matter-of-fact tone. 'By next summer he will have had time to adjust to the darker side of his manhood. When the dragonship is ready again, Chasse will also be ready. He is not the first Harbin warrior to feel guilty after his initial journey. And he won't be the last. It is all a part of the cycle that Nakiades' legend spawned.'

'But won't the Imperial soldiers be waiting again?'

'Perhaps. Perhaps not. Governments change their minds the way the wind changes direction. Next year is quite some time away. And the coastline is very long. The Dragon Fang is very small. Chances are next year they will find a place that hasn't heard of them. It's a big world, Tamesan, a very big world.'

Tam glanced back at the pedestal containing the

Seeing Waters. The world was bigger than she had ever imagined. And uglier. The Herbal Man had shown her things, things she wished she had never seen. But that wish was absurd. He had simply shown her the truth. He showed her why Chasse had changed, the horrible secret he was forced to hold. He had shown her the cause of the terrible sorrow that scarred Ashlee and then killed her. What would knowing the truth do to other people? she wondered. What would happen if she exposed the secret? How would the women—the wives, daughters, sisters, and mothers of the dragonwarriors—react? But Ashlee had known the truth. How many other women also knew where the Dragon Fang went each summer, and what they did? Were the children the only ones who didn't know? Was that what really separated childhood from adulthood—knowing the ugly truth about village life? The people of Harbin were living a lie, an enormous lie that kept them together as a group and threatened to tear them apart individually. Where, then, did that leave her?

Chapter Twenty-Six

Tam stood at the centre of a world without dragons. A world with dragons had its share of darkness and terror, but it also had reason and order. The legend of Nakiades, the story the village people shared to bind them to their past, to their present, to ensure they were not forgotten by the future, lay at the centre of that world. Now it was lost to Tam. Instead, she stood at the centre of an alien world made up of half-truths and lies. It was suddenly a very cruel and empty world.

There had been no Dragon Festival. The ship's return was so disheartening. The festival was abandoned while the people bore the brunt of their grief and buried their dead. No-one questioned or even mentioned the oversight. There was nothing to celebrate. Tam helped wherever she was needed. There was food to prepare for those who were in deepest grief, warriors to care for who were recovering, and people who simply needed to sit and talk in order to cope with their loss.

The Herbal Man's visits diminished and then ceased. He told Tam his work was done. He also hinted that it was unwise for him to visit. Ill-feeling towards the Herbal Man had grown, generated by those who simply refused to acknowledge the value of his healing, and fuelled by Trask's hunger for vengeance. Kevan ordered Trask to remain in the Warriors' Hall whenever the Herbal Man came down from the mountain. Marron's father obeyed, but Tam heard the rumours that he had sworn a blood oath on his spear to kill the old man for crippling his son. She was afraid for the Herbal Man, and said so, but the old man only remarked, 'There is nothing to be afraid of, young Tamesan, when you are as old as I am. Marron's father will not harm me.' She objected, but the old man waved her fear aside, and told her he had no more need to visit Harbin, for a while, anyway. Only later did she realise his decision at that moment was politic.

Marron's amputation healed very quickly, but once he could get out of bed, he disappeared into the Warriors' Hall with his father and refused to see anyone. When the women took food to the men, Marron avoided them, hiding in the darkest corner of the Hall. Tam tried to speak to him on one of her visits, but Trask brusquely intervened. He bluntly warned her not to meddle with his son. His manner was so aggressive that Jon steered Tam away, and advised her, for her own safety, not to go near Marron again. Outside the Hall, he told Kevan it would be better if his daughter did not bring food to the warriors, at least for a while, because of Trask's mood—especially as she was the Herbal Man's friend and had been present when Marron's arm was taken. Once Kevan curbed his initial anger, he realised Jon's advice was sensible for the well-being of all concerned. He told Eesa that Tam was not to go to the Hall.

But Tam faced another serious threat. Katris began a series of bitter attacks. The girls had avoided each other in the weeks while the dragonship was away. Tam was busy learning all the Herbal Man could teach her, and Katris and her friends were involved in learning how to be good young village women and prospective wives. The dragonship's return plunged Katris into deep mourning. Her father did not come home. Adding Marron's injury to her woes kept the distraught girl indoors, praying to Varst and Procra to guide her father's lost spirit, and to heal Marron, whom she adored. When Katris heard that the Herbal Man removed Marron's arm, she screamed her anguish into the night and wept for the mutilation of her love. She had lost her father, and now she had lost the man she wanted for her husband. Her dreams were haunted by the spectre of a one-armed lover who had Marron's charming smile. He always displayed his catch of fish to impress her. But she did not want to be a fisherwoman. She hated scaling fish. Or milking goats. What else could a crippled man offer her? Her man was as good as dead, as dead as her father.

Later, when she learned that Tamesan had been present while the Herbal Man amputated Marron's arm, that news gave her a focus for her loss, a target for her hatred. Tamesan had caused Marron to lose his arm. She must have deliberately let his arm become infected. Because she was jealous, because she knew Marron would choose Katris at Procra's Dance instead of her. She had made the Herbal Man take his arm out of spite. So Katris hated her.

Katris' first attack was verbal. In the middle of the village, three days after Marron's operation, she confronted Tam, who was carrying washed bed linen towards the Long Hall. Before Tam recognised who had burst out of the crowd of girls, Katris was loosing her venom.

'You dragon bitch!' she screamed. 'You did it! You made him take his arm! You made it happen! It was you!'

Flustered by the ferocity and suddenness of the attack, Tam was speechless. She stared open-mouthed at the dark-haired girl until several others pulled Katris back. Eesa took Tam's arm and drew her away.

'She has gone strange, that one,' Eesa confided as they entered the Long Hall. 'Some do not take their grief well.'

'What did she mean, "I did it"?' Tam asked, still grappling with the reason for Katris' outburst. 'What did I do?'

'It is nothing, girl,' her mother assured her. 'It will pass.'

Eesa was wrong. It did not pass. Katris harangued Tam on every occasion their paths crossed. Between incidents, Tam found out from the other young women why Katris was so angry. She spoke to Eesa, hoping her mother would have a solution to the unfortunate situation.

Eesa told her, 'I will talk to the girl, but it will not be easy. She blames you and won't listen to reason.'

'But I had nothing to do with Marron losing his arm. I cared for him. I cleaned his arm and helped the Herbal Man try to save it. Where was Katris then? How can she blame me?'

'Believe me, Tamesan, others are trying to bring her to her senses, but she does not want to listen. If it comes to the worst, as I fear it might, I will instruct her to stay home until she can be reasonable,' Eesa promised.

The thought that Katris might be made a prisoner in her own village, just as Trask had been forcibly confined while the Herbal Man came and went, did not appeal to Tam. It would only give Katris yet another reason for hating her. She begged Eesa not to intervene on her behalf. Nothing more was said on the issue.

Then came the stone-throwing. Early one morning, as Tam walked with Jaysin towards the goat pastures to collect a pail of goats' milk, Katris emerged from behind a hut and threw a stone. It hit Tam above the right eye. She collapsed, clutching her forehead. Katris took to her heels. Jaysin thought his sister was dead—she lay motionless on the path for several moments—but she was only stunned. When she collected her senses, she sat up and discovered a small cut on her forehead where the stone had struck. She dabbed at the trickle of blood, and studied the red stain on her fingertip.

'Are you all right?' Jaysin asked. His eyes were wide with shock, but Tam noticed that he was also regarding her cut with intense curiosity.

'I'm fine, little brother,' she answered. Several women were walking towards them, so she scrambled to her feet and said, 'Don't say anything to Mother or anyone else, please. Mother would get too angry with Katris if she knew.'

'But she tried to kill you,' Jaysin argued, still obsessed with his sister's injury.

'She didn't try to kill me,' she corrected, 'She just tried to scare me, that's all.'

'But why?'

'She thinks I hurt Marron.'

'That's silly,' Jaysin declared, frowning. 'We all know you helped him.'

Tam ruffled her little brother's hair and said, 'I know you know the truth. That's all that's important to me. Come on. Mother is expecting us back with the milk.' She urged Jaysin forward, and kept her hand over her forehead as she greeted the women who passed with their burdens of milk. Her mind was full of concern, though. Katris' attack was violent and premeditated. It made her worry just how far the dark-haired girl might go for vengeance. She had to find a way to make Katris listen to the truth, or face having to completely and permanently avoid her wherever she went. The latter would be far from easy in Harbin.

Her visits to the Herbal Man's home were limited by Eesa's and the village's needs. After her visions in the Seeing Waters, and the revelations they brought, she was reluctant to return to the mountain in a hurry. It wasn't because she did not like what the Herbal Man had shown her. As much as the truth horrified her, she knew within herself that she had to know. The truth revealed what tortured her brother. It gave her a real connection with Chasse's anguish. Now she knew why he suffered, and what had driven them apart.

Finding an opportunity to talk to Chasse proved difficult. Since running away from her on the mountain, he had remained distant. Like Marron, he hid in the safety of the Warriors' Hall, and Trask's ill-humour prevented Tam from visiting him while he was in there. Not that Chasse would have allowed her to see him. She sought her father's assistance to intercede and convince Chasse to meet with her, but he returned with sorry news.

'Chasse has made his decision,' Kevan growled. 'He does not want to see you.' He offered no further explanation, and when Tam asked him to speak to Chasse again on her behalf, her father frowned and declared, 'He is a man now. He has made a decision and it is his right to hold to it. He does not have to come to you if he chooses not to.'

'But he's my brother,' she insisted.

'He is a dragonwarrior first,' her father retorted. 'I will not force him to change his mind on this trivial matter.'

She wanted to argue that the matter was not trivial, but she knew that, as always, it would be futile. Kevan was not the least interested in her needs. Her brother was a man now. She was still a girl. The gulf between the two positions in Harbin was greater than the distance between the mountain peaks above the village. But she was determined. She knew the truth, and she had to show Chasse she understood what he was going through, and why. So she went about her daily duties while keeping a watchful eye on the movements of the men in the Warriors' Hall, hoping for a chance to follow her brother if he ventured out. She did not have to wait very long.

Two days after she had unsuccessfully sought her father's help, Chasse left the Hall alone and walked rapidly along the outward path towards Meltsparkle. Tam quickly delivered the basket of sharpened knives she had for Amarti, and excused herself from helping with the fish on the pretext of having another task to perform at home. Then she also headed towards the northern end of Harbin.

At Meltsparkle, the stream cascaded over the water-smoothed rocks sending fine mist into the air, which created a shimmering rainbow in the mid-morning light. Tam searched the rocks but Chasse was nowhere to be seen. She wondered if she had missed her brother somehow. Had he turned off the path and headed up the mountain? Or had he ventured deeper into Meltsparkle's gorge? She opted for the latter possibility, and began to pick her way across the slippery rocks.

Meltsparkle's gorge was much narrower than Watersdrop, and smaller. The water ran through it with greater velocity, and the way along the gorge was treacherous in the lower reaches and impossible higher up. She had never fully explored this gorge. She preferred to wander on the southern side of Dragon Mountain, above Watersdrop.

After clambering and slipping across the rocks for several metres, Tam considered turning back. The cliffs rose in steep angular blocks on either side. It seemed odd to her that Chasse would climb this far into Meltsparkle. She paused to reassess her situation, and then decided to ease around the base of a massive boulder that partially blocked the surging mountain stream's passage. If she remembered correctly, there was a ledge a short distance ahead where a portion of the cliff formed an alcove. She had sat in there to watch the tumbling water the last time she had been this deep in the gorge. There was a slim chance Chasse had gone that far, but beyond that point the vaulting cliffs closed right in, and it became impossible for anyone to continue further.

She slid down from the jutting rock and edged around the boulder. The stream surged around her ankles, foaming as it forced its way under the obstruction. She found her footing very difficult to maintain, and nearly slipped into the raging water twice. Only the strength in her wrists and fingers kept her secure. With a concerted effort she pushed herself around the last few centimetres and clambered onto the broader ledge beyond.

Chasse sat in the alcove, frowning at her. She shook out her damp hair and crawled across to join him. He made no attempt to speak, and turned to stare at the churning water thundering through the narrow gorge.

At first, Tam decided to be patient. She sat beside her brother and studied the rugged beauty of Meltsparkle. Cloud shadows flitted across the higher rocks like brief moments of thought and sorrow. Soft spray, drifting above the stream, created colourful rainbow fragments over the turbulence, and the moisture brought out the natural hues of the rocks—the greys and carmines and sepias of sediments trapped in the lower levels. Light glittered in the ever-changing current. She wondered what her brother was dwelling on. He was uncomfortable in her presence, and she sensed that if she didn't start the conversation soon, he would leave. She was also afraid that if she did start he would leave anyway. Some choice. But then she had waited too long not to speak to him now.

'I know the truth,' she announced finally. Chasse looked up, but he did not say anything. He glanced down at the water and looked back again. She realised then that he hadn't heard her above the roar of the rapids. She drew in her breath and repeated loudly, 'I know the truth!' He lifted an eyebrow. 'About the dragons!' she added. Chasse stiffened. His face registered a faint trace of fear. Tam made her decision and continued without hesitation. 'I know the dragonwarriors don't hunt dragons. They hunt people. I know what happened this summer.'

Her brother suddenly looked like a rabbit cornered by a wolf in the forest. He shifted his weight and started to push himself to his feet. Tam grabbed his arms to hold him down.

'Don't go, brother! Please don't!' she pleaded. 'I know the truth, and I want you to know I know. Don't you understand? I know what happened.'

He tried to break her hold, and she was frightened he would succeed, but then he acquiesced so suddenly he almost collapsed onto the ledge. He sighed in exasperation and hung his head forlornly. He muttered something, but the words were drowned by the thundering water. Tam put one hand under his chin and lifted it so that she could see his face. He looked devastated.

'I didn't hear you,' she said apologetically.

'I asked how you found out,' he murmured a little more clearly.

'The Herbal Man,' she answered. She would tell Chasse the truth. She could not expect her brother to be honest with her if she was not honest with him. 'He showed me what happens.'

Chasse's eyes widened in astonishment. Then he frowned in disbelief. 'What are you saying, Tam? How could you be shown what happened?'

'The Herbal Man is a wizard, Chasse. He uses the Seeing Waters. They show him the truth about things past,' she explained.

He pulled his chin away from her hand and snorted. 'Are you mocking me, sister?'

She shifted to look at him eye to eye. 'I'm telling you the truth. If I'm not, how do I know that the Dragon Fang was attacked by the Empress' Imperial Guard or whatever they're called? How could I know that Marron's arm was broken because he got it jammed between the dragonship and another ship that attacked you as you tried to escape? I know there are no dragons, Chasse. The Herbal Man showed me the truth.' Chasse's face registered increasing shock as his sister's revelation sank in. 'You see?' she said gently, trying to ease the visible pain on his face, 'I understand what you meant when you told me it's all a lie. I know what you mean now. I understand.'

Chasse began to shake. His face melted into a mask of grief, and tears glinted in the corners of his eyes. He shuddered and groaned, 'Oh, in all Varst's hells, Tam! What have I done? What have I done?' and then shuddered again as a convulsive sob racked his body. 'What have I done?'

Tam reached out and embraced him, and this time he did not resist as he had above Watersdrop. She cradled her brother against her as he poured out his disillusionment above the roiling waters in Melt-sparkle gorge. Then, after he caught his breath and pulled away from her embrace, no longer ashamed that he had let his deepest emotions escape in his sister's presence, they sat and talked.

Slowly, ever so reluctantly, Chasse revealed what his summer journey had unveiled to him. Each confession triggered more pain, but Tam held her brother's hands, and gave him the strength to go on. That was the least she could offer. He told her how the initiates were made to swear the Warrior's Oath once the dragonship sailed from Harbin, and how that oath bound them to keep secret what the journey really entailed. He described his revulsion when he learnt that their quarry was not a dragon but village folk, simple people like themselves.

'All the tales we used to hear around the hearths, all the talk of dragons, it was all half-truth,' he disclosed. 'The dragons are the warriors of the villages, Tam. That's what the men really mean when they tell their stories. When they brag about cutting off a dragon's head, they mean it the way we could mean it in our own village. They actually kill the village leader, a man like our father: the Dragon Head. See? They aren't lying. They just aren't telling the truth. All the treasures they bring home—they steal them from ordinary people. There were never any dragons. Never!'

When Chasse told her all he could, she shared her secrets with him concerning the Herbal Man. She knew the old man would forgive her for breaking her promise. Chasse could be trusted as much as she could.

'There is one thing,' she added as she finished telling Chasse about the Herbal Man's magic. 'There is a dragon.' Chasse, already amazed by his sister's confessions, was dumbfounded by this last one. 'It's true,' she assured him.

'Where?' he gasped.

'In the mountain. Her name is Claryssa,' she explained. 'She is the Herbal Man's companion.'

'A real dragon?' he asked in disbelief. 'Are you sure?'

'I've seen her,' she answered with genuine pride. 'She's very old, but she's still magnificent. She has enormous golden eyes,' she continued, and described the dragon in minute detail to her astonished brother.

The sharing of secrets, beautiful and dark, full of promise and despair, trust and betrayal, in the gorge above Meltsparkle renewed the bond that had drawn Tamesan and Chasse together as children. Yet they also realised neither of them would see the world through childlike eyes ever again. Their childhood beliefs, the heart of the village and of their lives, were shattered forever by the strange truths and experiences of the past summer. They had tasted the realities of adulthood, and were tainted by its bitter-sweet nectar.

Chapter Twenty-Seven

The sun had yet to light the peak of Dragon Mountain when Tam led Chasse across the goat pastures into the tree line. She had convinced her brother to climb the mountain with her, to meet the Herbal Man as he truly was—a wizard with a dragon.

Chasse had been reluctant to go at first. He was still struggling to come to terms with the enormity of the lie that lay at the core of Harbin. To have his sister lead him into a real dragon's lair above his own village was too fantastic, too grotesque an irony under the circumstances. All his childhood, adults had lied to him: lied to every boy and girl in Harbin. They perpetuated the myth of the dragonship's annual pilgrimage and the rites into manhood to hide the bloody reality of Harbin's heritage. The men told their tales of heroic dragon adventures while they slaughtered innocent people. His own father oversaw the butchery and pillaging and ensured it was done efficiently and ruthlessly. What other lies were hidden in the dark corners of the village? What other horrors had adulthood yet to reveal?

Tam took her brother up the mountain, aware that

he was still caught in a mass of confusion and frustration despite their mutual confessions. But for the moment she was also dealing with her own problems. Eesa would be furious with her for sneaking away this morning. The preparations for Procra's Dance were underway. Her mother insisted that the annual celebration would be the best remedy for the sorrow permeating Harbin. Because there had been no Dragon Festival, she saw it as all the more important to break the grief cycle and restore purpose to the lives of the people. It was true Chasse was the only new dragon-warrior who would choose a girl, and, for the parents of the young men who had not returned from the journey, Procra's dance would reopen their wounds, but that was not sufficient reason to cancel it. Some were sure to complain that Eesa only wanted the celebration because her own son had come of age, but those criticisms would not ruffle her. She had become too accustomed to regular criticism over the years as wife of the Dragon Head to be upset by it.

She pitied Marron, who remained in hiding in the Warriors' Hall and would be unlikely to choose a wife this year. Eesa believed the gods had been unnaturally cruel to him. Many villagers put the blame for his disfigurement solely on what they perceived as an act of butchery by the Herbal Man. They argued publicly that Varst, in his wisdom and his mercy, chose Marron for the dark journey through the shadows to his Eternal Paradise but the Herbal Man had unwisely interfered. As a consequence, he consigned the unfortunate lad to a longer stay in hell with one arm. Eesa was less inclined to condemn him—she did not condone unwarranted bitterness towards anyone—but the Herbal Man's popularity had never been high in Harbin, and in the end she succumbed to popular opinion. She informed Tam that she was worried by her daughter associating with a person considered to be an ill-omen, even a pariah, by many villagers. Tam knew Eesa would inevitably try to wean her off the relationship. It was probably even the reason behind why she made Tam responsible for organising decorations in the Long Hall, a duty normally entrusted to an older woman. It was Eesa's way of telling her she was becoming a trustworthy individual, a grown woman who would have too much to do to pursue a trivial and time-wasting hobby like herbalism. By sneaking away now, however, Tam risked losing the new status her mother offered her.

Tam hated the way people still distrusted the Herbal Man. All he wanted was to be able to mind his own business, but they wouldn't let him. They came to him for help whenever there was an illness or injury. Then they expected him to do the impossible. If he was successful, the villagers gave him begrudging respect. If he was seen to have failed— and the deaths of the badly injured warriors and the cutting off of Marron's arm were considered failures—he was reviled and ignored. Until the next time someone needed help. The village's selfish and narrow attitude was so unfair, so unwarranted.

Trask was constantly railing against the old man. He was obsessed with vengeance. He had threatened and attacked the Herbal Man, threatened Tam, and even shown he was close to disobeying Kevan's orders to exact revenge for the loss of Marron's dragonwarrior status. Chasse told Tam the disturbing news that Trask was gaining increasing sympathy and support from the dragonwarriors. He told her he was afraid some of them were looking for a way to vent their pent-up anger and frustration after the summer's debacle. Trask was inciting them to climb the mountain and punish the Herbal Man once and for all. Her father opposed such senseless action, but Chasse's news made her very afraid for the old man's safety.

Yet even she was ready to betray the Herbal Man's trust by bringing Chasse to him. Was she doing the right thing? She could still just tell Chasse that she had made it up and turn back. No. That was stupid. Chasse had been lied to far too much as it was. She had to prove to her brother that there was truth in the world, and that she could be trusted. He needed someone to trust; someone reliable. If she lied, he would have nothing to believe, and no-one to turn to. She was certain that's how Ashlee had felt in the end. There had to be other people in Harbin, present and past, who were equally disillusioned by the traditional lies. She could at least stop the lies for herself and her brother. It would be her first step towards changing her world for the better.

She had an unshakeable belief that the Herbal Man

would understand why she brought Chasse to him. The world of Harbin was so much confusion and mystery, like the churning waters of Meltsparkle gorge. The Herbal Man was like a solid rock of understanding, even safety, in the turmoil of living. Whatever lies came from the mouths of other people, she knew he would reveal only truth to them both.

The approach of footsteps and whispering voices surprised Katris. She quickly slid off the broad tree bough and melted into the dew-dampened foliage near the path. Who else would climb the mountain this early? she wondered. She had expected to ambush Tamesan. The Dragon Head's daughter was still sneaking off to the dirty old Herbal Man's hut. Katris had hidden every morning for the past four days at this point on the mountain path, lying in wait for an opportunity to punish Tamesan for what she had done to Marron. She had her grandfather's ornately decorated dagger wedged in her belt. The blade was honed on the whetstone of her hatred and it was wickedly sharp. At first she thought she would just kill Tamesan. But as she waited each morning, she entertained more unpleasant alternatives. She could wound Tamesan and let her slowly, agonisingly, bleed to death. She could cut out her tongue or eyes. She could maim her arm so it would have to be amputated just as Tam had arranged for Marron's arm to be taken. She could lacerate Tamesan's face so badly that no man would look at her. That appealed. Tamesan was far too pretty and far too proud. Without her pretty face she would be nothing in Harbin. No. She would be less than nothing. So that was what she would do.

Crouched in the underbrush, Katris waited for the walkers to pass. She glimpsed Tamesan's outline in the dull light and her fingers tightened on the hilt of her dagger. The gods had brought the wicked enemy to her. Then she saw the solid form of a man appear behind Tamesan, and hesitated. When she recognised Chasse, her hand slid restlessly over the dagger's pommel. It would be foolish to attack in the presence of a witness, especially one who would defend Tamesan. She silently cursed her luck and waited impatiently for the pair to climb past and disappear between the trees and rocks. Why was Chasse with his sister? Where were they going? Goaded by frustration and curiosity, Katris crept from her hiding place and peered up the rugged, twisting pathway. When she was certain she would not attract attention, she started to climb as well.

The higher sections of the mountain path were new territory for Katris. She and her friends had had no cause to explore there, and, apart from the short time in her life when she had been naive enough to consider Tamesan a friend, she had never been higher than the tree fringe at the mountain's base. Only grief and hunger for revenge had driven her to climb higher than usual in the past few days, to wait for

Tamesan. Those emotions were coupled to her curiosity now. She would see where Tamesan and her brother were going. It might give her a better opportunity to set a trap for the one she hated.

'Hallo?' Tam tentatively called when she reached the door to the old hut. There was no answer. She turned to Chasse and asked him to wait while she checked inside. She went to a window, forced the shutters open, much to Chasse's surprise, and climbed inside. A moment later her head reappeared.

'He's not here,' she announced, and climbed out.

'So now what?' Chasse asked. Tam sensed a note of despondency in her brother's voice.

'He'll be around somewhere. He's probably out collecting herbs. We can wait for a while.'

Her brother spun on his heels and studied the plateau. 'When I came up here before,' he started to say, 'to give messages to the Herbal Man for Father, I always thought this place felt odd. You know? Like it didn't quite belong.'

'Uh-uh,' she agreed. 'Everything here is always fresh. And there are so many plants growing in this small flat area. I still feel like that even now. It must have something to do with his magic.'

'What *is* this magic you keep talking about?' he inquired.

She stared at her brother and pulled a face. 'I'm not all that sure I know what it is myself. The Herbal

Man tried to explain it to me over summer. It's incredibly complicated.'

'Tell me what he told you.'

Tam shrugged. 'I'll try.' So she explained what she remembered being taught and shown: the theory about dragons and wizards, and fields of energy, and their interrelationships. Chasse's facial expressions moved through phases of confusion, disbelief, amusement and delight as she spoke. When she finished, their conversation drifted to the Herbal Man's secret home, and some of the wider mysteries he'd told Tam existed in the world beyond the mountains hemming in Harbin. The morning sun crept across the cloudy sky as they talked, until it was directly overhead.

'I don't think he's coming back, Tam,' Chasse observed finally. 'We had better go down. You'll be in enough trouble with Mother and Father as it is.'

'I'm not concerned about that any more. I'm old enough to make my own decisions,' she declared quietly.

'You've always been old enough to make your own decisions,' he chided with a smirking smile. 'That's why you are unique.'

'Where did you get that word from?' she asked, amused by the description.

'I heard it said about you once by old Sharmine. I haven't forgotten it.'

'But what's it mean?'

'It means you are remarkable: the only one of your kind,' announced a voice from within the hut. Tam and Chasse spun around to see the Herbal Man emerging.

'I thought you weren't in?' Tam sputtered in surprise. 'I looked.'

The Herbal Man laughed and winked at Chasse. 'I probably wasn't in when you looked, Tamesan, but you should know there are other ways in.'

She blushed at her own foolishness, then recovered and said, 'I brought Chasse to see you.'

'I can see that,' the old man observed with a wry grin beneath his flowing white beard.

'No,' corrected Tam, 'I mean I've told him. Everything,' she admitted, and lowered her gaze, as if to apologise.

'I know,' said the Herbal Man.

'You do?' she exclaimed. Her eyes widened and then filled with understanding even as he replied.

'Of course I know,' he said, and glanced at Chasse, who suddenly shifted his feet uncomfortably in the presence of the old man. 'I expected you to tell your brother. It was the right thing to do.'

The Herbal Man didn't mind after all, Tam decided. A surge of relief flowed through her body. 'I told him about Claryssa,' she added.

The Herbal Man nodded. 'Then Chasse had best come and meet her,' he offered, and motioned them to the door of the hut.

Chasse glanced at Tam. She smiled and said, 'She is beautiful, Chasse. You'll see. She is nothing like you imagine a dragon might be.'

*

From a thicket in the forest, Katris watched as Chasse and Tamesan entered the Herbal Man's hut. She was annoyed the pair had decided to wait so long for the old man, and now it seemed they were going to spend even longer with him since he had arrived. She strained to overhear the conversation that preceded their entry to the hut, but she was not close enough, and the words did not carry, so she was none the wiser as to their purpose for being so far up the mountain. She considered giving up and returning to the village, but then she noticed how the window shutters of the old hut were still closed even after the threesome disappeared inside. It might just be possible to creep closer and eavesdrop. She estimated which segment of greenery was nearest the hut and moved to it. A dozen heart-thumping steps later, she pressed against the wall, listening.

The interior was silent. She turned her head to listen with her right ear but still she could hear nothing. That was strange. She wondered if it was worth risking a peek through a crack in the wooden shutters. She gathered her courage and eased up to peer in. Yet another mystery. The hut was empty! There was some rudimentary furniture visible, but no people. This discovery annoyed and excited her. She went to the door and very cautiously tried the handle. It turned. With all the stealth she could muster, she crept inside.

Where could three people have gone? She studied each wall in case one concealed a door, and admonished herself for even bothering to check the three external walls. There were no additional doors. Perplexed, she even checked the hearth. The grate covering the fireplace was dirty and the fire-hole was very dark. It had a terribly disused appearance. She decided not to shift the grate in case she ended up coated with soot. Had they vanished? She shivered. The impossibility of what she had witnessed began to unnerve her.

She had started to back away towards the door when her heel caught on an uneven board in the hut's wooden floor and she stumbled. The dilapidated rug pulled away, exposing a section of floor which jutted higher than the rest of the boards. Closer inspection revealed a trapdoor, not fully pulled shut. Katris pressed her ear to the floor, and listened. When she was satisfied there was no noise below, she eased the trapdoor open, a centimetre at a time, until she discovered steps descending into a lighted space directly below. The blood pounded in her veins. What was hidden down there? What was this place? She slipped the dagger from her belt and measured its weight in her hand. Like all the girls in the village, she had never played with daggers, never been trained to use one. That was for boys and men. Now, for once, she wished she was a boy. She didn't have to look any further, she knew that, but her desperate curiosity was dragging her down the steps into this underground chamber, and she was scared.

She found two connecting chambers. The first was lit by a strange candle painted with red lines. An assortment of items cluttered the space. The second chamber was a bedroom. It was lit by a lantern hanging on the wall. There were two doors in that room. One was partially open. Katris crossed the room and listened at the door. When she opened it, she discovered a dark passageway. At the far end a bright light glowed from a doorway on the right.

She had come this far. She was no longer certain that Tamesan, or Chasse, or even the Herbal Man, had come this way. That consideration no longer weighed importantly on her mind. This strange underground habitation was unlike anything she had ever seen. It fascinated her. It was a puzzle she had to solve.

She crept along the passage, mesmerised by the brilliant flood of light at its end. The closer she came, the more she became aware of voices, soft voices, speaking. She recognised Tamesan's voice. Her luck held—she had found them. They were somewhere in the room of light. She forced herself to concentrate all her senses as she edged up to the doorway. Her eyes were slowly adjusting to the intense light. Then the light suddenly lost luminescence, becoming softer, more like a lantern glow. She tensed, ready to run if she heard any sound indicating that the occupants of the room were coming out. What she did hear was a voice, probably the Herbal Man's because of its timbre. She trained her ears on his voice, but he made no sense whatsoever. It sounded like elegant gibberish. She was pulled by her insistent curiosity to look.

Just once. Then she could sneak away. Just one, quick peek.

Slowly, very warily, her heart beating fiercely, Katris leaned around the doorjamb and peered into the chamber. The vision stunned her. The Herbal Man, Tamesan, and Chasse stood barely five metres away, their backs to her. All three faced something beyond the horror of Katris' worst imaginings. She had never seen a dragon. But she had heard all the village tales and the legends. The reptilian head, with its golden orbs for eyes, its protruding curved yellowed teeth, its scaly snout, could only belong to such a creature. She was standing not more than ten metres from the awesome beast, and, for whatever ungodly reason, the three people she had followed stood next to it.

She had seen too much for mere curiosity's sake. Fear gripped her stomach and threatened to turn her legs to water. She forced herself to stop staring at the scene, but, when she tried to ease herself back into the security of the darkness, she was seized by a fit of panic. She bolted along the passage and through the chambers, pursued by the knowledge that the most terrible of all Varst's creatures was nesting in the mountain above her home. By the time she scrambled up the ladder and burst out of the Herbal Man's false hut, Katris was running in blind terror from her darkest childhood nightmare.

Chapter Twenty-Eight

'What's happening?' Tam asked as they reached the edge of the goat pasture. People were milling in the centre of the village, crowding the entrance to the Long Hall.

'Something important,' Chasse responded. 'We'd best find out.'

The pair hurried towards the scene. It was late in the afternoon and they were just returning from the Herbal Man's hideaway. Chasse had met Claryssa for the first time, and was overwhelmed by the fearsome beauty of the Herbal Man's dragon companion. He also saw his sister in a new light, a girl truly unique in what she had seen and knew. She had shared her most treasured secret with him. Of all the people he knew, he would never doubt her trust again.

As they reached the Long Hall, the last few people squeezed through the door. Chasse and Tam followed. When they entered, the dragonwarrior Jon stared as if he was surprised to see them there, then he closed the door.

'What's going on?' Chasse asked.

'I thought you would know,' Jon replied.

Tam cast a quizzical glance at her brother and said to Jon, 'Know what?'

'Listen,' the warrior directed, and turned to look over the crowd. There was a buzz of voices around them, but it was quietening.

'I'm going further forward,' Tam said, and she pushed through the throng until she could see what was the centre of attention. Chasse tried to grab her arm as she moved away, but she moved too quickly. Jon's odd expression had warned him something was not quite right, something concerning himself and his sister. He considered following her, but he was reluctant to get entangled in the crowd. He did not understand why he felt apprehensive, just heeded a fear that sparked inside him. When some people in front shifted, he saw what was happening, and realised his fear was justified.

At the centre of the Long Hall, Kevan faced Trask. Anger flashed between the warriors. Katris stood between them. Her face was paler than usual, framed by the shining black hair that hung past her shoulders. She looked afraid, but her body leant towards Trask and away from Kevan. What was happening?

Tam pushed through almost to the front of the crowd. She saw Katris and her father and Trask, although none of the three noticed her. Tam spied Eesa with Amarti, and a number of the village women, to her right, and she was about to worm her way towards them when the low hubbub around her ceased. Trask was haranguing the gathering.

'All of you! Listen to me! Your lives are in great danger!' he yelled.

Tam saw her father take a step towards Trask as he interrupted. 'Hold your tongue, Trask. You speak out of turn!'

'I'll speak as I wish!' Trask retorted. 'The people don't need to hear your excuses. They must hear the truth!'

'Let the girl speak!' a warrior shouted from the left.

'Let the girl speak!' chorused others in the crowd. Tam was puzzled why Katris, of all people, would have cause to speak before the whole village assembly. What strange event had happened while she and Chasse were absent?

'You hear them?' Trask sneered at Kevan. 'Let this girl tell them what she has told us. They have a right to hear it.'

Kevan looked vexed. Tam could see from his expression that her father did not want Katris to speak. Was he simply being stubborn again, just because she was a girl? Would he realise one day that women had as much right to speak as men? The Dragon Head glanced past Trask's shoulder at the Dragon Heart priest. The priest added his affirmation to Trask's statement. Kevan's reaction told Tam he did not like the priest's response any more than he had liked Trask's challenge.

He swallowed and said, 'The girl can speak,' and added angrily, 'But I do not believe what she says.'

All eyes turned on Katris. Her face visibly whitened, and she suddenly looked as if she wanted to run from the massed attention. She was terrified. Tam felt a pang of pity for her, and wished she knew what terrible matter had dragged Katris here. She wished she could help her in some way.

'Go on, girl,' Trask growled with satisfaction. 'Tell the people what you have seen. Tell them the truth.' Katris was shaking. She hesitated, as if unable to force the words from her mouth. 'Speak!' Trask ordered gruffly. 'Tell us what you have seen.'

Katris stared blindly at the gathering. She opened her mouth, but nothing came out. She swallowed to control her nerves and finally said, in a harsh whisper, 'There is a dragon in the mountain.' The only sign that her revelation registered with the crowd was the sudden complete silence that followed. Tam felt a thrill of fear rip through her spine. Had she imagined what Katris said? Then a babble of voices filled the Hall, all questioning the news that a dragon lived in Dragon Mountain. She had not imagined it.

'Quiet!' Trask bellowed above the noise. 'Listen to the girl!' The frantic conversations died. Everyone focussed even more intently on Katris. 'Go on,' Trask prompted.

Katris shifted nervously and glanced fearfully at Kevan. The Dragon Head glared fiercely in return. 'I saw the Herbal Man and Chasse and Tamesan,' she announced. 'They were talking to it. It lives in the Herbal Man's home.'

Gasps of surprise and shock echoed through the hall. Tam saw Eesa stare in amazement at Kevan. Her father stiffened, and gave Trask a murderous look, the kind Tam had only ever seen from her father when he was infuriated beyond reason.

'What have you to say to that?' Trask challenged over the din. People stopped to hear Kevan's reply.

'The girl is obviously mad,' he responded. 'How can there be a dragon in the mountain? What kind of mad talk is that?'

'I'm not mad!' Katris screamed. 'I saw it! I followed them up the mountain and I saw it!'

'Where are your son and daughter?' Trask jeered. 'Why are they not here?'

'I am here,' Tam announced. She stepped out of the crowd so that she could be seen. Her heart raced and she felt sick. But what choice did she have? It might be the only chance she had to stop people listening to Katris.

Trask was surprised by her unanticipated presence, but he quickly gathered his wits and demanded, 'Where were you today when your mother was seeking you?'

Tam glanced in Eesa's direction and saw the despair on her mother's face. Her mother already believed Katris' tale. 'I was—' She hesitated. If she lied, she would be compromising her own principles. If she told the truth, she would condemn herself and Chasse. But there were too many lies already in Harbin. Too many.

'I was visiting the Herbal Man,' she answered, as calmly as she could. 'Is there anything wrong with that?' She heard her mother gasp. People whispered quickly to each other.

'And his dragon?' Trask queried.

The man's question was blunt. It caught her, but not unexpectedly. The Hall hushed as everyone awaited her answer. She wished she could lie as easily as the priest had lied about her rescue, as easily as her father lied about the summer dragon hunts. If she lied now, she could bluff her way out of the situation, make Trask and Katris look like fools, and save her father a lot of heartache. And there was the Herbal Man to think of. And Claryssa. But Katris clearly knew the truth. Tam had no idea how the girl had managed to spy on them in the Herbal Man's hideaway, but she must have done given her accurate description of what she claimed to have seen. Katris knew the truth, and it would only be a matter of time before she, or Trask, or someone else would try to establish it for themselves. Lies only bred more lies.

She fixed her gaze firmly on Katris' face and replied, 'Yes. We were with the dragon. I took Chasse to meet her.'

Protestations and cries of horror erupted. People shuffled restlessly. Again, Trask shouted above the din. 'You heard her admission!' he yelled triumphantly. 'There is a dragon in the mountain! A dragon over Harbin!'

'It will kill us!' another warrior cried. 'It will burn and destroy!'

'Not if we strike first!' Trask roared. 'Not if the Dragon Fang bring it down!' He brandished his spear as a sign of his intention.

'Stop this nonsense!' Kevan shouted. 'Hear me, people of Harbin! Hear me!'

'No-one listens to a liar!' snarled Trask. 'Your own children consort with a dragon! Your son and daughter speak to the enemy of Nakiades!'

'Hear me, Trask, or by Varst's mighty powers I will strike you down!' Kevan cried. He stepped in front of Trask and caught the end of the warrior's spear. Katris screamed and ran for safety. Members of the crowd started yelling encouragement to both warriors. Others cried for them to stop.

Tam was pinned in the crush of people who rushed forward to witness the confrontation. Trapped, she watched, horrified, as Trask and her father wrestled for possession of the spear. Muscles bulged in their arms and backs as they strained and twisted. Kevan forced Trask against an upright post supporting the roof. The Dragon Head used his greater bulk to advantage to pin his opponent, but he didn't anticipate Trask's left knee. It caught him sharply in the groin and forced him to loosen his grip on the spear. It was enough. Trask hit out with his elbow and sent Kevan reeling back. Before the Dragon Head recovered his balance, Trask drove his spear into Kevan's exposed thigh. Kevan roared with pain and staggered into the crowd. Eesa screamed. Tam broke free of the press of people, and leapt at Trask, but his reflexes were too quick. His right arm snaked out and caught her a stinging blow across the side of her face as she attempted to grapple his waist. She was thrown sideways against the wall of onlookers. Hands restrained her when she tried to scramble to her feet.

But her diversion had given her father time to recover. Someone handed him a sword. Blood flowed freely from his thigh.

'Stop them!' Tam desperately appealed as the two men circled each other.

'Hush, girl,' a man remonstrated above her. 'It is time this was resolved.'

Trask prodded at Kevan, trying to goad him into an attack. Tam was no expert at fighting, but she could see the advantage Trask had with a spear. It made his reach longer. Worse still, her father was already sorely wounded.

'Come on, old man,' Trask sneered. 'Come and taste Varst's bitter cup. No-one in Harbin will follow a man whose own children are dragon-spawn!'

Kevan circled silently, neatly dodging the probing point of Trask's spear, intense, controlled. She suddenly realised the odds were in her father's favour, even despite the wound in his thigh. He had more discipline than Trask. He seemed more resolute, more complete. Her fear for her father's life did not lessen, but she sensed he would win this encounter. She could feel it around her too. There were villagers cheering for Trask, predominantly the younger dragonwarriors, but most of the crowd favoured her father. He was the Dragon Head, after all.

Trask lunged. Kevan's sword steered the spear-point away from his side. Trask lunged again. Again Kevan easily turned his attack aside. This time he retaliated. A cut appeared on Trask's cheek. The warrior scowled and jabbed ineffectively as Kevan stepped back.

'Put the spear up, Trask,' he ordered quietly, as if he was unperturbed by Trask's threat. But Tam noticed how her father was breathing harder, and the bloodstain on his thigh had widened. It was running down his leg and smearing the floor.

'Go to hell!' Trask spat, and swung the spear in a wide arc. Kevan ducked but lost his footing, and a collective gasp rose from the crowd as the Dragon Head stumbled. Trask seized his chance. He stabbed. Even as Kevan twisted to avoid the spear-point, it pierced his shirt and dug into his side. His weight, as he fell, ripped the point out again. He collapsed like a dropped sack of grain, and rolled onto his back, his chest heaving. His sword clattered against the wall. With a satisfied grin spreading across his sweating face, Trask hefted his spear and swaggered towards his fallen opponent to deal the death blow.

In absolute desperation, Tam wrenched herself free from the restraining hands and leapt across the intervening space to stand between Trask and her stricken father.

'Get out of the way, girl!' Trask growled hungrily. 'I am going to kill your father.' He raised his spear.

Another figure scampered out of the hushed crowd to stand beside Tam. When she glanced to her side she saw Jaysin standing there, his eyes full of tears and his lower lip quivering.

'Touch my sister and my father and I will kill you!' he shrieked. He clenched his puny fists and stared defiantly at Trask. Tam was astonished by her brother's unexpected show of courage.

Trask hesitated. His grin widened as if he was amused by the young boy's defiance. Then he frowned and said, 'Pity your father never had your courage, boy,' and with a sweep of his broad arm, he flung both of them aside.

Tam screamed 'Father!' as she regained her feet, fearing she was too late to stop Trask's attack. She was surprised to see his spear still raised. Then she saw why. Two dragonwarriors stood between Trask and his victim. One was Jon, the other Raven. Neither held a weapon but both were determined in their stand.

Jon spoke sternly. 'You have won the fight, Trask,' he said. 'The people have witnessed it, and it is done with. Do not dishonour the Dragon Fang or your newly won title with a foolish or vengeful act. Give the old man his honour.'

Trask held his spear aloft a moment longer, as if he was unimpressed with Jon's speech. Then his fierce expression melted into a grin and he lowered his weapon. 'Fair words, Jon,' he acknowledged. 'Always the one with fair words.' As Eesa rushed forward to her husband, Trask spun on his heel and addressed the crowd.

'You witnessed this with your own eyes, people of my village. I am the new Dragon Head. Varst has given me the strength to make it so, and his will is done. The weaker man has fallen. So do all dragon worshippers perish. The task of Nakiades is never over so long as dragons live.' He drew a breath and continued his oration. 'Now the gods have shown us that a loathsome dragon roosts above our own village, in the mountain. Thankfully the girl Katris has warned us of its presence.'

'It's harmless!' Tam called from behind.

Trask ignored her. 'Dragons are the sworn enemy of our people!' he asserted sternly. 'And all dragons must die.'

Tam pushed beside him and pleaded, 'Claryssa is old! She's harmless! She will never hurt anyone!'

'Don't waste your foolish words here, girl!' Trask mocked, then addressed the gathering again. 'There is a dragon in the mountain, and it must be driven out and killed! If we do not do that, then it will steal down in the night, burn our homes, eat our children, and Harbin will perish. We know this is true. It is why Nakiades hunted the foul creatures. It is why the Dragon Fang journey every summer. All dragons must die!'

'There are no dragons!' Tam yelled in exasperation.

'You know that better than I do! You tell lies and say there are, but there are no dragons!'

'There are!' Katris screamed. 'I saw it! And you know I saw it!'

'Both of you be quiet!' Trask ordered. 'This is no longer a place for girls,' he announced. 'Or women,' he added. 'The Dragon Fang will meet and plan how to purge the mountain of this dragon and rid ourselves once and for all of the old fool who keeps it there. The rest of you go to your homes and stay there until the dragon is dead. The Dragon Head has spoken. Obey my words.'

People nodded knowingly, or shook their heads in concern, as they shuffled noisily out of the Long Hall. So much had happened. So much had suddenly changed. Some were confused by the turn of events, some happy, most worried. Tam saw Chasse, still near the door. He was pushing towards her against the tide of people. Then she was suddenly aware of a strong hand grabbing her arm. She looked around to discover a dragonwarrior at her side.

'Keep her and her family in the Long Hall,' she heard Trask instruct him. 'And find the boy Chasse.'

'Let go,' Tam warned.

She pulled against the warrior's grip, but he held her fast and hissed, 'Don't be stupid, Tamesan. Trask is Dragon Head now and you are no longer the Dragon Head's daughter.'

Suddenly realising the gravity of her predicament, she turned to her brother, who was emerging from the crowd, and yelled, 'Run, Chasse! Warn the Herbal Man! Please!' Chasse heard her plea. When he saw two dragonwarriors head towards him, and his sister being held prisoner, he understood the impending danger. He pushed through the stragglers filing out of the Hall and ran.

'Get him!' Trask roared. Two dragonwarriors raced out of the Hall in pursuit. Trask crossed to Tam and shook her chin roughly. 'He won't get there, girl,' he remarked sourly. 'The old man and his dragon are doomed.' She spat at him, but her retaliation only made him laugh. 'Never did have womanly manners, did you, girl?' he chuckled grimly. 'But a good man will teach you those. If any man will have you now.' Laughing heartily, he turned away to join a group of dragonwarriors waiting at the centre of the Long Hall, and he led them outside.

As darkness settled over the village, Tam dressed her father's wounds under guard in the Long Hall. Kevan was deathly pale: he had lost a lot of blood, and he slipped in and out of consciousness. She tried to enlist Jaysin's aid, but her little brother simply lay curled in a foetal position in a corner and refused to acknowledge anyone. Tam had been astonished by his stand against Trask. Jaysin always avoided fights with other children in Harbin, and hated anything that remotely looked like a weapon. He showed none of the fighting qualities expected of a boy. He preferred to remain alone, as he was that evening. He was interested in odd things like watching the stars, or learning to read and write. He sang songs. He did not belong. The word Chasse used to describe her suited Jaysin better. If anyone was unique, he was.

Eesa convinced their guards to let her fetch food, water and clean cloths to bandage Kevan. She kindled a fire and left Tam to do the healing work while she boiled water and organised a meal. She even provided food for the two guards. They expressed their appreciation of her kindness, and relaxed a little, but the tension in the air remained. Like Tam, they were eager to hear the Dragon Fang's decision regarding the fate of the dragon on the mountain.

Tam ate a morsel of the food Eesa offered, but her mind was on Chasse and the Herbal Man. Had her brother escaped the pursuing warriors? She assumed he must have, or else he would have already been thrown in here with the rest of them. Unless? She pushed the alternative from her mind. They wouldn't kill him. Surely they wouldn't kill him. She finished her meal and crossed to her father's bedding. Eesa sat stroking Kevan's greying hair. 'Mother?' she asked quietly.

'Yes?' Eesa responded. She did not look up from Kevan's sleeping face and kept stroking her husband's hair softly.

'Why didn't anyone stop Father and Trask from fighting? Theo would've.'

'Theo was a good man, a very good friend,' Eesa murmured, and added, 'Varst rest his soul.'

'But why didn't anyone else stop them?'

'Must you ask so many questions?' Eesa complained and lifted her tired eyes to look at her daughter.

'I need to know,' was all Tam could reply.

Her mother sighed and gazed wistfully at Kevan. 'This has all been a long time coming, child. He knew it would happen. If not Trask, then someone else. If not this summer, then perhaps the next.'

'Knew what, Mother?'

'Knew that someone else would become Dragon Head, that someone else would challenge and defeat him.'

'I don't understand,' Tam admitted quietly. 'Do you mean he knew Trask or someone else would try to kill him?'

'He knew someone would fight him. That's how a new Dragon Head is chosen. He must be the strongest warrior, one with the strength to lead unchallenged. Your father became Dragon Head by defeating Theo's father, Taen.'

'He killed Theo's father? I thought Theo was father's friend?'

Eesa chuckled, recalling a fond memory. 'Theo was. Kevan didn't kill Theo's father. He hardly even hurt him. It was all planned and agreed in advance. Taen chose your father to succeed him. I wasn't your father's wife then, just a girl like you. Kevan was the most handsome and wonderfully strong warrior in all Harbin. Everyone knew that. Even the older men respected him. He commanded respect. He was so perfect, so godlike.'

Tam listened in awe as her mother spoke. Never before had she heard her mother describe her father like this. Never had she imagined her parents as young people like herself or Chasse. They had always been old, and distant, and angry. Now Eesa was sounding like a young girl madly in love. It was a facet of her mother Tam had never seen, and it fascinated her.

'Anyway,' Eesa continued, composing her emotions, 'Taen didn't want to face any more challenges to his position. Like your father is now, he was getting old. He wanted less responsibility. He believed your father was the right warrior to replace him. So they held an arranged fight on the shore near the jetty. The whole village saw it, but no-one believed the fight was for real. People were laughing at some of the antics those two men got up to. They exchanged mock blows for a short while, no-one drew blood, and in the end Taen, Varst rest his soul, yielded, and declared Kevan was the new Dragon Head.'

'Why didn't Father name a successor like that?'

'He wanted to, but he wasn't satisfied with anyone. And there has always been Trask. Trask's father always told him he would be Dragon Head one day. He believed it. He has always been jealous of your father. But Trask will not make a good Dragon Head. He is too headstrong, too selfish. In recent years he has tried to take the title forcibly from Kevan.'

'You mean they've fought before?' Tam asked.

'Oh, yes,' Eesa affirmed quietly. 'Several times. But every other time your father put Trask back in his place.'

'Why didn't Father kill Trask?'

Eesa shook her head and said, 'Because your father knows how valuable a warrior Trask is to the Dragon Fang. He was always angry that Trask wanted to succeed him, but he never let that anger override the needs of Harbin.'

'Does Trask know that?' Tam asked.

'Of course he does, Tamesan. But he wanted to be Dragon Head and now he is. Perhaps he will mellow now that he has what he wants. Only time will tell.' Eesa yawned as she finished talking. 'I am tired,' she announced, and then smiled mildly at her daughter as she added, 'But for once you can answer my questions, Tamesan. Tell me about this dragon you have seen.'

It was time to tell all the truth, Tam decided. It gave her a warm feeling to share everything with her mother at last. She tucked her knees under her chin and began, 'She is the most beautiful thing I have ever seen.'

Chapter Twenty-Nine

Tam dreamed. She dreamt Chasse was whispering in her ear. He whispered that she had to climb the mountain with him. He started pulling at her arm. The strength of his pull and his voice became more insistent.

She woke up. Chasse squatted at her side in the semi-darkness, tugging at her arm. 'Shh,' he hissed as she went to speak. She sat up on the makeshift bed near the cold hearth in the Long Hall, and surveyed the immediate vicinity. The sleeping forms of her mother and father lay side by side. Jaysin was curled in the corner where he'd stayed all night.

'What about the guards?' she queried.

He shook his head and motioned for her to follow silently. Together they crept to the doorway. Chasse paused to peer around the door. Then he slipped outside. Tam followed.

Harbin was draped in thick fog. Tam could not even see the Warriors' Hall across the space separating it from the Long Hall. They sneaked along the path until they reached the last hut, and then cut across the goat pasture. Once they reached the tree fringe, Tam caught her brother's arm and broke the silence.

'What happened to the guards?' she asked.

'They're looking for me,' he grinned. 'I made an unexpected appearance and led them away towards Meltsparkle. Then I doubled back. We better hurry though, because they're sure to have gone back to the Long Hall by now.'

'Did you warn the Herbal Man?'

Chasse shook his head. 'I couldn't get up the path,' he confessed. 'The dragonwarriors cut me off. I hid in the forest last night until they gave up searching. Then I decided to come back for you, instead of going to the Herbal Man, in case Trask had done something stupid.'

'Then we'd better hurry,' Tam urged. 'The sooner we warn the Herbal Man, the sooner he and Claryssa can get to safety.' She leapt ahead of her brother and they climbed quickly.

As they clambered around a pile of tumbled boulders, a voice challenged them. 'Where are you going?' Two dragonwarriors emerged from hiding, holding their spears menacingly.

'I thought you said they had given up looking for you?' Tam complained.

'Trask thought it would be wise to put a guard up here in case Chasse convinced the Herbal Man to come back down,' explained the first warrior as he jumped down to confront brother and sister. 'We didn't quite expect to see you coming back up with your sister.' He smiled at Chasse.

'I didn't mean to be predictable, Alan,' Chasse replied.

'Stay here, Jarrod,' Alan instructed his companion. 'I'll take them down.' He turned to Chasse and rolled his spear smoothly in his hands and said, 'You wouldn't give me any trouble now, would you?'

'Me?' chuckled Chasse. 'Not with that thing in your hands, Alan.'

Alan laughed as well, then grunted, 'Let's go,' and prodded Chasse with the spear-point. Chasse turned and began to descend. Tam hesitated until Alan waved the spear at her, and then she fell into step with her brother.

'Now what?' she whispered as they walked.

'No scheming,' Alan chuckled. 'I think our new Dragon Head would thank me for skewering the off-spring of his enemy.'

'You wouldn't really do that for Trask?' Chasse suggested lightly.

'Of course I wouldn't,' Alan answered. 'I'd do it for the fun of it, really.'

'Improvise, Tam,' Chasse whispered.

Alan was about to warn them both again not to whisper when Tam suddenly stumbled and cried in agony, 'Oh my ankle! My ankle!' She collapsed and rolled between a pair of tree trunks.

Chasse bent forward to help her. 'What have you done?' he asked.

'Hurt my ankle, you idiot!' she exclaimed, and wrinkled her face in pain again as she clutched at her ankle. Chasse reached out to touch her, but before his fingers made contact she screamed, 'Touch it, you stupid boy, and I'll thrash you!' Alan started laughing in the background. 'What's so funny, you great heap of goat dung?' Tam cried.

Her outburst only made Alan laugh harder. 'I'm glad she's your sister, Chasse,' he chortled. 'Pity the man mad enough to choose her at Procra's Dance.'

'It won't be a half-wit like you!' she jeered.

Alan caught his breath and said, 'Get her up, Chasse. We have to get off this mountain.'

Chasse tried to lift her but she yelped with pain again, and her position between the trees made it awkward to manoeuvre her. 'Can you at least help me?' he appealed to Alan.

The young man cursed and came closer. 'Girls!' he lamented, as he realised Chasse could not lift her alone. 'Who needs them?' He leant his spear against a tree trunk and bent to pull Tam to her feet.

She protested that they were hurting her, as they shifted her into a more manageable position, but finally she had an arm over the shoulder of each young man. As they eased her back onto the path, she suddenly crumpled to her left, dragging Alan over as she clung to his neck. Unable to support her weight, he fell, and Tam quickly rolled away. By the time Alan pushed himself up on his elbows, Chasse stood over him with the spear pressed to his neck. Tam scrambled up beside her brother.

'Girls,' Chasse grinned in triumph. 'Pretty useful,

aren't they, Alan?' Alan cursed and went to call for help, but Chasse put more pressure on the spear and warned, 'I wouldn't, Alan. I have nothing to lose by killing you at present.'

Alan flinched at the spear-point nicking his throat. 'What do you want me to do?' he gasped.

'Roll over, face down,' Tam ordered. Alan complied, and she tore a strip from the hem of her skirt and bound his wrists. She used a second piece to gag the dragonwarrior. 'I've left your feet free, Alan,' she informed him. 'If you are silly enough, you can keep walking down the mountain, but I'd advise you to wait here. I'm sure Trask will be up here soon.' Alan mumbled something beneath the gag, but Tam and Chasse were already heading up the path.

Just before the point where Alan and Jarrod had ambushed them, the pair halted. 'Let me get a few metres up the path,' Chasse requested as they split up. Tam nodded, and Chasse slipped into the forest.

She waited quietly. Her brother's initial movements sounded too loud in the first seconds, but then she was left in silence. The dawn's light would be breaking over the top of the mountain very soon. They had to hurry. Suddenly she heard a cry further down the mountain. 'Jarrod! Watch out! They're coming back up!' Alan had obviously loosened his gag. Realising the imminent danger, she backed off the path into a thick bush and waited.

What would Jarrod do? Either he would come down to meet them or he would hope to ambush them again. But which? She waited until she thought Chasse should have reached the spot where he was going to wait for her. As she went to step out onto the path, she heard someone approaching, and ducked back into hiding. A stone clattered down the path. Then Chasse's familiar figure appeared.

'Where are you, Tam?' he whispered. She stepped out and startled him. He swung his spear up to defend himself and realised it was his sister. 'Come on!' he ordered. 'Time's running out.'

'Where's Jarrod?' she asked.

'Never mind,' he replied tersely. 'Come on.'

They ran wherever possible, and scrambled madly up the steeper sections of the path, alert to the possibility of further ambushes, until they reached the plateau and the old man's hut. Tam sprinted ahead and hammered on the door. As she expected, there was no answer, but when she tried the window shutters she discovered all of them were securely locked. That was abnormal.

'We'll go in through the goat cave,' she decided, and led her brother out of the clearing into the lush green forest.

Chasse was astonished at how easily his sister negotiated the forest. He presumed she was following goat tracks, but he wasn't always able to see how she found them in the tangled undergrowth. They emerged in a smaller clearing facing a low cliff. Chasse heard a goat bleat, and saw a small herd of the animals grazing on the dew-damp grass to his left.

A tiny cavern mouth, obscured by plants, opened in the cliff, and Tam headed directly for it. He followed, and dropped to his knees as he reached the cave to crawl in after her.

The interior was cold and dark, and stank of stale animal dung. After he'd crawled in some distance, he hoped it did not change into two tunnels—he could see nothing and would have no idea if his sister changed direction.

'Are you sure this is the right way?' he asked nervously after a few minutes.

'Yes,' he heard Tam respond. Then he ran head-on into her legs. 'You can stand up now, Chasse,' she informed him. 'But we have to feel our way around the wall. Careful. It's rough.'

He followed his sister blindly, hearing the scrape of his own feet and the echo of his breathing. He ran into her a second time, and asked 'What's wrong?'

'The door,' she replied. He noticed a hint of puzzlement in her voice. 'It should be somewhere here.'

'Perhaps we aren't far enough around,' he suggested.

'No. If anything we've gone too far. The door has—disappeared.'

'What now?' he asked, wondering if she had lost her way after all.

'Follow me,' she answered. 'There's another way.'

Chasse resumed the blind fumbling around the cavern until he hit his head on a lower ceiling and Tam told him to kneel. He crawled down the narrow tunnel towards the daylight, glad to be leaving the darkness and the stench of goat behind.

Back in the clearing, Tam oriented herself and then plunged into the forest again, dragging Chasse in her wake. This time, she shadowed the cliff until she found the foot of a narrow and very steep path cut into the mountainside. She clambered up, much to Chasse's chagrin. He followed reluctantly.

Some sections were no wider than a goat track, and Chasse clung to the mountain, afraid of falling as he edged after his sister. They slowly climbed to a higher ledge that hung directly over the plateau. The whole world of Harbin opened beneath them. But as they reached the ledge, Tam cried out in despair. She pointed down below them, where black smoke was rising into the sky.

'The Herbal Man's hut!' she moaned. 'Trask must already have the Dragon Fang there.' She reached the broad ledge and immediately disappeared into a cave. Chasse hurried after her.

Panic rose in Tam's chest. Her mind was spinning with a host of confusing thoughts. Katris had seen them with Claryssa in the crystal chamber so she knew there was a trapdoor entrance in the old hut. The disappearance of the door in the goat cave puzzled her. What if the Herbal Man was already out searching for herbs this morning? How could she warn him then? Her only hope was to get to Claryssa.

In the darkness, she carefully felt her way around the silken-smooth walls of the great cave that had once belonged to the Dawn People. Some day she hoped to show Chasse and Jaysin the ancient drawings daubed on the polished walls. She urged her brother to hurry, reassuring him that there was a tunnel and stairway soon. Progress down the flights of zigzagging stairs in the dark was slow. She knew she was leaving Chasse further behind as she descended, but time was urgent.

'Where are you?' she heard him call as she reached the base of the stairs. She estimated he had to be only halfway down.

'At the bottom,' she replied. 'It's only a little further. When you get here wait for me. Don't go anywhere. I'll come back for you.' He protested, but she had no other choice.

She edged across the space until she ran into a wall. She slid her fingers along it, searching for the doorway that opened into the corridor and the Herbal Man's hideaway. She couldn't locate it. She checked again. Nothing but cavern wall. Then she walked her fingers around the wall until she found an arched opening adorned with rough carvings. There were stairs leading up. She was certain she was in the right place. Carefully studying the wall with her fingertips, she retraced her footsteps, but still she could not find the door. It was as if it had never existed. She continued well past the point where she thought it should be until she discovered another arched opening, also intricately decorated. There was a stairwell beyond it which led down. Then she heard Chasse enter the chamber, breathing heavily.

'I can't find it,' she confessed.

'What?' he asked. He sounded unsettled in the dark.

'The door. It's gone. It just doesn't make sense. It was here but now it's gone.' She felt her way across to the central opening in the wall, which she knew led deeper into the mountain, but when she reached it she stopped and sucked in her breath. 'Chasse?' she whispered.

'What?'

'Come here.'

'Where are you?' he pleaded. He reached out in front of him and discovered Tam's shoulders.

'Look,' she said quietly.

'Where?' Chasse had no idea where he was supposed to look in the complete darkness, but then he saw a red glow.

'Do you see it?' she asked.

'Yes,' he replied. He stared at the light shining in the inky distance.

'Come on,' she whispered.

'What is it?'

'We'll find out.'

Brother and sister cautiously approached the glow. The corridor they traversed was smooth and level, and, as the red light spread around them, they could see that the corridor was square, built with crafted precision. The light emanated from a huge space beyond the corridor. When they reached it, they stood at the head of a wide flight of uniformly-cut steps that led into the heart of the chamber. The red glow emanated from a massive multifaceted crystal hanging from the ceiling. The air was unusually warm.

A reptilian form was curled in the centre of the floor: a dragon. Claryssa. Then Tam was aware of a figure striding briskly up the steps to meet them. His white flowing robes, hair and beard were pink in the weird light.

'So you came,' he called as he approached. 'I thought you would if it was possible.'

'We came to warn you,' Tam blurted quickly. 'I couldn't find any of the doors.'

'I've sealed them,' the Herbal Man explained. 'There are no more doors to here, only the way you've come in. And that can be sealed soon, if necessary.'

'The Dragon Fang know about Claryssa. They're coming to kill her. And you.'

The Herbal Man reached the top step and paused. 'I know,' he said in a matter-of-fact tone. 'The Seeing Waters told me.'

'They're burning your hut,' Chasse informed him.

'I thought they would. And the hideaway. The girl Katris saw it all, didn't she?' he said, shaking his head in disappointment. 'Very careless of me, that morning. Always thought I'd do something like that eventually,' he mumbled as much to himself as to Chasse or Tam. 'It had to happen.'

'It was my fault,' Tam muttered. 'I led her to you when I brought Chasse. I should never have brought him up here like that.'

'Nonsense, Tamesan,' he said tersely. 'She followed you. You had no way of knowing how her spite would vent itself. It was not your fault. Besides,' he added, 'it wasn't you who foolishly left things unlocked. I should have been more vigilant. Remember that.'

'But now your secret is lost,' she lamented. 'All your possessions are being destroyed.'

The Herbal Man chuckled conspiratorially. 'I said I knew they were coming. I retrieved everything of value and stored it safely away. What the Dragon Fang will find is of no use to anyone anyway. Just some old books and a few jars of herbs that can be replaced anytime.'

'But what about you and Claryssa? Where will you go now?' she asked with concern. 'The whole village knows the truth.'

'It was time the truth was told,' the old wizard replied and frowned. 'Too many lies make living impossible in the end, anyway. It is time for us both to go.'

'Where?'

'Away.' The Herbal Man turned his head to stare down at Claryssa's curled form and said, 'I think it is almost time.'

'For what?' Tam asked.

'For the last wizard and his dragon to be seen in this world of people,' he announced with a deft flourish of his arms. 'Claryssa and I have reached a decision, so now it is time to do what must be done.'

'What?' Tam was finding the Herbal Man's habitual ambiguity irritating.

'You will see. But first there are things that must be put in order.' He reached into his robes and withdrew three items which he passed to Tam. Into her hands, he pressed a set of keys, a parchment, and a ring.

'These are for you, my child,' the old man said. 'They are part of a gift from Claryssa and myself. I would have liked you to have completed a true apprenticeship, but that is no longer possible. You were a long time coming to us, Tamesan, and we were too long in hiding to find you. But these gifts are yours. Your brother can attest to any doubters that I gave them to you.' He clapped Chasse on the shoulder and said, 'Be her knight, young man. The path she has been chosen to walk is long, dangerous, and very lonely. But she is the right person to walk it. Claryssa knows that in her heart of hearts, and I have never doubted her wisdom, nor had cause to doubt it. Stand beside your sister and give her strength when she doubts herself. Trust her as she trusts you, and never abandon her, no matter what strange and terrible things you may both face in the times to come.'

Tam stared in amazement as the Herbal Man spoke to her brother. The old man's voice had changed. It was stronger, deeper than she remembered, as if it had a resonant power it had never possessed before. When he finished, she asked, 'But what do these things do? What are they for?'

'The keys will become obvious,' he promised. 'The ring is an heirloom, a gift from my great-grandfather to be passed from father to son in succession.'

'But I am not your son,' she protested.

'You are my inheritor,' the old man said firmly. 'You have the right to wear the ring.'

'And the parchment?'

'Must not be opened until Claryssa and I are gone,' the Herbal Man warned. 'Only then may you read what is inscribed there. It will reveal the last portion of our gift to you. You will be led to our treasure.'

'But I don't want any treasure,' she declared. 'I'd rather go with you and Claryssa. Why can't you take me?'

'You could not possibly go where we are about to go. One day, perhaps, but you are not yet ready. You have a harder path to travel than we do. I wish it was easier than I fear it will be, but that is not in my power to control. What it will become is for you to decide.'

A sudden movement in the chamber distracted Tam. The dragon uncurled its massive body and unfurled a pair of delicate bat-like wings that rustled as they spread out. Claryssa lifted her head and opened her eyes. The golden and russet colours Tam had seen on the dragon were drowned in the red glow from the gigantic crystal in the ceiling, and the unnatural hue gave the dragon a menacing aspect that sent a shiver down Tam's spine.

'It is time to go,' announced the Herbal Man. 'Take this light staff to see your way back up to the cave of the Dawn People. To make it work you need only shake it like this.' The old man shook the staff and it gave off a soft white glow like a small lantern. 'If you go out onto the ledge you will see what Claryssa and I have organised for the Dragon Fang. Be patient. My old friend and I are a lot slower than we used to be.' Tam and Chasse waited as the old man turned to descend the steps. As if sensing their hesitancy, he spun on his heel and entreated, 'Go now. Time is short. Go.'

Brother and sister backed into the long corridor. Then they turned and headed swiftly away from the red chamber where the wizard and his dragon communed in secret. As they walked, Tam clutched the Herbal Man's gifts, and wondered what fabulous treasure the old man and Claryssa were leaving behind, and what dark roads lay ahead.

Chapter Thirty

'We've searched everything,' Lance reported as he emerged from the smoking ruins of the Herbal Man's retreat. 'He's nowhere to be found. There's no dragon and no dragon cave, either.'

Trask spat on a charred hunk of wood that had formerly been the trapdoor to the lower chambers of the Herbal Man's retreat. 'It's a trick of some kind,' he growled. 'The girl swore she saw the dragon in a chamber beyond the crystal one. Even Kevan's daughter admitted there was a dragon here.'

'We found the crystal room. There's nothing beyond it but solid rock,' Lance explained. 'Maybe she imagined the dragon.'

'You don't imagine dragons,' Trask sneered contemptuously. 'Kevan's spawn must have warned the old man. When I get hold of them I'll use them as examples to the rest of the village of what happens to those who lie to the Dragon Head.'

'It might just as well be Varst's fortune we didn't find a real dragon here,' said Neal, who strolled from the forest where he and several of the Dragon Fang were searching for signs of the Herbal Man and his dragon. 'How do you fight a dragon, anyway?'

Trask spun and strode towards him, eyes brimming with anger. He struck Neal a solid blow with his spear shaft, sending the warrior sprawling at the feet of his startled companions.

'How do you think Nakiades fought his dragons, coward?' Trask roared. 'A dragonwarrior doesn't need to know how. He fights. It's in his blood! That's how it is. He fights!' He threw his spear across the clearing and impaled the trunk of a tree, and swore at the top of his voice. 'For years we've searched for dragons! For endless hell-blasted years! Now when there is one on the mountain right above us, we can't find it!' More dragonwarriors emerged from the smoking ruins, their faces blackened. Trask turned to them and asked, 'Any sign of the old man?'

'No,' Jon informed him. 'None.'

'I want him!' Trask bellowed. 'He crippled my son and he must pay for that! He will pay for that! On Varst's word I will make him pay for that!'

'Your personal vengeance isn't why we're here,' Jon reminded him. 'There is a dragon to kill.'

Trask whirled and retorted, 'I am Dragon Head now! If I want the old man dead, he will be! I am the law!' He fixed Jon with a threatening glare, but the warrior remained unperturbed. Finally, Trask spat on the ground at Jon's feet, and stalked away to retrieve his spear.

As he reached it, he heard Jon call, 'You wanted

the dragon, Trask? Here it comes!' He turned to see the dragonwarriors all gaping open-mouthed at the sky. Following the direction of their horrified gazes, he saw what they were staring at.

Sweeping across the western face of Dragon Mountain came a creature on broad wings thirty times the span of a man's arm. In the early afternoon light the creature's scales shone like burnished gold, and its long snaky tail, shifting in the air currents, stabilised the dragon's flight as it glided in a controlled arc towards the plateau. The first sighting of a dragon, the terrible child of Blitzart, Shaddho and Arkamroth, a creature out of Harbin's legends, stupefied the men. Trask felt a sickening surge of fear flood through his limbs. He had a mad urge to run, to flee the mountain and hide in the darkest corner he could find, but he steeled himself against his instinctive reactions, and raised his spear defiantly. The dragon drifted down, its scythe-like talons glinting in the sunlight as it descended to land amongst the astounded warriors, who retreated to the forest fringe.

On the dragon's back sat a white-haired wizard, his beard flowing down the front of his dazzling white robes. Chains and pendants, adorned with richly coloured jewels, hung from his neck, almost lost in the snowy mass of his beard, and he held a long gleaming black staff in his right hand. The dragon lowered its huge reptilian head, so that its slitted golden eyes fixed on several anxious dragonwarriors, and waited patiently for the wizard to dismount. The warriors directly under the dragon's piercing gaze lowered their spears and edged deeper into the trees, preparing to run. When the wizard had climbed down from its back, the dragon lifted its head again and started to preen its wings.

The wizard faced Trask, bowed politely, and said in a clear, commanding voice, 'I believe you wanted to see us.'

Tam watched in awe as Claryssa appeared above the north-western shoulder of Dragon Mountain, high over Meltsparkle gorge, and glided across the mountain's western face. The old dragon's scales shone in a way Tam had never imagined possible, and it was hard to believe Claryssa was anything but invincible. As she circled down towards the plateau she looked the image of the great dragon Arkamroth that Tam had so often heard described in the old legends.

'We won't see anything from up here once they've landed on the plateau,' Chasse complained.

'Then we'll climb down,' Tam decided. Chasse secretly cursed himself for opening his mouth. He had not enjoyed climbing the path to the ledge, and now he was already having to climb down. He started after his sister, but she turned and put a hand firmly on his chest. 'I've changed my mind,' she announced. 'I'm going down. You're staying here.'

'I don't think so,' he disputed.

'Someone has to guard this entrance in case any of the Dragon Fang find it, Chasse. You would do that better than I could. You are a warrior,' she argued.

'But—'

'It's important, Chasse. For me. Don't come down, no matter what happens. Stay here,' she pleaded. Against his better judgment he relented, but as Tam disappeared over the ledge he wondered if he had made a wise choice.

By the time she reached the base of the plateau, the Herbal Man was facing Trask. Behind Trask, the Dragon Fang fanned out in a broad arc, some holding their spears in readiness for battle, others standing less confidently in the fringe of trees looking nervously at the dragon. Claryssa had finished her preening and was eyeing the warriors warily.

'I don't care for your history, old man!' she heard Trask bellow as she nestled behind a bushy-leaved tree. 'The only dragon the people of Nakiades will ever praise is a dead dragon!'

The Herbal Man waggled his head sadly and replied, 'You speak the same tired and foolish words I've heard from the mouths of angry men for a thousand years. They are all forgotten dust in the winds of time. Learn from their bitter mistakes my friend. Bring the people of your village into the light of understanding.'

'Dust in the face of you and your abomination!' Trask cried. 'Nakiades taught us the truth about dragonkind. No man is a man until he slays the dragons that prey upon our homes. And I will be a man!'

The warrior suddenly hurled his spear. Tam screamed as she saw it strike the Herbal Man full in the chest, but before she could burst from her hiding place, the dragon's jaws opened, and a stream of raging fire poured over Trask. Some of the Dragon Fang panicked and ran. Others, Trask's closest friends and older warriors like Lance and Jon, courageously held their ground and raised their spears to fend off the legendary monster facing them. Seeing their intention, Claryssa rolled her head, lifted her wings until she reared on her haunches, and spat another stream of fire a metre in front of the remaining warriors. The intense flood of heat drove them back into the forest. More dropped their spears and ran in terror. The bare handful who remained, rallied beside Jon, but they all seemed bereft of any desire to confront the dragon on open ground.

Tam took a chance and sprinted across the space to the Herbal Man. Amazingly, he still stood upright despite having Trask's spear jutting from his chest. A bright red bloodstain was spreading across the front of his white robe. When she reached him, she caught his arm. The old man looked at her, though his eyes were glazed as if he could not see.

'Step away, child,' he gasped.

'You need help,' she insisted.

'Step away,' he repeated. 'You cánnot help now.' He turned from her and spread both arms wide. 'Get out of the clearing!' he ordered. 'Go, Te-Amen-San.'

She released the Herbal Man's arm, and retreated.

As she reached the trees, she heard him begin a litany in the ancient language, using words that flowed like the wild water over Watersdrop in springtime, words full of passion and power. She watched in fascination as a blue glow surrounded the wizard. It enveloped his entire body, but the colour was most intense around the spear that impaled him. The old man's chanting gained strength and volume, and the surviving dragonwarriors in the forest, like Tam, stared, enthralled by the wizard's display of magical power. Little by little, Trask's spear disintegrated, until only the nub piercing the old man's chest remained. Then it too dissolved. The blue aura flashed and vanished. An instant later, the wizard's chanting changed pitch, and his hands began to glow as if they were suddenly aflame. He motioned towards the trees where the dragonwarriors stood and a bush exploded. Another caught fire beside Jon. Terrified by the wizard's awesome power, the last dragonwarriors bolted in fear. Jon backed away, dropped his spear when another tree erupted in a ball of fire to his right, and then ran for his life. Once the dragonwarriors withdrew, the wizard ceased his spell-casting. The glow faded from his hands. He staggered and then crumpled at the knees. The dragon sagged beside him.

'We are much too old for that sort of thing any more,' the Herbal Man confessed, forcing a grin. Tam helped him to his feet, and he limped towards

Claryssa. The old dragon lowered her head. Behind her, the fires had already died, and only thin coils of smoke twisted into the air to testify that the confrontation between the dragon and the Dragon Fang had taken place.

'But you both looked so magnificent, so powerful,' Tam said, in a weak attempt to express what she had witnessed.

'Illusion,' the old man wheezed. 'All part of the show.'

'Claryssa's fire was no illusion,' she argued. She glanced at the ashen patch where Trask had perished, and felt a touch of nausea.

'That took just about every ounce of poor old Claryssa's energy. We had hoped we wouldn't need to resort to that,' the Herbal Man admitted. 'So many men choose to be so stupidly arrogant when instead they would be better served by admitting defeat and getting on with something else.' He coughed as he pulled himself aboard Claryssa's neck. 'Pass me my staff, please,' he requested once the coughing fit passed.

Tam picked up the staff. It was mirror-smooth to the touch, but beneath its glossy surface she saw myriad runes etched into its fibre. 'Is what you did magic?' she asked as she handed him the staff.

The wizard shook his head and said, 'It was a kind of magic. A very poor kind. Being able to scare or destroy things isn't very impressive magic. There is magic much greater than that.'

'Like what?' she asked.

The old man smiled and said softly, 'Like the magic you already have. Like being able to find answers to your questions, and earning a brother's trust. Helping people to see what is right and what is wrong. Honesty. Love. Make these things happen, Tamesan. That is real magic. Remember that.' He began coughing again.

'Aren't you going to at least wait until morning before you leave? The sun is already going down,' she entreated. She dreaded the thought of their leaving. Neither the wizard nor the dragon were well.

The Herbal Man studied the lengthening shadows and said, 'No. We've tarried here too long as it is. I didn't expect to have to take so much time to recover. But then I only wanted to try and talk reason into some heads. That way the road you have yet to travel might be a little easier at home. I fear I may have only succeeded in making it all that much harder for you now.'

'Chasse and I will sort things out,' Tam replied, although she was not terribly convinced by her own words. What would she do now?

'I'm sure you will,' he agreed. 'Claryssa believes that.'

Tam glanced to her left and saw the dragon's eye studying her. In daylight, the pool of golden liquid was condensed into a long yellow slit which made the dragon look much more sinister. But she remembered the great golden eye staring from the far wall in the crystal cavern. That eye seemed able to look through her, and draw her into its depths. That was what Tam would always see when she thought of Claryssa.

'Time to go, old girl,' the Herbal Man murmured quietly, and patted Claryssa's neck. The dragon lifted her great head and unfurled her wings. Despite having rested, she was noticeably unsteady, and still quite obviously exhausted. 'Tamesan,' the wizard called, 'don't forget the parchment. Don't read it yet,' he reminded her. Then he asked, 'Where's Chasse?'

'He's up on the ledge. I made him wait there,' she informed him.

'He is in your care, Tamesan,' the wizard said. 'And you are in his. And both of you must look to Jaysin. He has a destiny in a place beyond Harbin.'

'How do you know that?' Tam asked, startled by the wizard's prophetic words.

'It is in his eyes. I've seen it written there. Look to the boy.'

Claryssa shifted suddenly, turned her body, and rose on her hind legs. She was so huge, and yet also strangely fragile as her wings began to test the late afternoon breeze.

'I'm going to miss you!' Tam called out. 'Where will you go?'

'Away,' the Herbal Man replied. 'To the west.'

'Will I see you again?'

The Herbal Man laughed before he answered her. 'Wherever you go, Tamesan, Claryssa and I will be with you.'

'How?' she asked, confused yet again by his strangely twisted answers.

'Trust my word,' he said. 'You have the answer in your hands.' Tam fingered the ring, and parchment, and keys she still clutched. She held the answer. What was it though? Why always riddles?

Claryssa suddenly tensed and spread her wings. Tam ran back from the clearing as the tremendous downward push of air, generated by the dragon's wingbeats, stirred the trees and bushes. Dragon and wizard lifted into the air, and rose rapidly, circling to gain height, until they disappeared over the treetops.

Chasse came charging out of the forest. 'The dragon-ship! It's setting sail!' he cried. Tam stared at her brother as if she didn't understand him. 'Come on, Tam!' Chasse urged. 'I saw it from the ledge. It's already heading out into the bay. We've got to get back down to the village!'

She could hardly argue with him pulling on her arm. 'Come on!' he ordered. She followed him through the plateau forest and into the mad scramble down the mountain. Why would the dragonship be sailing? She had little time to consider anything else. Chasse was leaping ahead, plunging down the path in a mad helter-skelter towards the village, and Tam found for once she could not keep up with her brother. By the time she reached the edge of the goat pasture, Chasse was already disappearing amongst the huts, heading for the jetty. The sun was dipping low in the western sky and the last afternoon rays of sunlight were playing across the ice-capped peaks surrounding Harbin. At the furthest reach of the bay the solitary red sail of the dragonship was fast fading from view.

Tam could run no further. She stopped and caught her breath, exhausted by the mad downhill rush. Then she ventured across the pasture. A dozen goats grazing near the shelters lifted their snouts to watch her pass. The shadows of the nearest cottages and huts were rapidly lengthening, and the early evening chill was already creeping through the air. She noticed the absence of familiar twists of hearth-fire smoke from the open chimneys. Harbin looked cold and empty.

'You won't find anyone here,' a deep voice said. Tam turned to the source of the voice. Galt emerged from the shadows of a building.

'What do you mean?' she asked.

'They've all taken to the dragonship and sailed away,' he informed her with a sweep of his arm.

'Everyone?'

Galt shook his head. 'Near enough. Except a handful who stayed in the Long Hall with your folk. Your father wouldn't budge when they came for him. Thinks he's Nakiades now there's a dragon.'

'But why has everyone left so suddenly?'

'You ask such a foolish question?' Galt snorted and shook his head again in disbelief. 'You and your dragon friend scared them off. They think the dragon's going to come down to the village to fry them all.'

'So why didn't you go with them?'

Galt scratched his head and spat. 'Because I didn't. Maybe I'm too old to be frightened by much any more. Maybe I'm just an old fool,' he chuckled. 'But the way I see it is, if you and your brother aren't frightened of the old man on the mountain and his dragon, then why should I be frightened?' He laughed quietly to himself and jerked his thumb in the direction of the goats. 'I lost Derin this past summer. He was my only boy. I didn't want to lose that lot over there as well. They're all I've got left.' Tam glanced at the patchwork of moving colour the goats presented as they shuffled closer to the shelters, moving down from the pasture and the encroaching icy touch of evening air. The last of the sunlight had faded from the mountain peak, leaving the sky to deepen into dark blues and purples as dusk spread. She thought she heard the piping cry of a gull behind her, but when she turned towards the village again she heard a voice calling her.

'Tamesan!' She saw Jaysin running towards her along the path from the Long Hall. 'Tamesan!' he called again as he reached her. She held out her arms and scooped him up, full of joy to hold him. 'Jaysin! Where is everyone?' she asked as she released him.

'In the Long Hall,' he panted. 'Chasse told us you were coming, and that you were not hurt.'

'Of course I'm not hurt,' Tam smiled. 'The Herbal Man and Claryssa protected me.'

'I saw the dragon, Tam! I saw it fly away. It was magnificent! All golden and so big!' Jaysin's face was full of light and energy, brighter and stronger than Tam could ever remember. It sparked a memory, a moment in a dream when she'd seen Jaysin sitting astride a dragon and laughing with wild delight as he clung to the creature's neck. Her little brother had an affinity for dragonkind alien to the world of Harbin. He saw them as the Herbal Man saw Claryssa: as intelligent, awesome, beautiful creatures with the potential to be companions of the highest order. The Herbal Man's parting words came back to her: *Look to the boy*. What destiny awaited Jaysin? And where?

She gave his auburn hair her customary ruffle and said, 'Take me to the Long Hall.' Then she turned to Galt and asked, 'Are you going to come with us?'

He shook his head and answered, 'Not yet, young Tamesan. When I have the goats safely quartered, perhaps then I'll come to the Long Hall.' He looked up at the mountain and then cast a glance in the direction of his own dark hut. 'There's not a lot of point in going home tonight.'

'I will tell Father,' she said and smiled. Then she let herself be led away by Jaysin, who was anxious for her to follow him.

There were more people in the Long Hall than she had expected. Not all the Dragon Fang had sailed. Jon and Raven, and at least half a dozen more warriors were present, along with Banni, Amarti, and the fishermen, and a handful of other villagers. When she entered with Jaysin, the group were gathered at the centre of the hall with her mother Eesa, and her father, who was propped in a chair, listening to Chasse. He was furnishing them with the details of events on the mountain.

'I've brought Tam!' Jaysin yelled, and he proudly led his sister into the centre of the group. Then shyness got the better of him and he slunk self-consciously between his parents and withdrew to the outer edge.

Everyone's interest centred on Tam. Eesa greeted her with a warm hug, and Tam kissed Kevan, and then checked the state of his wound from the spear-fight with Trask. Banni also hugged her, as close as she could given her swollen tummy, and the girl and the woman laughed at the ridiculous image they must present to the gathering. Then the questions started. Tam answered and explained everything she could, including the details of the confrontation she had witnessed between Trask and the Herbal Man.

'He was only trying to talk sense to Trask,' she insisted. 'Trask just wouldn't listen.'

'It's true,' Jon agreed. 'Chasse did not see this as he has already said, but Tamesan did, and she will tell you that Trask attacked first. His spear—' He hesitated, remembering Trask's spear striking true and piercing the Herbal Man's chest, and the flow of healing magic that followed. 'His spear dissolved in the old man's chest.'

'Dissolved?' Eesa gasped. Everyone stared in disbelief at Jon.

'I saw it too,' Raven asserted. 'There was a blue glow and the spear disappeared.'

'Surely the old man was dead?' Kevan asked. He shifted his weight in the chair to be more comfortable and winced with pain from the wound in his side. Eesa squeezed his hand.

'No,' Jon replied. 'Not even hurt. Even the bloodstain on his chest vanished.'

'But how can this be?' Eesa asked.

'Magic,' Tam stated calmly. 'The Herbal Man is a wizard. He knows how to use magic to protect himself.'

The gathering stared at her. Only Chasse vaguely comprehended her statement.

'What do you mean, Tamesan?' Eesa spoke for all of them.

Tam shrugged her shoulders, aware Eesa's question could not be answered simply, and replied, 'I can't explain magic. I don't even really understand what it is myself. But it's a kind of way of doing things, making things happen that we can't normally make happen.' She knew her explanation hadn't made a lot of sense to the others, but then magic still did not make a lot of sense to her, either.

'Is it true the Herbal Man has gone?' Raven asked.

Tam nodded.

'And his dragon with him?'

'They've gone,' she confirmed. She felt a knot of sorrow in her throat.

'Where?' Kevan inquired. 'Where are they going?'

'I don't know,' Tam answered. 'Into the west.'

'But there's nothing to the west,' Jon argued. 'The ocean is endless, and only Shaddho the death dragon dares to fly there.'

'I saw the dragon flying west!' Jaysin interrupted. Everyone turned to look at him in the deepening shadows, and he blushed with embarrassment and he went quiet.

'Then they'll be coming back,' old Amarti croaked and nodded to Berikan, her husband.

'They won't be coming back,' Tam said. She knew her eyes were shining with tears. She sensed her mother's hand reaching for her and welcomed her comforting touch.

'How can you be so sure?' Raven asked.

'Because they're dying.' Her answer hung like an accusation. No-one spoke. It was as if the people in the Hall had turned to stone. Outside, the light was rapidly fading. Harbin was sinking into night. Tam felt the tears stream down her cheeks then. She accepted the gentle pull of her mother's arms, and melted gladly into Eesa's embrace. Her whole world had changed again, become a world of sadness and loss. She wept again for Harmi, and now for Eric and Claryssa, who had wanted only peace in their old age and could not stay.

Chapter Thirty-One

She dangled her feet over the edge of the jetty, letting the back of her legs press against the weathered edge of the wooden planks. The still morning air was brisk and biting, but she revelled in its crispness on her face and arms. Waves lapped against the barnacle-encrusted pylons. The creamy-grey face of the moon peered from the satin indigo sky, and its fading tapestry of stars. She had woken before daybreak, her dreams filled with images of Trask's fiery death, bright red blood spreading across the Herbal Man's chest, her father and Trask wrestling for possession of a spear, Eric and Claryssa flying into the red glow of the setting sun. She could not sleep.

The few who remained in Harbin after the dragonship set sail shared the night in the Long Hall. Tam cried into Eesa's arms for a time, then succumbed to a combination of emotional and physical exhaustion which swept her into the realm of sleep. When she did wake, the Hall was dark and the hearth-fire cold.

She lay listening to the sounds of sleep around her in the hope she would also fall back to sleep, but it eluded her. She held each of the gifts the Herbal Man had left behind in turn—the ring, the keys, and the parchment. There was a mystery yet to unravel before she could truly rest. She was certain the dragonship and its passengers would return to Harbin once they believed the dragon was gone. She wondered how the crippled Marron had greeted the news of his father's death and what Katris and her friends thought had happened to Chasse and herself when they did not come back down the mountain with the Dragon Fang. The mystery of the old wizard's gifts had to be solved before the dragonship and its cargo of disbelievers and rumour-mongers came back.

She finally slipped silently out of the Long Hall without disturbing anyone, and walked through the chilly pre-dawn gloom to the jetty. Her first thought had been to cross Watersdrop and climb onto the roof of her cottage. Then she could watch the dawning the way she used to do as a child, but as she left the Long Hall the water of the bay attracted her instead. So she crept down to the jetty.

Slowly, lighter hues began to appear in the sky, night blue fading inexorably to grey, that was in turn tinted by a lighter blue that began to seep into the air from the ridges of the brooding mountains. The ice atop Dragon Mountain gradually separated from the mountain's dark bulk, whitening as a precursor to the true morning light. A soft golden glow bloomed on the mountain peak—dawn's light. Te-Amen-San. She felt magic coursing through the sound of her name just as she used to when she was a child. Her name still whispered a promise of a greater destiny to her. Perhaps it was finally going to happen. The Herbal Man and Claryssa had left her their legacy. She would climb the mountain one more time to discover what lay at the heart of their promise.

Shadows of old Berikan the fisherman and his wife Amarti emerged from the Long Hall and headed down the worn path to their hut at the shoreline. A few moments later Galt also stumbled out, clapping his hands together to beat out the cold, his breath escaping in puffing billows of steam. Tam did not want any of them to see her, but their appearances this early in the morning were reassuring. Harbin life, the simple and honest daily routine, was continuing. It would be all right after all. She waited until the village was quiet again before she left the jetty and headed towards the mountain, deviating to avoid the Long Hall. She halted at the edge of the buildings until Galt drove the goats out of their overnight shelters and then she cut across the northern corner of the pasture behind a hillock that hid her from Galt should he look in that direction.

Once beyond the tree line, Tam stopped to extract the small bundle she carried inside her tunic. From the bundle she slipped the ring on her middle finger and studied it. It was silver-coloured, and yet, when she extended her hand and the ring caught scattered rays of the early morning light, it sparkled with greens and yellows and hints of gleaming red in the deeper lustre of the metal. It had an unusual texture that reminded Tam of the tessellated pattern of Claryssa's scales. It was a dragon ring, she decided fancifully.

Then she looked at the keys. Four were familiar—the keys to the Herbal Man's retreat that no longer existed. But there were three more keys Tam could not remember seeing when she had stayed with the Herbal Man last winter: keys made from a dark, dull metal. She assumed that they were for doors somewhere in the larger chamber where she had last seen Eric and Claryssa before their final confrontation with Trask. She attached the keys to a cord around her waist and then fingered the yellowing parchment. The Herbal Man had made her promise not to read it until Claryssa and he had gone. She had kept the promise. She was about to untie the thread encircling the rolled parchment when she heard a twig snap to her left. She turned hurriedly and saw a figure approaching between the trees. 'Chasse!' she gasped when she realised her brother had found her.

'Why didn't you wake me?' he asked as he reached her.

'I don't know,' she replied. 'I didn't want to disturb anyone else this morning.'

'You're quiet, Tam,' he grinned, 'But not that quiet. I heard you go out this morning.'

'Why didn't you say anything?'

'Because I know what it's like to want some time alone. You didn't want to disturb anyone. I didn't want to disturb you.'

Tam smiled. 'Thank you,' she said quietly. She felt ashamed for underestimating her brother's sensitivity. She had promised to be honest with Chasse. She had to remember to keep her promise.

Chasse's eyes rested on the furled parchment. 'Have you read it yet?'

She shook her head. 'No. I was about to. But I think I'll wait until we reach the top.' She hesitated, considering her next words carefully. 'Perhaps I should tell Mother and Father where we're going.'

'It's all right, Tam,' Chasse said. 'I explained where you were going before I came after you.'

Tam looked at him with questioning eyes. 'Truth.' he said quietly and smiled, 'Remember?'

She smiled and replied, 'I remember.'

They climbed the familiar path through the morning, clambering over rocks and between trees. Sunlight sparkled on the dewy rocks and moisture-laden leaves and their spirits were renewed by the pulsing beauty of the surrounding world. Even the mountain air smelt fresher and more invigorating. The blue sky, dotted with puffy white clumps of clouds, seemed to expand in all directions, and the western ocean lay deep blue and serene to the horizon. Only when the pair reached the plateau, where the ruin of the Herbal Man's hut lay like a dark smudge, did Tam's high spirits dissolve. Her memories flooded back; the mornings hunting for herbs through the forest, the days spent learning to painstakingly copy the alphabet, the frustrating nights reading by candlelight, struggling to recognise the words before her. And there were sharper moments—the very first vision of Claryssa, her great golden disc of a dragon eye staring back at Tam where a wall had been. She could hear Eric's voice calling her back from the chilly path she stumbled onto in the mountain blizzard, the radiating warmth and light that enveloped her, the whispering voice calling 'Te-Amen-San'.

'Tam?'

Chasse broke through her reverie, his hand on her arm. 'I'm all right,' she whispered hoarsely, choking back her sudden surge of sorrow.

'Look at the forest.'

Her brother's direction made her refocus. She opened her eyes and looked around. The plateau forest was dying. All the leaves were turning yellow and brown, and there were bare limbs on the higher branches. The lush ferns that had been taller than a dragonwarrior were wilting and colourless. No bird-life flitted through the rotting foliage. Tam stared in silence for a long moment. Then she turned abruptly and said, 'Come on,' and headed towards the path that led higher up the slope.

'Why is it dying?' Chasse asked as they passed the entrance to the goat cave.

'The magic is gone,' Tam replied. She suddenly wondered where the Herbal Man's goats were sheltering. They would have to be herded back down to the village.

Chasse didn't pursue the issue. His sister knew

more about magic than he ever wanted to know. It seemed pointless asking for an explanation concerning the dying forest. He suspected the answer would be too complicated.

When they reached the foot of the narrow and treacherous path that rose sharply up to the ledge overlooking the plateau, Chasse asked if he could go first.

'Why?' Tam asked.

'It's something I have to do,' he replied. 'I was scared yesterday when you led me up here. Now I need to prove to myself that I'm not scared.' He had never confessed to being scared before, at least, not quite so openly. She stepped aside and grinned at her brother as he went forward.

By the time Tam clambered onto the ledge to join her brother, the sun was sitting high over Dragon Mountain. 'This is a magnificent view!' Chasse exclaimed as he gazed out across the bay towards the expanse of the western ocean. 'Yesterday I was too overwhelmed by the height and rush when we scrambled up here to appreciate this, but this morning I see why the Herbal Man lived up here.'

'Did you see them leave?' Tam asked, and stared out to sea.

'Yes!' he said with no attempt to suppress his excitement. 'They circled the mountain three times, once really close to the ledge, and then they headed that way.' He pointed directly west across the ocean.

Tam wished she had been on the ledge with her brother to watch the Herbal Man and Claryssa fly away. But then if she had, she would not have had a chance to say goodbye. At least she had that. 'I want to read the parchment,' she murmured, lost momentarily in her memories again.

'Then open it,' Chasse suggested. Tam retrieved and unrolled the document, and studied the script. She recognised the Herbal Man's handwriting because she had been forced to copy it so thoroughly. 'Read it to me,' he asked.

She cleared her throat and read in a halting voice, '*Te-Amen-San: Of all things that can be given from one to another, the greatest gifts are life, trust, and knowledge. These three things Claryssa and I have shared, as all of our kind have shared through time. But all things have an ending just as they have a beginning. That is another universal law. So before our days are fully counted we entrust to you the fruits of our lives and knowledge. We choose to share with you the one treasure we value higher than even our own lives. Believe in what you are, Te-Amen-San, and the world will unfold before you.*'

The parchment carried no signature and no clue as to the nature of the treasure or where it lay. 'What does it mean?' Chasse asked as she finished reading.

'I don't know,' she replied. 'So many things the Herbal Man told me never seemed to make a lot of sense. At least not straightaway. Perhaps there's an answer in that red cavern we found him in yesterday.' So saying, she rolled the parchment and headed into the mountain.

'Wait, Tam,' Chasse called. He pulled a long rod from inside his tunic. 'We'll need this.' It was the light staff the Herbal Man had left with them, and he shook it into action.

Aided by the magical light, their progress was easy. Tam briefly showed Chasse the ochre wall art of the Dawn People as they passed through the upper caves, and then led him down the zigzag of stairs to the chamber where two stairways and a flat corridor met. Tam noted with grim disappointment that the wall where the entry to the Herbal Man's underground retreat had once been was still sealed solid. Whatever magic it was that bound the wall, it seemed permanent.

When they entered the long corridor Tam was pleased to discover the red crystal glowing at the far end. She led Chasse to the flight of steps that dropped into the vast chamber where Claryssa was resting when they first came to warn the Herbal Man about Trask and the Dragon Fang. Red light permeated everything, and the cavern was comfortably warm, as if a giant-sized hearth was burning somewhere near. In the centre, where Claryssa had lain, was a raised circular space, and at its hub was a large oval object that glowed soft pink.

Brother and sister descended the steps warily, half-expecting the dragon to suddenly reappear, even though they knew she had flown west. When they alighted at the base of the steps, they discovered that the object at the centre of the gigantic cavern sat on a huge grass pile which had been wound into a circular bed. It was then Tam realised what it was they were staring at.

'Chasse!' she cried, feeling both exhilaration and fear course through her veins. She ran forward.

'Wait, Tam!' her brother called. He ran after her, puzzled by his sister's sudden response. Before he could catch her, she had clambered onto the grass mound. He climbed up in pursuit, and found her sitting cross-legged in the centre of a nest, staring at the biggest egg he had ever seen. 'In Varst's name!' he blurted in astonishment. 'What is this?'

Tam, her face set in rapture, kept her eyes riveted on the soft oval shape resting in the grass nest, and whispered, 'A dragon's egg.'

'But how?'

'It's Claryssa's. It's her egg,' she confided. She reached out and stroked the smooth skin. It was not like a bird's egg. She had often collected birds' eggs. This shell was soft, flexible, leathery, and warm to touch.

'But if it's Claryssa's, why has she left it?' Chasse persisted.

'It's her gift,' Tam explained, finally understanding what was happening. 'This is what the parchment is about. Don't you see? This is Claryssa and Eric's treasure. The egg. It's life and trust and knowledge all wrapped up in one thing. And they've passed it to me, to protect and care for.'

'But I thought Claryssa was the last dragon?' Chasse murmured as he settled in the nest beside his sister and stared at the shell glowing pink in the chamber's eerie light.

'No. Not any more,' she answered as she stroked the egg. 'The last dragon is still here, Chasse, it's still here, and we have been made its guardians. What greater gift could we have been given?'